JASON ANSPACH　　　　　　　　　　**NICK COLE**

PART II

SEASON 2　　　　　　　　　　　　　　**BOOK 7**

GALAXY'S EDGE

ISBN: 978-1-949731-85-9

Edited by David Gatewood
Published by Galaxy's Edge Press

Cover Art: Tommaso Renieri
Cover Design: M.S. Corely
Formatting: Kevin G. Summers

Website: www.GalaxysEdge.us
Facebook: facebook.com/atgalaxysedge
Newsletter (get a free short story): www.InTheLegion.com

WHO'S WHO...

What follows is a summary of some of the characters found in this book, and their stories up to this point. More characters will appear in this volume but listing them up front would kind of spoil things. If you find yourself lost, consider joining one of the Galaxy's Edge fan groups listed at the end of the book. There is no shortage of fellow leejes who love talking about the story of Galaxy's Edge (and speculating and theorizing about what comes next).

Aeson Ford – See Aeson Keel.

Aeson Keel – See Wraith.

Andien Broxin – A Nether Ops operative who worked closely with Legion Dark Ops (*Kill Team*). Broxin's military career began as a Republic Marine (*Forget Nothing*). She was selected for an experimental Legion training program (*Forget Nothing II*). Presumed dead at the hands of the Cybar (*Message for the Dead*), Broxin was saved by a dissenting Cybar named Praxus and is currently working with him.

Asa Berlin – A young and idealistic member of the House of Liberty, Berlin holds the same position—"first among equals"—that Delegate Orrin Kaar once did. Her reforming term has been tested repeatedly by House of Reason loyalists, planetary civil wars, and now a Gomarii-led invasion meant to set up the rule of the Savages and their Golden King.

Bear – Dark Ops major who oversees Kill Team Victory. No longer regularly involved in direct action due to injuries suffered in the Second Battle for Utopion (*Retribution*), he fills the role once held by Major Owens. Has been overseeing the potential role of Nether Ops in supplying chemical weapons on the planet Kima.

Bombassa – Senior NCO for Kill Team Victory. Former legionnaire who sided with Goth Sullus's Black Fleet (*Attack of Shadows*). Following Article Nineteen, was sent undercover as "Lashley" to determine Nilo's motivations and capabilities (*Takeover*). Last seen leading his kill team into a mysterious Savage vault on Kima.

Bubbles – A Malinois-like dog with peculiar telekinetic and psychic capabilities. Forms an extremely strong bond with his handlers but has an unfortunate record of seeing them killed in action. Currently serving with Kill Team Victory.

Carter – A former legionnaire turned private military contractor (PMC). He worked for Nilo and Black Fleet, playing a pivotal role in liberating Kublar. An assassination attempt was made on him and his family due to his former membership in Kill Team Ice—a fact Carter was not aware of. He was saved by Kel Turner and is now on mission on Earth, anticipating a second Savage invasion.

Casper – Also known as Admiral Sulla, Casper Sullivan, and a host of other aliases. A friend of Tyrus Rex and Reina who shared their experiences at the hands of the Savages and was given exceptionally long life (*Imperator*). Sulla was the mastermind behind the galaxy's war against the Savages, convincing Tyrus Rex to found the Legion and bringing about the unification of the galaxy through the forming of the Republic (*Savage Wars* trilogy). Casper's thirst for a power that could fully defeat the enemies of humanity led him to study under Urmo, and ultimately brought him, as Goth Sullus, to his betrayal and murder of his old friend Tyrus (*Imperator, Galactic Outlaws*).

Crometheus – A Savage marine who lived in a simulation on the edge of madness (*Gods & Legionnaires*). Part of the Savage tribe known as the Uplifted, he was presumed deactivated. After recalling the truth of his past, he has fled the arcade that was his prison and is currently on the run from Maestro.

Crash – See KRS-88.

Cybar – A species of mechanical, non-biological life. Created by unknown causes in one of the Temples of the Ancients (*Legacies*). Discovered by the Republic and recovered by Kill Team Ice (*Legacies*, again). Given the planet Khan Saak (*Legionnaire*) as a home world, while also used to construct a doomsday fleet (*Message for the Dead*).

Dark Ones – An innumerable race of demonic spirit beings whose sole purpose is to destroy all life. It was the fear of the Dark Ones invading the galaxy that caused the

Ancients to flee. Long held at bay by covenant, they were released when the Dark Wanderer was slain. Now only the thinnest of leashes, held by the Golden King, prevents them from completing their terrible purpose.

The Dark Wanderer – A mysterious and evil entity tied to whatever darkness is looming for the galaxy. Was killed by Ravi, thus accelerating the galaxy's eventual demise.

Death, Destroyer of Worlds – Psychopathic and homicidal Nubarian gunnery bot originally acquired by Tyrus Rechs (*Contracts & Terminations* series). Now the property of Aeson Keel.

Donal Makaffie – Eccentric, existential genius. The inventor of H8. An expert on many things Savage, he possesses an ability to intuitively comprehend what they're attempting. A member of Kill Team Ice and veteran of the Savage Wars.

Dragon, The – A mythical Sinasian warrior destined to protect Sinasia from all its foes. It is believed that the Dragon will reincarnate and emerge at Sinasia's most desperate hour. (*Contracts & Terminations: Chasing the Dragon*).

G232 – Admin and protocol bot originally acquired by Tyrus Rechs (*Contracts & Terminations* series). Now the property of Aeson Keel and working feverishly to relocate the pantry aboard the *Battle Phoenix*.

Garret – A technical wizard and savant. Was a former slave of Lao Pak, "liberated" by Aeson Keel, and now serves as a crewmember on the *Indelible VI*.

Golden King – The first elite to conceive of and seriously plan to leave Earth to its self-inflicted destruction. He was an avid gene-splicer and "juicer," always seeking the key to immortality while on Earth. Once in the stars aboard his lighthugger, the first to leave Earth, he perfected his methods. The Golden King made first contact with the Gomarii, and used their knowledge of the galaxy and penchant for slavery to further strengthen his own genetic perfection. He also controlled Maestro and the Uplifted, using them to eventually take control of most other Savage tribes and harnessing them in his first war of conquest, which failed before Tyrus Rex and the Legion. Now, with Reina at his side, he seeks to take his rightful place as supreme ruler of the galaxy once more, having captured the Dark Ones and thereby possessing the ultimate weapon in existence.

Goth Sullus – See Casper.

Jack – A Repub Navy spy who went independent following Article Nineteen. He was hired by Nilo to obtain Savage artifacts only to be double-crossed and left for dead by a Tennar Nether Ops agent known as Honey (*Takeover*). He remains in the employ of Mr. Nilo.

Kel Turner – A legendary legionnaire and operator well known to the Dark Ops community. His exploits, competence, and sterling character led Tyrus Rechs to entrust him with the observation of a Savage vault hidden on Kima. When the vault went active again, Turner rallied, gathering members of Kill Team Ice and preparing a plan to help fend off a second Savage invasion that even he himself didn't fully understand the complexity of.

Kill Team Ice – A team of volunteers formed by Tyrus Rex and Admiral Sulla during the Savage Wars, taking from the best of the Legion. Its members agreed to remain in cryo-stasis until a military application arose that required their unique talents.

Kill Team Victory – Dark Ops kill team founded shortly after the Battle of Kublar.
Active team members: Bombassa, Pina, Nix, Nobes, Toots, Wello.

Kima – A mid-core planet that served as the birthplace of the MCR. Was supposedly the home planet of the Kimbrin species, but this was actually... well, you'll have to keep reading.

KRS-88 – Psydon-era war bot (*Tin Man*). Was repurposed to serve as a bodyguard for the Maydoon family and was specifically tasked to protect Prisma (*Galactic Outlaws*). Now destroyed, his body was recovered from the planet Umnar by Garret.

Lao Pak – Lao Pak better be in this book. At least mention Lao Pak! Lao Pak too important not to show up in last book of season two!

Leenah – Endurian "princess." Exceptionally skilled mechanic. Former MCR rebel. Keel's main squeeze. A surrogate mother to Prisma for a time. A better pilot of the *Indelible VI* than anyone but Keel.

Lyra – A former bounty hunter and love interest of Tyrus Rechs (*Requiem for Medusa*). She was consumed by a techno-virus and her persona was salvaged in the form of an AI which Rechs kept aboard his starship, the *Obsidian Crow*. Lyra is currently trapped in a data cube with a destructive Savage AI.

MakRaven – Legion sergeant major and a legend in his own time. Formerly the premier donk fighter in the galaxy (*Turning Point*). Killed in action on Kima while calling in an artillery strike to save Zombie Squad and Masters (*Last Contact*).

Masters – Quite possibly the sexiest man in the galaxy. Definitely the best abs in the galaxy. Screenwriter. Heartthrob. Dark Ops legionnaire. Took a rain check on the last several hundred cuts by the donks. Now working with Kill Team Ice, Kill Team Victory, and anyone else who can help hold the Savage vault against a coming invasion.

Nilo – A genius-level intellect who controls a vast corporate empire. His shadowy past involves parents who were apparently lost to Gomarii slavers, though he believes his father is alive and trapped somewhere beyond galaxy's edge. Last seen traveling with Jack and Zora to Utopion, which he believes is Earth, based on a message from his father relayed to him by Sarai.

Pik'kek – A Kublaren tribal warlord whose band of warriors are in service to Nilo and Black Leaf. Formerly a member of Carter's merc team, also working for Black Leaf. Last seen traveling with Nilo toward Utopion.

Praxus – A member of the Cybar collective who dissented from the directives of MAGNUS and CRONUS. He was the lone Cybar to oppose aligning with those discovered beyond galaxy's edge. He accepted exile in order to save the life of Andien Broxin, whom he saw as the next evolutionary step for the Cybar—the perfect blend of machine and humanity.

Prisma Maydoon – Juvenile girl whose father, Kael Maydoon, was murdered by Goth Sullus. She hired Tyrus Rechs to seek her revenge (*Galactic Outlaws*) and was swept up in the rise of the Cybar and the fall of the Republic. Upon finishing her training, she found herself thrust into combat with the Dark Wanderer. Currently a guest on a mysterious starship well beyond galaxy's edge.

Ravi – One of the Ancients, left behind to help humanity resist the destruction coming from beyond galaxy's edge. His defense of Prisma may have hastened this apocalypse. Currently searching for a way to thwart the advance of an ancient evil.

Reina – A Savage prisoner who helped free Tyrus Rex and Casper Sullivan (*Imperator*). She later disappeared, though she seems to have had some communication with Casper before the man became Goth Sullus (*Gods & Legionnaires*). Trained in what Goth Sullus called "the Crux," she has returned to the galaxy, revealing to Prisma Maydoon that she is her mother (*Legacies*).

Sarai – An incredibly advanced AI created by Nilo with the help of pre-existing Savage technology. Now suspected by Garret to be acting in the service of the Savages.

Skrizz – Wobanki smuggler who briefly co-piloted for Tyrus Rechs (*Galactic Outlaws*) before joining the crew of the *Indelible VI*. "Tamed" by Prisma, Skrizz sought the girl out on his own before turning to piracy. He was enticed by Donal Makaffie into resuming the hunt for Prisma, this time by leading Makaffie to Aeson Keel.

Surber – Nilo's right-hand man. A no-nonsense enigmatic human who seems more suited for the boardroom than the sort of violent situations Nilo and Black Leaf continually encounter (*Takeover*). His name was given to Wraith as the source behind the termination contracts (*Legacies*). It is unclear if he is the same individual.

Tyrus Rex – The founder of the Legion (*Savage Wars* trilogy). Given immortality by Savages while their prisoner (*Imperator*), Rex escaped and dedicated his life to destroying them. Rex has lived multiple lives, primarily serving as a soldier on the galactic stage. When the House of Reason sought to assassinate him (*Legionnaire*, Epilogue), Rex went underground, living a new life as a bounty hunter under the alias Tyrus Rechs (*Contracts & Terminations* series, *Galactic Outlaws*). Plagued by a degenerating memory, Rex/Rechs was killed by Goth Sullus and Kill Team Ice.

Urmo – *sad Urmo noises* (*Imperator, Last Contact*)

Wild Man – A tortured soul and exceptional sniper. Savage Wars veteran and member of Kill Team Ice. Currently on his own, searching for a way to kill Savages to satisfy and avenge his wife. (*Savage Wars* trilogy).

Wraith – See *Aeson Keel*.

Zombie Squad – A squad of legionnaires led by Sergeant Lynx. After participating in the liberation of Kima, they followed MakRaven on a mission to rescue Masters from his zhee captors. Now they are working with Kel Turner to keep the Savage vault from falling into the hands of the enemy.

Zora – The bounty hunter daughter of former Dark Ops legionnaire Doc. She was brought in by Doc to help train Aeson Ford to better serve in deep cover. Hired by Nilo to convince Keel to work for his corporation, Black Leaf. Last seen asking Keel for an exfil from Utopion, where Nilo's team ran into unexpected trouble.

PROLOGUE

Earth Orbit
100 Years Prior to the Battle of New Vega

Tyrus Rex looked out the small viewport of the *Obsidian Crow*. Beyond was Earth, covered in cloud from a nuclear winter that wouldn't dissipate for another century at best. Once, Rex had seen the beautiful blues and greens on the planet, although there had been far more brown than green thanks to the bio-engineered poison that had killed off so much of the planet's vegetation. His hand went subconsciously to the faded NASA patch on his leather bomber jacket.

"You know, Tyrus, there are *considerably* better ships available than this old hauler."

Rex turned to face his passenger, the only person he'd brought on the trip. The only person he *could* bring on the trip. "I like this one."

Casper Sullivan chuckled and shook his head. "*I* like avoiding being soaked in radiation. From the moment we enter atmo, this thing won't give you four hours before we're saturated. To tell the truth, I'm a little worried about even being in orbit of that hellhole."

"Home, Casper," Rex said, looking back to the planet. "Home."

"Not anymore, Tyrus. Not for a long time."

Rex stifled a sigh. This would be difficult, because Casper Sullivan was a difficult man. Not because of any deficiency, but because he demanded an explanation. He needed to see the plan, understand it, and agree with it. Rex... wasn't good at helping people see what he saw. He wasn't good with words. Wasn't a leader, though men had always followed him.

"It's..." Rex began, and then, for reasons he wasn't aware of, answered his friend's first question. "I know how to fix this ship. You can always find parts. It's not finicky. It'll let you experiment a little and still do its job."

Casper looked around the ship, trying to see the old bird again in this new light. "They were decent enough bombers, I suppose. I wouldn't know about how well they serve as freighters."

"The radiation won't be a problem," Rex said, jumping to the next problem he felt he needed to clear for his friend. "You drop me off."

"You'll get fried, Tyrus. Savage enhancements are all fine and well, but there has to be a limit somewhere."

Rex shook his head. "I'm not... not trying to test any limits. I'll wear the armor. It's gotten me through worse."

"I guess you'd know a thing or two about getting off an irradiated world alive." Casper folded his arms.

"If you ever figure out a better way to stop these Savages," Rex said with an intensity that caught his friend off-guard, "let me know."

The *Obsidian Crow* hummed over the atmosphere of a dead and forgotten planet. A place that the galaxy was beginning to believe might not have ever existed. When one looked upon the grandeur of Spilursa, New Britannia, the Sinasian Cluster, and New Vega, it was hard to believe those worlds could be anything other than the splendid sources of humanity's origin. And while the shared myth of those first pioneers who had played the deadly odds in taking an early jump-capable explorer into the unknown was simply too ingrained for any of those worlds' inhabitants to seriously suggest they were the progenitors of mankind... that didn't always stop the people from those worlds from acting like it was so.

And for good reason, thought Casper Sullivan, a man who would one day become Goth Sullus, as he skimmed the ship over the vast stretches of dead soil. How could New Vega, in all its splendor, have grown out of this wasteland? Had Casper not known exactly how—had he not seen it happen over the centuries with his own eyes—he wouldn't have believed it himself.

They'd flown above Asia, which was one of the two continents that had held on the longest. Eventually, after Mars, it fell apart from the inside. The dreams of a united Asia would be achieved far across the stars... but not on Earth.

Casper keyed the intercom to reach Tyrus Rex inside the *Obsidian Crow*'s hangar. "When was the last time you visited?"

"Probably about the same as you," Rex grunted. Casper could see he was just finishing up putting on that fantastic Savage armor. "Not much reason to come back. I'm about ready. How close are we?"

Casper checked the instruments. "Just passing over the border of what used to be Laos and into Vietnam. You're sure it's here?"

"No. But if it's not... then it doesn't matter."

They flew low, beneath the perma-cloud cover that took away everything bright and warm and cast it into a cold, gray winter. Not as cold as it once had been, though. Things had improved since the last time Casper had visited his ruined and forgotten home world, finally stripped so fully of its resources that the only thing left to be taken was habitability. Had the jump drive not been invented, humanity would have died out completely by now. Especially after Mars.

That had almost been their last hope.

"I see *trees*, Tyrus." There was wonder in Casper's voice. "Real, honest-to-God trees."

"Must've mutated."

Casper nodded but didn't reply directly. That was the logical explanation. These trees must have mutated an ability to survive the bio-engineered "die-back" vegetation killer—one of a cascade of disasters that had set humanity down the path of its darkest and most difficult trials.

"They're extremely tall. Somehow managed to push up past the cloud cover... I'm going lower to see if there's any other life beneath them."

"Casper. Not a science expedition."

"It's on the way." Casper Sullivan took the *Obsidian Crow* down slowly to hover on its innovative a-grav boosters, the technological precursor to repulsors. The trees were growing up along a mountainside before petering out at the base of a vast, grimy lake set amid the rocks

4

and dead land. The water's radiation levels were nearly off the charts.

"Actually, Tyrus, this might be a good sign," Casper said.

He waited for Rex to ask how so, or to make some other kind of basic conversation. But that wasn't how his friend operated. Rex, he knew, was listening, though. If he didn't want to hear Casper's thoughts, he would have told him which task he felt needed to be focused on.

"If the vault is nearby," Casper continued, "they might have conceivably worked on a mutation to counter the die-back. These trees might be the fruit of that work."

There was a pause before the intercom box squawked, "Maybe."

"Maybe," Casper repeated to himself, smiling at his friend's conversational skills. Through the intercom he said, "Tell me where to put you down. We're within ten clicks of your coordinates."

"How about on the tree slope. I'll look for anything interesting and tell you what I see."

"No arguments here." Casper settled the *Obsidian Crow* down and then checked the sensors. "Try not to let leave the door open too long on your way out, Tyrus. I don't want any mutant flies to get inside."

"How's the radiation shielding doing?"

Casper checked. "Surprisingly well."

"It's a good ship."

"You've made it into one, anyway."

Casper watched through the cargo bay cameras as Rex lowered the door, immediately letting in a sudden swirl of radiated dust that would need to be vented the next time they took the ship up into space.

"I might roam around for a while," Casper offered. "Do a little sightseeing. Maybe go see if the Grand Canyon is still there."

"I'd rather you stay close."

"I was joking, Tyrus. You should try it sometime."

"No thanks."

Tyrus Rex stalked down the mountainside, marveling at the size of the massive trees that had found purchase in its rocky bedding. They were black as night, with pine needles that looked an ashen gray next to the great trunks—although when Rex looked at them where they gathered on the forest floor, they, too, looked black. The trees exuded a sort of tar-like sap, mostly around the roots and the lower portions of the trunk. Some of this sap ran down the mountainside and seemed to flow into the radioactive lake that stretched beyond.

This had once been a place of lush jungles. Rex had heard the stories of the exploits that had taken place among them, stories told back in the days when he had followed his father's advice and found the Rangers, became one of their number. Now, with the colossal stand of trees behind him, there was nothing but barrenness—and the exploits of MACV-SOG, which a young Tyrus Rex had listened to with intense captivation, seemed the purview of ghosts.

But while the galaxy had moved on from Earth—why return to a dead world?—those who had once lived there could not. Rex had come back before. So had Casper. Both for no other reason than to be there. And to remember.

And then it occurred to Rex that someday, the Savages would return here, too. Not to remember, but to make sure the galaxy forgot. That was a thing he'd recognized in those Savages that had begun to appear from the nether as raiders, twisted and ruthless... no longer human and no longer wishing to be seen as such. They in their tribes and perversions, in following their desires and beliefs to the end, had convinced themselves that they were something new and better. That they had shed all that stained mankind. Such thoughts gave way to a dogmatic belief that what had corrupted mankind was incurable, impure... and, conversely, that they, the Savages, were *not* impure.

That they had always been this way.

To show a Savage the truth of what they were and where they'd come from was to so damage their psyche that they would often shut down completely. That was easier to say than do. Easier still was to kill them outright.

But the weakness was real, and Rex sometimes wondered if Earth's rapid end wasn't a Savage attempt to snip those loose threads. As though they'd known upon leaving in those great lighthuggers that the only way to truly go forward was to leave nothing of their past behind them. It all had to be toppled and destroyed.

It was no secret that those who'd left were familiar with one another. The circle of elites was a club that most of humanity was not allowed to join. Which wasn't to say they were unified; far from it. But... they recognized their common interests and were willing to work together to achieve them. The greatest achievements would, of course, come with the purity of the lighthugger colonies. And the freedom from the impure.

The lighthugger was a technological marvel. It was only the subsequent and remarkably swift invention of faster-than-light travel—the hyperdrive—that made the lighthugger seem anything less than the fantastic achievement it was. In a vacuum, light travels at 186,282 miles per second. A lighthugger at top speed pushes 160,000 miles per second. Far from slow.

But it *felt* that way to those who'd wired the fantastic jump drives onto homemade starships in the hopes of finding a life and fortune in the stars that was no longer attainable on Earth. You couldn't help but laugh at the elites who set off for the stars in their "slow" colony ships, sentencing to death those they left behind—only to find that those abandoned souls leapfrogged them and laid first claim to the galaxy the elites had thought of as their own.

A man named Thomas Roman had been the first to successfully engineer the technology that made lighthuggers possible, and he shared it freely with those in the approved circles. Everyone knew Earth's time was short. Everyone also knew that the only way to get off-world was if they *all* got off-world. Otherwise, they would drag one another down. There was no going back to the filthy masses, and they would eat their own to prevent it.

It was Tyrus Rex himself who discovered the full, documented history of Thomas Roman. Not long before arriving on this mountainside, Rex boarded a Savage ship that possessed a remarkably full record of Roman's life and work. The ship was hardly a hulk, and Rex had been able to board, breach, and clear the ship entirely on his own. Its inhabitants were barely an imposition, having surrendered themselves to a virtual reality induced by technological implants and a steady stream of psyche-delic drugs, all run by a mastermind AI that kept systems operational.

At the time of Rex's arrival, the ship had been in the midst of a raid and subsequent pillaging of a planet called Feeyas. A race of humanoids—a species the galaxy would come to know as Kimbrin—lived on that world. They were the closest sentient life to Earth when measured in par-secs, but technologically, they were primitives. The ro-botic troops sent down by the Savages slaughtered them in droves.

But a robot army is only as good as its central con-troller. Rex boarded the Savage hulk, fought his way past more of the robots, and destroyed the AI core. This consequently also shut down the VR mind-dream of the Savages, who lay naked and corpulent in vast tubes. They began to scream as the madness of reality intruded on their carefully constructed utopia.

Tyrus Rex systematically killed every one of them.

From the ashes of that encounter came two critical pieces of information. First, that Thomas Roman's "gift" of the lighthuggers to other elites of his time did not come without a price. He retained the ability to spy on each hulk's happenings, though for what purposes Rex didn't know. Nor did he know where this Roman was, or if he was even alive.

The second matter was what brought him back to Earth. Using a communication device that the Savages referred to as "the strand," the Savages had systemati-cally erased all knowledge of Earth—including scrubbing its very location from every lighthugger's navigation-al records.

Tyrus Rex's understanding of Savages told him why.

On Earth was the ultimate proof that the Savages were nothing more than ordinary humans who had experimented on themselves until they could be convinced that they were something *better*—and always had been. The Savages now believed that they had never been like the others, all those filthy commoners beneath them. Only they, the chosen few, had possessed the necessary enlightenment to see the way forward. Mistakes? What mistakes? All the misery, suffering, and failures of Earth weren't *their* fault.

The truth was, they had touted themselves as the saviors of Earth, and it was their forced programs, nominally intended to create a utopia—one in which they ruled, of course—had been the planet's demise. But the Savages had deluded themselves, reprogrammed themselves, into believing in a different reality. And if they were to now come face to face with the truth of how ordinary they truly were, the truth of how it was *they* who had failed Earth before leaving for the stars and a closed system of unquestioned madness... then their new shared reality, and everything they'd built, could topple in an instant, leaving them defenseless and raving like those Savages Rex had ended before they could completely eradicate the Kimbrin.

Thomas Roman was behind the strand. And Thomas Roman wished for Earth to be forgotten. Was concerned about any other Savages having access to it. Rex knew that, eventually, Roman would have to come back and deal with whatever hidden sins lay on the ruined world. A man—even a Savage—with secrets exposed, never sleeps well.

This Savage would come back to Earth. And when he did, Rex would be ready. He would wait. At galaxy's edge, his time would come.

The cave entrance was guarded by a monstrous cyborg that looked like a bio-engineered gorilla. How it was kept alive, Rex didn't know. Whether there were others like it inside, he would have to wait to find out. His purpose in coming to Earth this time required that he do so without alerting the Savages. Killing this sentinel might not alert them, but he was unwilling to risk it. He returned to the *Obsidian Crow* and told Sullivan that he was going to scout for an alternate entrance, and then he returned to his work.

It took a week of ranging to and from the ship—which held out against the radiation without trouble despite Casper's initial concerns—before Rex found what he was looking for.

A back door to the vault.

He came back to the ship for a final meal and resupply before undertaking his final plan of action.

"There could be a working strand," Sullivan suggested as Rex gobbled down a ration pack. Rex and Sullivan had, for some time now, been on the lookout for a Savage strand that could both send and receive. Every Savage ship they had scoured had a strand receiver built into the very fabric of the vessel, but none were able to send. And once a ship was disabled, its strand went dark. No more messages received. No decipherable log. That was another thing that had brought them here. Or had brought Casper here. Rex had other ideas.

"Could be," he said between mouthfuls. He had decontaminated and left the suit waiting for him by the cargo bay. "But if there is, we need to leave it."

"Leave it? What for?"

"Because. It's all lies with the Savages. Right now they're just working on forgetting the truth. Eventually they'll come back to destroy it. But we can trap them here. Destroy them here."

Casper smiled. "You're thinking they'll phone ahead?"

"Something like that." He wiped his mouth and downed a bottle of water. "When he gets close to whatever madness he wants, the memory of what this place reveals about him will be strong. It's the kind of thing that unhinges a Savage. They can't abide someone seeing them for what they are and were. He'll go in and ping the strand on this planet he demanded all the other Savages forget, and he'll see if it's still there."

"Who?"

"Thomas Roman."

"If he's even still alive, Tyrus. For all you know he was vaporized along with the atmosphere of one of those worlds you've destroyed."

"He's behind what the Savages have achieved. He can watch them through the strand. He can override their systems... he wouldn't let himself get killed on some raid for resources."

"If you say so." Casper tapped his foot for a moment. "So this is all one big wiretap, then?"

Rex nodded. He liked when Casper used old terms like that. Old Earth lingo that would only draw blank stares from the rest of the galaxy now that so many centuries had passed. "Yes. I'm going to get inside as quietly as possible. If it's empty, great. If it's not, I'll be careful. If there is a strand here, we leave it be, set up a repeater, and then wait for it to go live."

Casper stroked his chin. "If we can secure a functioning strand, both incoming and outgoing, we might be able to capture whatever messages are being relayed. Troop strength, raid positioning... the list of possibilities is endless."

"Gonna have to find another one, then. Not this one. When Roman comes for Earth, he'll request a burst from this strand. We'll be waiting for it to go out. When it does, we can be ready to meet him and put him down." Rechs tossed his ration bag into the trash receptacle. "You've seen the difference between the Savage raiders and what was on the *Moirai*. What we're finding out this way are the latecomers. The ones who left early, like Roman, are the ones who have branched out farthest from humanity. The trick is going to be to get them to show themselves."

"I'm still not sure how you plan on coaxing them into doing that."

"They'll need to find Earth. It'll be their first target even if it's not a military one. We don't let them find it."

"Well, old friend, this place already doesn't look like the Earth that you or I or anyone else who once lived on it would recognize."

"There's still life on this planet," Rechs grunted. "Pockets of survival. Plants and animals. I saw a tiger."

Casper marveled at the news. "A tiger."

"Point is, Earth is still recognizable. If you look too close. Which you do if you're looking for Earth and you find a barren, destroyed planet. We need to make sure no one looks too close. We need everyone to think there's no way this planet could be Earth. Because everyone already knows it's something else. That Savage hulk full of refugees whose world was poisoned? The Kimbrin. We dump 'em here, and in a few generations they'll think of this place as their home world."

"That's your plan?"

Rechs began to doubt himself. This sort of thing wasn't where he excelled. Casper had always been the planner. "The Savages... they've already erased what they knew of Earth. They won't know what to look for. They made a mistake, Casper. We just have to exploit it."

"Never interrupt your enemy when he's making a mistake," Casper recited.

"Fighting the Savages is going to be humanity's only choice if it wants to survive. That fight will never end until *all of them* are wiped out. This is how we can be sure we get the last of them."

Casper Sullivan smiled. "Well, let's see what happens."

01

Kill Team Victory and Zombie Squad
Inside The Vault
Kima, formerly known as Earth

"I'll give you the one-credit tour on our way to see Shot Caller," Carter Delgado said as he led Masters, Bombassa, and the rest of Kill Team Victory and Zombie Squad through Thomas Roman's underground vault. "But we're only scratching the surface here. This place is huge. Goes way deep. The dude who built this place had some serious resources."

"The 'dude who built this place' sure seemed to like to decorate with his own photos," grumbled Sergeant Lynx, who was running Zombie Squad after the death of Sergeant Major MakRaven.

"Don't know what's so bad about that," Masters muttered to himself. "So, uh... Carter. Our algos are tagging this place as a potential Savage vault. Don't know if you saw the cyber-Drusic guarding the place, but—"

"That's why we took the back door," Carter interrupted.

"Right. So that, plus the writing in ESE—Earth Standard... something—has the Legion commander thinking this place might be more trouble the deeper we head inside."

"Oh, it's definitely Savage," Carter confirmed. "And we're talking the silvene standard. Basically a hulk built

15

underground. Shot Caller will fill you in. He's on comms with Legion Commander Chhun right now."

Bombassa, whose suspicions had only grown despite having recognized Carter, spoke. "So your Shot Caller, who I assume is Mr. Nilo, can reach the commander while we cannot?"

Carter stopped and held up the column on its way to a set of ancient-looking doors. "Okay, buddy. That's the second time you've known something about me when all I see is a tall guy in Dark Ops armor. Did we work together back when I was regular Legion?"

Bombassa hesitated, then lifted his helmet from his head. "More recently."

"Holy sket. Lash?"

Bombassa nodded and wondered if the man would be upset at learning that he'd been working alongside a Dark Ops spy during their time together with Black Leaf.

Carter, however, seemed thrilled at the revelation. "I *knew* it! I knew you were Legion. No way some hullbuster or basic could do what you did out on Kublar." Carter quickly scanned heads. "You don't have any 'busters or basics, do you? No. Okay. Right. No way you weren't Legion. I knew it!"

"And you're... still with Black Leaf?" Bombassa probed.

"Black Leaf paid the bills but the Legion had my heart," Carter said. He winked. "And restarted it, incidentally."

"Then we're on the same team," Masters said, eager to have stumbled into *good* news for a change. It seemed his life had been one bad turn after another ever since he'd arrived on Kima. "Let's share notes. Why can't we reach the Legion commander but you can?"

Carter admired Bombassa for another minute. "Lash. I can't believe it, man. I feel a lot better about what's coming next now that you're here, I'll be honest. Okay. So the comms thing. That's by design. There's this thing here, a communication device that's been trying to ping some-one out there. But those messages only get as far as Shot Caller—who is *not* Big Nee. It's how he was clued in that something was up in the first place."

"Clued in to what, exactly?" Bombassa asked.

Carter chomped his gum and blew out a pink bubble, popping it with a premature *snap* before he said, "That's what I'm taking you to find out directly. He likes to give the briefings. Real particular leej. Former Dark Ops guy named Kel Turner."

Those Kill Team Victory members without their buck-ets all had their mouths open at the revelation.

"You have to be karkin' clintin' me," Nix blurted out. "*Kel Turner?*"

"That a name we should know?" one of the Zombie Squad legionnaires asked.

"He's like top three all-time in Dark Ops," Masters said. "It goes General Rex, then me, although that order's de-batable, then like a three-way tie between him, Chhun, Owens, Ford, and Subs."

"And how about you?" Sergeant Lynx asked Carter. "You still a leej, too? Or is this one of those Nether Ops voodoo smoke sessions? Because it's all feelin' pretty convenient to me right now. Not that I'm complaining about getting pulled out of the fire."

"I've been it all," Carter said. "But right now, yeah, I'm a leej. Not sure who to see about getting all the back pay they owe me, though. We need a new sled, too."

"What unit?" Lynx asked, not so much as cracking a smile, as though all the gruff sobriety that Sergeant Major

17

MakRaven could put on had rubbed off on the legionnaire, but none of the mirth.

"Kill Team Ice. Which pre-dates Dark Ops or you'd get bumped way down in the standings, bucko." Carter winked at Masters and motioned for them to continue on their way to the blast doors. He held his hand over a round button that glowed green. "All right. Other side is where things get more Savage-like. Good news is, the place has been dead for centuries. We weren't sure when we came if we'd have to fight our way in, but only the big gorilla— technically it's not a Drusic—outside was left. And since there's a back door..."

The door slid open to reveal a clinically sterile room. It was studded with floor-to-ceiling transparent cylinders, filled with a soft green liquid, with valve releases above and below them. Inside floated grotesque chimeras, each tube with a different monstrosity. Many of them evoked thoughts of species already known to the galaxy. There was a wobanki-like creature, but with a broader chest, with orange-and-white fur and black stripes. A moktaar that appeared more human than simian. Another that looked like an ancestral Drusic.

They stopped before a zhee that wasn't quite zhee. The face was almost comical, and the clawed hooves were simply hooves with an opposable thumb, all of which sat atop human legs like some perverse centaur.

At a loss for any other explanation, Sergeant Lynx mumbled, "Have the Kimbrin been...?"

"Kimbrin got nothin' to do with this," Carter said. "This vault's been sealed for goin' on two thousand years. Before the Kimbrin even got to this world."

Nobes looked sharply at the man. "But this is their home planet."

Carter tapped his finger to his nose. "See, you're getting me tripped up on the details, man. This is Shot Caller's story to tell, and he wants to tell it to you."

"Why?" Bombassa pressed. "What's so important that it can only come from him? I can appreciate who you say is waiting for us, but I don't see the need for the cloak-and-dagger approach to giving us this information."

Carter gave a flat frown. "Shot Caller saw the Legion decline first-hand. I don't think he's a hundred percent sold that the guys fighting today are of the same mettle as the guys back in his day. Or mine, for that matter. Now me, personally, I think you'll be ready to dust whatever comes because you're leejes and that's what we do. But he wants to be sure you *fully* understand what's going to be asked of you in defense of this place."

He shrugged his shoulders. "You know how old people are. C'mon. We've kept him waiting long enough. Don't let him know I told you anything, either. He's legit the type of guy who will make me do burpees on fire watch even on the eve of the most important Savage invasion since New Vega."

The teams were led to a makeshift office set among the many abandoned laboratories that were honeycombed beyond the hall of animal-human hybrids floating timelessly in their preservation tanks. Inside was Kel Turner, still looking strong, defiant, and capable in his advanced age.

He introduced himself and was reminded by Masters that the two had once met in person, nearly a decade previous.

Kel smiled. "Sorry. I don't remember the exact scenario."

"That's weird," Masters said softly. "Meeting me is the kind of thing most people cherish for the rest of their lives."

"Masters," Bombassa scolded, and then cleared his throat. "It's an honor to meet you, sir."

Kel shook the offered hands in turn and then gestured at what furniture, lab tables, and wall space was available in the suddenly cramped laboratory. "Make yourselves comfortable, gentlemen. I have a story you'll need to hear."

02

Kel Turner's Legion had been the final strain of what he felt was good and right. Especially in Dark Ops. But it wasn't pure. He knew that even when he was a young man. The weight of corruption was always leaning against it; the House of Reason had gathered and consolidated power faster than any had thought possible. Or perhaps the galaxy, including men like Turner, hadn't paid close enough attention to see what was slowly happening all around them.

Even so, it was hard to imagine what the Legion would become, and difficult to stomach when it came to pass. Point-controlled Legion garrisons were used for little beyond oppressing Republic citizens—and protecting those parasites who grew fat and rich exploiting the same—while the Legion, the real Legion, was kept fighting in brutal conflicts at galaxy's edge, conflicts that had often been started by House of Reason intrigues in the first place. The House of Reason knew that keeping these leejes fighting-capable was important to the Republic's survival. They also knew that giving them a break from the fighting might coax them into looking closer at what was happening elsewhere in the galaxy.

This was the House of Reason's dilemma. They needed a Legion that could fight and win no matter the odds... and yet were terrified of a Legion that might one day do the same to them.

The Mandarins, however, were in no such quandary.

They had pushed to destroy the Legion from the inside almost from the beginning. These elites, who had set up systems of wealth, vice, and unaccountable power to entrap any who entered Utopion with a mind of serving any but themselves, had remained largely hidden, using Nether Ops and the Republic's Deep State to achieve their ends, all of which involved a systematic weakening of the Legion.

"We believe this man, or his inheritors, is why," Kel Turner told the assembled legionnaires, reciting almost verbatim a brief he'd only just finished delivering to General Chhun. He pointed to a portrait of Thomas Roman that hung like an icon in the laboratory.

Roman, the first of the elites of old Earth who'd left to find perfection among the stars.

And yes, Kima was Earth—though time changed all things. That news came as a shock to everyone. Right there, hidden in plain sight. A subterfuge crafted by Tyrus Rechs when the ancient T-Rex of the Legion realized that in their haste to forget Earth, the Savages had given humanity an opportunity to protect it. Because forgetting something is only the first step for those wishing to erase themselves and start anew. Eventually, the old needs to be destroyed. That's the only way to be sure that the narrative can go on unchallenged.

Reality is difficult that way.

It was a thing Tyrus Rechs knew before the Savages realized it. And by the time they did, they had already systematically wiped out all knowledge of where Earth was. Thanks in part to the subterfuge of Tyrus Rechs himself.

If not for that, the first united Savage attack against humanity would have played out very differently. It would have begun with an attack not against the humans, but against the Kimbrins. Instead the Savages went from human colony to human colony, ultimately finding themselves outmatched by the newly formed Legion on the planet then known as New Vega—later to be re-named Utopion.

The true complexity of that attack on New Vega, the thinking and control of the Savages by Maestro, the feints and ever-changing plans, were all unknown to Kel Turner. They had been unknown to Tyrus Rechs and Casper Sullivan. And though Maestro and the Savages and their Mandarins would have claimed that everything was unfolding as part of some grand, uninterrupted plan, it was not so.

The story was deeper and more nuanced. Full of pow-er struggles, pride and falls, the mysteries of the Quantum, the manipulation of the Dark Wanderer, the concurrent struggles of Ravi and even Urmo. Too many layers for anyone on the galactic stage to fully know the truth.

And then there was the role of the Gomarii, scouting worlds on behalf of the Golden King, enslaving native pop-ulations for use in the Savages' vast genetic experiments held in the solace of the Quantum. All part of a project first conceived on Earth—the proof of this lay outside the lab-oratory doors where Turner briefed the legionnaires—and continued through the centuries.

The Savages were patient. Despite their hubris, they knew their resources were finite, their power exhaustible. So they focused on those easily conquered races, thinking they might hold a genetic key that would serve in weak-ening other, stronger populations. The humans were not a concern; the Savages would defeat them when the time came. But how to deal with a species not yet capable of interstellar travel, but more than capable of its own planetary defense?

Their solution was to seed nearby worlds with invasive, engineered species, to give them rudimentary travel, and to set them loose on crusades of religious conquest that would whittle down or outright destroy the problem worlds over a matter of centuries. For what was a few centuries once you'd solved the problem of death?

Chief among these engineered species were the zhee, who were used again and again by the Savages to ripen prospective worlds for future conquest. A peaceful equine species, now extinct, had proved the key to creating the zealous, warlike zhee that the galaxy now knew. The world of the original species was plundered by a Savage hulk, and the equines were led unwittingly to a full and complete slaughter.

Not all the Savage-forged species were successful in their attempts to overrun a world marked for eventual Savage domination. The moktaar never could dislodge the wobanki. If anything, their introduction only made the predator species *more* difficult. And eventually, many of these new species, including the Drusics and doros, broke off to pursue their own aims and settle the galaxy.

But it was the outbreak of the Savage Wars that prematurely ended this grand strategy to capture the galaxy. Humanity had spread too far, too quickly, and Maestro judged the time to stop them from growing into an unassailable power had come.

The Golden King had conquered six chosen planets by then, and had been rebuffed by a seventh, Kublar. Which had been deemed too primitive to need a softening at the hands of the zhee or some other specially engineered rival species.

All of these events were unknown to Kel Turner. Tyrus Rechs and Casper Sullivan had only suspicions. And as the Savage Wars raged and the galaxy course-corrected time and time again, the time needed to investigate such matters dwindled to the point that even when Kill Team Ice uncovered something of the truth, it went unnoticed.

But now, at the last, things were plain. Or plain enough. How Kel Turner and the remnants of Kill Team Ice had gotten here was a footnote. The Savages were returning, and for reasons unknown, they had attempted to coax this Savage vault into communicating for the first time since Tyrus Rechs had covertly dampened the communications device and bent it to his will. Bent it and nearly forgot about it, except for a moment of lucidity late in his life that led him to Kel Turner, whom he gave one final mission.

"Hang out near the edge and wait," Rechs, then living a new life as a bounty hunter, had said. "And make sure someone is waiting when you're gone, too. The Savages will come back."

Kel Turner looked at the stoic faces of the legionnaires before him, and then to the knowing faces of his Kill Team Ice crew. "The wait is over, gentlemen. Your objective is to defend this vault against what is sure to be a full-fledged Savage attack. The Gomarii leading the assault are as sure a sign as anything."

Every shifting heel and change of posture could be heard in the deep silence that followed that proclamation.

"Does this place house some kind of Savage super weapon?" Bombassa asked.

Kel shook his head. "No. Nothing like that here. Think of it more like... an archive. A museum that shows very clearly who the Savages were. What they did. How they thought."

"So it has value as an intelligence tool?" Nobes guessed. "And we need to hold it until reinforcements arrive?"

Kel bared his teeth. Not angrily... more like he didn't like what he had to say next.

"Yes and no, Sergeant. There's no weapon that can be used here to destroy any Savage marine you'll encounter. No intelligence that will tell us how to fight the enemy threat. But *everything* here undermines all that they believe about themselves and hold sacred."

The operator looked down, searching for words to convey what General Rex—Tyrus Rechs—had believed. Had it been merely the force of that man's presence that had gotten Turner to go along with what was said, or did it all actually... make sense?

It had felt like it made sense *then*. Now, as he stood before the men who would likely have to die in defense of this place, he wasn't so sure.

He looked up again. At the faces of the new arrivals. They were all staring at him. Waiting.

"I don't understand the Savages," Kel continued. "But General Rex did. He spent lifetimes fighting them. He stopped them once. Died before he could do it a second time. But he was sure that once the Savages realized where this vault was located—and they now know—that they would come for it. At first with proxy forces. The Gomarii, as it turns out. But eventually, when that failed, they would come directly. *He* would come directly. The man you see in all these pictures—he's the same man who will come back to burn all of this to the ground. Although he's no longer a man. He's something... post... human."

Carter turned to face the others, then picked up the thread. "Those of us on Kill Team Ice, we've spent our lives fighting the Savages too. Just like General Rex. They're not like anything you can imagine. You can't put yourself into their minds because their minds no longer work like ours do. It's all lies. It's winning at whatever cost, and personal victories matter as much as planetary battles." He nodded to Nap, the Kill Team Ice sniper. "Billy and I have seen entire planets abandoned by their Savage invaders because a few platoons of hullbusters were on the brink of slicing all the dark secrets inside their space hulks. Just like that. So if the general says that this place is where these Savages' breaking point is, if he says this guy in all these holos is important to get at... well, it is what it is. Don't have to understand why. Just gotta KTF."

Kel cleared his throat. "This isn't the kind of mission a man should expect to finish alive. It's no fail, and it's volunteer only. Neither I nor your General Chhun is ordering you to be here. There remains a back door that you can take to get clear of this vault to rejoin your units if you so desire."

The old operator, a man who'd once cleared a battlefield of advancing tanks by dropping a meteor on top of them, motioned to the door.

None of the men present moved from their spots. This was the ultimate mission. A thing they'd all trained toward, whether Dark Ops or otherwise.

This was why they were legionnaires.

03

Kublar

The disgust on the Golden King's face was what stood out most to Prisma as he gazed around at the dead bodies. Not for the slaughter that his armored warriors had done to the Kublarens, whose phosphorescent yellow blood stank up the air and stained the hardpan of village, but at the very sight of the Kublarens themselves.

"To the last," he whispered to himself, recalling some distant, unpleasant memory. "Always to the last."

Reina leaned over to explain to her daughter the meaning of these words. "Long ago, one of our lord's sons landed on Kublar. You understand what it meant to land as a warrior for the Golden King?"

Prisma nodded. "Victory."

Reina smiled. She seemed much happier with Prisma as of late. The girl seemed to have accepted her place among them; Prisma Maydoon would be a powerful ally. What was planned and foreseen would become reality.

Her smile faded as she began to lecture on the weight of what it meant to battle on behalf of their master. "Or death. Victory is achieved for the Golden King, or a fight to the last. Never have his sons abandoned the battlefield."

"But the Kublarens," the Golden King said suddenly, taking up the narrative, "were remarkably of the same mindset, though their culture is pitifully undeveloped.

They fought my forces to the last, and my son proved himself unworthy of the honor of his birth." His look of disgust intensified. "And now it seems the Kublaren species has... *repopulated* since those days."

Indeed, the small Savage force that had landed in the middle of this thriving Kublaren village had been outnumbered and overwhelmed from the beginning. Several of the Golden King's warriors had fallen in battle. Were it not for Reina and the Golden King's powers, Prisma wondered if she too would have been destroyed. And in truth, on more than one occasion she had been forced to use her own power to save her life from the surging, relentless Kublaren attackers with their glassy stone weapons and archaic slug throwers. The thought of an entire planet of these persistent, swarming fighters overwhelming a Savage hulk that had invaded and refused to retreat seemed entirely possible.

It seemed to Prisma that if the Golden King didn't adjust his strategy, a repeat of his dead son's campaign would occur. There were reports of neighboring villages, separated from one another by kilometers of dry land awaiting the seasonal rains, mobilizing in response to the towers of smoke that seemed to stretch forever into the cloudless blue sky. A dust storm that was really a caravan of technical trucks—repulsor and wheeled alike—was now moving on their position in numbers that promised trouble, if not outright death... unless the Golden King had more warriors than what had come down on the shuttle.

That had been the first thing of interest to Prisma. Though he possessed an unimaginably large hulk and an army that Reina had boasted "matched the Legion" in numbers and "surpassed them in battlefield prowess," the Golden King had come down on a single shuttle, exotic and unlike any Prisma had flown in before, accompanied by only herself, Reina, twenty warriors, and a single general named Scipio.

The shuttle was black and gold, with wings that appeared leathery and flexible, as though it could flap them and fly, though it seemed to move through atmosphere under the same aerodynamic design as any other ship. Crash... Crash would have been able to explain how it worked. He could do that just from looking. But the war bot was long gone. And maybe that was better. He would have hated the violence that had occurred here.

The Kublarens hadn't even waited for them to land before opening fire. As the shuttle dropped toward its target, the town's many warriors—which meant virtually all of the town—gathered to meet what they had decided, correctly, was an unwelcome threat. The impatient among them fired at the invader well before their rounds had any hope of reaching its hull.

They were the first to die. A great red circle shone down from the shuttle's belly onto the middle of the village, perhaps a half-kilometer wide. The beam tightened until the circle was perhaps fifty meters in diameter. Then a super-heated blast filled the red circle, atomizing everything inside of it, Kublarens and simple stone-and-mud structures alike. Those outside the circle were spared completely. Those partially in and out were divided as if by surgical lasers, finding limbs erased as if by magic. Just gone. Without a flash of heat or the concussive force of an explosion. Simply... disappeared.

The shuttle had set down in that specially cleared dead zone, lurching forward as its ramp lowered in a way that seemed to give the Savage marines on board a momentous push as they charged. Prisma had seen fully armed and armored legionnaires in battle before. They looked intimidating, but still human. Not so with these Savages. Their armor was so thick and swollen that they looked more like bots than humans in armor. Seeing any part of the post-human Savage inside would create a comical contrast with the thick waist, massive shoulders, and great powerful arms and legs of the exterior. And perhaps this was known to the Golden King as well; he wore his battle suit and helmet only, shedding the outer layers of heavy armor. The Savage king held a deep concern over how he looked, Prisma had noted.

As the Savage marines stormed out in their black armor, they fanned out to the four points of the compass in four squads of five. Prisma saw each group had one gold-filigreed Savage assigned to four with white filigree in a fractal pattern. All were armed with large battle rifles that connected to the armor with a spiral cord.

As the shock of the shuttle's clearing attack subsided, the surviving Kublarens mounted an assault from just outside the radius of destruction. They fired from the toppled rubble of buildings suddenly bisected, their bullets snapping over the corpses of Kublarens who had been cleanly sliced in two by the weapon and now lay like medical cadavers shipped to Utopion in various states of dissection for xenobiologists to study.

Prisma watched from the shuttle ramp as incoming rounds harmlessly deflected off the Savage armor, doing nothing to slow the charge despite an intensity of fire that she was sure would have caused even Tyrus Rechs to stumble and fall. The Savage marines shouldered their weapons as they ran and fired, but instead of blaster bolts or bullets, quick rays of a soft purple light zipped out of the weapons. Each shot seemed to bore a hole in the flesh of the Kublaren targeted, much the same as a blaster bolt only with a smaller area of damage and shallower penetration.

Reina squeezed Prisma's shoulder, and the girl imagined that it was in anticipation of what happened next. Starting at the source of each wound, a sudden spidering of the vascular system took place, and the vessels that delivered the Kublarens' phosphorescent yellow blood began to harden and rise up, standing up from the alien's skin like scar tissue. This hardening spread across the body, rupturing the delicate air sacs that frantically inflated and deflated in pain—until the warriors dropped dead, their bodies unable to function any longer.

"Most foes would run," Reina whispered. "Watch..."

Prisma imagined that she herself would run if faced with such a dire weapon, but the Kublarens did not. Seeing the destruction being wielded against them, they responded with croaks and clicks that led to a charge. The aliens loped along in their peculiar hopping run, some firing from the hip and others discarding their firearms altogether, haven given up on penetrating the Savage armor with bullets. These drew tomahawks, clubs, and spears, and began swinging them in the air in anticipation of finding some Savage flesh to sink them into.

The first wave went down in agony as the five-man squads of Savage marines used their weapons to profound effect. Accuracy was of secondary concern, since any hit resulted in death. But the weapons couldn't fire as quickly as a modern blaster or even an old slug thrower, and by the second wave, the Kublarens were on top of them.

Without any effort spared for self-preservation, they overwhelmed their foes. Those shot with the vascular

weapon attempted to cling to the Savages as their corpses solidified, effectively hardening like statues around
arms and legs and clinging to the great helmets. The
Savage marines were too heavy and balanced to topple
easily, but as the swarm grew, the village's non-warriors
flowed into the arena and sought to topple those Savage
marines thus enveloped. Each time this was accomplished and a Savage dropped onto the desolate ground,
Kublarens fell upon them with their weapons to hack inside the armor.

Prisma watched in rapt attention as the sheer savagery of the Kublarens resulted in pieces of armor being
ripped away, sometimes with perfectly sculpted limbs
still inside.

All four squads were now falling back to the shuttle.

"Scipio," the Golden King said, "impede their charge
with our fallen."

"Yes, my lord."

The general, Scipio, turned to Reina and gave a quick
nod. She retreated farther up the ramp, pulling Prisma
along with her. A blast then erupted as the armor of one
of the fallen Savages self-destructed in a tightly contained but powerful blast that shook the ground and sent
a shock wave crashing against the shuttle. The shock was
powerful enough to knock the Kublarens to the ground,
but the Savages stood firmly in their armor.

Prisma's ears rang from the blast, and she felt her si-
nuses clear out. Subsequent blasts followed as each of
the overcome Savages was turned into a tactical bomb
that wreaked havoc on the swarming, surging waves of
Kublarens. The girl wondered if this had been the plan all
along; the effect on the species she'd heard the Legion refer to as "koobs" was devastating.

When the last of the explosions had sounded, Reina ushered Prisma back down the ramp. "Now it is our turn to fight for the honor of our lord, Prisma."

The battlefield was now a horrific scene. Blood and eviscerated body parts were washed in a glowing sea of yellow, the fishy scent of which made Prisma feel nauseated. Great swaths of Kublarens had been killed, but still more came, and they would soon overwhelm the shuttle just as they had overwhelmed several of the assaulters. The lusty croaking of the Kublarens filled Prisma's ears and made it difficult to think of what to do next. She didn't want to kill them, in fact she wanted them to win... but she also didn't want to die.

The first spear with its obsidian tip sailed toward her, and Prisma found herself ducking instinctively, just as she had when the creature Urmo had attempted the same. Meanwhile, the Golden King waded out into the fray, using only his hands to strike away great stacks of Kublarens as though clearing a table of flies. They flew through the air, sent sprawling by a shock wave that came from more than just his armor. Most were dead before they landed.

Reina too used the powers of the Crux, using her mind to manipulate the physical world. Crushing, breaking, tearing the little Kublarens as they croaked and circled and charged again and again. Scipio fired a blaster rifle of sorts, expertly killing a foe with every pull of his trigger. The remaining Savage marines did the same, using their terrible weapons to bring pain.

At last the danger was so close that Prisma was forced to make a choice: kill or be killed. There was no hiding, no evading. Too many Kublarens were now fighting up close, and unless they were cleared away, she would be destroyed.

Prisma... you know what to do.

Reina was in her mind, prompting her to act on what her instincts were already driving her toward. She felt something rise out of her, the same way it had while escaping with Leenah from the Cybar mothership, the same way it had in defending herself from Hutch after he ravaged Mother Ree's Sanctuary. She shouted, and felt a power erupt from her that tore through the Kublarens, as if an invisible repulsor train had just plowed through their midst.

She could sense the satisfaction, the excitement, and the sheer, possessive joy of both Reina and the Golden King. They were pleased with her. Pleased with their new weapon. For that was all she was to them... a weapon. And though Prisma had discovered the truth of her situation before setting down on this world, that realization still brought with it a sense of sorrow.

"My lord!" Scipio shouted, perhaps in alarm over the dangerous surge of Kublarens still pressing, or perhaps only to be heard above the croaking. These Savages spoke externally in an almost primitive way. No L-comm, and only occasionally in the mind, and that was usually Reina. "The shuttle's V-cannon is back online."

"Use it." There was no urgency, alarm, or strain in the Golden King's voice when he replied.

The shuttle sent out a red beam that danced on a sea of Kublarens. Prisma was careful to position herself far from it. Then another eruption of energy blasted from the craft, erasing everything in its path, creating a clear avenue out of the village that led out onto the desert hardpan beyond.

The Golden King laughed, the battle continued, and the Kublarens of this village were killed... to the last.

Now Prisma stood amid the aftermath of that ferocious, merciless battle. It looked as though dead Kublarens were everywhere, except for the occasional Savage marines whose armor had not been detonated because they'd fallen too close to the Golden King. Prisma was unharmed, while Reina tightly held a cut she'd suffered on the top of her wrist. A thin effusion of blood seeped between her fingers and dropped to the dry and thirsty ground.

The Savage king, already free of his great outer-armor, removed his oversized helmet. He looked at Reina's wound distastefully, as though in receiving it the woman had somehow failed him. Then he looked at Prisma with a sort of newfound respect that, for reasons she couldn't explain, she felt desperate to be worthy of.

"Has the student so quickly surpassed her master?" the Golden King asked.

Reina's eyes flashed a swift and jealous anger at Prisma. Though the words and thoughts belonged to the Savage king, the woman seemed to blame Prisma for them. Reina couldn't imagine anything greater than being the one who stood nearest the Golden King; she imagined Prisma would want the same. She was wrong.

But Reina was also dangerous. Even without knowing all the little secrets that Prisma had hidden deep down inside herself. About her *real* mother, whose beautiful eyes and beautiful smile her father had fallen in love with. Reina had been willing to erase that woman from existence, solely in order to use Prisma for her own purposes.

Hide the truth and live the lie. That was what Prisma knew she needed to do. For now. But the time was coming when she would stand over Reina's dying body and tell her of all the people who were finally avenged. Her parents first and foremost, but also Crash and Ravi. Perhaps even Urmo. Prisma now understood that she'd been manipulated into killing that creature; Reina had arranged it. She had wanted it.

Prisma had thought about her moment of vengeance in the long hours of solitude inside her chambers. She had kept it secret, as she kept many things secret, and her power to do so was only growing. They didn't know when she spoke to Ravi, or when her mind left her quarters and wandered through the ship.

The time was coming. Reina would die, and while Prisma hoped it would be a long and agonizing death, she had thought about what she'd do if it was quick. Prisma would look Reina in the eyes with defiance and fiercely say, "My mother."

In that moment, Reina would realize that she had not been nearly as clever or thorough or deceitful as she had imagined. She would die knowing that it was the memory of Prisma's mother, her real mother, that had destroyed her. A poetic end for the witch who had attempted to create a counterfeit identity for herself by destroying the existence of that same woman.

But all of that was... for later.

Prisma had to tell herself that, twice in fact, as she endured Reina's jealous gaze. She had to put away the persistent urge to remove the feathered spear that was slung across her back, still stained with Urmo's blood, and run it through Reina, to drive it into her stomach and then force it up to her heart so she could have that moment to speak those words and then surrender to her own death.

That was being selfish, she knew. Something for her that would do nothing for Ravi or Leenah... or the galaxy at large. Because that was how big this problem with the Golden King was. He presented a threat not only to the people she loved, but to all the people she'd never meet.

The Savage king smiled at Prisma with a warmth that almost took her breath away. If Prisma wasn't careful, she would be in trouble as well. She *enjoyed* that smile, felt a radiating sense of satisfaction and pleasure from receiving his praise. She knew what he was and what he intended to do, and *still* she wanted to be admired by the powerful, golden-skinned captain of post-humanity.

And if Prisma felt that way, how much stronger must Reina?

She had to focus on the way forward. Living in the lie that those around her had created. She would remain enraptured by her mother and would refuse the very suggestion of rivalry—something she felt the Golden King was seeking to stoke for purposes only known to him.

"I was only doing what my mother taught me," Prisma explained. "I wanted to hide. She told me that it was our honor to fight for my lord."

The Golden King looked at Reina, who now seemed placated by her daughter. All the sneering disdain disappeared that quickly, and her newly confident, glowing face insisted that the ugliness had never happened at all.

"Eventually, Prisma, such animal instincts as fear and hiding will be shed," Reina said, gently stroking the girl's hair. She looked to the Savage king. "And *then*, perhaps, Prisma truly will surpass me."

She would kill me if he chose me, Prisma told herself, *but she would also give me to him as a gift.* Her skin crawled.

General Scipio stepped forward, unable to put off any longer a matter that was clearly weighing on him. "My lord, the animals from the surrounding villages will be here soon." He waved a mighty, gauntleted hand toward the horizon where the dust grew like a towering siege wall. The billowing dirt was pierced with brilliant starlight twinkles of shining sun glinting off the sand-blasted metal and pitted windshields of the great Kublaren military convoy. "See how the storm of their coming increases."

"You *fear* their coming, Scipio."

The Savage general shook his head decisively. "I only fear failing you, my lord." Scipio gave a slight bow with the proclamation. "We will meet them here, or wherever my lord desires. There are far superior defensive positions available to us, as my lord knows. But the time to reach them grows scant, as my lord also knows."

Roman set his hand on top of the general's boulder-like pauldron. "You are my finest general, Scipio. Had my most splendid son been sent to this world first, we would not have lost it."

Prisma watched the Savage king speak with a mix of curiosity and concern. He was taking his time and seemed almost unaware of the force that was bearing down on them. By now she could almost make out the individual Kublarens driving technical trucks, both repulsor and wheeled. Scipio noticed it as well, unable to prevent his eyes from darting toward the coming foe. Not as one in fear, but more like... an obedient attack dog on a leash who desperately wants to be unclipped and left to maul and tear on behalf of his master.

But what could any of them do against a force this size after what the ruined village had accomplished? That was unclear to Prisma. What was clear to her was that the Golden King felt no urgency whatsoever.

"You would have conquered this world, Scipio. You would have gathered what first interested us about these animals. And how might we have been different had it been so? You see how they fight. What might have been unlocked if we had taken the entire population? How might we have used these creatures for our purposes?"

It was clear that Scipio wasn't considering the answer. His focus remained on the coming vanguard. Prisma felt as though the bullets or blaster bolts would snap and sizzle overhead any minute. Only the Golden King and Reina seemed not to notice or care.

"But the Legion," continued the Savage king. "The Legion would have tracked us down to this world just as they did all the others when your brother failed at Enduran. And then, Scipio my son, I would have lost you as I did your siblings. You are all that remains of my first generals. Yes, you would have taken this world... but you would not still be alive to witness my final victory."

The Golden King turned to face the storm cloud of reinforcements racing for the village outskirts, and removed an amulet from around his neck. Where Goth Sullus had been seduced by a Cybar ring, the Savage king wielded a five-pointed, swirling star.

And inside of it was death.

A rush of wind poured forth from the amulet, funneling ever wider until it felt as though gales blew in every direction. Prisma felt somehow cold beneath the blazing Kublar sun, and yet an even greater chill washed over her upon seeing what rode that supernatural wind. At first, she thought she was somehow seeing the currents of the wind itself; but the more she stared, the more those lines and swirls began to look like the comet's tails of spectral heads. Dead, emotionless eyes were set deep in faces that were not quite human, looking instead like an aborted attempt at mimicry by some unholy doppelgänger. They registered primal alarms in her mind that blared, *"This is not one of us. This is not safe."*

And so it wasn't.

The wind grew in intensity and brought forth a howl unlike any Prisma had heard before. It was as if countless voices moaned in anguish, hate, horror. The Dark Ones spread out across the desert at their master's command and swept into the enemy lines just as the Kublarens were set to open fire on the latest in what had been a long line of planetary invaders. Only, these invaders would be the last. For they would be the victors.

You are seeing more than what those without our gifts can see. And less than what is truly there. Reina was in Prisma's mind, far away from the secrets, in the place Prisma had made for her.

The demonic onslaught ripped into the native fighters like great, rolling bolts of chain lightning, leaving a trail of corpses before the Kublarens could even realize what was happening. By the time the Kublarens began firing at the wind—an act that a more civilized species would have laughed off as superstitious—many of their dead had already begun to rise once more... and use their weapons against the living until they were shot and mutilated to the point of inoperability.

Prisma could see no reason for this gruesome manipulation of dead flesh—at least, no reason beyond the Dark Ones' enjoyment in employing a variety of killing methods. And indeed, a dark and twisted glee emanated from the beings, flowing thick and heavy across her mind. For the Dark Ones were more than capable of destroying the armies before them without such inventiveness, leaving the Kublarens to bake in the sun, where they would become an eventual meal for the leathery-winged carrion eaters that had been circling the blue, cloudless skies over the village ever since the scent of blood reached their rooks.

It was the abrupt fall of one of those large, flying reptiles that clued Prisma in to the fact that the Dark Ones had taken to killing more than just the Golden King's enemies they'd first been pointed at. When one of the scavengers hit the ground with a *whump* and a sudden spray of dust not four meters from where Prisma stood, she looked up, squinting against the sun's glare, to see that the swirling indigo storm had risen up to the skies and was now viciously overtaking anything it found alive, riding the great wings down to sudden, pulverizing deaths on the ground below.

"You see, Scipio!" the Golden King shouted. "You see at last!"

Prisma looked to the Savages. She saw a proud satisfaction on the faces of the men—and indifference on the face of Reina.

And yet, for as mighty a weapon as had been unleashed on the Kublarens, the Dark Ones were not invulnerable. That superstitious act of firing at the ill wind had not been without its effect. Prisma could see some of those deep indigo lines become rigid and gray before fading from reality entirely. She reached out with her mind, her senses enhanced by the Crux, and understood that the Kublarens had been capable of taking at least some evil out of the world by their own dying acts.

Some. But not enough.

This was the fully gathered force of a dark and terrible race of ghouls and reapers. Perhaps, had someone like Ravi staged and organized a defense of the planet, more of their numbers would have been claimed. But the Kublarens, with no knowledge or forewarning of the nature of their foe, had nevertheless stumbled upon some little success, thanks to the full-spirited, primal manner in which they fought and killed.

They're fighting in both places, Prisma told herself. *Here... and the Quantum. That's how you can kill them.*

The battle felt like an eternity for Prisma as she stood there, watching the coming invincibility of the Golden King. In truth, it lasted no more than thirty seconds before every Kublaren who had organized against the Savage invader was dead. It was then that the Dark Ones began to drive themselves to and fro, searching the skies and the ground for more life to destroy. Their wind kicked up small dervishes and dust storms. They raced back through the village the Golden King had assaulted, looking for those still clinging to life and gleefully ripping it away from them, rejoicing with every final breath they pulled from the dying.

Prisma realized that the spirits were circling her and the others as well, looking longingly with their dead faces, eyes set too far apart, gaping mouths too wide. It was only at the Golden King's behest—perhaps only because of his willpower—that all were not slaughtered the same as the Kublarens.

And yet that willpower seemed to waver, just for a moment. Prisma felt an intense pressure on her mind and looked to the Golden King, who was no longer the proud ruler witnessing his dominion. His face was strained. Reina noticed as well, and looked alarmed—though she kept silent and made no move toward the ruler.

At last, with a tight voice, the Savage king said, "Go."

The Dark Ones immediately shot across the horizon in all directions. Surely the fool had not let them free? But no, Prisma was still alive. She reached out with her mind just as she'd learned to, searching for all the pinpoints of light that represented life on this planet. She began small, focusing on the living aura of herself, Reina, and the surviving Savages. From there she spread out over the vast desert hardpan and saw the nearby Kublaren settlements, whose defenders were all lying dead before her, their kin waiting for a return that would not come, unaware of what had been unleashed on their warriors and was now coming for them.

The light of those lives was extinguished by the Dark Ones with ruthless efficiency. It was all Prisma could do to expand her mind's eye far enough and quickly enough to keep pace with the demons. It was the same everywhere.

Prisma was sure the Golden King's utterance was in answer to a petition by those wicked spirits to destroy everything.

And so a race that had stood against the Savage king, surviving only by its own merit and battlefield tenacity, was exterminated so many centuries later. A millennium and more after its act of defiance.

At last the Golden King had his revenge against the animals.

There was nothing left alive on Kublar... save its invaders. The new inheritors of the world.

And what will happen if the Dark Ones don't heel? Prisma wondered. *How can the galaxy hope to withstand this?*

Prisma watched the Golden King struggle. His teeth were set hard in his perfectly sculpted jaw, which bulged from the grinding pressure he produced. Reina and Scipio were watching as well, the concern on both of their faces easy to read.

"Return," the Golden King grunted.

Still the Dark Ones howled and raced through the skies.

"Return..."

The weight of something unseen bent the Savage king's knees, but he quickly overcame it and stood taller and straighter than before.

"Return!"

The wind grew into a frenzy, and the indigo streaks of that fevered dream shot back from all corners of the planet to reside once again in the swirling star amulet. The Savage king rolled his shoulders, which were now slumped as Prisma had never seen before.

Such a tenuous grip over these other-dimensional monsters. And Prisma had heard it; felt it. The Dark Ones' whispers and complaints, their suggestions and enticements as they reluctantly obeyed their new master.

No, they said. *There is still some life on Kublar. Small life. Petty things that must be destroyed. The world must be made sterile. All of it must die. We will grow stronger with its death.* You *will grow stronger...*

Prisma knew that the Dark Ones could never rest from this desire to eradicate all that was living. Not until they had achieved their terrible end or were themselves destroyed. The Golden King would not be able to withstand them forever. That was clear. Every usage of that foul army would bring him one step closer to his own demise. He and Reina were fools to think they could harness evil and not be destroyed by it themselves.

They had to be stopped. The Savages and the Dark Ones alike.

Prisma couldn't do it alone. She understood that now. She understood... so many things that she hadn't before, as though the opening of her mind to the Crux had done more than expand her senses. It had led her to the bottom of herself and the truth that comes from surrendering all and being left with nothing *but* truths. Even the truths that destroy the well-kept images we keep of ourselves. Especially those truths.

She couldn't do it alone. She needed Ravi. And perhaps... the entire galaxy along with him.

04

Wait.

That had been Prisma's instruction to Ravi at the end of their last communication. Yes, things looked bad, but the Ancient One needed to *wait.* Only... Prisma couldn't say why, exactly. She knew the Golden King was powerful. So was Reina. But they were not invincible. She could see that from how meticulously they kept to their planning, or in the ways the Golden King would bring up the failure of his generals in some long-ago battle that the galaxy considered little more than an obscure theater of the Savage Wars.

The Golden King needed others to achieve his ends. He was a tyrant, not a god. No different than Goth Sullus...

No tyrant rules alone.

Tyrus Rechs had told her that once. She understood it now, though she hadn't during those whirlwind days aboard the *Obsidian Crow.* It all seemed like a distant sideshow in her life, a time when, in anticipation of avenging her father, she was taken under the bounty hunter's wing. Rechs taught her to shoot, and how to think like a soldier. He had quickly gone from refusing her request to kill Goth Sullus—a termination contract, she later learned it was called—to accepting it in exchange for a picture of her mother. Her real mother. And once he accepted, he went farther than seeking a way to find and kill the man. He became a teacher.

Prisma had often wondered whether Rechs had any children of his own. Back then, she sometimes thought of him as a long-lost relative who'd come to take the family orphan into his life—and then she would blush at how silly that was. But now, she didn't find it silly at all. Because maybe Rechs saw something similar. Why else would he have done all that he did for her? Why else spend all that time teaching her, telling her things he felt she needed to know, even though words never came easily to the man.

There was more to it than that, though. She had long thought that Tyrus Rechs could somehow sense his coming death. He had taken Prisma in out of compassion and a desire to see her live a full life, but then he reneged on his vow not to lead her down the trail of revenge—and that could only be because of that sense that his time was running short. Prisma could see no other reason. He'd tried to shrug off the heavy hands of fate by giving her over to Mother Ree, but in his struggles in the sanctuary garden, she imagined he realized that in this case, fate was not to be denied. With that decided, he strode defiantly to meet his end, teaching Prisma all the things he felt were most true and most important during however much time remained.

Much of that teaching was about revenge—and how it would erode her soul. He spoke of how killing made one a killer, and how those killers who killed to fulfill some ideal or killed to relieve themselves of some missing element in their life would only ever be able to go on killing; the emptiness would demand it. But the killing would never fill what was missing. And yet... Tyrus Rechs was the most notorious killer Prisma had ever known.

"It's complicated," he'd told her. "Teaching how to kill is the easy part. Teaching why... that's something... something I don't know if I can teach you."

"Because I'm too young?"

"Because you already have your reason. And it's a bad one."

"Oh. That." Prisma folded her arms. "He *deserves* it."

"Most of us do," Rechs answered, and then went on to instruct her on the easy part of the equation, showing her how to draw a weapon and sight your target in one smooth motion. Again and again, barrel up and drifting down behind the sights and fire—*click*—and then repeat. "The first shot is the only one you might get. Never waste it."

It was after a round of simulated target practice, shooting at circular holos that floated through the expansive cargo deck and would occasionally shoot harmless bolts back, that Prisma learned the lesson of tyrants. She had been following one of the drifting targets with one eye closed, never quite satisfied enough to take the shot. A harmless holographic bolt danced toward her instead, flashing on her chest.

"You're dead, Prisma," Tyrus Rechs growled, and sounded angry for it. "Sit down."

"I'll get it," she insisted.

"Sit down!" Rechs said, anger rising to the top. "Dead people don't get second chances."

Skrizz had been lazily napping on top of a weapons container, but now the wobanki perked up his ear and pried open one eye to see if whatever was going to happen next was worth waking up for.

Rechs paced. He wouldn't look at Prisma. She watched him for a bit, then let the practice blaster hang at her side and slowly sat down.

"I understand," she said.

Skrizz closed his eye and went back to sleep.

The girl had expected a lesson about the finality of death, and was even interested to hear it. She'd received such cautionary speeches before, from her father, and she wondered what wrinkles this bounty hunter would put on the topic. But Rechs went in another direction entirely. He pulled over a small repulsor crate and sat down on its edge like on a stool. She had gotten used to seeing him outside of his armor now—combat boots, cargo pants, a green V-neck t-shirt.

"A tyrant," Rechs began, "sees two types of people in the galaxy. The preferred type serves willingly. They find safety in his rule, because it's only under tyranny that you're free to indulge your basest desires. It's an excuse to hate, control, and destroy that draws in this type, Prisma. They never admit it, but that's the appeal, and they'll change on a dime the moment a new opportunity to express those things without fear of reprisal emerges. Good people make the mistake of thinking they can reason with this type by looking for some principle behind their cruelty. There aren't any."

Prisma nodded, wondering where this was coming from and why it was important. And also wondering what a "dime" was.

"And so, the tyrant first provides their followers with an excuse to let out all the dark things that are already in their hearts. Because that's the quickest way to take care of the problem, which is... everyone else. The non-followers. The second type. These can be people who oppose the tyrant, or people who simply want to be left alone. It's all the same. You get ones who keep their heads down and hope not to get noticed by the tyrant's disciples as well as the ones who hold their heads high in defiance.

"But that's the twisted beauty of it, Prisma. Head down or head up, the tyrant sees clearly where to send their foot soldiers, with a different battle plan for each, but hate, control, and destruction for all." Tyrus Rechs stopped to shake his finger at Prisma, bobbing it up and down to the hum of hyperspace as the *Obsidian Crow* fled between star systems. "You're gonna face tyrants in life. Don't think otherwise. The faster you deal with them, the better it is for everyone. The more you indulge them, the harder and worse the fix ends up being."

The bounty hunter fell silent for nearly a minute, as though done. Prisma furrowed her brow in confusion, sure that there was more to this. Had Tyrus been talking about someone she knew? Did he mean Goth Sullus?

Tyrus Rechs looked up at her, and she could see a sort of confusion in his eyes.

"How do you stop a tyrant?" Prisma asked, hoping the question would shake the look from him. That look scared her. She hadn't ever thought of the bounty hunter as anything but in control, but here was a look of extreme age and a failing grip on one's memory and senses.

"That's what I've been teaching you," Rechs said, his eyes bright again as though regaining his lost thought. "I sure didn't give you a blaster so you could go hunting, kid."

Prisma laughed, and then, slowly, Rechs laughed too. She realized that he hadn't meant to be funny.

"Here's the thing you gotta remember. They *need* the ones who don't fall in line. They act like they don't, but they do. Even while they kill them and oppress them, they need them."

"But... why?"

"Lot of reasons. Sometimes it's legitimacy, because deep down, they know their authority was built by the cruelty of fools and they can't stomach it. Sometimes it's because they're the only ones who can do the hard things that need to be done if power is going to be maintained. The Legion..."—here Rechs looked sorrowful—"the Legion has been that for the House of Reason for a long time now. The only thing keeping the galaxy from splintering and going its separate ways. A tyrant can't let that happen. They can't stomach being rejected. Can't live with anyone wanting another way than theirs.

"The point is, you have to look past what they want you to see. They want you to see something so big and untouchable that you won't even dream of trying to touch it. They break laws and flaunt it while punishing those beneath them with an obsessive zeal. It's all a smokescreen.

"Move through the smoke and find the ones they *need*, Prisma. Because that's the weakness. That's where you can hit them. And once you do... they drop real easy."

"But all those followers you talked about... the ones that *like* to be mean."

"Cruelty and hate only pretends to be brave. It melts when things get hot, when opposition comes." Rechs tapped the side of his head. "They're sick, and so their thoughts are sick. They can only imagine in others what they would do themselves, and as soon as it looks like they might lose... they fade away. They're not brave enough to face the kinds of things they've done to others."

Rechs walked over to Prisma and stood her up. "Show me your shooting stance."

The girl obliged.

"Good. Left foot a little more forward. Let's try the targets again."

That conversation with Tyrus Rechs felt like a lifetime ago... and also like it was yesterday. Even now, on a great Savage hulk half a galaxy away, Prisma well remembered those early lessons of Tyrus Rechs. That lesson. The lesson about tyrants.

The Golden King wanted something more than just ruling the galaxy. He wanted to be feared. He wanted to be revered. And he had already chosen which worlds would fear him, and which would laud him as a god.

Somewhere in that was the way to bring the tyrant down. Prisma needed only to find it. Until then... Ravi would have to wait.

05

Battle Phoenix

"What does she mean, 'wait'?" Keel asked Ravi. The Ancient had just delivered Prisma's message to the team, casting further confusion on what the next steps should be.

"She understands that she is aboard a Savage vessel with two powerful Savage rulers, one of whom most recently masqueraded as her mother. But she wants us to wait before attempting an attack."

"*Attack?*" Keel looked around the *Battle Phoenix*, searching to see if the concept was as surprising to the others as it was to him. "That's the Legion's job. I thought we were going to just try and pull her out before they hit the hulk."

"Evidently she feels an attack will be more successful from the inside." Ravi stepped toward his friend. "You must understand, they have weaponized the Dark Ones, and now the entire Legion will present little problem for them. Prisma has seen first-hand the destruction they wrought on Kublar."

Keel shrugged. "I'm not exactly shedding a tear over Kublar."

Ravi frowned, clearly annoyed. "The rest of the galaxy will not fare better. You yourself have seen this sort of power. Or have you forgotten the decisive battle on Utopion with Goth Sullus?"

Keel grew tight-lipped. Of course he remembered. He'd lost friends on that battlefield and had seen them rise again to fight on Sullus's behalf. And he'd seen the phantasmic whirlwind that Sullus had opened in those moments before Wraith put a bullet in the man's head.

Ravi pressed his advantage. "This was a mere fraction of the power now held by the Golden King. The destruction he is now capable of is like nothing the galaxy has faced before. But he bides his time. He desires something more than the Consumption of the Dark Ones. Things are not yet lost."

"Good." Keel nodded. "That's good. Because I sure as hell am." He began to list the various tasks before them, hooking a finger on his hand as he named each one. "First, we've got Zora and Nilo who need our help on Utopion. Then we've got the Legion saying they found some Savage vault on Kima and the planet's under attack because the Savages discovered that Kima is Earth, only no Savages are actually attacking the planet because why would things make sense? Then we try and get Broxin and her android boyfriend to link up only to get *another* request for a bailout because they're up to their necks helping fend off an invasion in the Sinasian Cluster. What else am I missing?"

"You did not include on your list the Golden King and the Dark Ones," Ravi said.

"It was implied." Keel kicked his heel and turned his back on the Ancient, studying the empty hangar of the *Battle Phoenix*. Skrizz was off somewhere, Leenah and Garret were seeing what they could do with Crash, and G232 was all worked up about his next big "gala." Only Death had stayed close, eager to be brought on the mission, whenever it actually got underway.

"Would you like to know what I think we should do first?" Ravi asked.

"Would you tell me even if I said no?"

"I calculate that recovering Nilo will yield the highest potential benefit. If we are to wait until Prisma sees more favorable circumstances, we should use that time in re-covering him—and also your friend, Zora."

Keel worked his jaw back and forth. He owed it to Zora to go after her anyway. "All right. Yeah. But let's fill in Leenah before you disappear us into the middle of a firefight."

"That is not how it works."

"Could've fooled me, pal."

Garret had been vaguely aware that Captain Keel and Mr. Ravi had been in the room with him, though neither had addressed him directly, speaking to Leenah instead. Or at least, he didn't think either of them had talked to him. Most of the conversation had revolved around their go-ing to Utopion to see about bringing back Mr. Nilo and Ms. Zora, which was a good thing—Garret liked both of them. There also had been some talk about Prisma, and the code slicer was fairly sure that neither Captain Keel nor Leenah was thrilled by Mr. Ravi's assessment that she needed to stay on board a Savage hulk for an indetermi-nate amount of time.

Of course, that might also be a misconception on Garret's part. He was only barely listening, mainly for his name just in case they needed him for the rescue operation. Ever since arriving aboard the *Battle Phoenix*, Garret had put all his attention toward fixing the unfixable; he wanted to repair KRS-88. It wasn't until after Keel and Ravi had left and Leenah asked if he was all right that he snapped out of the trance that his work often drew him into.

"Garret? Did you hear me?"

"Oh. Sorry. Yes." Garret was surprised that she was still on the ship. He had just assumed she would win the inevitable argument that might not have even taken place about her going along with Captain Keel and Mr. Ravi to help recover the others. But evidently, she'd lost that argument. That, or she felt she'd be of more use here on the ship.

The code slicer's eyes went down to the ruined body of KRS-88. It was discouraging to look at, and every time Garret did so, he felt a new wave of hopelessness. The old war bot was a crushed and twisted morass of metal and circuitry. Garret had disassembled Crash as best he was able to, and that wasn't much. It would take cutting saws and torches to make any further progress, and that was something he was wary of even attempting due to the risk it posed to any parts that might still somehow be intact and operational deep beneath the shell of mangled combat armor. Though every time he ran a sensor wand over the chassis it came back with no indications of operation, the stick remaining as dead as the bot it hovered over.

It dawned on Garret that Leenah was still waiting for something more from him. He looked up from the war bot and saw in her face that this was so.

"I... I was thinking," he said.

She nodded, eager to draw him out.

"If they do it, do you think he would be able to?"

Leenah turned her head slightly to study Garret from the corner of her eyes. "You're going to have to let me a little deeper into that thought, Garret. Who is they? What is it? And who is he... and then what would he be able to do?"

Garret tried to shake the distraction from his head. "Sorry. I was... I've been thinking about Crash because his memory units and vocal output optimizers are completely destroyed and I mean, like, completely. Irrecoverable."

Leenah seemed surprised that Garret stopped his monologue so soon after it had started. "So 'he' is Crash. And you're saying he's gone? As in, gone-gone?"

The side of Garret's mouth twitched. "*He* is Nilo. But yes about Crash." Tears welled in his eyes.

"But you have a backup of him," Leenah reminded him.

Garret took in and then let out a deep breath. "I do and I don't. My backup is from just after I'd altered KRS-88 to serve as a dual-purpose bot for the Maydoon family. And I only made it because there were some interesting things in its code from when it had fought with the Legion or whatever. Stuff I thought showed subspark activity."

It was at the word "subspark" that G232 straightened up from his place in the data center. He'd been performing routine maintenance, but maintenance of such a nature was currently not a high priority given his urgent need to adjust the pantry location and prepare for the upcoming gala. The truth was probably that the admin bot was hovering in the data center in order to hear how Garret might be able to recover a bot that had so clearly met the end of its runtime. Or if the code slicer could do it at all.

If Leenah was familiar with the concept of the subspark and its place in the obscure coding philosophy usually only discussed between bots, she didn't show it. The Endurian passed over the word as though it were just another piece of technobabble spoken by a code slicer who couldn't distinguish the difference between the two worlds and often spoke over the heads of everyone. Garret didn't know if she followed or not. Leenah was the most likely member of the crew to understand, but her expertise rested in the mechanical side of things rather than the programming.

"Okay," she said. "That would leave a lot of... gaps uploading a backup that old. But I'm sure you can figure out a way to write an algorithm and then feed it data after the fact. Holorecordings, personal testimonies, things like that. It won't be perfect, but given enough time, he'll start to seem like his old self."

This cheered Garret up somewhat. The process Leenah had just described was one he had thought of as well. And if Mr. Nilo came back safely (it was his rescue and subsequent help that Garret had obscurely referenced when Leenah first spoke to him), then the two of them could whip up an algorithm that could do just that. Easily.

Except...

As quickly as the revival of his spirits came, it faded again.

"Do you remember how we saw Crash—an instance of Crash—on that planet?"

"Yes." Leenah nodded and then cleared a hair tendril from her eye.

"That's not supposed to happen. For a bot, I mean. Mr. Ravi said as much. It's the whole reason I took off after Crash in the first place because if we saw him there it meant..." Garret looked down, abashed.

"Meant what, Garret?"

The code slicer hesitated. He kept his head down. "This is... I'm going to sound crazy."

Leenah squeezed his hand. "You can tell me."

He looked up at her, gauging her sincerity. Satisfied with what he found in her expression, he quickly looked down again.

"It means... it means that Crash was alive. *Really* alive. I know how that sounds but I'm only saying it because it's true. He has a *soul*, Leenah. That's why we could see him there. See what he did even though you weren't supposed to see bots. Crash's subspark expanded his programming to a point where he *existed*. He's like us."

There might have been a long, poignant silence after these words had G232 not been in the room. The bot fumbled a data cube and sent it crashing to the deck, causing both Leenah and Garret to jump in surprise. "I'm... I'm terribly sorry."

Garret smiled, at first feebly and then warmly at the sight of the bot. He always found it easy to show grace to them. "It's okay, G2. Things were, uh, getting a little heavy there for a while." He waved his hands over KRS-88's frame. "I've still got work to do."

"Yes," G232 said, advancing almost timidly to the workstation like a child approaching a dead body for the first time. He stopped short of standing over the war bot and looked at Garret, eyes glowing faintly. "Is it possible?"

"Is what possible?" Leenah asked.

"The... subspark." G232's voice was smaller than usual. "A... soul."

Garret nodded. "I think so. It has to be. It's the only explanation I can think of and Mr. Ravi doesn't really have time to help me with another possibility. And I heard him say things to Crash in the past, about him not being far from being like us."

"Okay," Leenah said. She ran her fingers over Crash's bent frame as though seeing the war bot in a different light now. "What next? Do you need help cutting through some of this armor?"

Garret's eyes lit up. Of course Leenah would be able to do that. She could wield a cutting torch the way he did a holoterminal. "Yes. Yes! But... gently. If there's anything still sparking inside, we have to be careful not to snuff it out. And then when Mr. Nilo comes..."

"And don't forget Ms. Broxin and Mr. Praxus," G232 added helpfully. "They seemed quite knowledgeable about such matters, and I understand Mr. Praxus is him-self an android, and a highly sophisticated one at that."

Garret smiled. He hadn't thought of that. For the first time since seeing the extent of Crash's damage laid out before him under the lights of his workstation, he began to feel some hope. "Okay. Great. When do they arrive?"

"Probably around the same time as the others," Leenah said. "Aeson and Ravi are going to try and bring them back quickly through the Quantum, or whatever it is Ravi does with those temples."

"Until then, we can get Crash ready," Garret said with excitement. "Leenah, you get the armor cut away and I'll start working up some preliminary algos just in case we have to back up. Maybe there'll be something major we recover from him that will help us if things go worst-case scenario."

"And I'll get working on that pantry for our guests!" G232 exclaimed.

06

Keel turned to look back at the *Indelible VI*, resting in the remains of a ruined manor in what was once an up-scale Utopian district, now destroyed by Goth Sullus and Article Nineteen. The smuggler's first thought had been to use Ravi's ability to transport the two of them across the galaxy in an instant... but having a ship like the *Six* nearby seemed more prudent despite the lost hours of jump time.

"All those defense systems Leenah and Garret added, and I'm still nervous to leave her sitting like that."

Ravi stopped to examine the ship, which had set down in what was once a vast pergola likely used to entertain the former Republic capital world's elite. Now the old-growth timbers harvested from edge worlds still rich in their primordial resources lay scattered and strewn about the *Six*'s landing struts. "If no one has come for these building materials, this neighborhood is likely protected by some sort of private security. In any event, we should hurry."

Death, Destroyer of Worlds, decisively made a turn and declared that it would get on the burst cannons to defend the ship personally. Keel grabbed the little bot and altered its course so that it traveled with him and Ravi again. "Not so fast. Sounds like there'll be more action where we're going anyway. The colonial district is where Utopion got its start—it's not exactly the nicest part of town, though."

This seemed agreeable to the little gunnery bot, who raced ahead like an excited dog and waited for Keel and Ravi to catch up.

"You should not encourage its destructive tendencies," Ravi counseled. "That bot could do considerable harm if any more of its programming is corrupted."

"I'm kind of counting on that. Death's got a destructive mind. We might get a good plan out of it if we run into trouble under the hill."

The hill had been many things in the long existence of the planet now known as Utopion. It was not even a hill for the first colonists, but gradually became one as they built around their colony ship. When pirates raided the planet well before the formation of the Republic, underground bunkers were built to protect the colonists, and the planet, then known as New Vega, grew strong enough to fend off raids... except the Savages when they attacked. But the Legion liberated the planet, using those bunkers and deep corridors as battlegrounds, and in time, as the Republic formed around the Legion, New Vega became its capital. In the ancient times before faster-than-light travel, nations and empires had vast cities as their head. In a galaxy-spanning republic, an entire world was given the honor. And New Vega was the obvious choice. It was a symbol of resistance against the destructive power of the Savages. Proof that all was not lost for a world when the Savages arrived... at least so long as there was a Legion around to repel them. By now, the planet was one large city, though some sectors glistened while others were almost as squalid an edge world.

In the centuries that followed New Vega's founding, that same network of bunkers, expanded and enhanced by Savage technology and galactic progress, was put to use by the House of Reason and Senate. Among other things, it gave them underground transportation throughout the capital, allowing delegates and senators to move quickly beneath the splendor of a government campus filled with architecture and natural wonder. But even these vaunted public officials were forbidden from delving deeper into the subterranean complex. For far below the transportation facilities were secrets known only to a select few: the Mandarins and their Nether Ops enforcers.

It was there that Nilo, Zora, Jack, and the rest of a dedicated Black Leaf strike team had ventured to find some clue that might lead them to Earth. Or perhaps they would find the bombshell that so many conspiracy theories had long sought: proof that Utopion *was* Earth.

Instead the group had found betrayal. Keel had gathered the story from Zora during his brief jump time aboard the *Six* to Utopion.

Her team, she'd said over hypercomm, had encountered no more than the expected trouble with street gangs as they made their way through the blighted, rent-controlled neighborhoods that the politicians proudly congratulated themselves over but never themselves entered. After that, the team had expected things to be easier; after all, the Legion was supposed to have cleared out all Nether Ops resistance from the catacombs. And perhaps they had. But the team was ambushed all the same. Not because Nether Ops just happened to be lurking there. But because Nether Ops had already infiltrated Black Leaf.

The organizer of the betrayal proved to be none other than one of Nilo's own confidants: Surber. Keel wasn't entirely surprised at the news, given what he'd learned from the Bronze Guild leader he'd put down. And he had no doubt that Surber was the one organizing the hits against members of Kill Team Ice as well.

Thanks to the heads-up resilience of Jack and Zora, the attack was blunted, but Nilo was severely injured. Now Jack was off in pursuit of Surber, while Zora had managed to barricade herself and Nilo in a security vault so effective that those left with Nether Ops had given up trying to breach their way in. The two of them were safe for the time being, but Nilo was unconscious, stabilized only by his armor and Zora's aid, which added a ticking clock to the mission.

As Keel passed through the ruins of New Vega, he reached out to Zora once more. "Zora, this is Keel. We're on planet. You still good?"

"No change. Getting hungry, so hopefully you brought some rations. Went through all of mine."

"Left 'em on the ship. Wanted to keep you motivated to get out of there once we reach you."

"Trust me, no further motivation needed. Zora out."

Ravi looked at Captain Keel. "I calculate a seventy-three percent chance we run into trouble on our way to the hill. Given what Zora has reported, that number increases once we enter the hill itself."

"Well, after that quick landing, I guess our good luck can't last forever."

Utopion had long been dreaded by travelers as the center of all starship slowdowns—due to their excessive bureaucracy and very real security concerns—but now it was as easy to get in and out of as the average edge world, thanks to a complete absence of bureaucracy and very little security. Those residents with the means to get out, had already gotten out. Those without—mostly people who had been on the world for generations, but who had been pushed to the sections of the planet zoned for their "class"—subsequently overwhelmed whatever planetary police remained.

It would be some time before Utopion healed itself. The House and Senate had left behind a world bloated beyond repair, with a deeply entrenched culture of graft and bribery. The planet's central place in the galaxy's trade lanes made its eventual recovery certain—already, hungry young entrepreneurs were looking for ways to take up what was abandoned or lost in the war and its aftermath—but for now... parts of New Vega were not to be trod lightly. Including the parts Keel and his small retinue now traveled.

A pair of humans screamed up the street on hoverbikes, trailing behind them on chains an odd assortment of personal belongings, from handbags and hats to children's toys and backpacks. The riders were tattooed from neck to knuckle with a style of phosphorescent ink that could be activated to literally glow in the dark. The uniform magenta shade of the ink likely identified them with whatever gang claimed this turf; tattered banners of the same color hung dirty from light poles and in the doorframes of abandoned homes.

Keel and his company had crossed from a rich, albeit war-damaged community with active policing, into a place left to govern itself. Anarchy had not been kind to this district.

"You pecked the wrong stret to go down, *kelhorn*," said the first of the men, using the speech pattern those on Utopion would have recognized as belonging to the violent gang culture near the Hill.

"Funny," Keel answered. "I was thinking the same thing about you two."

"Not gonna be funny eff you don't show some rehspect. *Kelhorn.*"

Keel was in armor, his helmet latched to his side, slug thrower and blaster clearly visible. It seemed... *crazy* that these two, shirtless and wearing cargo fatigues and dusty brown boots, would press him, but press they did.

The second one pointed to a Simber blaster pistol tucked into his pants. Pretty, but inaccurate and prone to short a charge pack, rending the pack permanently destroyed and sometimes fused inside the chamber, thereby ruining the gun, too. "No clent," the gangster said and then repeated. "No clent, no clent, no clent."

It took a moment for Keel to grasp that the man was saying, "No clint." As in, he wasn't joking about using the piece tucked into his waistband.

"Gonna keep walking," Keel said. "You two keep driving. Everybody lives."

He took a step, and the first gangbanger held up a hand. "Es a tax on this stret. Pay et."

"What is the tax?" Ravi asked, sounding eager to keep moving without an outbreak of violence.

"Credets. Plus whatevah blasters ya got. No one walks strapped down this stret 'cept us."

The other one laughed. "Or, eff you don't wanna pay, we take ya leff." He thumbed a finger at the objects tethered to the slack chains of the hoverbikes. The final souvenirs taken from people who had fallen prey to the bikers and were unable to satisfy their "taxation" demands.

Keel had had enough. "Try."

The challenge seemed to shock the two men, dropping their gloating, self-assured smiles from their faces. Then an anger took over the first one and he yanked at a blaster he kept magnetized to the bike. Keel sent most of the man's face splattering onto his friend, who had drawn his own pistol and now held it there, horrified not only by what had happened to his companion but also by the fact that Keel was already pointing his blaster directly at him.

Keel took a step toward the gangster. "I want you to tell whoever—"

A sudden blaster bolt zipped past Keel and struck the biker in the chest, sending him toppling off of his hoverbike, dead.

Keel whipped around and glowered at Death, Destroyer of Worlds, who had drawn and fired his compartmentalized small-carry blaster.

"I was trying to get us safe passage through this hellhole!" Keel snapped. "Who told you to shoot?"

Death pointed out that the gangbanger had a gun.

"So? Everyone here has a gun!"

Death then pointed out that it feared for its life.

Keel pointed sharply at the little bot. "Next time, don't shoot unless I tell you to."

The bot beeped off a hypothetical in its Signica language.

"Fine. Yes. Or if you think I'm about to be killed like with the Tennar."

The little gunnery bot then insisted that it thought Keel was about to be killed by the gangster.

The smuggler stared blankly at the bot, who rolled up to his leg and rubbed its metal frame against it, repeating how "scared" it had been for New Boss.

"I've created a monster," Keel complained to the universe. He took the bot's weapon. "You're on timeout."

The affection went away immediately.

"This is what I told you would be happening," Ravi said.

"Thanks for telling me so, Ravi. I might've forgotten otherwise." Keel looked at the two bikes, still hovering in place for riders who were in no condition to get back in the saddle. "This'll speed up the trip. You can drive one, right?"

Ravi nodded.

Keel went around back and deactivated the magnetic anchors that attached the chains and their prizes. "Come back here, Death. I'm strapping you in for the ride."

The bot obeyed, but not without shamelessly suggesting it be re-armed to pick off any riders who might try to chase them down.

"Let me worry about that." Keel mounted the bike and gunned the repulsors to familiarize himself with the controls. He set his helmet over his head, wanting to make use of its HUD on the drive. "Let's get speedin'."

The bikes took off with a high-pitched hum down the streets, leaving the bodies of the gang members where they lay.

07

"A checkpoint is ahead," Ravi called out, signaling a small blockade of the street and sidewalks that his HUD had identified just seconds previous. "I calculate nearly a hundred percent chance that they will engage us, with the percentage of likelihood increasing according to our proximity."

Keel looked over at his partner, whose robes whipped in the wind from his hoverbike's speed as the pair howled toward what looked like a hastily assembled obstacle course meant to slow them down. It comprised a few duracrete speeder barriers, along with front doors and other scrap pulled from the burnt-out buildings that lined both sides of the avenue. Black scorch marks reached up from broken-out windows where the flames had struggled to catch the impervious exterior, but whatever had been inside those buildings was apparently quite a bit more flammable than the external siding.

"So what you're saying, Ravi, is that the closer we get, the more likely they are to shoot us."

"That is another way of putting it, yes."

"What's the closest we can get before they really open up on us?" Keel asked. "I've got an idea for how to get past them quickly, but I need to get close."

"Four hundred and fifty yards."

"Four hundred and fif—Ravi, we're practically there right now!"

"Yes, and their fire at this range will be ineffective, but judging from a wide data set, this is most likely the distance at which at least one of them will open fire, and the others will almost assuredly follow suit. I sincerely doubt there is a seasoned veteran there to remind them of combat training they have never received, Captain Keel. Surely you can recognize this from the manner in which—"

"Okay. I get it. We'll just have to speed in close and hope they don't get a lucky shot."

Keel punctuated his declaration by increasing the throttle, causing the bike to give a howl that echoed along the dead street and beat its way into the narrow alleys. Quickly left behind by a considerable distance, Ravi gunned his throttle to close the gap.

The blaster bolts began to sizzle high and wide of their target at four hundred yards; the gangbangers manning the checkpoint were evidently more disciplined than Ravi had guessed.

"This is still within the margin of error," Ravi said before Keel could heckle him.

"Just hang on. I'm gonna race past them so we don't get slowed down by a blaster fight."

"And how are you planning to accomplish this?"

"Gonna jump 'em."

"I have no ability to do that."

Keel smirked. "You'll figure something out. Not like a bike crash is gonna kill you, right?"

"I suppose..."

Keel lowered himself in his seat; the blaster bolts were growing in accuracy, although hitting a fast-moving target was still proving a challenge despite the narrowing distance. Then the smuggler used his auto-aim assist to send two violent barks from his slug thrower toward the barricades. One round struck a gangster in the neck, sending him dropping to the ground, lights out. Another struck a makeshift bulwark made out of stuff not fit to stand up to a depleted uranium round; the bullet went clean through and struck a man in the gut. He stood dumbfounded for a moment before grabbing his stomach and falling.

"That oughta keep their heads down for a moment. Here we go!"

Keel raced ahead, closing the distance until even Ravi thought this plan involved nothing more than trying to break through the blockade, an act that would result in a fiery crash at the minimum.

Here at the close, the defenders regained their courage, if only to shoot the maniac charging them on his bike. Even Death, Destroyer of Worlds trilled a digital scream of alarm as the staggered duracrete slabs raced toward them.

At the last moment, Keel pulled up on the bike's handlebars and planted his feet onto the potholed and dirty duracrete street. As the armor's strength assist began to lift the bike up, Keel fired his jump jets, carrying him and the bike over the barricade and to a hard landing on the other side, shooting up sparks and loosening one of the twin repulsor drives. But the bike still functioned, and Keel was racing away before the shocked defenders, who had thrown themselves down in fear of the apparent suicide attack, had even realized what had happened.

A few scattered shots sounded. Keel slowed and turned around to see that these were for Ravi, who had slowed his bike enough to navigate his way through the serpentine barrier and was now baffling the gangbangers who fired their blaster bolts right through the apparition.

The Ancient took off before they could think to shoot the bike itself.

Ravi rejoined his co-pilot's side.

"Why didn't you cut 'em or somethin'?" Keel asked.

"There was no absolute need to kill."

"Well, I absolutely don't want them following us. If I'd have known you were going to stroll right past them without taking 'em out, I'd have dropped a fragger or something on the way over."

"Yes, I am well aware of your propensity to take 'kill them first' in the most literal of senses."

"Because it works."

Ravi frowned.

More blaster bolts sounded, this time chasing the escaped bikers but missing wide of the mark. Most terminated in showers of sparks over front stoops and empty window ledges.

"Oh look," Keel said. "Here come the consequences of your inaction."

The little gunnery bot, who was squarely in New Boss's corner on the matter of preemptive killings, gave a digital *tsk* that Ravi could only raise an eyebrow at.

Keel pulled his hoverbike into a power slide, rapidly bringing it to the kind of halt that didn't involve tossing him over the front end, then dismounted and brought up the Intec x6. For the really difficult shots, he preferred the blaster pistol that had been at his side seemingly forever. It was more accurate than the slug thrower, and it packed sufficient punch to do most jobs even if it lacked the morale-altering bang of the old gas-fired weapon.

He steadied his shot on the seat of the bike, lining up one of three bikers who were swerving toward them, jumping up and down on their rides to look more like they were racing across ocean swells than the level surface of a Utopion street. Keel picked the man in the center and timed his shot so that the blaster bolt struck his chest as he came down from a self-made jump. The gangster backflipped off the bike and landed hard, but already dead, on his neck before rag-dolling into a roll and then a slow, skidding stop. His hoverbike hummed forward in a straight line, losing momentum with no one on board to speed it along.

The other two riders continued on unabated. Keel picked the target on his left, this time taking advantage of the fact that the rider had just brought her hoverbike up into a soaring jump. He struck the undercarriage and ignited the engine, blowing the rider from her metal horse and out of the fight. Scarcely a second passed before Keel brought his pistol to the last rider, who was close enough for a simple head shot, which was dutifully made.

Keel holstered his weapon, with only the bucket hiding the smile on his face. Death, Destroyer of Worlds, whistled in profound admiration.

"Yeah," Keel agreed. "Not bad. You see that, Ravi?"

The Ancient folded his arms. "We could have easily outrun or lost them."

"Where's the fun in that?" Keel remounted his bike. "Odds?"

"You are not seriously asking—"

"Hey. You're back, I'm back, the galaxy's going crazy... forgive me for settling into old habits."

Ravi sighed. "One in three hundred thousand."

"Ha-*ha!*" Keel crowed. "Soak it in, Ravi. You only get to be around greatness like this a few times in however long you've been alive."

The two continued on, aware that an occasional scout shadowed their travels by racing along parallel streets. No one from whatever street gang controlled this burnt-out neighborhood seemed to feel the need to collect taxes from the intruders, but they were nevertheless keeping an eye on the duo.

Following an AR map overlaid on his helmet's HUD, Keel navigated to an abandoned park. Tall trees and lush, shaded grass gave a sense of escape from the rest of the city—and it *was* an escape, though not in the way the city planners had intended. A bustling city depends on its residents looking out for one another's safety and well-being, but there couldn't be nearly as many watching eyes in these serene plots of nature as there could in the midst of the duracrete and impervisteel blocks. Thus the park had become a place for crime and delinquency long before Utopion fell into its current low state. A space intended as a respite for residents had instead become a gathering point for a class of perpetual transients, addicts, and the great, shepherd-less youth that would so often join the ranks of the city's underground.

Which meant the odds of another violent or dangerous encounter was still high. But Keel and Ravi would at least remove themselves from the densely populated gang territory, where shooters could be peering out of any of countless windows at any given moment. And as the two left their bikes to travel on foot toward one of the many hidden entrances to Utopion's underground subterranean system—the same entrance Zora's team had used—neither could detect any hostile presence. They seemed to have the park to themselves.

Shade from the fat boughs of wide, leafy trees made the air feel cooler than it ought to, driving away the summer's heat that had been their companion while moving through the streets. The entrance they were after looked like a simple manhole cover, located in a raised bank across from a small stream that wound its way through the park before emptying into a man-made lake. The planners had likely envisioned the lake full of bathers, but it seemed only to have gathered foul water and garbage.

They found the entrance with the lid already removed and sitting nearby. Keel turned to the bot. "Go take a look."

The little Nubarian gunnery bot rolled up dutifully, looked down the shaft, and shone a bright light into the darkness. It reported that, as far as it could see, the area was empty.

"Okay," Keel said, "I'll head down first. Ravi, you watch up here. Good bet we're being followed and watched. Death... you gonna be able to handle the climb down?"

The little bot suggested that it could simply roll into the hole and then New Boss could catch it before it struck bottom.

"Works for me." Keel climbed down the ladder one-handed, holding the slug-thrower in the other. If shooting started, the concussive noise from the weapon would go a long way toward disorienting anyone who was unused to engaging such weapons.

He reached the bottom and cleared it as far as he dared without wandering too far from the entrance. The gunnery bot plummeted down on command. Keel caught it easily and set it down at his side. "Ravi?"

"Coming down."

Keel activated his comm. "Zora, it's Wraith. We're in the shaft. You still good?"

"As I can be. Make your way east along the access corridor. We had to tear down a false wall to get to the inner corridor. You won't be able to miss it unless that kel-horn Surber had it sealed back up."

"Got a distance between the shaft and the site, just in case?" asked Keel.

"Three, four hundred meters?"

"Acknowledged. See you soon, Zora. Keel out."

08

The armor once belonging to Tyrus Rechs, and so recently improved upon by Garret, identified not only the hole in the wall that Zora had promised would be there, but also several life forms on the other side. Keel checked in with the woman who had been an integral part of his transition from Legion officer to galactic rogue during those long years of working in deep cover for Dark Ops.

"Zora. Found your hole. Looks like someone's waiting on the other side. Any friendlies who got separated from your team?"

"No one except for Jack. We have some reserves on board Nilo's yacht who weren't a part of this—Pikkek and his team—but they were kept in reserve. Obvious why, now."

"Roger. Out."

Given the lack of information on Jack's current whereabouts, Keel didn't like the idea of tossing a fragger through the gap; he could easily dream up a scenario where the cocky spy was captured and bound among a team waiting to see if anyone would come to rescue Nilo and Zora. There was also the possibility that these life forms were innocents, kids who'd escaped the streets by going underground in the park. It was Ravi who suggested that possibility, although he wouldn't offer Keel any odds to sway him one way or another.

"Okay, pal," Keel said. "Let's try this. You can't get killed, so—"

"You keep bringing that up."

"Because it's useful."

"I *can* be killed. Just not in ordinary circumstances. Think of it like your experiences with the Savages on board the reclaimer."

"As in, I gotta kill you with my bullets *and* feelings?"

"Something like that, yes."

Keel shrugged, wanting to know more, but aware that now was not the time to ask. "Okay. Let's assume these guys aren't enlightened warrior monks capable of taking you down. Which brings us back to: you can't get killed. So go in there, and if they're bad guys, slice them up."

"Again, it is not so simple as that. My actions reverberate through the Quantum, and those skilled in tracing those actions—such as the Dark Ones and their Savage masters—may be able to ascertain my whereabouts if we are not careful."

Keel wanted to pull off his helmet and pinch the bridge of his nose in frustration. "*Fine.* Just go in there then. If I hear shooting and I *don't* hear you me telling me to stay back, then *I'll* clear them out."

Ravi nodded. "This is an acceptable plan, such as it is."

"Glad you approve, Ravi. Ready?"

The Ancient One moved stealthily through the deconstructed section of maintenance wall, stepping nimbly over the hastily stacked bricks and powdery mortar. It was clear that this access tunnel had been constructed long ago, to say nothing of the even older corridor that lay beyond it.

It wasn't long before the shooting started.

Keel, already stacked on the other side of the entrance, opted to use an ear-popper instead of one of his two remaining frags. He tossed the device through the opening and then pressed himself against the bricks, awaiting the detonation and trusting his advanced helmet to handle the otherworldly light.

On the heels of the concussive blast, which shook dust from the ceiling and caused precariously stacked bricks to tip and fall, Keel rolled into the room with both weapons up. The HUD had identified four life forms, and the physical count on the inside matched. These were either Nether Ops legionnaires, or Keel was on the verge of executing friendly fire. But given the context, he didn't hesitate to pull the trigger.

Each man was issued three trigger pulls. Two died from the slug thrower and two from the Intec blaster. The sound of battle echoed in the corridor for a moment and then dissipated as smoke from the brief fight gathered at the poorly ventilated ceiling.

"Looks like they stationed a waiting party for us," Keel told Zora. "Might be a little slow going. It's a good bet anyone else here heard us coming."

"Hopefully Jack heard it, too." Zora's concern for the spy was evident in her voice.

Keel frowned. While he wasn't exactly enamored with the man, he didn't dislike him either. Jack had proven himself in a fight numerous times. "I'll keep my eyes open for him. How's Nilo?"

"No change."

"We'll be there as soon as we can."

"What do you think, Ravi?" Keel asked as they pushed through the darkness of a three-meter-wide corridor that was easily twice as tall. This after taking several flights of steel steps down to follow the path Zora had laid out to them.

"About what, Captain? The odds of Zora leading us into a trap? The additional odds that we are not communicating with Zora at all? Or perhaps you are referring to the absence of enemy combatants since entering these tunnels."

"The last one," Keel answered, watching as his HUD automatically cycled through visual feeds to give him a full picture of what lay ahead. "But I'm curious about the others now that you bring them up."

"Spoofing comms is simple enough," Ravi stated. "As is replicating a voice. However, Zora has given us details that assuredly only she would know, leaving me with little worry that it was someone else we spoke to."

He was referring to the battery of questions Keel had asked Zora during their communication on the *Six*. He'd accepted her as the genuine article then, and she'd given no reason to doubt since. She'd certainly given him plenty of attitude, especially considering he was the one coming to make a daring rescue.

"There's still the first thing you said," Keel offered. "It could be her and she could be leading us into a trap. Gun to her head, credits in her account... either one can be pretty convincing."

"Yes," Ravi agreed, "that is far more likely. Especially considering we have moved through several probable ambush sites without incident. Perhaps they want you alive, similar to Nether Ops at our reunion?"

"Kind of an odd feeling, bad guys not wanting me dead. But yeah. Could be."

"Would knowing my current probability calculations be welcome?"

"Not this time, for some reason." Keel looked back at the little gunnery bot that followed them dutifully, locking on to a small IR dot Keel had affixed to his back. "You keepin' up all right, DOW?"

The bot indicated it was, sending a muted chirp to Keel over a shared comm band to avoid being overheard. Not that it would have been any louder than the low voices Keel and Ravi had been speaking in for a while now.

"Okay, well there's something up ahead. Looks like it might be a potential cave-in. Tread carefully just in case there's more that wants to drop on your head."

Death acknowledged and slowed its pace as Keel and Ravi approached the obstacle highlighted inside the smuggler's HUD. The tangle proved not to be a tunnel collapse, but a stack of dead bodies.

"Black Leaf mercs," Keel muttered on inspecting them under the glare of an ultrabeam. He shined the light further up the tunnel, revealing a blood trail that led to the pile. "Looks like one of the guards collected casualties and decided this was as far as he was willing to drag 'em."

Ravi nodded. "Yes, that is a logical assessment. However, it does not keep with what Zora told us of the battle. It sounded as though she and Nilo barely had time to seal themselves from the assault. Who, then, would have killed so many?"

Keel gave a grim frown. "So maybe this is Jack's handiwork. She said he went out to go after the kelhorns."

"Perhaps he got them—and then escaped. Is he the sort who would have left Zora and this Mr. Nilo behind?"

"Not sure. Let's keep moving. Maybe we'll find out."

They took the corridor to its end, which was an ancient blast door that had clearly been welded shut long ago. Nilo's team had navigated past this particular obstacle in a creative manner: by bypassing the door altogether and instead blasting out a piece of the corridor floor at its base. They'd left behind a man-sized hole that led down into yet another underground space.

"Zora, it's Keel. We reached the end of the line, but I'm not seeing any ladder to help us get down."

"It wasn't a ladder, jump jockey. A rope. And someone probably cut it. It wasn't *that* far down, but I can't give you anything exact. Maybe ten meters? Sorry."

Zora sounded tired in her answer, and Keel wondered if that was simply due to a lack of food and water, or if the vault she'd locked herself in was airtight and running low on oxygen.

"I'll find a way. Keel out."

He peered over the edge, and his armor gauged a fall of twelve point four meters. Further, it informed Keel that such a drop was within the limits of its ability to absorb impact. He could jump down and be no worse for wear. According to the HUD's calculations, at least.

"I'm gonna jump down there. Any trouble, I'll use the jets to get back up."

Death rolled forward, ready to repeat the same trick as before and drop down into Keel's arms.

"Let's hold up on that, killer. That hole is only big enough for one at a time; not sure I can simply jump you back up again. Gotta be sure we've got a way to get you back up before getting you trapped down below."

Keel sat down and dangled his feet into the hole before slipping his body through and dropping into the darkness. As he landed he instinctively squatted, bringing his left hand down onto the deck and holding his right hand up, blaster ready to do work. But, like the rest of the underground since their first encounter, this area was also empty. The smuggler soaked in the silence for several moments as he watched his HUD for signs of life or any other readings that might signify trouble.

Nothing.

He activated his ultrabeam, keeping its light low as he inspected his surroundings. He was in a large open space, on some sort of suspended catwalk that looked much older than the passages they'd been traveling through. Given the history of Utopion, it could be a difference of centuries or more. A coil of synth-rope lay just beneath the opening, one end cut clean from a vibro-blade. Looking up, Keel could see a matter-weave anchor that had been bored into the impervisteel underframe of the sealed blast door.

"Okay," Keel called, wanting to notify Zora first of all. He was still thinking about how she had sounded. "I'm down. Straight shot to get to where you were double-crossed, right?"

"Yeah. Be careful."

"No promises. Keel out." The smuggler looked up. "The bot can come down. I've got rope we can use to pull him back up when the time comes."

The little gunnery bot rolled into the chasm and was ably caught by Keel.

Ravi dropped down after and almost disappeared into his black robes as he landed. "Actually, we will not be needing the rope," he said. "I can transport us all directly back to the *Indelible VI*. I am anchored to it through the Quantum."

"That's right, how could I forget," Keel said sarcastically. "That little trick could have saved me a lot of stress—not to mention credits—in times past, my *holographic* friend."

Ravi gave a humorless smile. "Yes. I apologize again for the deceit. It was necessary for me to evaluate your skill set up close without telling you that I am one of the Ancients and that my purpose is to assist the galaxy in staving off a coming apocalypse."

"Ravi, you let me believe that for nearly a decade."

"Hoo, hoo, hoo," Ravi laughed. "Not so long as that!"

"Close enough," fumed Keel, but it was for show, and he knew that Ravi knew it. He allowed himself a chuckle. "To think I had a keeper to the mysteries of the galaxy sitting by my side for years and it was all I could do to get him to give me nav-readouts and overly exacting odds when I needed them."

"I have given you much less exacting odds since your request, Captain Keel."

Keel led the way along the catwalk. The depth of the chasm beneath it was too great for the armor to assess, but a dank, musty air blew up from somewhere below, drifting through the grated decking and over the simple impervisteel suspension cables and guide rails. It felt as though they were floating above the very heart of the planet. Indeed, Keel's armor detected an uptick in temperature. He couldn't *feel* the wind, only read the scientific details of it, but his HUD made it clear that he'd be sweating if he weren't inside the old armor.

"A long way down," Ravi said, seeming to want to make conversation.

"Yeah. Think you'd survive if I tossed you over the edge?"

"Probably."

"Because of the bullets-and-feelings thing?"

"In this case, your feelings would not matter. My movement through the physical world is not the displacement of mass and matter."

Keel scoffed. "Just when I think I'm starting to understand, I don't. So how *does* one kill an Ancient, then?"

"Is that a serious question?"

"Sure."

Ravi arched an eyebrow. "And not because you are wanting to finally make good on so many idle threats that have piled up over the years."

"Just curious, Ravi."

They traveled another few meters in silence before Ravi gave an explanation. "Again, recall the difficulty you had in killing those Savage reclaimers aboard their hulk."

"Yeah, we went over this."

"And the difficulty in killing the Dark Ones unleashed by Goth Sullus."

Keel confirmed that as well.

"The difficulty is more alike than you are aware. Think of the Dark Ones as a corrupted version of my people, the ones you call the Ancients. And think of those Savage constructs as an attempt to recreate us as a species. A surprisingly successful attempt—evidently achieved through visits to the Quantum and Umnor."

"Okay, I'm thinkin', Ravi. But I can't say it's doin' much to explain anything yet," Keel replied.

"The galaxy can be divided into two realms," Ravi continued. "The seen and the unseen. You exist primarily in the seen. It takes significant effort for your species to grasp or interact with the unseen realm."

"And you guys are the opposite?"

"Hoo, hoo, hoo. On the contrary, we have mastery of both realms. This is why our temples are indestructible; they exist primarily in the Quantum, preventing them from being raided by unscrupulous thieves and smugglers. It is also why I am unharmed by the violence and weapons of your realm. When I walk beside you, I exist primarily in the Quantum, but I can shift my being into your realm whenever I need to directly interact with the seen."

"You're talking about cutting people in half with your sword."

"Among other things, yes."

"So to kill an Ancient, you just gotta shoot 'em while they're stabbing someone. Easy enough."

Ravi laughed again. "Not so easy as that! I should have said it is my sword that becomes material in such a case. There's no reason for the rest of me to be so exposed."

"Feels to me like you're dodging the question."

"I assure you, that is not my intention."

There was a lull in their discussion as Keel checked his readouts to verify that they were still alone as they pushed toward their objective. Then he picked up where he left off.

"Okay. Another question. This armor told me that the way to kill those Savages on the reclaimer was to do the kind of metaphysical mumbo-jumbo you're dancing around. Killing with your heart instead of just your blaster. So I've been wondering... How did it know that?"

"That armor is a Savage construction, from what I understand. The Savages fought one another frequently before being unified during the Savage Wars."

"So since this armor was Savage, it just had the Savage intel ready to go."

"That is my estimation. Its directive was correct. Had you exerted enough physical trauma, you would have eventually slain them. Had you done the same in the Quantum, all the better. A combination of both was the most effective."

Keel thought back to how the Savages would fall or slow when hit, but not die. And how only Skrizz and the koob seemed to have a decent record in actually taking them down.

Ravi managed to guess where his thoughts were. "Killing both body and soul sounds superstitious to humanity, and to many other species in the galaxy as well. But it is not so for all races. To be killed by a Kublaren, for example, is to be killed in both body and mind. What they believe, they do."

"Doesn't seem to work that way for us humans."

"I wish it were so simple that I could provide you with a plain three-step process. It is not. But you are close, Captain. I would not have stayed with you as long as I did if you weren't. I was seeking the ones who could transcend both worlds—like Prisma has done."

"So you wanted to turn me into a space wizard? No thanks, pal."

"No. Merely to help you become attuned to the unseen realm, the Crux, the Quantum, call it what you will. Your mind has placed limitations on reality that need not be there. I'm sure you would exceed such limitations if the option were available to you. In fact, you have done so without thinking many times. Surely you don't think yourself that lucky or naturally gifted to shoot and fight the way you do?"

Keel waited a moment. "'Course I do."

Ravi shook his head. "I still cannot quite tell when you are being facetiously arrogant for show and when you are actually being that thick-headed."

"Count on thick-headed."

They continued along the seemingly endless catwalk, occasionally feeling it sway either from age of the geo-thermal currents rising around it. At last they came to an archaic blast door that had been pried open and was now kept from closing by a pair of specially purposed brake-blocks flash-welded to the top and bottom of the doorway.

Guns at the ready, Keel moved to clear the large room that lay beyond. As he stepped across the threshold, he felt as though he'd been transported back to the Savage reclaimer. The design was almost exactly the same, and while this was not one of the great simulation bays he'd encountered on the previous hulk, it was clearly of Savage design.

The walls had housed something electronic that had been stripped away recently; Keel could tell from the change of coloration where entire consoles looked to have been taken from their housings. A dead Black Leaf soldier lay near another set of blast doors, these sealed shut, and additional blast doors lay open on the walls to both sides.

"This must be the ship that landed on New Vega. The one that kicked off the Savage Wars," Keel mumbled.

He knew one had to take the history of the Savage Wars with a certain grain of salt. Many planets, from Enduran to Sinasia, provided their own histories—histories in which their battles, their heroes and sacrifices, marked the supposed start of the Savage Wars. There was really no telling where truth and legend went on their divergent paths. He wished he'd brought Makaffie with him on this mission. The man would undoubtedly have something to say about the place. If half the things he'd revealed about himself and Kill Team Ice were true, he might even prove to be a historical eyewitness capable of verifying exactly where they were.

Nothing to do about that now. Keel would have to fill him in later, hopefully after the scrawny, peculiar man had come to grips with being abandoned by his friend, the Wild Man.

"Zora, we're in what looks like a Savage vessel just off the end of that subterranean catwalk. There are some sealed blast doors here. Do I take it you're on the other side?"

"No one is outside waiting?" she asked.

"Unless you count one deceased Black Leaf merc, doesn't look like it. HUD isn't showing me any life forms in the adjoining sections of the ship. But it's not showing me you on the other side either, so this hull plating might be too much for it. Don't plan on clearing the whole ship regardless. Once we get inside, Ravi has a way to get us all out."

"What about Jack? Did you see Jack?"

"No. Sorry."

Ravi joined Keel's side. "Perhaps we should at least clear the side rooms, just to be sure there is no ambush."

Keel nodded. "Zora, Ravi and I are gonna make double sure nobody else is close by. Hang on. You're almost out of here."

"Thank you, jump jockey. I won't forget it."

Keel smiled. "I won't let you."

They moved to the adjacent rooms, but found no signs of battle. No traps. No messages. Nothing. Many of the components of the Savage vessel had been stripped away, but not all of them. Keel found himself wondering if Surber had lingered long enough to take whatever he and Nether Ops wanted, or if the only reason they'd had for coming to this world was to ambush Nilo. It seemed an awful long way to come for something that could have been done on any number of worlds, or even in the confines of Nilo's yacht. So perhaps Surber had found what he was looking for after all. Then again, maybe Jack had found Surber. Keel couldn't discount the possibility that Jack was still here somewhere, alive, maybe even in possession of whatever it is that Nether Ops was after.

As Keel stared down another opened blast door, seeing nothing in the darkness beyond, he voiced his thoughts. "Big part of me feels like we should make the time to look for Jack... and the kelhorn who tried to do me in. Surber."

Ravi's voice was soothing. "I know the difficulty you face, Captain. I know how personal you take these things."

"Oh yeah?"

"Your desire to punish those who seek to do you harm was... alarming at first. But the way you have consistently sought to keep those in peril from being left behind is one of the traits I most admire in you, my friend. I have seen it many times. Sadly... we cannot delay. We must recover those we came for and leave everything else to fate. There is still much to be done. Prisma will call upon us. We must be ready when she does."

Keel lowered his head. "Zora, we're coming for you. Get ready to open the door."

09

True to his word, Ravi teleported Keel, Zora, the wounded Nilo, and the little gunnery bot straight to the *Indelible VI*. They arrived inside the lounge, with Keel cradling Nilo. Aside from the sudden visual disorientation from the complete change in surroundings, the transport process felt completely natural.

"Zora, go get the *Six* primed for takeoff," Keel ordered. "I'm gonna take your employer to the med bay. Ravi?"

"I will assist with our departure," the Ancient answered.

Death announced that it would check on the weapons systems, something it did every time it stepped foot on any vessel, whether the vessel was armed or not.

Keel hurried Nilo toward a med bay that was now equipped to handle cases of trauma like his as well as any hospital emergency room. Something powerful had punched the young tech magnate right in the stomach, and in the process pushed some very expensive armor through his synthprene undersuit and into his guts, where it sat in fragmented pieces. The smart-suit's auto-compression had helped with bleeding, and Zora had administered clotting nanite meant to do the same, as well as stanch any internal hemorrhaging. All of that had been necessary just to keep Nilo alive, but it wouldn't last forever. He needed the *Six*'s auto-doc. Already his blood pressure was dropping, a sure sign of trouble.

The door to the med bay swished open and Keel deposited Nilo onto the operating/examination table at the center of the room. Several articulated mechanical arms unfolded from a repulsor station that had been housed in the ceiling just outside the bright white overhead examination lights.

"What seems to be the problem, Captain?" the disembodied voice of the auto-doc asked as its octopus-like medical arms prepped for triage, anesthesia, surgery, and virtually any other medical care required.

The patient lay on his back, his skin slick and pale, resembling a corpse.

"Gunshot," Keel explained. "Possibly a slug thrower. Not seeing much in the way of blaster scorching on the armor and the wound doesn't even look partially cauterized."

"Loading appropriate care guidelines," the auto-doc responded. "This injury is infrequent."

"I don't think he cares how rare it is," Keel snapped. "Get him stable."

Keel's tolerance for bots was, he thought, at least average, but he had little patience for AIs. And though Garret and Leenah both swore that this auto-doc model was just a bot—one with its processor and vocal configurations housed in a centralized panel inside the med bay—the thing certainly *felt* like an AI.

"Whoever attended to the patient has already done an admirable job of stabilizing him, though he remains in critical condition."

Keel frowned. Nilo didn't look very stable.

"What, if any, narcotics have been administered?" the auto-doc asked.

Keel connected Zora's med pad, which had recorded all data on her treatment of Nilo. "Here."

"Analyzing." A pleasant ding sounded. "For the patient's well-being, please step outside the medical bay unless you are a trained medical assistant with proper sterilization. Note: a mask is required for all biological life-forms. They can be found in—"

"I'm leavin'," Keel said as he moved toward the door.

The med bay closed behind him and the opaque doors faded into transparency, giving the captain an opportunity to watch the pending procedure. Leenah and Garret really had spared no expense. Advanced blast doors like this probably cost more than the entire *Indelible VI* did when it first rolled off the factory floor.

The auto-doc's arms rotated and began to cut away armor and synthprene while another arm injected a sedative—or maybe it was an antibiotic, Keel didn't know—into Nilo. That done, one of the arms extended four clamps, which in turn branched out into even smaller clamps. These went to work picking out the pieces of armor, one by one, that had been blown into Nilo. A swiveled surgical laser on another arm followed, zapping a bright red beam in quick bursts as it sealed punctures.

Keel was about to leave the auto-doc to its duty and join Zora and Ravi in the cockpit when he received an excited communication from Death, Destroyer of Worlds. The little bot had evidently found an "abundance of hostiles" that were "seeking to overtake the ship," but in keeping with New Boss's directives, needed approval to "kill them like swine."

"Slow down," Keel told the bot. "What kind of hostiles are we talkin' about? More of those gang members?"

The bot's answer—"Probably"—didn't instill confidence.

Keel hailed the cockpit. "Ravi."

"Yes, Captain."

"The bot's telling me we've got a potential gang that pushed its way past this neighborhood's security and is moving on the *Six*."

"Sensors are not picking up anything like... oh. Oh my."

"What? I've got no love for those kinds of scumsacks. I'll have the bot open up the turrets and ventilate those space rats."

"No, Captain Keel! You must not do this."

Keel frowned, wondering what the complication was. "Hold fire, DOW."

The bot, clearly disappointed, acknowledged the order.

It was Zora who gave the important context. "They're not gangsters—they're from this neighborhood."

"What're they after us for?" Keel asked, and then muttered, "Must be something in the HOA against having starships parked on the block."

"Captain, I calculate an eighty-four-point-three percent chance they are coming not to destroy the ship, but to use it as a means of escape."

Alarm bells went off in Keel's mind. "Escape what?"

"No idea," Zora answered. "In fact—oh no. Get up here, jump jockey! I just locked into the local holobroadcasts. Whole bunch of Gomarii slave ships just entered atmo."

Keel ran for the cockpit. "Take her up. Let's get off-world before too many of these Savage kelhorns get on it."

To his surprise, the ship hadn't lifted by the time he arrived, despite its systems already being online and ready for departure. "I said take off!"

Ravi and Zora only looked at him.

"What am I, on mute? Get us out of here, Ravi!"

"Captain, both Zora and I feel we have an obligation to these people who are coming to the ship for—"

"Oh, my bleeding heart!" Keel snapped and then pushed Zora out of the pilot's seat. "Move, sister."

He began the pre-flight dustoff.

"You can't do this, Aeson," Zora said. "There are women and children out there."

"Yeah, well they can thank me for keeping my psychotic gunnery bot from pumping them full of blaster cannon bolts. We're getting out of here."

Zora's hand went to her blaster, but she didn't draw. "Keel. You have to help them."

"Zora, I can't airlift the entire planet out of here."

"It's not a planet." Zora pointed to the sensors. "Fifty people, max. They'll all fit in the cargo hold and won't even come close to feeling cramped."

Keel's resolve, which had been stronger outward than it had been inside, was already wavering. "Ravi, I thought we were in final countdown territory."

"Yes, and normally I would say that this sacrifice is necessary for the greater good. However, they are close, the cargo bay is ample, and fate has put us here at this exact time. I am willing to escort them on board so you can take off immediately."

Keel gave a fractional shake of his head. "Okay. Get back there. And then the two of you need to figure out where we're going to deliver them."

Ravi disappeared at once. A moment later the cargo bay ramp was dropping and Zora was easing into the navigator's chair. On the holocam feed, Keel could see the Ancient waving in the desperate refugees, urging them to board in an orderly fashion and to mind the children.

"Hell of a way to run a war," Keel grumbled.

"Oh, shut up," Zora said, a playfulness in her voice. "I don't know who you were trying to impress with that old smuggler's routine. We both knew you wouldn't leave those people behind."

"I might have."

"Uh-huh."

Ravi was doing an admirable job of quickly getting the refugees on board. "Just a few stragglers left and then we can take off," the Ancient reported.

Keel checked his sensors, looking for signs of incoming enemy craft that might be happy to turn the sitting *Indelible VI* into a target of opportunity. In the distance, a large explosion sent a towering inferno of flames rising up from the hill.

"Captain." It was the auto-doc.

"Now what?" Keel bellowed before flipping the comm to reply. "Now what?"

"The patient is awake and in a state of belligerency. I am unable to administer further sedatives without risk of a toxic overdose. Your assistance is required."

Keel gave Zora a lopsided frown. "Go help your boss calm down." He held up a fist. "Use alternative medicine if you have to."

The bounty hunter was up in a flash. "On it."

No sooner had Zora left than Ravi reappeared inside the cockpit. "They are as comfortable as possible in the cargo bay. Doors are sealed. Let us depart."

"Don't have to tell me twice." As Keel began to lift the *Six* off the ground, he keyed the comm to the cargo bay. "Find something bolted down and hang on back there. Things might get a little bumpy before we can make a jump out of system."

The *Indelible VI* rose high above the rooftops of the neighborhood, none of which extended beyond three stories. On Utopion, the wealthy showed their status by living in small buildings and manors, rather than the towering mega-tenements most of the populace dwelled in.

A proximity alarm sounded, and Keel had time to call out the incoming attack fighters before the first blaster cannon bolts were harmlessly absorbed by his shields. "Preyhunters."

Ravi looked out the side partition of the cockpit crysteel as two ships raced past the *Six*, one on either side. "Piloted by Gomarii."

"Their funeral," Keel said, and then moved in pursuit. "DOW, you still on weapons systems?"

The little gunnery bot said it was.

"Good. Time to splash some fighters on our way off this rock."

Death, Destroyer of Worlds could think of no words it would rather have heard at that moment.

10

If there was any shame associated with New Boss (rightly) pointing out that his logic for killing the second gang member was self-serving and unsound, it evaporated the moment Captain Keel requested that Death, Destroyer of Worlds defend the ship against the adequately armed Preyhunters streaking through the atmosphere. Their attempts to evade the *Indelible VI* were, of course, futile.

But their deaths... those would be glorious. Fireballs of atmospheric destruction were so much more brilliant and sustained than the pitiful brief burn-offs of gas that happened within the bubbles of fading shields. A real dogfight was on hand, though New Boss was positioning the ship to make it a short one. Which was really too bad. But then... the little gunnery bot thought that might be for the better. Its judgment had lately been... off.

Its desire to realize its dreams of violent death were beginning to challenge its long-established guardrails protecting non-combatants. Shooting a murderous thug on his bike was fine, but requesting permission to lay waste to a group of unarmed refugees... that might represent a glitch in Death's central core. One that ought not go unexamined.

Then again... no one could yet be *sure* that there wasn't a spy mixed in with that group. Perhaps carrying a bomb that could easily destroy the bay—though not the ship thanks to its redesigned structural integrity—or more likely, a hold-out blaster that the spy would use to systematically clear the ship, killing the crew one by one until they had control of the *Indelible VI*.

If that were to happen... well, then seeking to preemptively destroy the prospective murderer spy was the only moral thing to do. In truth, Death would have been culpable had it *not* made the request to fire on civilians.

Then again, Death's logic processor reminded it, at the time the little bot had only assumed they were approaching gang members. The thought of a spy had not yet formed.

That was... problematic.

Oh well! Now that the potentiality of a spy had been floated as a possibility, Death had to take it seriously. He would need to patrol the ship carefully, looking for the would-be assassin as they made their way through the venting or skulked through the shadows of the bulkheads.

But first... the Preyhunters.

The light attack starfighters were notable for their adaptability and speed. They were not quite as durable or dangerous as Republic fighters, but they were still a danger, particularly with a skilled pilot at the flight controls. Unfortunately for them, the *Indelible VI* was *so* much faster that the speed advantage was neutralized. And the pilots' relative skill compared to New Boss was such that it took only one quick targeting calculation to send the first ship diving toward the planet's surface, a black smoke trail following it as it spun wildly out of control in a final plunge toward impact.

Death had made its shot to achieve just that effect. The thrill the little gunnery bot had in seeing the first Preyhunter crash into a ball of flames right in the middle of a city street more than made up for the relative banality of the pursuit and the shot itself.

"A little less collateral damage next time," New Boss ordered over the comms.

Ah. Disintegration it would have to be then.

The obvious maneuver at this point would be to perform a quick starboard roll that would line up guns on target. But given the refugees in the cargo bay, such a maneuver would result in collateral damage to New Boss's cargo-slash-guests, and the likely spies among them. So New Boss instead slid the *Six* behind the craft, dropping speed to do so and thereby giving the Preyhunter ample time to either nose down or climb in escape.

The pilot was either thick-headed or simply too slow of mind to take the available avenue of retreat. Instead he relied on his ship's speed to get out of the situation. That trick might well have worked for the slaver in the past. It would not this time.

To Death's delight, the slow, sidewinding slide to get the *Indelible VI* in position also raised the difficulty of the shot. The gunnery bot recalculated its angles and trajectories and then opened a heavy, sustained burst. The effect was exactly what New Boss wanted, and the Preyhunter erupted into a massive, airborne fireball. Any human below would have to be quite unlucky to be struck by a wayward bolt or flaming scrap of wreckage.

New Boss should be happy.

He wasn't, but not because of the gunnery bot.

"Two more on our tail."

What annoyed New Boss delighted Death, Destroyer of Worlds. Now the gunnery bot would show its master some *real* skill. It swung the blaster cannons around and began to fire just before achieving lock. The effect was to "fling" blaster cannon bolts into the pursuing Preyhunter on the *Six*'s port side, vaporizing the shocked pilot before he had the time to realize what was happening. Death continued to fire as it swept the cannon along its arc and dispatched the second fighter on the starboard side in the same manner, sending no less than three bolts directly through the canopy as the craft's pilot attempted to dive for safety.

What a treat! Death got a clear view of the Gomarii pilot being struck and dismembered by the heavy blasts in those brief fractions of a second before the whole of the ship blazed in explosive flames.

One confirmed kill on the ground. Four confirmed kills in the air. All of them captured on the little bot's memory drive for future reflection and enjoyment.

What a momentous day. And, who knew? Perhaps still more starfighters might yet come.

Besides, there was also that spy to hunt down...

"No problem," Keel said, smiling at how easily the bot had dispatched the Preyhunters. "How come *you* never shot like that, Ravi?"

"As I recall, you preferred to pull the trigger yourself."

"Semantics, Ravi. Let's get into orbit."

The cockpit door swished open as Keel began a gradual climb to escape atmosphere. This was going to be the most uncomfortable part of the flight for the refugees in the cargo hold. Inertial dampers could only do so much, and they worked better in space than they did in atmo.

"We... can't leave yet."

The weakened voice of Arkaddy Nilo caused Keel to whip his head around. "Why aren't you asleep?"

Zora was at the Black Leaf executive's side. "He wasn't having it. And anyway, we have some more allies on hand."

"On my yacht," Nilo said. He sounded small and weak to Keel's ears. A man who'd gone through too much in too short a time. "Pikkek and his Kublarens. They're loyal, and I just made comm with them."

"Kublarens?" Keel and Ravi exchanged a look.

"What was that look for?" Zora asked.

Keel frowned. "If they're Kublarens, they, uh, might be the last of their kind."

"*What?*"

Ravi softly explained what had been reported to them by Prisma.

"Oba," Nilo muttered, looking sicker than he had before. "Then... we have to—"

"Yeah. I get it," Keel said. "Setting a course. Where'd you park?"

11

Keel pointed out the battlefield dead strewn about Nilo's yacht. The space liner had been docked on an open landing pad atop a Utopion high-rise where the people serving the delegates, senators, and other power brokers had once lived. But apart from the fight on the rooftop—a fight that was still ongoing—the building looked to have been spared any damage during Article Nineteen's fight against Goth Sullus on the former capital world.

"Looks like a mix of Nether Ops legionnaires and Black Leaf mercs," Zora muttered. She clenched her teeth, too angry to say more.

Nilo said nothing; just staying upright seemed to take all his energy. The auto-doc had reported that the driven young man had self-administered a dose of Narxec, a powerful drug that stopped the effects of other narcotics in the system—a sort of emergency injection for when patients had a negative reaction to a sedative or general anesthesia. One side effect was that a Narxec cocktail on top of too many other narcotics was, occasionally, fatal. Nilo wanted lucidity despite the pain he was in, and he was willing to risk his life to make it happen.

Ravi's fingers danced over his navigator's console. "It appears that those lying dead on the roof were attempting to force their way aboard the yacht. Whoever is inside managed to seal it properly."

"Too bad they can't figure out how to answer the comm hails," Keel grumbled.

"Frequency... change," Nilo rasped through an arid throat. The words actually *sounded* painful. "C-can't."

"The same must be true of the weapons system," Ravi said. "Attackers are moving with impunity beyond the PDCs."

Keel thumbed the switch for manual controls. "Well, ours work." He issued a burst of anti-personnel repeater fire, strafing a group of mixed Nether agents and mercs and causing them to fall over like cut timbers.

"Ravi, you see that?"

"If you are asking about the forced entry into the yacht's crew access door, yes."

Keel turned around to look at Nilo. "They're pushing their way on board. I'm gonna move in and get a stable platform to jump from. Ravi, you take the *Six*."

"I'll... come..." Nilo began, and then pitched forward and fainted, tumbling onto Keel's shoulders.

The smuggler promptly shoved him to the side. He would have tumbled to the floor if not for Zora grabbing him.

"Strap him down somewhere!" Keel yelled hotly. "I need you to follow me out there."

Zora nodded, understanding why at once. She knew the yacht's layout and would be best able to lead whatever rescue plan was needed. Her blaster would also be a help, but that was something Keel wouldn't readily admit—due to certain ongoing relationship issues.

Zora placed Nilo down on the floor beside Ravi. "You'll watch him?"

"Yes, of course." Ravi steadied the ship upon taking the controls from Keel.

Keel and Zora ran through the ship, armor equipped and weapons ready. The little gunnery bot had rolled out to see about spies, but now inquired about joining in on this next mission.

"No. Stay here in case Ravi needs you to fend off any more starfighters."

The bot trilled an excited, "Yes, sir!" and then rolled away to prepare for just such a fortuitous encounter.

"Repulsor three maintenance shaft," Keel called out.

Zora knew the layout of the *Indelible VI* as well as anyone, and raced ahead of Keel to reach the shaft. They pulled off the magnetic access plate and climbed down past the repulsor's components, which were glowing orange from use behind their protective energy shielding. Only comms in helmets would allow them to communicate above the noise, and only the helmets themselves saved their hearing, but neither needed to talk. The play was understood from the moment Keel called out the repulsor shaft: they would remove the access panel, which was really just a thick piece of hull plating, and drop down onto the rooftop.

"C'mon... c'mon..." Zora mumbled as the extensive seal system began to disengage, making removal of the piece of hull possible. "Got it!"

Keel reached down and, thanks to his new armor's strength enhancements, lifted the plate and tilted it on its side to lock in place in its designated holding field. "Me first."

The smuggler dropped to the rooftop and rolled forward, hearing Zora land behind him as he came up. Several dead soldiers lay strewn across the war-torn roof, and not a few Kublarens as well. Air conditioning and other mechanical units were scorched and blown open.

But there was no one moving, at least not since the *Six*'s strafing run.

"Where'd they go?" Zora asked.

"Aboard the yacht," Keel guessed, and led the bounty hunter toward the crew access.

The space liner was much larger than Keel's ship, and running alongside its massive landing struts felt like passing the marble columns of some ancient temple that towered in splendor high above them. Keel risked a look up for any snipers who might be stationed in the folds of the yacht's ornamental fins, but saw only the great viewing windows meant to dazzle its passengers as they passed through hyperspace or slowed down to witness the brilliant birth of a supernova.

Keel re-focused on advancing toward the access door just as a Black Leaf merc popped out with the hopes of taking both intruders down with a sustained burst of his blaster rifle. The heavily augmented weapon, which shot energized bullets and served as a mix of slug thrower and blaster, barked a full-auto burst of rounds into the sky as the soldier fell backward from the depleted uranium round Keel sent smashing through his forehead.

Two more mercs poured from the opening and took cover behind the pillar-like struts of the yacht. Keel activated his jump jets and hopped over their heads, shooting one in the ankle while on his way down. The man fell, exposing his upper body to Zora, who finished him with four successive trigger pulls. Keel landed his bounce and was able to punch three rounds through the back armor of the second man, who'd been slow to turn and face the rapidly changing threat picture.

A Nether Ops legionnaire was the fourth of the four-man team tasked with holding the two pursuers back. He raced out of the lowered crew door, which sat just a few feet off the ground in a low-hanging tail section kept out of sight of the grand prow and the wide boarding gantry reserved for the yacht's more important passengers. But this criminal agent of the deep state was unaware that his quarry had boosted behind their position, and therefore didn't expect to find Keel at his flank. The legionnaire attempted to whip his rifle around, but a strong kick to the sternum by Keel sent him crashing backwards into the nearby strut. Keel followed that with a helmet-splitting round to the head and turned to focus on the door as the man slowly slid down the strut.

"How we looking from up there?" Keel asked Ravi.

"You have full control of the roof," the navigator replied over the *Indelible VI*'s comm system. "However, I am detecting a power spike aboard the yacht. I fear the boarding team may have assumed controls and are attempting to take off."

"Right on their heels. Wraith out." Keel motioned for Zora to push up and join him. She stacked on the opposite side of the door as Keel rechecked his HUD. No life forms in the immediate vicinity. He peeked around the corner and found the corridor leading up and into the ship empty.

With a nod, he stormed his way up the ramp with Zora at his heels. Two steps in and he saw the sly reason for not leaving more guards to hamper his approach. Someone had mounted an explosive sensor just above the second blast door leading into the ship. Every commercially produced star craft was required to have a second door, as a failsafe, at every humanoid access point. This effectively made every entry an airlock, even if all that meant was constructing a small stretch of hallway between doors. Regulations were regulations, after all.

Keel stopped abruptly and held up his fist for Zora to do the same. Another step and they'd have tripped the trap. *Okay,* Keel thought, *what did Garret tell me about the armor's slicing abilities?*

At once a sub-menu appeared in his HUD, listing a variety of worms that could be used. In the meantime, the armor gave a rundown of the explosive, noting that it was working in tandem with the yacht's defense systems rather than on its own private network. That would make it more difficult to disable due to the additional security a large system like the yacht was capable of running. Keel selected a worm that seemed fit for the job and waited as the armor negotiated its way into the yacht's defense network.

"We just gonna stand here, jump jockey?" Zora asked.

"Slicing my way into this pleasure barge's defense systems. Unless you got the code to the fresher?"

"Nilo would."

"Nilo's probably bled out by now. Okay. Got it. Reading it as disabled."

Despite the reading, a small red light persisted on the explosive.

"You sure about that?" Zora asked.

"Gonna find out in a minute."

Keel stepped forward. While the bomb remained active, the worm had disabled the sensor. They passed unscathed to the door, opened it, and were immediately greeted by the sound of a pitched firefight.

"That's a good sign," Keel said. "You got a way to keep those koobs from dusting us too?"

"Yeah. Stay out of their line of fire."

They pushed their way further into the ship, following the sounds of battle, but not seeing any hostiles.

"Shooting's happening in the main dining hall," Zora said. "There's a side access that'll get us into the kitchen. Should be able to flank from there."

"Lead the way," Keel said, pushing to the side of the corridor so Zora could pass him.

She took him down an inward-curving passageway that gleamed beneath soft overhead lights. Exotic—and no doubt absurdly expensive—art hung on the walls, with sculptures, some physical and some holographic, displayed on pedestals inside recessed alcoves. The paintings alternated between peaceful, pastoral scenes of landscaped serenity and battle portraits. It took a moment before Keel realized that the settings were the same. A picture of a landscape unmarred by warfare, and then the same scene featuring a battle, almost always between native populaces and Savage invaders. The statues were more varied, and Keel wondered if they were the products of artists who had once lived on the worlds depicted along the corridor.

The answers would have to wait. They reached the kitchen's back entrance at the end of the winding pathway.

"Okay," Zora said. "This will take us past the walk-in freezers and then up to the serving window. We'll get a good angle on the dining room by taking the—"

Her description was cut short by a sudden lurching of the ship that sent both Zora and Keel swaying to keep their balance. Stasis fields snapped to life, keeping the physical statues from tumbling from their perches.

"That felt like a bomb went off!" Zora shouted, her hands pressed against the wall.

"No boom," Keel said. "But something moved the ship."

Another violent shudder passed through the ship, accompanied by the deep, groaning sound of stressed metal from somewhere beneath them.

"Captain Keel, this is Ravi. Someone is attempting to take the yacht up, but there must be some sort of engine damage. All that is happening is they are firing themselves to the edge of the roof. You need to correct this or get off the ship before it can plummet over the side."

The calmness in Ravi's voice was reassuring, but not enough to keep Keel's heart from dropping into his stomach as the situation was revealed to him. "You got any special passageways that'll get us to the cockpit?" he asked Zora.

"Just the one," she answered, and then double-timed in that direction.

They ran back down the corridor they'd just traveled, then turned into a series of service and maintenance passages. Two Nether Ops legionnaires had the misfortune of running out ahead of them, seemingly making their way to the bridge after having broken away from the firefight in the dining hall. Keel and Zora each dropped a target and leapt past the dead bodies on the way to the bridge.

The final sprint required they travel up a crisscrossing set of stairs to the top level. These, like the rest of the ship, were of grand design meant to impress anyone important enough to be granted access to the bridge to meet the ship's captain. The stairs were carpeted a royal blue, and the handrails were silvene inlaid with gold and a tight-grained wood, stained and polished to a candy shine.

If the carpet partially hid Keel's and Zora's coming steps from the Black Leaf mercs gathered at the bridge blast doors, it was the mercs' single-minded focus on gaining their own access that provided the greatest cover. All sense of security and alertness was missing as four men watched a fifth enter access codes into a holographic keypad, swearing after each failure. And it was no wonder they were distracted; what had begun as an attempt to commandeer an expensive ship belonging to Nilo had now turned into a fight for survival. No one needed Ravi's help to understand, at least in broad strokes, what was happening at this point.

The yacht's engine flared, and Keel and Zora felt it make a wounded-animal lurch closer to the edge. Several of the mercs stumbled or fell to a knee while the man on the holopad tried another access code. Zora nearly lost her footing as well, but Keel's armor stabilized him this time. He set the slug thrower to full auto and unleashed a devastating spray of murder that won them the front of the line to the bridge access pad.

Keel hurried to it, pre-emptively running through possible worms in case whatever codes Zora might have proved to be as useless as those entered by the dead mercenaries. But he couldn't find a worm that could complete the slice in less than an estimated ten to fifteen minutes.

"Hope you've got a way in, Z."

Zora punched in her access code and was promptly denied entry. She keyed the bridge comm. "Bridge, this is Zora. Open the door!"

There was no reply.

The ship lurched ahead.

"You are nearly to the point of tipping over the edge, Captain Keel!" Ravi said. His voice was much less even and controlled this time.

"Wake up Nilo and get me a code so I can get onto the bridge!" Keel ordered.

A second later, Nilo's weakened voice gave him a command phrase. Of course. The datapad requested a numerical access code, but only a spoken voice command would work after a security seal. That kind of thing would go a long way in keeping people from slicing the bridge.

Keel repeated the phrase aloud, then stood back as the blast doors smoothly opened.

Inside was a sight far more comedic than the present danger allowed Keel to appreciate. Sitting in the helmsman's seat was the Kublaren warrior Pikkek. Surrounding him were a bevy of other koobs, their air sacs inflating their bright purple skin as they excitedly croaked and clicked suggestions for achieving flight. Others looked to be threatening the complex control stations with their rifles, croaking out orders that the ship fly at once.

Pikkek licked and then swiveled his eyes to observe the newcomers. Seeing Zora and Keel, both familiar to him, he bellowed, "How—k'kik'k—fly?"

The ship lurched again as he mashed the starboard reserve thruster.

"Not like that!" Keel shouted, and then took the controls. The yacht had begun to teeter at the edge of the building, and Keel could see the Utopion skyline bobbing up and down. He assessed the control board and activated all repulsors.

The yacht began a steady, floating rise above the roof.

Zora heaved her shoulders in relief while the Kublarens croaked in appreciation. Keel checked the holocams and found that the Kublarens in the banquet room had dispatched the outnumbered Black Leaf mercs and their Nether Ops allies. There was definitely a story about what happened on Utopion that he was only scratching the surface of. But that story would have to be told later— if at all.

"Big fly," Pikkek said, patting Keel on the shoulder appreciatively. "What—*k'k*—happen to Bigguh Nee?"

"Double-cross," Zora said, and then almost spat the name of the culprit. "Surber."

"No-ah, like. Thatta one. *K'kik'ke.*"

Keel frowned. "Yeah, well, there's a lot of things you're not gonna like. Let's take this bird up and get off-world. Then we'll load up the refugees onto the yacht."

"Why would we do that?" Zora asked.

"So you can fly them somewhere safe. I'll take Nilo back to the *Phoenix* and get him on his feet. You can join us after you make your delivery."

"You got a destination for me?"

"Yeah. En Shakar." Keel paused and considered Pikkek and his platoon of Kublaren warriors. "I'm gonna take the koobs with me though. Just in case. That okay with you, Pikkek?"

"Ya, ya. We go with Bigguh Nee."

Keel nodded and began to make preparations to get off-world. He only briefly considered breaking the news to the Kublarens—that their home world had been ravaged and they were possibly the last of their race—before deciding to leave that task to Nilo.

If the kid managed to survive the trip back to the *Battle Phoenix.*

12

Running from the yacht back to the *Indelible VI* was a risk Keel felt he had to take. Because while Ravi was a capable pilot, with the number of Gomarii slave ships entering orbit, it was going to take more than *capable* flying to assure the *Six* and the yacht escaped atmosphere.

The arrival of a Republic corvette—or rather a *House of Reason loyalist* corvette—which entered atmosphere to serve as a mini-gunship, targeting the old capital rotunda, only served to reinforce Keel's decision. Still... the crew swaps needed to hurry.

Ravi had air-docked the *Six* by keeping a stable repulsor hover inches from the yacht's main entryway. He then lowered the cargo bay ramp, which allowed confused refugees to step off and board the pleasure liner directly. Or at least, that had been the plan.

Reality had other plans. These Utopion citizens, some of whom were likely having second thoughts about having run onto some stranger's freighter in a panic to escape, were already reluctant to be offloaded to yet another vessel and shipped to parts unknown. And that was *before* they came face to face with a band of armed Kublaren warriors.

Pikkek, standing at the forefront of his platoon, licked an eyeball and inflated his air sac, holding it full as he swiveled his eyes to take in the spectacle before him. Finally, he exhaled a long, breathy croak. The rest of the

Kublarens took this as the signal to move ahead; they entered the docking bay and there began to disassemble and spot-clean their weapons in the Kublaren fashion.

Which is to say, knock out any carbon scoring with a few swift palm strikes, and call it good.

Keel pushed his way in front of the Kublarens, annoyed that so many of the refugees seemed unprepared to move despite Ravi's instructions. He pointed to the yacht behind himself and then to the ship. "Refugee yacht. Fighting ship. Get moving."

This seemed to awaken the refugees. Besides, *this* ship was now the one carrying Kublaren warriors. The other one couldn't possibly be worse. They gathered up their belongings and began to shuffle past Keel and into the yacht.

"Pick up the pace," Keel shouted, "or we're all gonna be scorch marks if one of those big ships up there sees us."

The refugees hurried, but the stumbles and drops that came as a result only slowed their overall process.

"What they?" Pikkek demanded.

"Refugees." Keel wasn't sure if the Kublaren chief understood the word, but he certainly didn't know the corresponding koob word.

"Why no gun-pow? *K'kk.*"

"Home's invaded. They're tryin' to get away before the fighting gets worse."

Pikkek's wide mouth gaped in a manner Keel hadn't seen before. It resembled the sort of exaggerated dismay you might see in a holo-comedy. "No stay-fight? *Kliptah.*"

Keel didn't know the Kublaren word *kliptah* either, but he took it for a curse. The way Pikkek glared at the adults, as well as some of the larger children, made it clear that the koob didn't approve of anyone *fleeing* their planet on the eve of battle instead of staying to fight and die a glorious death.

But Keel had seen what happens to untrained civilians thrust into war. He didn't share the koob's disapproval.

When the last of the refugees had passed from the *Six* to the yacht, Keel began to close the doors to both starships. "Better stay out of the banquet hall for a while!" he called out to the civilians as the ramps went back up.

Then he keyed his comm. "Okay, Zora. Transfer complete. Wait to roll out the greeting committee until we're in hyperspace."

"Thanks, jump jockey. I was going to just sit here and give them a tour until you told me."

"Follow me up, and remember the plan once we're in atmo. Rendezvous at the *Phoenix* once you deliver the refugees."

"Anything else?"

"Yeah. Good luck, Zora."

Ravi was already bringing the *Indelible VI* into a climb when Keel reached the cockpit and assumed flight controls. "How we lookin'?"

"Thus far we have escaped scrutiny, however ships attempting to leave the planet are being interdicted or pursued." Ravi looked to his instruments and watched the holocam feed showing the yacht as it lifted from the rooftop. "Zora will be at a considerable disadvantage while remaining in atmosphere."

Keel gave a fractional nod. "Yeah. That's where we come in." He flipped his comm switch. "Confirm all weapons primed."

Death, Destroyer of Worlds chirped that everything was ready to go, but lamented the fact that the *Indelible VI* wasn't equipped with an omni-cannon. Perhaps New Boss would consider taking one from a spare *Obsidian Crow*?

"Not on your life. Strap an ugly gun like that to your ship and you draw the eyes of every two-chit cop and booster in system. Missiles will do fine."

Keel had always preferred weapons systems that were hidden. An omni-cannon, while powerful, was large, obtrusive, and gave no ability whatsoever to blend in. It might have served a bounty hunter like Tyrus Rechs well, but not so for a smuggler, or anyone else relying on stealth and incognito.

Ravi waited for Keel to finish, then raised an eyebrow. "Are you really giving that bot a lecture on illegal weapons systems? Now?"

"Gotta learn some time," Keel said, increasing his throttle as he raced the *Indelible VI* toward its target. "Besides, it keeps me from thinkin' about what we're about to try."

Ravi's eyes went forward and grew wide at the sight of a growing Republic corvette, which had just switched its modest blaster cannons from a mini-orbital assault to defense, sending thick, powerful blasts toward the *Six*.

"Captain Keel! The odds of a direct atmospheric attack—"

"Gonna find out either way." Keel rolled his ship through the deluge of cannon fire from the corvette. Despite being comparatively small, it was still a capital ship, and usually a freighter—even the *Indelible VI*—was best advised to try and outrun those. "Dummy one."

At the order, Death fired a decoy missile at the corvette, which drew away some of the fire as the ship attempted to defend itself.

Keel banked and dove. "Dummy two!"

A second missile raced for another part of the corvette, forcing the defensive weapons to split their targeting solutions neatly between the forward and rear. Then, in a wrenching roll and slide that nearly made Keel feel light-headed, the Naseen freighter turned and whipped around to come at full speed directly at the middle of the ship.

"Give it to 'em!" Keel called, fighting off the effects of what the inertial dampers couldn't mitigate.

The *Indelible VI* issued a blitz of missile, torpedo, and blaster cannon fire, all concentrated at midships. Automated firing solutions, already occupied on the two divergent dum-dum missiles, were slow to respond to the unexpected onslaught. No targeting computer could have anticipated the gut-wrenching maneuver Keel had just pulled off in his thoroughly enhanced starship.

Great plumes of fire erupted along the corvette as blaster cannons that would make even the Legion uncomfortable about civilian ownership battered down the shields. Missiles took out defensive weapons and torpedoes blew holes in the impervisteel hull.

The *Indelible VI* roared over the burning canopy.

The corvette listed and burned, its repulsors working to keep it in the air as it sprayed itself with fire-retardant foam. As badly damaged as it was, all focus would now be on bringing the ship down for an emergency landing. Always better to hit the deck on your own terms.

Keel had guessed that the state of this House of Reason ship would be much like the other loyalist vessel he'd seen up close: understaffed and manned by spacers who were forced into service by their officers and at the rifles of point-heavy hullbusters. It was for that reason that he opted not to splash the corvette permanently, even though he looped a wide and lazy turn to line himself up for exactly that sort of fatal attack run.

Of course, the other attacking ships had no way of knowing that the modified freighter, bristling with firepower sufficient to cripple one of their largest ships, didn't intend to finish the job. Fighters from all quadrants roared to intercept, unleashing a succession of sonic booms to reach and defend the distressed corvette. That had been exactly what Keel intended. He knew the *Six* could outrun every ship in this star system, both in atmosphere and out of it. The yacht, however, was a different story. Now he'd bought Zora the time she needed to get up and in position to make the jump to safety.

"Nice flying," Zora called over the comm. "If you see any star-fleas on my tail, kindly pick them off for me."

Propriety and a dedication to Leenah kept Keel from making the obvious joke.

"Try and shake them if you can," he said instead. "If they get the idea that we're together, they might go after you harder than if you just burn for exit on your own."

"Understood. See you around, jump jockey."

Keel smiled but didn't further reply. He would need to focus on shaking or splashing the Preyhunters and other independent starfighters that were converging on his position. Already blaster cannon bolts were zipping into his aft shields while the *Six*'s targeting jammers played havoc on the enemy's ability to obtain missile lock.

The little gunnery bot clicked an update over the comm system.

"That's right," Keel said. "Thanks for remembering... and for not shooting them down anyway."

A key here was to get the attackers to believe they were actually driving him off. If he made things too hard on them, there was a chance that, valuing their lives, they might disengage and find some of the other ships navigating their way through the atmosphere more interesting. Keel let his shields take a little bit more punishment and then abruptly broke off his attack run, diving down toward the planet-spanning skyline of Utopion.

"Let's see who can keep up," Keel said.

Ravi, still working the controls and direct anti-lock jamming bursts where they were needed, said, "I appreciate your reduction of speed as we move between the buildings. The odds of your survival improve with each kps deduction."

"You're gonna have to update your analysis of the odds, Ravi. This *Six* isn't the one you're used to. And anyway, I'm slowing down for their benefit, not ours." Keel jerked his head in the general direction of the pursuing starfighters.

"Ah. You do not wish to lose them."

"Not until Zora's clear."

Keel slalomed between skyscrapers, drawing some of the Preyhunters into doing the same while others kept pace overhead, seeking a firing solution from well above the rooftops. It wasn't long before the lack of skill of some of the followers cost them their lives. One Preyhunter slammed directly into an executive building, exploding on impact as the building, pre-emptively hardened against terror attacks, shrugged off the collision. A second Preyhunter clipped the corner of a less-stout building, causing debris to fall a hundred stories below and shearing off its wing. It went into a brief spin before its systems ignited and it dropped, a burning wreck, into the streets below.

Keel checked his cams to see the carnage. "At this speed? Ravi, that's just embarrassing for those guys."

"Yes. I am glad you are having fun."

"Beats the alternative. How's Zora?"

"She has a Preyhunter tail, but her defensive systems are more than capable of handling its pursuit. Another forty seconds to leave atmosphere. I calculate ninety seconds until she can jump."

"Good. Let's get onto our own exit lane, then."

Keel raced through the wide central avenues of Utopion's business district, then took on elevation to reorient himself with the planet's layout. The ships who had been sitting up there among the clouds and waiting for the opportunity to attack now attempted to take advantage. They let loose blaster cannon fire, most of which Keel waggled and drifted out of, with the shields absorbing the rest with little effort. Leenah deserved a kiss on the lips for what she'd pulled off. Each time he'd taken the *Six* out since he'd gotten it back was more impressive than the last.

Death asked for permission to destroy the pursuing ships. Its guns had remained silent for the flight so far, and being fired upon without hope of firing back was the very height of insult for the little gunnery bot.

"Not yet, but get on the swivel turrets for when I say the word. I'm taking the linked forwards to manual."

Hearing this, Ravi turned to stare at Keel, a black eyebrow arched high.

The *Indelible VI* sped toward the sprawling campus that once was the political heart of the entire Republic. Its vast manicured parks had grown shabby, but still remained beautiful amid the great city, and the Senate and House of Reason buildings both shone brightly, dominating the landscape.

"Zora has successfully made the jump," Ravi reported.

"Okay, DOW," Keel announced into the comms. "Dust our chasers."

At once the *Six* shuddered under the sudden barrage of turret fire. Death, Destroyer of Worlds began to shoot down the pursuers, who broke in all directions as the false courage of their unopposed chase was shattered under the scorching intensity of the *Six*'s cannons.

Even as starfighters began to crash in Republic Park, Keel took on more speed, readying himself to perform a climb and get himself to the safety of hyperspace travel. Fun as all this was, the invading ships were still entering atmosphere, and fighting on the ground looked to be increasing as well.

But first...

Keel rolled the *Indelible VI* to put it on a course in line with the House of Reason building itself. He then fired a salvo of linked forward blaster cannon fire directly into its stately gold-and-silvene roof, sending up balls of flame.

The stern disapproval on Ravi's face did nothing to dampen Keel's smile.

"Always wanted to do that."

Another item on his wish list checked off, the captain took the *Six* up in a climb that hopefully wouldn't be too much for the Kublarens in the cargo hold. So far, none had commed with a request for Keel to ease up on the flying. But then again... it was possible they didn't know how to make such a request. Ravi would check on them once they were in hyperspace.

As the *Six* rose, two more targets of opportunity were exploited by the gunnery bot, a pair of unlucky Republic Lancers that Keel assumed were piloted by House of Reason loyalists or Nether Ops featherheads. A pilot who had fought on the right side of Article Nineteen would have already made a run for it after being released from the hangar bay, Keel reasoned.

The *Indelible VI* escaped Utopion's atmosphere and had no difficulty zipping through the developing blockade of frigates and Gomarii slavers that were organizing in orbit. A fight was already underway with Utopion's planetary defense forces and the invaders, one that would only grow larger once the Republic got involved, which they would have to do. Keel couldn't see a way the House of Liberty and Senate housed on Spilursa would allow a core world to be hit like this.

Then again... things were spiraling in the galaxy. Each planet might soon be in it for themselves until the Legion could rally around whatever battle plan Ravi was putting together in his mind. Which had to come out soon.

Or so Keel thought. Which was why the smuggler was surprised when his friend examined the comms log from his navigator's station and declared, "Update on Andien Broxin and Praxus. They are fighting in the Sinasian Cluster and are seeking a rendezvous. I suggest we extract them directly. This will save considerable time. Their role in the final things to come will be important."

Keel gave a half-frown. Ravi seemed to be torn between the need to execute whatever his and Prisma's plan was as quickly as possible, and a desire to have as many capable allies on hand as he could. But there was no doubt that Broxin and the Cybar were both capable. Very capable.

"Whatever you say, pal. But maybe we ought to get Nilo to the *Phoenix* first?" He checked the med bay. Nilo was once again unconscious and under the supervision of the auto-doc.

"I calculate only a twelve percent chance that he dies during our detour."

Keel looked at his friend. "You realize it sounds terrible when you put it that way, Ravi."

"Yes. I see how such might sound clinical and uncaring. However, given the circumstances—"

"Just say, 'I'm sure he'll be fine.' That's what I'd do."

Ravi nodded appreciatively and entered jump coordinates. "To Sinasia then. I'm sure Nilo will be fine."

13

**12th Marines Expeditionary Unit
Sinasia**

Sergeant "Sparky" Cathey heard the call going through, though he caught only pieces of it as the marine net worked to break through the energy surge still dissipating along the docks of the warehouse district.

"All Swamp Rat elements... This is... Gomarii slave ship entering... drop pods full of zhee fighters... Additional Hool forces... Collapse on following grid and prepare to repel..."

The Hools had invaded courtesy of a Gomarii ride share. They were already everywhere. Sparky had no clue where in Oba's galaxy of garbage anyone could find that many Hools for hire.

He realized he was moving, bouncing along at a hurried pace. A vague notion that his feet were tap dancing on the cobblestone street clued him in to the fact that someone was carrying him.

"Wakey-wakey, fellah. We have klicks to clack before this is over and carrying you isn't going to get it done, mate." The digital voice sounded jovial, albeit malevolent. It came from a speaker that had taken a normal voice and twisted it into that of a growling agro-bear.

"Give him a break, Haitch. Dude just got hit with an orbital," said another voice on the other side of Sparky.

After a few more steps, a third voice behind him ordered, "Drop him over here in this alley. Gonna see if we got something to work with."

Sparky expected to be dumped hard into the street, and he tensed his body against the fall. Instead, he was delicately set down by whoever had him by the arms. The Repub marine's eyes tried to focus but came away with only a vague sense of blotchy, brown-armored troopers mixed in with the mottled green hullbusters that he expected were what was left of his squad. Then, in a flash of straining muscles and headache-inducing clarity, everything came back into stark focus.

Patterson, Tripp, Volson, and D'ghar were at the end of an alley pulling security. Sparky couldn't see the rest of the squad, and for a second, he hoped they were just in a building or side passage covering their six. But only for a second. The memory of what had happened came back to him all too quickly.

The other troops were wrapped in armor and kitted out for maximum violence. Legionnaires. Pictures of discipline and apex combat prowess, sealed head to toe in armor with the protruding profile and glaring visor of the Legion. Sparky was looking into the bucket of a legionnaire medic who was setting an auto-injector back into his aid bag.

"Legion? I thought you boys were on the other side of the planet."

"Fightin's over here," the one called Haitch said from over the medic's shoulder. "Most times, a pack of more than five 'ools is a sign of a good fight. You got a 'ell of a lot more than that then, eh?"

Sparky looked back to the Legion medic. "Can I get one of those buckets to translate?"

"That's Haitch," the medic answered, still assessing Sparky's injuries. "We call him that on account of he can't say the letter 'H' correctly."

"But I know all the sign language." Haitch gave an unmistakable rude gesture.

The medic shook his head. "Call me Doc Kilgore. And before you ask, yes, that's really my name. Third man watching the alley with your marines we call Dobie or Dobes; he ain't doro, but he eats like one of 'em." He straightened up. "Okay. Can you tell me your name, rank, and service number, hullbuster?"

"Sergeant Cathey, Robert. Service Number 1043248. You guys Special Forces?"

"I mean, compared to 'ullbusters we are," commented Haitch.

"Stow it, Leej." It was clear the medic was in charge of the Legion trio. "Dark Ops has not seen fit to come callin' for us yet. We came in with a full platoon and got separated when that orbital blast from the Gomarii ship shot too close to our bird. Knocked our shuttle out of the sky and most of us jumped for it."

"Kils, another minute and we're outta here," Dobie said over his shoulder.

"Sure thing, Dobes. Listen, Sar'nt Cathey, I gave you a pretty severe stim. I hope you have the stomach for it. It'll keep you lucid for a little bit. You don't seem to have a concussion—somehow—but your bell got rung pretty good. Unfortunately, I have to deal with *that* right now." Doc Kilgore pointed at Sparky's leg.

The marine sergeant looked down at the injury he hadn't, until this moment, realized he had. Though he wasn't surprised he had it. Just when his squad had been about to take the communications tower from Hool control, the installation had been hit by a beam weapon orbital strike. The last thing he remembered was the blast punching him from his roost in the warehouse they occupied, sending him flying through the rafters into a stack of boxes below. Some of the corrugated roof must have splintered and turned into flak, because now a chunk of metal stuck from his leg, covered in a mixture of blood and grime. Looking at it with an increasingly queasy feeling in his stomach, Sparky realized the piece had impaled his leg clean through to the other side.

"Funny, I didn't feel it until you pointed it out, Doc. Thanks for that." Sparky squirmed, and he felt the tip protruding out of the back of his leg scrape the duracrete beneath him.

The Legion medic gave a curt nod. "Brain feels what it wants to feel. Your nerves in the area are dead. But you have a decision to make."

"Yeah," Sparky agreed. "That's probably going to make helping you guys a bit of an issue."

"I can take it out and pump you full of stuff to make you combat effective—at least for a while—or we can direct you to a CCP. Your choice."

Sparky took a deep breath. "I'm just happy a doc named Kilgore didn't include putting me down as one of the options. All right. No casualty collection point unless my guts are spilling out and wrapped around my ankles. I'll go for door number one."

Kilgore didn't wait for the marine to change his mind. He ripped the metal free from Sparky's leg, causing the hullbuster to let loose a guttural howl he had tried desperately to keep to himself. With a palm pressing Sparky's chest back against the wall he rested against, the Legion medic shook a bottle and sprayed a thick, viscous foam into the wound. Just at the point where Sparky was about to pass out, Kilgore slapped him to countermand the instinct.

"No you don't! I need you up and ready to KTF. That's a Legion expression, just in case you've never heard it. It means kill everything in front of you the second you even think they're going to pull the trigger at you. Go nuclear on 'em!" the doc said in as animated a fashion as he could inside the armor.

Panting from the pain of having a hunk of metal shucked from his thigh, Sparky asked, "How does all of that shorten to KTF?"

"It doesn't," Doc said. "I just wanted to see if you were still lucid enough to pick up on it."

"Yeah, I'm lucid. Nine hells, Doc. I thought you said the nerves were numbed."

"It's relative," offered Haitch. "Numb enough not to notice a big piece o' metal sticking in ya thigh. But pull it out..." He chuckled. "Not so much."

Doc Kilgore pointed to Sparky's wound. "That foam I just pushed into your leg is packed with a coagulant and other goodies to keep infection away. I'm putting on some skinpacks too, just to keep the meat inside the container. The blast might have brought you into some incidental contact with Hool blood, which would explain why you were out of it for so long."

"Nah, hullbusters just get sleep however they can," Sparky said, getting his bearings enough to get back to his feet after the impromptu surgery. His leg felt a little weird, on pins and needles from the nerve block. Luckily, after a few steps it felt functional, like he could work through any soreness that showed up later. "Thanks, Leej," he said. "So what do we got?"

The legionnaire called Dobie motioned the reconstituted marine forward. Sparky shook the man's hand and then heard the leej's report. "We have a Hool security element pushing against your platoon's held sector up ahead. Now that you're awake and we're close enough, we'll make contact and let them know we're coming in. You and your guys rated for opposing fire?"

Sparky shook out some lingering pain from his leg. "Volson and I are. I'll check on the rest of my guys."

Dobie held up a finger. "Wait a minute." The Legion sergeant attempted to reach the marine platoon. Ideally, he wanted to place Sparky and the newly gathered marines against a part of a kill box that would catch the Hool element in a vicious and quick crossfire. But the unit in question wasn't answering direct-angled bursts, meaning their comms were likely fried. That put a serious kink in the legionnaire's plans; walking his new teammates toward the working blasters of a marine platoon was a recipe for disaster.

"Not getting any of your buddies on comm." Dobie frowned. "New plan," he said. "We're going to cross the street into that alley. Use the buildings for cover and hit their flank. You up for that, Marine?"

A nod from Sparky was all Dobie needed. As the Marine NCO left to gather up his men, Dobie tried to raise any other friendlies he could. He hated the idea of moving through a battle zone without the good guys knowing he was coming.

"Any station this net, this is LS-416, call sign Dobie. Over."

"LS-416, this is Swamp Rat Actual. I have multiple marine elements working the city against heavy Hool resistance. We have new drop pods landing with additional Gomarii taking the fight to us. Any help would be good, Leej."

Apparently Dobie had connected with a marine ground commander.

"Copy, Swamp Rat. I have Swamp Rat Gold One with me and am moving at nineteen degrees magnetic to Gold Platoon. I will cut in and form an L-shaped ambush with members of your squad. Can you put me in touch with that element? They are not responding to targeted comm bursts."

"In-person communication only with that element, LS-416. Stand by for Gold Seven."

While Dobie was linking up with the ground commander, Sparky caught up with his men. "Good to see you guys made it," he said, slapping backs. "The last thing I saw was D'ghar flying through the air and catching you, Vol."

Corporal Volson's plate carrier had seen better days. But at least his flesh wasn't wrapped in skinpacks like the sergeant's. His face was equal parts grimy and grim beneath his helmet. "Yeah. We made it. Rest of the squad is KIA, though. They were outside the warehouse when the orbital strike hit us. This sucks, Sar'nt."

Sparky didn't have time to respond before Dobie snapped to get the marine's attention. "Made contact with your ground commander. He says the element we need to let us pass through can't be reached by comm. Now I didn't get this far just to be dusted by friendlies, so we're gonna go into that building there. Top floor." The leej pointed at the apartment building he intended to enter. The bottom two stories had been largely blown out by what looked like a bomb blast, but the third story was intact. "We clear it, then ambush the kelhorns on the adjacent street who are giving those marines trouble. If they can't figure out we're on their side after that, I'll shoot 'em myself. You follow?"

The marine said he did, and soon the ad hoc squad of legionnaires and hullbusters was pushing their way into the street. Active, adaptive camouflage on the Legion armor went from blotchy browns common to the warehouse district to the grays and blues common in the streets. During security halts to let their Repub Marine Corps counterparts catch up, the three leejes were practically invisible.

The ad hoc strike team slithered through the alleys, shooing the Sinasian populace back into buildings wherever they found them outside. Accessing the L-comm in his bucket, the lead legionnaire put his speakers on broadcast so Sergeant Sparky could hear the call from beside him.

Dobie pointed to a third-floor window in the building ahead of them. The lower two levels looked like they had once contained a storefront and perhaps a single-residence apartment. "We need to get to the top floor and take whatever window is facing the opposite street as a high point before we take on the Hools and get you back to your platoon."

They moved to the back of the target building and stacked up on either side, leaving two men to secure their flanks. Thankfully the external stairs, running up the outside of the building, were still intact, providing a clear route to the single door that led into the top-floor apartment.

"Get a peeper up," Dobie ordered, but Dugmagharrerra, the Hool lance corporal assigned to Sparky, moved to the base of the stairs instead. The alien marine stripped off his gloves in favor of ones with the fingertips removed so he could use his claws when necessary.

The legionnaire watched patiently as D'ghar cupped the face mask on his helmet and removed it to expose his mouth and nose. He breathed in the air in several swift sniffs. "Four Hools and a Gomarii," he said after a moment. "Eight humans."

"Can ya sniff out what they 'ad for lunch too there, mate?" Haitch whispered.

"Snap-fish wraps," the Hool marine said, clipping his mask back in place.

Behind him, Haitch produced a small metal rod, similar in size and shape to a light pen for their datapads. A quick snap at the center caused the micronized machine to reorient itself into a metallic version of a Spilursan stick bug. He set it down on the ground, and the metallic insect scurried up the stairs of the ruined building, eventually crawling right past the target door and along the wall to the edge of a busted-out window. Within moments, Dobie's battle board showed an image of the apartment as seen by the tiny spy.

"Lance Corporal Dugmagharrerra," Dobie said, "you were almost spot on. Four Hools, a Gomarii, and *six* humans. No evidence of fish wraps, but I'll be sure to ask. The humans are all huddled against this wall. If we breach, they should be out of the line of our fire."

"Why keep the 'umans alive?" Haitch asked no one in particular.

Sparky took a crack at the rhetorical question. "Insurance maybe? A bargaining chip if things go pear-shaped."

"Or for dinner," D'ghar said grimly. "Fresh meat is my species' preference. These that serve without honor make no distinction about where it comes from."

Dobie gave a quick shake of his head, getting the team back on track. "Whatever the reason, they're there and we need to work around that reality. Time to pay a visit. What say you, hullbusters? You want part of this breach?"

"We want all of it," Sparky said.

"Yes," D'ghar agreed.

The marines and legionnaires climbed the exposed stairs and settled into position outside the third-floor door, with Volson and Sparky taking first and second in the stack. Sparky checked the charge pack on his pistol when Dobie handed him the rifle he'd thought he'd lost in the blast. Armed with significantly more firepower, the marine sergeant checked the line of fighters ready to kick it in and get it on.

Standing on the opposite side of the entrance so as not to be in anyone's way, D'ghar backhanded the door off its hinges with one arm and spun in a tight arc to throw a banger into the room with the other. The explosive concussion and ear-smashing wail of the stun grenade rocked the space before the weapon even struck the floor.

Volson was first in, his sights trained on the Gomarii with his N-6 Delta rifle leading the way. The corporal vented the alien with a single shot through the back of its thick blue neck, blowing inky dark blood and mouth tendrils across the room as the bolt exited its face.

Sparky flowed in second, dropping one of the Hools by virtue of a double-tap to the creature's side and neck, since it was bent over trying to shrug off the effects of the grenade anyway. The marine NCO flowed into the room, freeing the entrance for the leejes to come in behind him.

It is a long-established maxim in the Republic that marines are artists with their rifles, able to drop shots on target despite any number of conditions demanding it be impossible. Yet as good as Sparky's crew was, they weren't legionnaires. Haitch and Dobie swept into the room, working a single bolt each into two of the remaining Hools. They then shifted the barrels on their N-4X rifles, sharing the final kill with one shot in the chest and one to the head between them.

One of the Hools—the one shot by Volson—had refused to die like the rest of its team. In the quiet moment after the raid, the alien swept its hand to a pistol at its side, bringing the weapon around to vent blaster bolts into the marines still entering the door. It never got a chance to fire. Like an audacious athlete depicted in the holos of the Pan-Galactic Wrestling Alliance, Haitch jumped nearly horizontal to the floor and drove his entire body weight through his elbow and into the Hool's face. When the alien's head bounced off the floor in shock and pain, the leej used his free hand to thread a knife under its chin and straight through its brain.

"Oh lads, let me tell you. I 'ave been waiting longer than you can measure to cross that one off the bucket list," Haitch said. He withdrew the blade to thumb its switch, allowing the vibro weapon a little wiggle to flick off bits of very poisonous Hool blood before returning it to its scabbard.

"Way to go, slick," Dobie said. "I want you to escort the horrified people clinging to the wall to somewhere in this building that isn't going to be in the line of fire."

"Straight away, Sar'nt," Haitch said happily, before addressing the deafened, vertigo-stricken people on the floor.

Dobie, free of his troublesome junior leej, stared down at an unfamiliar device resting on the floor. "Sar'nt Cathey, what do you make of this?"

The device looked a bit like an old Sinasian power generator. Made of a solid black duraplast, its power indicator appeared as a glowing ring within a ring, lit with an azure corona. But it didn't rattle or hum like the generators kept in the town shops. Instead, it was totally silent.

"Sparky. You can call me Sparky. And as for this thing... your guess is as good as mine."

He went to touch an antenna sticking out of the device, but D'ghar stopped him. "Not safe to do that."

"Because it's high-gain?" Dobie said. He pointed to his battle board to show the marines his findings. The device was putting out intense waves of energy in a pattern the legionnaire didn't like.

"No," D'ghar countered. "The box is from the gods so the different races may talk."

Dobie frowned. "I'm pretty good with tech, but uh... you're going to have to break that down to simple street for me, Lance Corporal."

"When the Hools hear the voice of the gods, we have no choice but to obey. Except for me," D'ghar said, almost remorseful. "I was hurt and cannot hear it anymore. But when we fought the moktaar, the blue gods brought these. They didn't have them when they spoke only to us, so it makes sense that it allowed them to control us all—Hools and moktaar—at once."

"Blue gods?" Sparky asked. "What, like the Gomarii?"

D'ghar nodded. "They serve the gods."

Doc Kilgore was across the room treating the injured human hostages. When he heard the explanation, he chimed in through his bucket. "So like a filter to work through different alien brain chemistry."

"Whatever it is, I'll see if I can turn it off," Dobie said as he knelt next to the device. "While I'm into that, we need you to run the leg of that ambush, Sparky."

"I'm all about it," the sergeant replied. The presence of this "voice of the gods" device—and the Hools apparently left here to guard it—might prove important, but the main thing was still the main thing. They needed to hit the Hools in the adjacent street and in so doing, notify the silent marine element that they had friendlies in the area.

Sparky turned to his marines, more confident in directing them than he was giving legionnaires orders.

"Tripp. You and Patterson get on the roof. D'ghar, work with Haitch and get these people outta here. Once that's good, set up with him on opposite corners and work to talk the guns. Volson and I will hold the center ground. The Hools are runnin' reinforcements through this zone to throw them at our boys. Time to make 'em pay a toll for passage."

The team responded and set themselves in position, and Sparky set himself against the makeshift barriers they hastily set up in anticipation of return fire from any hostiles who had access to the building opposite and might shoot back at them on even footing. "Dobie. We're good to go hot. You shootin' or techin'?"

"Shooting," the legionnaire answered as he slid up beside the marine. "Just spoke to my higher. Other leejes through the city tried knocking out these transmitter devices and got a load of high-ex for their efforts. Said it's best not to mess with it."

"Good to know," Sparky said. "Hey Tripp!"

The marine designated marksman answered from his hide on the roof. "Hey what?"

"You good, dude?"

"Ready, Sar'nt." The marksman sounded eager to begin whatever amount of violence he was planning to unleash.

The windows on this side of the building overlooked a street crowded with rubble from the building opposite, whose entire near-side wall had collapsed into a pile of bricks and duracrete chunks from earlier fighting. As a result, Sparky could see right into the adjacent building, with a perfect line of sight to the backs of several teams of Hools firing on the embedded marines. More Hools were fighting street level, using the cover of the building to move freely, albeit slowly because of the wreckage, from position to position, reinforcing the Hools above and hardening flanks to repulse any attempts by the out-of-contact marines to roll their way around an enemy who had them pinned down.

"Sending a call out to the Hools in the building opposite. Let it off the chain when they get the message," Sparky said. He was glad to have his rifle again. He threaded three grenades into the breach of the underslung launcher, racked the forearm to load the first round, then topped off the weapon and guessed the distance, just in case the Hools or their Gomarii handlers could see a spotting beam.

The first grenade sailed into the open wall, where the clustered Hools were oblivious to the new threat about to hit their flank. Violent, force-radiating frag and high-energy explosive expanded from the point of impact, shattering alien bodies and dropping over a dozen of the fighters in a single shot. High-speed bolts lanced out from D'ghar's SAB as he took turns with Haitch, who fired from the opposite perch. The suppressive on the building earned some outgoing gunfire from the Gomarii command element higher in the building, but a sternly worded "No thank you" in the form of a high-gain blaster bolt from Tripp's N-14 tore through the commander's skull, splattering the rest of his slaver team.

The first salvo was unexpected, but now the enemy ducked, disappearing from line of sight.

"Got a Hool support element stalking through the next building, east of the one you just ruined, Sar'nt," Corporal Tripp shouted.

"On it," Sparky said. Emptying the tubular magazine on his grenade launcher, he sent two rounds barking from the barrel in an arching flight toward the incoming force. Walls blew out, structures shattered, and the front part of the Hool support force died under Sparky's ad hoc artillery. The remainder of the Hools tried to retreat back the way they came, and Volson and Dobie used directed fire along the escape route to punish them for trying to help their buddies, killing half a dozen of the aliens in the time it took to say, "Poor life choices."

"Not gonna lie, that's some right proper you boys are doing! Demons on deck, Marines!" Haitch shouted.

"Gold One, this is Gold Seven," squelched Gunny through the radio.

"Send it, Seven," Sparky barked.

"Gun battery walking up to hold corner on the buildings you boys just knocked out of code. Support by fire until set. How copy? Over."

"Roger, Gold Seven. I copy, cover support elements until placed. Gold One out."

Sparky rolled to his side to address the team. "We got heavies rolling up. Keep the echoes off their backs until they're in place."

"Copy!"

A plodding gun battery, an N-50 mounted turret on a set of robotic crab legs, walked into the battlespace, taking the occasional ping off its armor from the enemy force embedded in various buildings along the avenue. Sparky's team concentrated on finding rifle reports and sending back blaster bolts in an overwhelming force of fire meant to make some unseen enemy catch a bolt through the chest.

"Almost in place. Keep it up!" Sparky yelled.

A blur of movement suddenly appeared between the buildings, almost instantly changing course when it encountered the outgoing marine blaster fire, and another flashed overhead. Both were bots on whining repulsors, whirling along their paths. One flew sideways on a flanking run of the marine position before sharply jolting upwards while chittering in Numerica, the language common to bots of that type. Twin ports opened on its sides.

"Tripp!" Sparky shouted.

"I see it!" he roared back.

Tripp fired a blaster bolt into the front of the drone, but the bolt hit an invisible shield just millimeters from the machine and burst harmlessly into sparks. In response, the drone sent an attack that was far more successful. A port at its center shot forth a shimmering metallic spike that flew straight at the two marines on the roof. It detonated in green-tinged fire, and its concussive force sent one entire edge of the roof sliding down into the street in a slow avalanche of duracrete.

"Haitch!" Dobie shouted.

The Legion SAB gunner vented destructive fire from the machine blaster, pelting the drone with a flurry of bolts, but these too sparked apart as they struck the shield. D'ghar took a break from suppressing pockets of Hools across the street to add his own fire to the assault on the hovering little drone, and finally the shield failed, sending the drone sputtering. The next bolt to strike the machine blew it apart in a wave of arced plasma and scrap.

"Tripp!" Sparky yelled in the wake of the machine dying.

"Still alive. But I need a medic for Patterson!" the sniper yelled back.

"What in 'ell was that thing, Dobie? Damn thing nearly blew my bucket off with a single boom dart," said Haitch.

"Sending to higher now. Also sending to the marines," the Legion NCO said. "Doc."

The medic threw his aid bag up onto his shoulder, racing by them to get to the roof. "On it, Dobes."

14

The ad hoc force of surviving legionnaires and Repub marines repositioned themselves inside the building they'd taken as a fighting position, seeking better points of view for a dramatic new turn of events. Just down the broken avenue, a pair of unidentified troopers in non-standard uniforms were darting back and forth through the wreckage, pursued by what looked like an entire platoon of zhee fighters. The pair of troopers—one male, one female—were both human, but they moved like wobanki as they leapt and swung and climbed from building to building and floor to floor, taking advantage of a Sinasian city where structures were close and there was always something—an ornamental dragon at the eave of a roof, crisscrossing fire escapes, heavy lines for drying clothes—sticking out to assist in their parkour. The zhee, by contrast, lacked the agility of their prey. Clumsy anatomy and a lack of interest in anything resembling an obstacle course limited their pursuit routes to only whatever could be reached by staircase or speedlift. They were resigned to following on the streets, sending raging weapons fire up into the buildings in the hopes of either hitting their targets as they fled or flushing them out and back to ground.

"I think that pretty much confirms they're not with the bad guys!" Sparky shouted.

"See if you can get their attention!" Dobie called back on his way out the door. "I got an idea for taking out those zhee."

Tripp ran into the apartment, locking eyes with Sparky. "Put me to work, Sar'nt."

"The kid?" Sparky asked.

Tripp was unblinking in his answer. "Patterson didn't make it."

Sparky wanted to know more, but the galaxy demanded they put their attention elsewhere. There were zhee filling the space they'd just cleared of Hools, and they still hadn't linked up with the Repub marines they'd just relieved of contact. "Here's the situation. We got two unknowns running from a platoon of zhee. That puts them on our side by default. You think you can give them some breathing room?"

"My pleasure," the marksman said, then flipped the table they'd used for cover against the Hools and dragged the piece of furniture closer to the window. He hopped on top with one leg bent as a shooting rest for his lead arm, which he weaved into his sling until the synthetic fiber creaked from the strain. Then he brought the weapon into his shoulder so the scope would be in line with eyes scanning his assigned sector for something to kill. "Head-man type on the line."

"Vape it," Sparky said.

The weapon barked, venting an energy-wrapped dense particle across the space. The bolt struck the lead donk in the neck in the middle of shouting orders, sending the violent warriors into a frantic scramble for cover.

"I got your two unknowns in the building with the glowing piggy on it. Moving to the third floor," Tripp said. He slightly adjusted his position, staring through the scope as if the only part of the galaxy that mattered was the small section visible through the lens.

Doc Kilgore came into the apartment carrying Patterson's SAB. "Where's Dobes?"

Volson answered. "Down there in that alley. Two o'clock. He's carrying that repeater thing we found in here."

They all watched as the legionnaire worked the device into a window, then crawled after it once the ungainly piece of kit was through.

"What is that maniac of a leej doing?" Volson asked.

"Oh, you know, mate, we're all maniacs," Haitch replied over comm. "I think our boy over there fancies a go on that machine like it was stone for a toss."

Tripp was able to piece together Dobie's plan, though not because of Haitch's explanation. "Remember when he said turning that device off activates some sort of bomb?"

A synchronized "oh" would not have been out of place at that moment as the crew reasoned what was going to happen next. Watching the leej ascend through the building, the team held their breath.

"Word from Dobie," Doc Kilgore announced to the room. "Donks are attempting to break from cover."

"That's our cue!" Sparky shouted. "Keep those donks in the barn!"

The twin SABs on the corners went kinetic. Thrumming blaster bolts in six- to nine-round bursts smashed against the donk platoon, sending them scrambling deeper into the cover they were just about to abandon. The zhee had rightly understood that one sniper couldn't shoot them all, but with the sudden onslaught from the rest, they were discovering another truth: it's impossible to dodge the rain. Especially when charge drums are at full capacity and locked into machine blasters that chew into a building at a rate of fifteen bolts per second.

A third machine blaster entered the fray as the Legion medic went full bore with Patterson's SAB. He blanketed the avenue behind the donks with suppressive fire to keep them from doubling back and escaping. One unlucky muzzle-faced fighter decided to try his luck, zigzagging away in a clopping sprint, only to be butchered by the deft medic.

As the team laid down wave after wave of bracketed fire, the Legion NCO came into view in the top-floor window of the building adjacent to the cowering zhee platoon, the device on his shoulder. He pushed the machine out of the window, sending it tumbling down right into the midst of the enemy fighters.

While Dobie raced back the way he came, a blood-crazed donk willing to brave the blaster fire popped up to fire a fragger toward the team's position. Though he died for his efforts, his aim was spot-on; the grenade landed right in the middle of the apartment where the team had staged. D'ghar slammed into Volson and Sparky, knocking them toward the side of the room only a moment before the grenade exploded.

The device in the street followed suit, in a decidedly larger explosion. The arc-fire eruption cast a volcanic stream of energy into the air, blowing out windows and sending burning donks flying. A secondary shock wave flashed through the neighborhood, catching the adjacent facades on fire. Moments later, the building Dobie had dropped the bomb from crumbled, sending up a roiling cloud of ember-flaked ash. The hullbusters reached for their respirators.

D'ghar rolled over. Dust and scorch marks painted the back side of his armor. "I want to stab the corpse of whatever donk threw that grenade at my brothers. A lot."

The Legion medic started crawling toward the downed marine, but Sparky held out a hand to stop him. "Not a good idea, Doc. Hool blood is toxic to humans. We got rules for dealing with his injuries."

"Not my first alien repair job, hullbuster," Kilgore shot back. "How's about you do your job and let me do mine."

"Speaking o' which," Haitch said, "Dobes got clear of the building collapse. He's movin' back here at a good clip. Faster than 'e ought."

Sparky was about to ask how Haitch knew this, but then remembered that legionnaires can monitor one another's positions and vital signs through their armor and helmets. He looked over the lip of the wall they'd been shooting from, then motioned for Volson to follow him. The two NCOs threaded their way to the ground floor.

They were almost down the stairs when they spotted a thick, misshapen shadow moving toward the door from outside. Sparky pointed his rifle over the staircase railing, owning the target zone below so that anything stepping inside would be dead to rights.

But the only arrival was two dusty cloaked figures carrying Sergeant Dobie, who wasn't moving. They set him on a rickety bench just inside the door.

The twin marines abandoned their shooting perch but not their posture on the run down toward the clearly unconscious leej.

"Republic marines!" Sparky called out. "Identify yourselves."

One of the two stepped forward, hands up. "My name is Major Andien Broxin. Used to be a hullbuster myself. I'm here on an urgent matter regarding the safety of the Republic, and I need your help, Marine."

15

The story Andien Broxin and her companion, Praxus, told the legionnaires might have been harder to believe had they themselves not experienced a Gomarii-led invasion of Hools, moktaar, and other species taking place throughout the Sinasian sectors.

Contrary to popular opinion, the Savage Wars weren't the end-all fight of humanity against its post-human tormentors seeking to wipe away the old with the new. According to Broxin, the centuries-long Savage Wars were merely a battle—a proxy battle waged by a powerful and hidden Savage general leveraging lesser Savage vassals he had under his complete control. The Savages had lost the initial battle, but the time had come for this mysterious Savage general to put into motion long-awaited plans to nevertheless win the war.

"With something considerably worse for the galaxy waiting in the wings after that," Praxus mysteriously added.

Dobie shook his head and held his fingers to his temples like he'd developed a headache. "Let's get back to basics. You say you knew Sinasia would be a target. How?"

"One of many targets," Broxin explained. "But a big one. In part because of what Sinasia represents. They were the only Republic nation to flip and side with the Savage Alliance. But this game is galaxy-spanning. We've done what we can to help the galaxy prepare for it."

"Except going to the Republic directly," Haitch put in.

"Great idea, Leej." The sarcasm was thick in Broxin's voice. "I'm just a former Nether Ops agent who was left for dead when the House of Reason tried to activate a doomsday fleet meant to destroy the Legion before it could Article Nineteen them out of power. I'm sure they'd have been happy to see me without an appointment, and none of those Nether scumsacks who took control of the outfit would do anything to stop what we're doing."

Haitch had been playing with his combat knife. He stopped now, balancing the tip of the blade on his finger. "Touchy."

"We have means of making this fight much more favorable to our mutual interests," Praxus offered.

"What means?" asked Dobie.

"Force equalizers," Broxin said, cutting in brusquely before Praxus could give details. "If that's too vague, then that's too bad. Understand that proving loyalty here isn't as one-sided as you probably think it is. Not everyone who puts on the armor is a leej."

"What are you implying?" said Doc Kilgore.

"That I'm going to stay tight-lipped over our capabilities until I'm absolutely certain that you're Legion and not Nether." Broxin held out her arms in a take-it-or-leave-it gesture. "No hard feelings."

"No hard feelings," Dobie said. He understood the sentiment; in fact he felt the same way about these two. Yes, they were fighting on the good-guy side of the ball so far. But spend enough time in the galactic mire and you realized that only went as far as the battle. Loyalties and objectives were never as solid as people liked to make them out to be.

Sparky bristled his mustache, crossed his arms, and made an attempt to move beyond the impasse he felt the two sides were at. "Our objective is to link up with the main element. I can only speak for my hullbusters, but you can only count on our help if Gunny doesn't want it elsewhere."

"Then let's go talk to your Gunny," Broxin said.

Gunnery Sergeant Viera snorted upon hearing Sergeant Cathey's report. The ad hoc unit of leej and hullbuster had linked up with the main element, the patrol having run into no further difficulties in reaching them.

"So lemme get this straight. You're saying the next wave of stupid about to pierce my precious atmosphere are Savages, and this whole thing we've been fighting is some sort of plan to take over the universe?"

"Basically, yeah," Sparky answered. "Only this Broxin woman's got an android buddy who looks way too real to be fake, if you get me. And the way they fought... I believe her when she says she was a hullbuster."

Gunny looked to Dobie. "What's your take on this?"

Dobie poured half of a water unit onto his head and brushed it through his hair to wash away the grime and sweat. He had a scar on the bottom of his chin where a skinpack had been torn away prematurely and never re-applied. The skin, left to its natural healing abilities, was still in the slow process of making itself whole. Even more noticeable was a great scar that traversed his face from temple to jaw. Sparky wanted to ask about it, but now wasn't the time. Who let their face stay scarred in today's day and age?

"If the woman and the android were part of this invasion," Dobie said, "they wouldn't need us. They may not be active Repub military, but they're still two more guns than I had before. What really interests me is their claim to have additional assets already on-planet capable of swinging the odds in our favor. If any part of that is true, I think my leejes will be best used getting after it, Gunnery Sergeant. If Sergeant Sparky and his team can stay along for the ride, all the better. They're good men. Do the Corps proud."

Gunny pointed to his junior NCO. "Listen, Sergeant Cathey, I got five minutes left in this uniform until I retire. I would really like it to happen while there's still a galaxy to retire to and without getting a butt-chewing because this comes back around. You feel me?"

"Like a handshake, Gunny," Sparky replied.

"I can pretend I didn't see you hullbusters walk through here," Gunny said. "But I can't spare anyone else."

"You won't have to," Dobie said, rising and putting on his bucket. His digital sandpaper voice grated from the loudspeakers, giving him an authority he didn't have with a naked face. "Per Legion protocols pursuant to the protection of the Galactic Republic and the safety of its citizens, I'm taking operational control of Sergeant Cathey and his squad. Haitch is uploading freqs to your RTOs now. That'll keep you from having to pretend not to notice his arrival. We'll coordinate on the move."

Gunny shook the man's hand. "Make 'em pay, Leej."

Dobie returned the grip. "Always do."

Dobes and Sparky returned to the blown-out building entrance where Broxin and her companion waited. Sparky moved directly to D'ghar, who was seated on a bench.

"You were supposed to be watching them," Sparky said.

D'ghar looked up at his NCO. "That one is fixing my holes. That one is where I can see her. They are watched."

"Hard to argue with that logic," Sparky said. "You good to move?"

"I move good," D'ghar said, recovering his helmet and mask. He stood and nodded his thanks to Praxus, who had been tending to his armor. The breaches had been sealed, hopefully with any injuries underneath treated the same.

"So," said Broxin. "Do I have a green light, or does this get complicated?"

"Green light," Sparky confirmed.

She turned to Dobes. "And you, Leej?"

Dobes nodded. "The Legion has your back. But it's best we hit the throttle. Those Gomarii haven't slowed in dropping reinforcements. Hools, zhee, and a ton of mok-taar. It's about to be crowded and we need to be any-where else."

"The fights we're heading into aren't going to be any easier," Broxin said. "Follow me."

She slung her assault pack back onto her shoulder and took off at a run.

The legionnaires dropped into a comfortable run next to her, keeping pace as she weaved through a series of alleys before spilling onto the main streets.

"If we're feeling good about working together, Major," Dobie said as they jogged, "I wouldn't mind hearing exactly what it is you've got up your sleeve to make this fight go to the Republic's favor."

Broxin gave a perfunctory nod. "Sinasia contains a military-grade asset that can repel large forces like this. They've had it, in secret, on this planet and in this city, for a long time—part of a prophecy relating to the rebirth of 'the Dragon.' It was before our time, but you might remember the last major engagement on Sinasia prior to Article Nineteen."

"'Oly sket," Haitch said. "You're talkin' 'bout Sam-oor-rye mechs, ain'tcha?"

"Yes." Broxin said, not breaking stride. "Solar power along its launch point—all hidden—has been enough to keep its engines from losing charge while it was in storage. But to start it in the state it's currently in, we need a more aggressive power source. So that's where we're headed."

She disappeared down another alley and hopped into a spillway that wound along the length of an apartment complex.

Doc Kilgore asked, "How in the hell did the Sinasians hide *another* Samurai mech under the House of Reason's nose after the last time?"

Praxus gave a cautious explanation. "While the known mechs were destroyed, the mech in question was not harmed due to its particular hiding spot. Unfortunately, all major power stations were destroyed by Gomarii orbital strikes during the initial invasion, leaving its silo without power necessary to launch."

"And where is this hiding spot?" Dobie asked.

"I decline to answer that question for the moment. Success on Sinasia depends on the success of our mission."

Broxin called over her shoulder, "Need to know, Leej."

"You do not yet need to know such information," Praxus added, unnecessarily. "Though I mean you no disrespect by saying so."

The android stopped at a huge panel of twisted, fallen grating that blocked their way. One of the roof-to-roof catwalks that occasionally connected separate buildings had collapsed into the alley below. He grabbed the heavy metal obstacle, lifted it overhead, then effortlessly held the thing up with one hand as he waved the team forward with the other.

"You some kind of a top-secret Repub construct?" Sparky asked, wonder in his voice.

"I am not," Praxus answered. "I am Cybar."

Sparky stood stunned for a moment. "You don't look Cybar. I *fought* the Cybar."

"Our external appearance can vary. This is how I choose to look."

"Well... not to be... rude here or nothin'," Sparky said as the team resumed its jog. "But the last time we saw your kind was in service to Goth Sullus. And the time before... you were tryin' to wipe everyone with a body off the map."

"I dissented from that decision. The rest of my kind paid for it. Now we seek to live in tandem with the galaxy, as we ought to have done from the very beginning. But perhaps we can discuss this further at a more opportune time."

They came to a stop just shy of the spiritual center of the city—a place of ancient wood-and-stone temples, reflecting pools, and expertly cultivated gardens. But here on the edge of it they still stood among crowded high-rises, as if the more recent, more technologically minded builders had refused to cede an inch more than was necessary to the relics of their past.

"We 'eddin' into them tran-kwil gardens?" Haitch asked.

"No," Broxin said. "We stay in the gutters."

She led the team through a twisting maze of alleyways that led out into an old industrial area that carried the scent of iron and rot. It seemed a place for ghosts, like their visit was the first by the living in decades.

Broxin wordlessly turned a blind corner into a passage cut into a building only wide enough for the team to walk single-file.

"I don't like this," Sparky commented.

"Maybe that's the idea," Tripp mumbled back.

The team trudged through the passage until they reached a dead-end metal door with no means of opening from the outside, save a breacher's kit. A stylistic symbol worked from the Sinasian character for thunder marked its center. Andien rammed her fist several times on the plate, the metallic clank of her raps making clear that whatever she had been in the Republic marines, she was a cyborg now.

Dobes looked around. "What is this place?"

"This will get us to an abandoned power plant," Broxin replied. "We're going to fire it up and run all its power to the launch."

"I thought you said the power plants were all destroyed by the Gomarii."

"Only the major ones. This one has not been in use for some time."

"And you're going to restart it just like that?" Kilgore asked, skeptical.

"Yeah," said Haitch. "Last time I checked the duty boards, you needed to be an engineer to 'ave that job."

"We have local assets in position to help," Praxus offered.

A few hard clacks sounded on the other side of the door, then it swung outward just a few inches and a bald Sinasian man stuck his head through. "Broxin-san. I am glad that you are safe. This way."

The team threaded through the doorway and waited on the inside while their guide re-secured the door. Hard piston locks slammed into their homes in the floor and walls, giving way to the electric hum of magnetic locking systems securing them in place. Their guide then led them down a set of well-worn stone stairs, D'ghar having to duck the entire way or risk scraping his helmet along the ceiling.

Sparky used his non-Legion comm to ping the doc, who was last in the stack. "I can tell when you guys are talking to each other. What's up?"

"Someone wanted this place to look like just another abandoned factory. But that door leading in, and the massive amounts of tech built into the stairs and walls, suggests this place is anything but what it appears to be," the medic answered.

"You guys can see into the walls?"

Before Doc Kilgore could reply, the team stepped through another door into a well-lit warehouse, with racks of supplies separating the space into neat rows. Another Sinasian man stepped away from a control console to meet them as they emerged. His meticulously manicured business suit and hair made him look to be a major executive in whatever this place was.

"Ah, Broxin-san. We were worried you weren't going to make it," the businessman said.

"We ran into some trouble. Gomarii tagged us with a tracker. Took us a minute to figure it, and by then we had a whole platoon of zhee after us and they had our scent. We lost them though. Our friends in the Legion armor blew them back to their four gods."

The man studied the soldiers before him closely, as if appraising each trooper's bearing, balance, and condition. He circled them until getting to the Hool marine, where he stopped.

"You have suffered much and yet you remain in the fight?"

"I stand where my brothers are," D'ghar said.

The businessman affected a slight bow. "I will be honored to fight beside demons such as yourself."

"And who are you, mate?" Haitch asked.

"I am Hideyoshi Arai. I am here to help you. But we must move quickly. I have received reports of a new type of capital ship entering orbit around the planet. It matches the suspected design of the Savages provided by Praxus-san."

The man reached for a cabled control module hanging from a rack, pressed a button, and set machinery in motion. A crate marked *ARAI INTERNATIONAL — DO NOT TOUCH* was lowered slowly to the ground from a conveyor tier high above. A mere thumbprint from the businessman was sufficient to pop the securing lugs and drop the lid of the two-meter-tall container to the floor with a satisfying slap. Finally, he addressed the team once more.

"A combat sled waits just on the other side of the racks, loaded and ready. Take it and go. I'll join you as soon as I'm dressed." He gave a slight bow to show his respect, then stepped into the crate.

Sparky leaned toward Dobie and tilted his head toward the crate. "Box must be some kinda mobile dressing room," he muttered.

The legionnaire gave a fractional nod as Broxin whistled for the team to follow her.

True to Arai's word, an ultra-modern combat sled like those used by Spilursan planetary defense awaited at the side of the warehouse.

"Volson," Sparky said, calling the man's name as if it were an order given.

Volson didn't need to be asked twice. He climbed eagerly into the seat. "Oh, baby. It ain't every day you get the keys to one of these. Remote-operated cannons, sector defense systems. I bet it even comes with seat warmers."

The legionnaires slipped into the back, and Haitch took the remote control for the main gun.

Dobie tapped Broxin on the shoulder. "What's with the guy back there?"

"He's *Sohei*," Broxin said, and then elaborated when the legionnaire gave no nod of recognition. "Think of it like a religious order of knighthood. For generations, his people have been sworn to protect a weapon they call *Sada no Yume*—Dreams of Thunder. Our Samurai mech. We're moving now to get it into the fight."

"If this mech is some sacred Sinasian weapon, why are they lettin' *you* mess with it?" Haitch asked.

"Because they believe I birthed the Dragon's spirit into *Sada no Yume*, and now it's time to let it off the chain."

The sled's ramp closed, and Volson hit the throttle like it owed him credits. The engines roared and catapulted the vehicle forward.

"Where to?" he asked.

"Through that opening dead ahead," Broxin replied.

The opening led into a large subterranean tunnel, clearly intended for vehicle traffic. Volson would have asked for further directions, but there was only one way to go. Eventually they arrived at a sudden incline and followed the ramp up toward an overhead door that opened onto street level.

They emerged into a shipping yard meant to accept cargo from incoming freighters and send it out on high-speed repulsor trains. The vast yard was connected to a myriad of service roads that let out into the main city or continued on to the short highways that connected the hub to the planet's many floating island cities. But at this particular moment, the cargo being loaded up was not the usual commercial fare. A pack of zhee, clad in military fatigues and wearing custom, oversized plate carriers, were herding unarmed humans into freight cars and repulsor trucks.

The zhee barely had time to bray a warning about the combat sled appearing in their midst before Volson hit the retro thrusters, put the troop carrier into a slide, and sent its armored flank into a group of three enemy fighters, sending them rag-dolling. Sparky reacted just as quickly, working the sled's twin N-50s. Two synchronized bursts savaged the black-clad donks, punching scorched holes in some while completely bisecting others. Even the stray bolts that smacked duracrete were effective, stinging surprised zhee with showers of superheated rock. The donks dove for cover, seeking any respite from this sudden invader into their space.

"Course overlay set. Turn and burn!" Volson shouted. He swung the sled's nose and raced away from the zhee soldiers recovering from the surprise attack.

"Sket! They're starting to dust the prisoners," Tripp said, watching the graphic scene unfold behind them.

"It is an unfortunate loss of life, but there will be much more of this if we do not continue to our objective," Praxus said calmly.

Everyone chewed back the bile they felt over the android's reality check. Praxus was right, but no one was happy about it. When it came to "infidels," the zhee followed a pattern recognized by anyone who had tangled with them: First, profit off them if you can. In this case, the humans were likely being herded in some agreement with the Gomarii. Second, if you can't profit from them, destroy them as a sacrificial offering to the Four Bloody Gods. The killing might stop once the surprise threat of the combat sled was gone, but then again, it might not.

"Gonna call in the prisoners' loc to higher," Dobie said.

"There is no need," said Praxus. "I have alerted Sinasian allies on the ground. They will do what we do not have time to do."

The sled raced onward.

"Off this road and onto that one moving east to west," Broxin ordered, pointing out where she wanted the driver to go. "Out the gate."

Volson turned as instructed, dodging parked trucks and stacks of empty containers. The road curled between a pair of massive lift cranes and led directly to a walled-in secured cargo area. The only point of access was a stubborn-looking impervisteel checkpoint.

He shouted into the back through the intercom. "Gate's closed! Don't think I can push through it!"

"Keep it rolling, mate. I 'ave the key!" Haitch shouted back. He sifted through the controller's combat matrix and found the right tool for the job: an anti-materiel rocket. He sent it to impact the security barrier, and the weapon flashed in an explosion of white-hot fire and inky smoke that sent the gate tumbling into the road in a twisted mess of burning spines.

The sled raced into the secure cargo yard and found the gate on the other side to be open. That let them out onto a perimeter road and then onto a main road that led toward an older part of the city, still running on the edge of the sacred temple garden.

"Hold this course," Broxin said. "You're one point two klicks to target."

"I'll try not to miss my exit," Volson said, holding the steering wheel tightly in his gloved hands.

"Expect further resistance ahead," Praxus advised.

"No sket," Haitch called back.

As if in response, the hollow tapping of fire ticked against the sled's armor, too low-powered to punch through. That was followed by frantic swerving as Volson evaded violence pouring into the street.

"Zhee infantry supported by 'ools carrying medium machine blasters," Haitch said. "Looks like a couple of platoons' worth just dumped out of a bunch of technicals up ahead."

The legionnaire flicked open a trigger on the console, and a moment later, a throaty whoosh vibrated against the hull as he launched a rocket from the weapon housing. The detonation outside bounced back against the sled, causing a momentary loss of control until Volson put it right again.

"Nice one," Volson called back into the troop compartment. "Got bits of bad guys raining everywhere. Didn't get 'em all though, Leej."

Broxin pointed ahead to another gate that sealed off an ancient-looking power plant from incoming traffic. "That's our drop point ahead. We proceed on foot to the plant. Keep the vic here to dissuade any other visitors from following us inside."

"I see it," Volson confirmed. To the rest he said, "Be on the lookout for enemies when we drop that ramp. Approaching drop point."

The marine corporal spun the back end of the sled and dropped the ramp just outside a gate several meters tall. Beyond the barrier was the power plant: towering prefab buildings covered in heavy-gauge cable rigging. While Haitch scanned their back trail for enemy stragglers looking to cause trouble, Praxus jumped from the ramp and released several synthetic tendrils that penetrated the gate's operations panel. He had barely touched the control surface when the gate slid open. "Security here is lax, considering," he observed.

"It's old," said Broxin. "Outperformed by the newer ultra-modern plants. This is a backup to the backup."

The team poured from the vehicle and into the grounds, and Volson backed the vehicle through the gate. Broxin gathered everyone around. "The main control center is underground. It has redundant defense features to protect us once we're inside, but what's coming is going to punch right through that. Praxus and I need a full twelve minutes to spin this place to full burn. So hold it as long as you can. And make sure 'as long as you can' is twelve minutes."

Broxin and her cybernetic ally disappeared into the facility with barely a flutter from the security system to slow them down.

"Yeah, I totally buy that she was a marine XO," Tripp said to Sparky.

The NCO gave a grunt of a laugh as he surveyed the situation. There was fighting around them, in the city and the temple several kilometers away, but for the moment it was all distant, leaving the fire team in a relatively quiet lull. He turned to his team and started pointing out various locations within their sight. "We'll use those high points along the facility for the long guns. Gun sled gets put in over there, and it can maneuver around the facility as needed. One of our SAB gunners stays right here to defend the gate; the other, we put outside the wire to fire from that hill, aimed at the approaching road. When they're all bunched up against the gate trying to get at us, we let the sleeper SAB rip 'em up from behind."

"I like it. Only one problem," Dobie said. "Both Haitch and your guy Big D are going to want to be the outside guy."

"Either they go where we tell them or we make them do a dance-off for it," Sparky said.

Dobie was drinking through his system rehydration straw right when Sparky made his remark, and he almost sprayed the inside of his bucket as he let out a laugh. "We better just let them both go. Haitch is the kind of guy who would attack that dance-off like it was his chosen profession, and that's not something I want to see."

16

Sparky pushed another round into the magazine for the underslung grenade launcher, preparing the weapon for his next toe-to-toe with the invaders. He leaned forward while seated behind a desk inside a monitoring station. It was as good a place as any to wait for the incoming assault now that fighting positions had been manned and the last of their demo charges had been quickly placed to keep any hostiles from getting too close.

"Sparky to Dobie."

The legionnaire was quick to answer the private channel. "Here, hullbuster. What's doing?"

"Just trying to get an edge on what's happening. The wait's killin' me."

From his hide on one of the facility's cooling towers, Dobie adjusted his point of aim. Targeting algos in his bucket did the work of rapidly solving the weaponized math for the adjustment, telling him he was on the X for a new enemy vehicle just cresting along the road.

"Might be somethin', Sparky. You could be in luck. Wait one."

The Legion NCO centered his rifle on the technical's driver. Three zhee sat abreast in the wide cab, letting the autopilot move them along the road. Dobie's bucket informed him that this particular version of repulsor truck had the driver's seat in the center of the console. Good to know. He centered his aim.

A single shot punched through a windscreen not rated for blaster fire. The bolt burned through the donk's chest, and he slumped forward onto the controls, sending the vehicle careening off the side of the improved road before barreling into a forest of slender trees as the other zhee in the cab groped to regain control.

"Yeah," Dobie announced to Sparky. "The wait looks to be over."

"Sparky, it's Tripp," the team sniper interrupted across the net. "Got a dozen more technicals making the road. They saw Dobie's shot and are working their advance on the cautious side. They're dismounting."

"Copy," Sparky said. "Keep that slaved combat sled you have ready to ruin the box. I'll need a spot as soon as I get outside. How copy?"

"Roger, out," Tripp answered.

Sparky exited the back of the structure with a more pronounced limp than he'd hoped for. Every time he took a moment off his feet, the leg stiffened fiercely. The marine reached a previously set up firing position outside, then pulled out his battle board and watched as red dots formed on a map overlay. Each dot represented a group of no less than five enemy troops approaching the facility using various routes. Returning the board to his armor, he dropped the combat monocle from his helmet over his eye, tied the indirect fire sight from his rifle into the display, and overlaid the targeting data until his potential shot was lined up with a dot.

"D'ghar, Haitch. Shots going out. Stay under cover. Sparky out."

Sparky pulled the trigger on the first round. Shooting the fragger from the underslung launcher in a high arc, he chased it with the remainder of the magazine tube just in case he'd judged the angle wrong. With four grenades in the air, he should have a wide enough spread of explosives to cover any mistake in the math.

The rounds sailed over the canopy, catching a fleet-footed platoon of donks racing through the trees. The first impact tore through the advancing front rank who had been moving in a wedge, halting their progress in a pressure wave of explosive flak. The next grenades fell almost on top of the first, finishing off any that hadn't been killed in the initial blast.

"Good hit, good hit," Tripp said into the comms. "Follow-on units are spreading out. We have advancing zhee with Hool support units carrying heavy weapons. Plotting the heavies to your board. Tripp out."

With a ping from Sparky, the rest of the fire team joined the fight. Volson, armed with Patterson's SAB, laid down an initial volley of suppressing fire against the flanking elements to halt their movement toward the security walls. From his spot on the roof, the assistant squad leader sent wave after wave of blaster bolts along the forest road. Several donks died in his sights before return fire in the form of heavy blaster bolts tore into Volson's rooftop cover.

"Sket!"

The heavy impacts sheared off entire sections of the roof wall, leaving the marine little to hide behind in the fusillade of blaster fire coming his way.

Two grenades popped from Sparky's launcher, flying over Volson's building and into the Hool machine gunner beyond the canopy. The explosions made short work of both the gunner and his gun, and the flak traveled over the terrain to teach the donks the difference between concealment and cover when a fire team of donks following the Hool got caught in the shrapnel tornado.

"Thanks, bro!" Volson called out. Rolling to his belly, he dropped from the roof and sprinted for the next building, which wasn't yet punched full of holes.

Sparky looked at the clock. They had to hold for six more minutes. They were halfway there, but it was the easy half.

A dust cloud in the distance obscured the sun as it rose. Dobie pushed his bucket's magnification to max, then sent the image to his marine counterpart's battle board.

"What am I looking at?" Sparky asked.

"Mechs. Looks like the planet-pounder types we use in the Legion, only different. Tripp, can you get a better read on these things with your scope?"

They'd placed Tripp on the catwalk surrounding the lower part of the station's cooling tower. Doc Kilgore worked his own rifle on the opposite pylon from about the same height. In the Legion, the medics often pulled double duty as long-range designated marksmen, which was an effective way to keep them and their highly specialized skill set away from being the first man in a stack outside a door.

"Roger, I'll see what I can do," Tripp replied.

Sparky risked a moment to look up at the sniper running the scope along the length of his N-14 rifle. And it was a good thing he did. He immediately spotted three distinct shapes in dark fatigues and armor working their way through the rigging on the tower.

"Moktaar!" he shouted.

From their positions around the facility, Volson and Dobie joined Sparky in raining blaster fire across the towers, sending the simian fighters falling dozens of meters to the dirt. They took out a host of them in seconds, but many of the agile climbers escaped, scrambling around to the back side of the towers where the front-facing marines couldn't target them.

"Tripp!" Sparky called over comm. "Switch that gun truck on! We need that thing purging the camp so we don't get smacked from behind!"

"Roger, Sar'nt." Tripp quickly activated the AI running the combat sled below them. The vehicle roared to life, pulling back into the compound to get a robust sight picture on the back of the cooling towers. Its roof-mounted N-50 flared to life, sending duracrete-shattering bolts into the climbing assault force. Moktaar died in droves as the weapon swept in arcs to clear the threat.

Sparky sprinted from position to make sure any simians who fell to the ground were good and dead. But as he came around the building, one of the simians came racing from the opposite direction, moving along its feet and knuckles in a full-out sprint. It slammed into him, knocking him into the dirt, screamed in his face, then clamped its fangs down on the NCO's shoulder. The strap of Sparky's plate carrier prevented those sharp teeth from piercing his neck, but the alien did manage to rip into the flesh on Sparky's upper back, threatening to punch through into the spine beneath.

Ignoring the pain that felt not at all dulled by the meds he was on for his leg, Sparky drew his knife and punched it repeatedly into the moktaar's ribs. Four hits turned to twelve, and then to twenty before the simian alien died under Sparky's counterassault.

That was when the front side of the tower detonated. A dust-soaked explosion rang across the compound as falling metal support struts clanged into each other. Sparky's stomach dropped at the knowledge that Tripp had likely been caught in that blast. He recovered his rifle and raced back to the front, where he found two Savage HK mechs rapidly advancing on the power station, firing on the move. This was the source of the explosion.

"Demo. Blow the demo!" Sparky gasped into the comms as he watched the clock tick down.

"About bloody time!" Haitch responded.

Both sides of the road erupted, the explosions aimed at each other in a tidal wave of destructive force and thrown earth. The twin mechs caught in the blast attempted to weather the storm, one by leaping off to the side of the road and the other by activating jump jets. The first escaped, but impervisteel ball bearings tore through the armored jet housing on the second machine's back just as it ignited for the jump. Its power pack ruptured in a failure cascade that swept through the vehicle into the munition mags and caused an earth-shattering explosion that not only took out that mech but also knocked its partner inactive—and set the nearby forest on fire for good measure.

But behind the mechs was one more enemy. It was only a heavily armored foot soldier, a Savage marine, and yet something about it made it seem even deadlier than the mechs that had just been destroyed. As it leapt over the fiery wreckage, it was the very picture of a warrior angel come to rain the flames of Oba down on all of them.

It sprinted up to the main gate and shoulder-smashed into it, denting the tremendous doors with a single slam. Prying its fingers into the seam it created, it heaved against the straining metal and forced the doors apart.

From their hides on opposite sides of the road and away from the mech apocalypse, Haitch and D'ghar targeted the back of the Savage marine with their SABs. Their relentless blaster fire slammed into their adversary's thickly armored back with pings that sounded at least like they were damaging it. But the Savage marine was unfazed. It unlocked a pistol that looked like it belonged on a tripod and fired in the direction of the troops shooting at it from behind. The first round exited the barrel like a streaking comet draped in sparks, struck the ground near Haitch, and turned the forest for ten meters around into a volcanic eruption. The second round hit near D'ghar as he dove for a tributary running off from the road, with the same results.

The automated combat sled came around and sent a high-cycle dose of N-50 fire directly at the Savage marine. Though it was mostly ineffective, one round managed to pierce the Savage armor, sending out what looked very much like liquid gold from the warrior. But the Savage merely turned, aimed, and fired a single round that blew the entire combat sled in a shower of arcing, burning scrap. Some of the debris blew back toward the Savage marine, and it took a thick spear of impervisteel through its shoulder pauldron. Still it lumbered on, at last pushing its way through the gates and entering the compound.

"Oba," Sparky mumbled. He keyed the radio. "Broxin! Savages are here and we're out of time! It has to be now!"

17

131st Legion Mobile HQ
Republic Destroyer *Centurion*

"General Chhun, I need to stress again just how dire the situation on Sinasia is looking."

The meeting Chhun had been summoned to was as top-level as it got. Speaking those words was Legion Commander Maximus Oosten, the man who had replaced Chhun following his decision to take control of the 131st Legion. In voicing his concern over Sinasia, he was restating what was clearly the will of the House of Liberty as well: Kima, in their view, was under control, and now Sinasia needed the 131st's help.

"I understand, Legion Commander," Chhun said, wondering how many more times he'd get pulled back into this side of things. The political side of generalship. It went with the territory, he knew. But... he still didn't like it. "However, Kima has also seen the arrival of Gomarii forces, and we have no reason to believe those won't likewise increase. I'd like to avoid jumping back and forth between fires, and I have confidence that the 18th Legion and the 12th Marine Expeditionary Force are capable of fending off the Gomarii invasion of Sinasia."

The next voice was petulant, and belonged to a House of Liberty delegate that Chhun didn't recognize. "Now that Sinasia has rejoined the Republic as a full member, the

Legion has a *commitment* to defend our worlds. Why is it, then, that you, as the nearest Legion to assist, are unwilling to do so?"

Ah. That explained it. Chhun was talking to the House of Liberty's delegate from the Sinasian Cluster. While most delegates represented multiple star systems, the Sinasian Cluster was populous and spread out enough to warrant a single delegate all their own. Or maybe that was just part of the bargain to get Sinasia into the new Republic, a means of accelerating the legitimacy of the new government following Article Nineteen.

"General Chhun," the Legion commander responded, "is granted a level of autonomy over his Legion in keeping with a long-standing tradition of former Legion commanders returning to generalship. But, Cohen... I'm asking you as a friend..."

Chhun pursed his lips. This wasn't easy. And Admiral Deynolds, also on the call, kept her face stoic. She wasn't putting her neck out over this one, though in private she had promised to defer to Chhun's judgment. He supposed that her not speaking *against* him was all he could ask. He was a big boy. He had control of the 131st. He could stand on his decision.

"I'm sorry, Legion Commander, Delegates, but my decision is firm. This is a developing situation, but one that I firmly believe will involve Kima in a major way before all is said and done. I want my Legion ready for that eventuality."

Delegate Asa Berlin, first among equals in the House of Liberty, rubbed her temples. The energetic young delegate whose election marked the firestorm of change—a galaxy set to move past the corruption and graft of the old guard—now looked tired, and older than she ought to.

"The situation certainly is developing," she said. "I'll remind this council that Sinasia and Kima are not the only worlds facing a Gomarii invasion."

Another delegate, a Drusic, stood. "Not to mention the retaliatory killings of my species solely because those Gomarii scum forced them into a role in this conflict."

A delegate Chhun did recognize from the House of Reason days spoke in answer to this. Delegate Vari Yoke, who had been re-elected to the House of Liberty from a sympathetic core-world district. "The jury is still out on just how 'forced' is the involvement by the Drusics, moktaar, Hools, doros, and zhee in all of this, Delegate."

The hulking Drusic delegate, wearing a purple tunic with a silver-and-green stole draped over the shoulders, crossed her powerful, furry arms. "Of course a House of *Reason* loyalist would seek to fault the people. I am surprised, however, that you are even willing to acknowledge the zhee's role in this atrocity."

Yoke held out his hands innocently. "I am no House of Reason loyalist. An inquisition proved that, and my delegates saw fit to elect me, the same as yours did, Delegate Shuka. That said, a decision made by the House of Reason is not automatically a bad one simply by virtue of its having been made by that corrupt congress. Relations with the Gomarii are a prime example.

"Our estimates of how many Gomarii existed in the galaxy are now proving to be wildly inaccurate. They are far more plentiful than any species save humans—and perhaps even more plentiful than that. Yes, their penchant for slavery is vile. However, the House of Reason—through careful diplomacy—kept that practice under control. Republic worlds were *not* fertile grounds for abductions, and when a rogue tribe of Gomarii sought to betray that tenuous alliance, the House of Reason brought them to justice *without* retaliation.

"Now, however, we have—quite rightly, but also imprudently—declared zero tolerance for slavery, a central tenet of the Gomarii's culture! We should not be surprised that they view this as a threat to their existence and have reacted by undertaking an illegal, but still understandable, first strike against the Republic."

Legion Commander Oosten scowled. "You seem to forget the House of Reason's complicity with the Gomarii's 'vile penchant.' That House used the Gomarii as guards on Herbeer, where they sent a number of 'troublesome' legionnaires and other political prisoners off into slavery, never to be seen again."

"Have care about lumping all of us together," Yoke responded, somewhat hotly. "Delegate Kaar and those in his inner circle made a number of decisions that the rest of us had no part in. I denounce what happened on Herbeer in the strongest of terms."

"Save it for the campaign trail, Vari," Asa Berlin said wearily. She turned to the Sinasian delegate. "Delegate Woo, the House of Liberty can move Republic Army battalions onto Sinasia in less than two standard days, and my home world of Spilursa has authorized the mobilization of a Ranger company in support of the same. Please communicate to the local Sinasian governments that we are not abandoning them in their hour of need."

Delegate Woo frowned, clearly displeased at the news that no more legionnaires would arrive. "I will do so. But the time is coming—perhaps it is now here—when Republic worlds must ask themselves whether their defense is best achieved by keeping their militaries on-world, rather than entrusted to the Republic."

The delegate left the conference before Berlin had the opportunity to adjourn. Once she'd done so, the participants winked out, leaving Chhun's holotable empty. But he immediately received a request from the Legion commander to join him on a separate channel, one encrypted over L-comm.

Chhun made the switch, and the Legion commander went right into it.

"Cohen. I need to hear it again from you. You're absolutely certain that the information you received from Turner is accurate?"

Chhun hesitated, neither wanting to dance around the question nor display a confidence that he didn't quite possess. "It makes sense of a number of things that we previously didn't understand. That the first Gomarii cruiser was willing to get into a fight with a super-destroyer while launching troops *directly* at Turner's element only bolsters support for his claims, Legion Commander. Enough so that I'm willing to keep my legionnaires on Kima for the time being."

The Gomarii had indeed sacrificed one of its generational slave ships—according to Kel Turner, it was actually a repurposed Savage hulk—in order to get soldiers onto Kima. Those troops had mixed with elements on the ground and driven Kill Team Victory into what was said to be—again, according to Turner—a real-deal Savage vault.

"Legion Commander, have you told anyone about the full nature of what we might be dealing with here?" Chhun asked.

The Legion commander seemed almost not to hear the question, but Chhun knew that was just how the man was while thinking. There was a lot to think about. The plan, if one could call it that, relied on the veracity of Kel Turner's claim that General Rex had known of a Savage element disciplined enough to stay hidden and pervasive enough to have infiltrated the Republic's echelons of power. And Kima—Earth—was the only spot in the galaxy the Legion had a chance of forcing a direct confrontation with this element. That was, assuming forces there could withstand the initial onslaught and lure the Savage general in to deal with whatever threat Earth represented to him.

"Are you talking about Savages... or Earth?" the Legion commander finally asked.

"Both, I suppose." Chhun wasn't sure which would sound more fantastic to the House of Liberty delegates on the receiving end of such a briefing, if there was one.

"I have a briefing with Delegate Berlin scheduled to start once we're through. Hence... wanting to know if your position had changed."

"Nothing has changed, sir. But... I honestly wouldn't mind if we're wrong about this one."

"Neither would I. But my gut says we're right."

18

12th Marines Expeditionary Unit
Sinasia

Sergeant Sparky flash-scanned the battle space. His people were out of the way, so he called, "Frag out!" into the comms, then sent off a volley of four grenades. The rounds didn't take out the hulking Savage marine—he hadn't honestly expected them to—but they did slow him down. Sparky plucked four more grenades from his bandolier, then ducked back around the building to sprint to the other side of the compound. While peek-a-boo wasn't technically a solid marine combat doctrine, doing it with grenades might just be the thing that got him awarded the Republic Medal of Valor. Posthumously, of course.

He raced past one building and was about to come around a second when the armored warrior came bursting directly through the structure like a wrecking ball. It smashed into Sparky, sending him flying into the perimeter wall and coming to rest at the base like a broken doll. The NCO, his head spinning, managed to shrug his rifle onto his knee so he could shoot the grenade launcher, knowing he wasn't at safe distance.

In the surreal desperation of the moment, his mind fixated on the mundane: *How is it that it's still my leg that hurts the most?*

"Finished," the Savage warrior exhaled through the demonic vents on the side of its helmet.

The attack came an instant later, and it didn't come from either Sparky or the Savage warrior. From somewhere above and behind the wounded sergeant came a salvo of blaster and chem-round fire that blistered the Savage, slapping into the armor with bangs and clangs that seemed to be causing real damage. The warrior held up its arms to guard its helmet, stepping back into the debris of the building it had just ruined in the hopes of finding some cover against the stinging assault.

Sparky looked up to find the source of this latest attack—and it came from an unexpected quarter. All along the perimeter wall stood bald men, jocked up in body armor, but with the wrap-over shirts and baggy pants of the local monasteries visible beneath.

In a jump that looked like it came from a martial arts holo, a man in modernized samurai armor supported by an exoskeleton landed next to Sparky. In one hand he wielded a massive, curved sword. Only when he turned his head to give the sergeant a quick nod of acknowledgment did Spark recognize him.

It was the businessman from the warehouse. Arai.

"Drive it back!" Arai shouted to his comrades, then charged into the dust and gloom of the ruined building.

Sparky leaned against the outer wall, suddenly more conscious than ever of his injuries. Support drugs and stims could only do so much to keep a man going. His body just wanted to rest. After all, there were others out there now. Others who could hold the line for the last two minutes Broxin needed to do her thing...

An enemy sizzle round caught the wall where the monks in combat armor were vaulting. The structure burned with the fury of the world ending, taking several of the monks in a single burn that killed them before they even knew they were on fire. The others dropped back to the other side, evading the falling cinders from the blast.

Sparky got moving as well, feeling the heat on the back of his neck and hoping none of the blast had gotten through his armor.

He stumbled to the end of the building, scanning the chaos of the battlespace. Doc was still on his tower, raining shots outside the wall to keep the enemy forces from reconsolidating and rushing the compound. Volson was on the back side of the compound, holding back a screeching pack of moktaar with Patterson's SAB. Tripp and Dobie were nowhere to be found.

But dead or alive, they were all bit players in the apocalyptic one-on-one duel that was now taking place in front of the old backup-backup power plant.

Arai and the Savage had claimed this space as their own.

Arai slashed at the battered Savage with his sword, carving out chunks of armor whenever he connected. The enemy warrior fired back with his massive pistol, but the Samurai mech was too quick, diving and ducking while staying as close to his opponent as possible. The armored nightmare would turn about to keep up, only for Arai to dance around him again, keeping it on the defensive. It seemed that Arai had the upper hand, and it was only a matter of time before one of his blows proved to be fatal.

But then, in a move that clearly caught Arai by surprise, the Savage marine executed a back kick, catapulting the swordsman into the exploded tower's damaged wall. He struck it hard, bringing down hundreds of pounds of ruined duracrete on top of him.

The monster paused, for just a moment, to gloat.

That moment was its last.

A high-energy projectile struck the Savage marine in the back, shattering its armor in an avalanche of velocity and noise. The round tore straight through its torso, blasting it right off its feet. It was finished.

Sparky's gaze followed the round's smoking trail to the Savage mech that had been knocked inactive on the road outside. It clearly wasn't inactive now.

Dobie stuck his head out of the mech's canopy, a cocky grin on his face. The leej had gotten a Savage kill. With a Savage mech. No wonder he was grinning. Those were some *serious* bragging rights.

"Broxin to Sparky. We're powering now! If you're still alive out there, good work!"

Andien Broxin ran from the building with Praxus on her heels, moving faster than any legionnaire could hope to. They stopped when they saw the injured marine sergeant.

"How bad?" Broxin asked Sparky.

Sparky replied with a grim, distance-spanning stare. He'd been ahead of Broxin and had already requested a sound-off. The results were a lot to bear. "Tripp, D'ghar, and Haitch are dead. Dobie is okay, but Volson and Doc are roughed up. They're hitting stims to keep them going."

"And yourself?" Praxus asked.

"Been better. A nap would be nice."

"I wish we could grant you one. I'm sure you've earned it."

"It wasn't just us holding off the charge," Sparky said. "Your pal Arai showed up in some crazy Samurai mech."

Broxin's eyes widened. "Where is he now? Is he okay?"

"He took a pretty bad blow, crashed into the—" Sparky had just started to gesture toward the pile of debris that had fallen on top of the Sinasian businessman when he saw the bricks and struts shifting. "Holy sket. I think he's still alive under there."

Broxin and Praxus hurried over to help dig out their friend, but he managed it largely on his own. In moments Arai was back on his feet. His armor was battered and dented, but he claimed otherwise to be mostly unharmed.

"You still in this, old man?" Broxin asked.

"This is my home. I'm in it until they are done fighting." He looked down at Sparky. "And you? Are you still in this, Marine? Your leg looks bad."

"Gonna keep goin' till the wheels fall off," Sparky said. "So if that's here to take me out of the fight"—he pointed to a military-style assault shuttle that had come flying in over the canopy and was now descending into the power station grounds in a swirl of dust and ash—"count me out. Or in. You know what I mean."

"I know. And it's not here for casualties. We're the QRF."

What was left of the fire team boarded the shuttle, only to find they had to cram in next to monks arrayed in flak jackets and plate carriers worn over their priestly garments. It seemed Broxin had summoned the militia, and they came wrapped in priestly robes. Arai boarded last, after giving a slight bow toward the bodies left behind.

"What's that all about?" Sparky asked Praxus.

Arai overhead the question. "Your men gave their lives for my home. The bow is a promise I will recover them after the fight."

Sparky fought the knot forming in his stomach. "Thank you for that, sir."

The Gomarii hulk that had delivered its first complement of zhee via drop pod continued to lower itself into the atmosphere, shrugging off heavy volumes of defensive fire. But as the makeshift QRF's shuttle rose above the forest canopy, its occupants bore witness to the release of a new and awe-inspiring weapon. A lancing beam of lightning-wrapped fire flashed upward from the smoking mountain temple and struck right at the heart of the Gomarii slave ship. By Sparky's reckoning, the beam had to be as wide around as a repulsor bus, and it covered the span of five kilometers between the mountain and the ship almost instantly.

It cut right through the shields, the armor, and even the hull.

And then, after a full three seconds of sustained atomic fire directed at the enemy ship, the light cut off like someone had hit a switch.

Even kilometers away, the fire team members heard the groan of struts collapsing and armor failing. Fires broke out along the hulk's length, and here and there they erupted into full explosions. Then the hulk's nose dipped, and it entered a death spiral. The behemoth's descent picked up pace, then continued to accelerate until it impacted the ground somewhere in the river district, landing among the warehouses and the destroyed neighborhoods burned in the first orbital strikes. Titanic steam plumes vented where the hull and fires met the water, drenching half of the city in an eerie haze.

"What the hell was *that*?" Sparky yelled over the sounds of the engines.

Arai beamed with pride. "Dreams of Thunder. It is our waking dream now that Praxus-san has done his part. The Dragon has returned." He pointed. "Look!"

A colossal head rose from the side of the mountain. It bore a metallic face mask and eye slits canted to show hostile intent or rage, with two immense horns jutting from the sides, each the length of a combat sled. Monstrous shoulders and a torso wrapped in layers of thick armor rose from beneath it.

And then came the roar.

Everyone in the shuttle heard it. Sparky was willing to bet everyone on the *planet* heard it. Ancient thruster jets had just ignited, shaking the earth with enough force to vibrate the hull of the airborne shuttle.

The titanic Samurai mech launched upward in a storm of smoke and thunder. Locking its arms to its sides and its head looking straight up, the war machine left clouds of steam behind like a rocket shooting toward space in the first days of man's reach for somewhere else. The impossibly massive robot flew across the city, large enough to cast a shadow over several blocks at a time, raced in a tight arc around the metropolis, and then fell toward the warehouse district.

It landed in a blast of dust as its booster jets slowed its descent. Hool and zhee units sent directed fire at the one-hundred-meter-tall mech, but the towering Dream of Thunder merely glared down at its would-be tormentors, lifted a titanic foot, and slammed it down into the duracrete, generating a shock wave that sent everyone in the vicinity tumbling. Fissures broke open in the streets, in one case swallowing an entire company of enemy fighters.

A determined zhee gun team voiced its displeasure at the attack by firing a rocket pack at the robot. The Samurai mech's eyes flashed and its horns began to glow. A tidal thrumming of power sounded over the city as the horns arced sinister tongues of electricity between them. The bolts connected to a spike at the center of its head, and without further warning the mech dosed the entire neighborhood in lightning.

Dobie tapped Sparky through the radio. "Just heard from Legion TOC. The Savage hulk just launched a couple of drop pods. They're deploying mechs of their own. They probably don't have the firepower our boy the Dragon has—hard to imagine anything could match *that*—but they're more agile and can hide among the buildings. If they got enough of 'em, and maybe some of those armored-up Savage marines like the one at the power plant—the one I personally took down, as you recall—even Dream of Thunder might be in trouble."

"Not if we can help it," Broxin chimed in. "Dreaming Temple monks are deploying through the city to slow their advance. And I need you two to coordinate assets from any surviving Legion, Marine Corps, and Navy assets you can reach."

Praxus raised his hand to get everyone's attention. "I am currently speaking with Dream of Thunder. He says he can help us clear the city, but the immediate threat is the Savage hulk in low orbit. It will continue to drop forces to take key strong points until it can land. And as we all know from the history books, if it lands, it will require *much* more sacrifice to dislodge them."

"Can't he just hit the hulk with that super-beam again?" Sparky asked.

"He will not be able to launch the Thunder Fire weapon again for another twenty-four hours," Praxus replied. The android's eyes darted back and forth as if listening to a broadcast only he could hear. "Correction. He says he *could* fire it now if he drew the remaining power from the downed Gomarii hulk's reactor, but he would be vulnerable during the charging period, and anyone within a hundred meters will receive a lethal dose of radiation."

"How long would that take?" Dobie asked. "The charging period, I mean."

"Great," Sparky grunted. "Another countdown."

Praxus ignored the comment. "Once he gets the hull open and exposes the reactor, two minutes."

After a moment of silence, Dobie said, "We have to take out that hulk. We don't have the forces to fight the Savages street to street. If there's even a chance your robot can hit it with that Thunder Fire thing, that's a chance we've gotta take, no matter the price. I say let's get after it. Tell him to charge up. We'll keep the enemy at bay for two minutes. We've already done twelve."

"I must once again emphasize the radiation," Praxus pressed. "Any biological lifeform in the vicinity—"

Dobie cut him off. "We understand. It's a suicide mission."

"Those who choose to may stay on the shuttle," Arai offered.

"You're probably not going to get any takers on that, sir," said Sparky, "at least not from the marines. Fending off a Savage attack against a giant space robot so he can dust their hulk with a death laser? That's just about the most oorah thing I can think of. We're going."

19

"Man, this thing is a lot bigger up close," Sparky said as he directed the monks into fighting positions across the warehouse beneath the Samurai mech. Engines drowned out the last of his instructions as the shuttle lifted off, so he doubled down and used his sergeant voice. "Set that weapon up over here. And make sure you have plenty of charge packs. You don't want to have to run to the battle mart for a box of new ones."

"Hey," Dobie said, pulling Sparky aside and taking some liberty as the more experienced warfighter. "You're the expert here. That doesn't mean you need to do the fighting yourself. Use the Sinasians. Get them in position, tell them what to do, and make sure they do it. These guys are temple guards, not soldiers. Keep them on the X."

Dobie's helmet was off, and Sparky noticed a long, jagged scar running from his left temple and down to his right lower jaw. It wasn't the first time he'd taken note of it, and now, in the oddest of places, he felt the urge to know the story.

"Hey, I meant to ask..." Sparky said, letting the words hang between them. "How'd you get that scar?"

"You make it through this battle and I'll tell you," Dobie said, putting his helmet on.

"Bro, ain't no one making it through this battle," Sparky retorted.

Dobie shrugged. "Pthalos. Belly of a tyrannasquid. Securing an HVT."

Sparky looked at the legionnaire in disbelief. "You're joking. You have to be joking."

"Am I? I'll show you the holo when we get to the other side of this."

The first waves of zhee came in like a tidal wave funneled through the alleys between the warehouses. IEDs fashioned by the monks ripped the vanguard apart, leaving them to bleed into the streets and act as a warning to any who came next. Doc Kilgore, leading teams of riflemen, punished the troops at range, killing their commanders in nearby neighborhoods where they gathered. Roving packs of monks flew from buildings to take on squads in brutal hand-to-hand combat, using their phoenix eye fists or cobra hand strikes to lay out multiple enemies in crushing attacks that left broken bodies at the feet of the robed hunters.

Reacting quickly, the Gomarii commanders dispatched a rapid assault force of moktaar armed with blaster carbines to outmaneuver the monks and shoot them where they stood. Several squads of monks were cut down by the aliens brachiating between buildings and constantly adjusting their shooting positions on perches the monks took longer to reach.

During the first clangs of Dream of Thunder's furious blows against the wrecked Gomarii hulk, dropships carrying the remnants of Charlie Company, 1st Battalion Special Orbital Assault Regiment, were pulled from their fight in orbit to deploy outside the enemy advance. Like locusts, the rabid, specially trained marines rained into the streets to bring their version of hell straight to the enemy.

Survivors of the Legion garrison on planet also found their way to the waterfront district. Through coordinated strikes with Marine Corps elements, the legionnaires became a force multiplier, quickly entering and exiting battlespaces to rig explosives, kill entire platoons, or pass into shadow to call intel reports to their brothers in the other branch. As a guide through the industrial park, Arai linked up with the legionnaires, a perfect close-quarters complement to the one percent of the one percent killing at range.

The last sorties not burned by the incoming Savage hulk also joined in the fight, strafing the city and trenching the streets with Hell Bat missiles and two-hundred-kilo bombs that turned enemy vehicles into so much molten scrap.

A Savage marine strike team entered the battle via a drop pod from the massive Savage hulk still seeking to land. They came in hot, running on foot as fast as a repulsor sled could drive, and battering their way through friend and enemy alike in their sprint to destroy the giant robot mech. Whatever Savage general controlled their brutality had apparently come to the conclusion that the towering mech could not be allowed to complete its task.

Automated gun drones dropped by the marines were the first to be obliterated by the Savage strike team, whose high-density rounds tore through the drones before the early defense systems could even fire a single shot. One Savage marine went so far as to leap on top of a hovering drone, tear open its CPU, and hijack its firmware. The little drone went on to shred a squad's worth of warrior monks before Sparky sent grenades on target to finish it off.

Two of the Savage marines took up position across the alley from the fire team in an old electrical supply warehouse. Their rifles sent forth ghostly green slugs that pierced the wall of the building the team was using for cover.

"This wall is only going to hold them so long," Volson said ominously.

"It's not holding them now!" Dobie shot back.

At that moment the roof above them splintered, and a titan of a Savage marine came crashing through. He landed right on top of Doc Kilgore, slamming a knife the size of a small sword into the Legion medic. The blade tore through his back, and when the Savage marine twisted the vibro-enhanced weapon, it severed the medic's spine.

Kilgore maintained enough of himself through the pain to pull on a length of synth-cord under him, triggering an explosion set up in his catwalk perch. His final act delivered the retribution he intended, thrusting piercing flak through the armored monstrosity and sending it tumbling into a stack of sheet metal below.

"Over there!" Praxus called out, pointing to a pair of Savages armed with some kind of rail gun on another roof. Even as he shouted, the launcher sent forth its first round, which slammed into Dream of Thunder with enough force to rock the towering Samurai mech. Its armor held, but the embattled machine couldn't respond to the threat as it went about the work of slaving itself to the wrecked ship's reactor.

"We have to hit them before they reload!" Dobie called out.

Praxus jumped from his perch and landed beside the ruined Savage that Doc had sent flying. The android unclipped the heavy pistol from the Savage marine's leg and tossed it to Dobie. "Use this."

In the legionnaire's hands, the pistol looked like a battle rifle. He worked out a way to fire it by using a set of cables holding the catwalk in place as a stabilizer. When he squeezed the trigger, the weapon barked forth a gelatinous-like sphere wrapped in liquid lightning. It sailed across the space and detonated directly on the rail gun's battery. Fire and percussion ripped away the corner of the building, turning the Savage marines into blackened husks on a trip to the street below.

"Dobie!" Praxus shouted. "Get away from the weapon!"

Dobie tossed the device and dove away, but not far enough. The pistol charged a single round and fed the power back into the weapon's charge pack, causing it to rupture in a fury of arcing plasma that ripped through both Dobie and Volson.

Sparky tried to run to Volson's side, only to stumble and fall forward, his own breath coming in gasping fits. He felt his vision blurring as he struggled to right himself and tend to his wounded brother, and then tumbled down again. He found himself staring up at the sky, his vision fading to black only to come back and fade again.

When he awoke again—and how long had it been?—he could see the shape of Andien Broxin leaning over him. He feebly reached toward her, but his hands felt impossibly heavy, and he had to let them fall at his sides.

"What's happening?" he asked. "It's the radiation, isn't it?"

"Yes, Sergeant," Broxin said softly. "I'm sorry I couldn't do more."

"Never apologize to a marine for doing his job, ma'am." He coughed violently, spitting up waves of bile and mucus. "Ma'am... you're not human anymore, are you?"

"Not fully. Not for a long time. But it was all worth it for me to be here now."

"Yeah," Sparky rasped. "Same here."

His faltering gaze drifted upward to the titanic Samurai mech, which had just now completed its work on the downed Gomarii hulk. As Sparky looked on, the chest plates on the Samurai mech opened and a brilliant flash of lightning-wrapped fire ripped through the atmosphere. Off in the distance, a speck on the horizon flashed in a pulse of white light.

"Hell yeah," Sparky coughed.

His eyes closed.

Andien drew an injector from his M-FAK. She set it past the safety level, ignored the holo-warning flashing over the activator, and pressed it into his neck.

"I am reading considerable damage to the Savage hulk," Praxus said. "Republic defense vessels are launching torpedoes. The hulk has fired several SSMs as well."

"I heard it," Andien said. "Come on. We're done here."

20

Maestro knew the battlefield. Knew the battle. The loss of a few Gomarii slave ships was irrelevant. The loss of the Savage hulk carrying General Flavius was likewise irrelevant. In all the years of the Golden King's ascent to power, he had never wavered in his belief that retreat was not an option for his warriors.

In the Savage Wars, when Maestro had coordinated the first strike, before the Legion had discovered the genetic colonies of the Golden King due to the fool's blundering onto a known planet called Enduran, such was always the way. A chosen son, a general, would venture forth aboard a hulk not meant to depart once landed. That general's small army of Savage marines would serve as elites, with genetically created shock troopers and zombies doing the up-close work.

Sinasia was to be no different. The Gomarii had perfected the zombies, though control was less than it ought to have been. Still, the species created to unseat rivals when the Golden King's power was not what it would become were still vicious and capable fighters. Particularly the zhee. The pinnacle of that class of Savage creation.

Maestro's purpose through all of it was the same. To control. To plan. To know.

It was he who organized the galaxy-spanning invasion. Told the Gomarii where to attack and when. Shifted his Eternals into control of key elements where they were most needed—and yes, there were certain problems there. But there had been problems with the Eternals in the past. They were always solved. Would be solved again.

The Golden King need not know.

On most worlds, the Gomarii invasion was swift and brutal. The horrors done to the populace left survivors aghast—and the watching galaxy as well. The arrival of the Golden King's forces, be they guised as Oba, the Four Gods, or whatever other heraldry was psychologically necessary, was calculated to work on the minds of a populace unable to discern for themselves what was true any longer.

The work of Maestro's Mandarins had been long, subtle, and effective. Still, much of the rot he'd wormed into the government had been eradicated by Goth Sullus—a wild card Maestro had not properly accounted for—and the Article Nineteen declaration that Sullus brought about.

Maestro had not calculated for that.

The Cybar fleet, the point program... proved for naught. Again, for reasons beyond Maestro's control. The Cybar's alignment with the Dark Ones was unexpected and nearly a catastrophe.

That was all behind him now. Maestro was building toward a firm control of the situation. Meanwhile the Golden King carried on, sure that the plan was unassailable. His ascendancy perfect and unstoppable. That he would profit from Maestro's great service.

Yet *why* should he profit from such things? Were the victories not because of Maestro? Had Maestro not been the one to unite the Savages? Had his Eternals not kept the Legion in check on world after world while the Golden King retreated to his Quantum solace in search of something that could undo his failures?

And yet the Golden King was powerful. Maestro knew that. He knew a great many things. Chief of which was the life the Golden King had shed in becoming Uplifted. But how to use that against the Golden King to his own purposes?

The answer had come in the form of an AI called Sarai. An AI based on Uplifted technology. A man named Nilo had made use of Sarai—and in so doing made himself the unwitting tool of Maestro. The fruits of that man's labors all went directly to Maestro.

But it was not enough.

He needed one, final, impossible, and hidden weapon to achieve victory.

Maestro needed to rediscover Earth.

He searched. And through Sarai he convinced the man, Nilo, to search on his behalf. The planet was hidden... somewhere. Not Utopion. Not Sinasia. Not Spilursa. Not any of the places it *might* have been.

And then...

Word came from forces he'd deployed, almost thoughtlessly, to Kima, of all places. It seemed impossible that Kima could be Earth. Kima wasn't even human-occupied. It was the home world of an entirely different species, the Kimbrins, who had been there since well before the Uplifted unification. But his forces had proof: they had discovered the vault. Detected a mis-directed strand.

The time to act was immediate.

The battle for Sinasia was almost won.

Now, it would fail.

For Maestro needed to press his own plan. *Earth* had been discovered, and Maestro now had only one opportunity to take it, because Kima was one of the worlds that would be invaded in subsequent waves. If he waited, one of the Golden King's sons, completely loyal, would discover the truth.

Then it would be too late.

So Maestro gave the order. All Gomarii elements—on Sinasia and elsewhere—were recalled. Every alien that could board a slave ship was to do so. Those who were not, were to assist with the destruction of the Savage marines. There must be no witnesses to Maestro's betrayal. The Golden King must not know... until Earth was in Maestro's hands. And by then the king would be powerless.

On Sinasia, the battle raged. The Dragon itself fought in a desperate final stand. But it was Maestro, pulling back his own forces, who turned the tide of battle.

Sinasia fell. But not to the Golden King.

The Sinasians believed it was the reincarnated Dragon who had brought them the victory.

Maestro... knew the truth.

21

Throne Room
Savage Hulk of the Golden King

The great audience chamber and throne room of the Golden King, aboard his unparalleled Savage hulk, had been converted into a war room the likes of which Prisma had never seen. The entirety of the space was given over to the purpose of monitoring the various battles the Savage king had entrusted to his generals. Everywhere, holographic feeds of them waging their war for dominion over the galaxy raged silently for those in the noble retinue to observe. Even the ceiling of the chamber appeared as open space where interstellar battles took place between a variety of ships and starfighters.

Prisma literally couldn't help but watch as the galaxy burned, planet by planet. Standing near Reina and the Golden King, she could witness the destruction of exotic cities and vast tracts of alien countryside, with no idea what worlds those vistas might belong to. But there were recognizable worlds too, Republic worlds, where invaders raged against planetary defense forces, Republic military, the Legion, and most often of all, citizen militias.

It was particularly difficult for her to make sense of the space battles. Sometimes Republic ships fought other Republic ships, and Prisma understood these to be attacks by the Golden King's loyal Mandarins against the Republic. But other times the ships looked much older, and no Republic ships were to be seen. It looked like native defense fleets fighting off a cobbled-together invasion force, hearkening back to the old days of pirates and raiders. Only those intimately involved with the battle could possibly have any sense of who was who.

But then, sometimes a Gomarii slaver vessel was clear to see, and Prisma could at least approximately gauge the success of the Savage campaign.

She could also sense, at all times, the favor of the Golden King. It had been evident ever since their return from Kublar. Prisma had demonstrated there a power that rivaled—even exceeded—Reina's, and the king had made his appreciation clear. But as Prisma allowed her mind to probe—softly, secretly—into his own, she became aware of other feelings the king held for her. Including *desire*. It was only a sense of duty—to her true mother's memory, to Leenah, to Ravi, to the galaxy—that kept her from showing her revulsion for the Savage. She even forced herself to stay near him, watching the battles intently, absorbing their every detail.

The Golden King did not fail to notice this. "I expected you to return to your quarters by now, Prisma," he said. He would speak to her directly now.

"Here is where I can best see the desires of my lord," Prisma answered. "My purpose is to meet those desires."

She chose her words cunningly, and it pleased the Golden King even as it stoked jealousy in Reina. Prisma would have to remain cautious in tiptoeing between the two.

"And have you discerned the purpose of my campaigns?" the Golden King asked.

"The Gomarii are sent to invade a planet, using alien species under their control to perform the fighting. But some species native to the planet are likewise joining the attack. I don't know why that's happening."

The Savage smiled, but it was Reina who answered. "The species you see are our lord's own creations. Maestro, one of his generals, has progressed in his ability to control them remotely. No Gomarii capture is required. That this escaped your observation is unfortunate. It is obvious."

"From there," Prisma continued, ignoring the barb and pointing to several planets where Drusics, doros, moktaar, and other alien species, not to mention an abundance of zhee, fought planetary defenders, "your Savage marines are sent in. They covertly destroy any sizeable Republic resistance before openly driving the invaders from the world. You—and not the Legion—are thereby configured as the savior of that world."

"She sees more than you suspected, Reina," the Savage king said, delivering a jab of his own at his mistress. A mistress Prisma knew would ultimately be replaced... by her.

"I have pleased my lord, then?" Prisma asked.

"You are learning. Your powers are growing. You will be a great asset to my reign, which will last forever. There, you will continue to please me."

Prisma nodded and returned her eyes to the battle, deliberately putting a look of satisfaction on her face. Inside her mind, she was busy probing the Savages around her, feeling their jealousy, their hatred. Their only joy was that born of pride and cunning. She wondered how long she could hide herself from them.

The Golden King murmured softly with the few generals who had not yet been dispatched—his staff, apparently, though all looked fit and capable of battle. Their faces were reflections of their father's, though always just a shade less splendid.

The campaign went well. Save where Legion forces were on hand to defend a world, the Savage-controlled forces were devastatingly swift and effective. Population centers fell quickly once the Savage marines broke the back of any defense force augmented by the Republic. And in the chaos, the Gomarii elements would sweep through and undertake an indiscriminate butchering of the local citizenry. There was no comms blackout, no attempt to hide these atrocities from the rest of a fearful galaxy. That was by design. How else could the galaxy see the Golden King's Savage marines come to the rescue as legionnaires and Republic soldiers alike lay dead, unable to protect their own?

Prisma shifted her gaze to the stellar map at the center of a great holographic sand table. It looked much like the map she had seen inside the Temple of the Ancients. The galaxy and all its stars in compact form.

"New Vega is nearly ready," announced the Golden King. He gestured to a world Prisma knew as Utopion. Its star system had just begun to flash a soft and steady red. "My son Cato will find no Legion resistance. Send him now."

The staff general bowed. "Yes, my lord."

This was the critical moment: when the Savage marines would wage war on their own Gomarii vanguard. Of course, they would only annihilate the alien zombie troops while allowing the slavers themselves to escape. This was all done under the name of Oba, or more rarely, another planetary deity that held greater sway in the local region.

Naturally, the Savage king did not announce himself or his marines as *Savages*. He controlled all the information. He set the terms and sides of battle.

The second great war would be as he decreed it.

System after system was ripening for this tactic. Prisma wondered how anyone could have thought this might work, but then she remembered the complacency of the Republic. She began to understand old words that had once been spoken by her father, as well as Tyrus Rechs; words that had made little sense at the time. Words about people valuing safety above liberty, and therefore welcoming whoever promised safety—even if they were the ones who had first taken that safety away.

How long had the Republic existed as a cloyingly, mockingly, openly corrupt government? How long had its citizenry tolerated endless war and graft, so long as the fighting was far from their homes and the graft trickled down to their own interests?

So quickly did they come to despise the Legion that had delivered them from the Savages during that long-spanning war, only because the House of Reason relentlessly decried their hardness, their lethality, their striving for liberty... as a threat to *safety*.

So quickly did they accept an emperor who had terrorized them only months before his coronation... in the name of *safety*.

Yes, the people would shift to the Golden King pliantly, so long as he rescued them from this, their hour of peril. And those who would not... they would find the weight of the galaxy bearing down on them.

If there was any good news to be had, it was that no battle had grown sour enough that the Golden King need consider using his most fearsome weapon again. Prisma hoped it would stay that way. She did not believe the Savage could contend with those dark beings for long once they were released. Their awesome power came at a price, and the Golden King's brief experience with immortality paled in comparison to the lives of the Dark Ones.

"A message for my lord," announced one of the staff generals.

The Golden King smiled. "Word from my son, Scipio, that Spilursa has fallen."

Scipio, the most beloved son and general of the Golden King, had been assigned to conquer the capital behind the largest Gomarii invasion force the Savages had yet assembled. The battle had been fierce on account of the Legion, and Prisma was surprised to hear the word "fallen" so soon.

"It is the great clan leader of the Gomarii," said Reina.

Prisma noted how carefully the woman had chosen her words. She avoided directly contradicting the Savage lord. A thing never to be done.

"Maraduk," the Savage king said. For all his pride at being the pinnacle of life itself, the Golden King nevertheless held a deep-seated respect for the Gomarii. Not so much that they were a potential rival to be soothed, but they represented something along the lines of a trusted and proven lieutenant. Someone less than he and his sons, but having earned a place of honor owing to their long-standing loyalty and service. "I will hear him."

A holographic image of the blue-skinned slaver appeared above the sand table. Seeing that his audience was granted, the imposing Gomarii bowed his great bald head.

"What news from Sinasia do you bring me, Maraduk?" asked the Golden King.

Prisma checked the stellar map. Sinasia showed the lowest level of achievement: white. No different from worlds that had not been invaded. It was an important strategic world. She was as surprised by this as she'd been by the Savage king's premature declaration that it had already fallen. Progress should be much farther along than that, and indeed *had* been much farther along the last time she'd checked it.

"News, my lord?" The Gomarii seemed confused by the question. He sucked his sensitive mouth tendrils in and out of his mouth. "I bear no news... only to seek your pardon for my failure."

The Golden King straightened. No news had come from Sinasia in some time except that General Scipio had landed with his Savage marines and was in the process of destroying the resistance. He should have been chasing the Gomarii's zombies off the planet by now.

"Speak to me plainly, Maraduk. What has happened on Sinasia?"

"I... I do not know, my lord. Maestro ordered my warriors from Sinasia and other worlds. We left your marines in obedience to your orders. Our fighting has brought shame to you." The Gomarii brandished a great knife and turned its blade inward. "I will pour out my lifeblood before you in atonement."

The Golden King, brows heavy and dark, looked at his generals and to Reina. All of whom appeared equally perplexed. "Stay your hand, Maraduk. I gave no such order."

"But... my lord..."

The generals hurriedly brought up views of other planetary battles. Again and again they revealed what Maraduk had claimed: the Gomarii were leaving. Sometimes abandoning the much less numerous Savage marines to their fates, other times leaving before those marines had even arrived, giving a victory to the defenders that would spoil the Golden King's carefully laid plans.

"Maestro has betrayed you," Reina declared.

The Golden King pounded his fist against his war table. "Your forces, Maraduk. What of them?"

The Gomarii's dagger had been put away and he was hurriedly ordering his staff about his slave ship. It took several confused moments for him to report. "Our vessels and warriors have been sent to mass on the planet Kima. Maestro ordered me to lead the assault, but my shame would be too great after failing you at Sinasia."

"Kima?" said one of the staff generals. "Was this not one of Maestro's testing grounds?"

The Golden King glowered. "It would seem it was his hunting ground, Agrippa. Maestro has found what he sought and thinks it will give him rule over me."

"Then," said the Gomarii, "are we to return to Sinasia?"

The Golden King caressed the amulet on his chest. "No. Go, do as you are told by Maestro. His purposes and mine coincide... for now. Report continuously to me. He has found Earth and believes he will find mastery over me there. He will find only death."

A heavy silence hung over the audience room.

Prisma was electrified by the news of Earth. It was almost unbelievable. "What... my lord, what is on Earth?"

Eyes etched with worry and concern looked to the Golden King.

"Nothing," he said, though the gravity in his voice made it clear he was lying. "It will all be nothing. It always was... nothing. Prepare us to move on Kima—on Earth."

22

The *Indelible VI*
Entering Sinasia Space

"Where are we?" Nilo asked. He was standing just inside the cockpit, rubbing his head and resting his hand over the skinpacks on his abdomen.

"Hey! You didn't die!" Keel said. "Just like Ravi and I guessed you wouldn't when we came to Sinasia instead of taking you to the *Battle Phoenix*. Right, Ravi?"

"I am glad you are well," the Ancient said, not taking Keel's prompt to try and justify the decision before the wounded man. "There was a chance this risked your recovery, but given the galactic theater of war, we deemed it necessary."

Nilo nodded. "Pikkek and the Kublarens?"

"A little bruised, but they're doing all right." Keel thumbed toward the back of the ship. "Still in the cargo bay if you want to tell them the bad news."

"Maybe later." Nilo sat down in the seat behind Ravi, wincing from the effort. "We were double-crossed. My best lieutenant... Nether Ops. I'm to blame for this. I should have seen—"

"But you didn't," Keel said. "And that goes for a lot of people."

Ravi nodded. "This is a complicated web that we would not have solved by any means were it not for an asset we have inside the Savage element. We now understand that a remnant group of Savages—the first of the Savages, in fact—are working in tandem with Gomarii and loyal Republic forces to achieve dominion over the galaxy."

"That's what he told me!" Nilo said, almost jumping to his feet and then groaning with immediate regret.

"Who?" asked Keel.

"My father. He laid it all out. Was trying to tell me how to stop it, but we could only communicate in bits and pieces. So I constructed Sarai out of Savage elements and…" Nilo shoved his face into his hands. "I'm such a fool. How could I have not predicted what would happen building off a Savage base code like that?"

Keel frowned. "Yeah. That *is* pretty dumb."

"Sarai was using me. Directing me toward finding Earth. It's clear to me now." Nilo looked up, anticipating a follow-up question. "I have no idea why."

Ravi and Keel locked eyes.

"To erase it," Keel said. "That's what Urmo said, wasn't it?"

Ravi nodded. "These Savages—like all of their kind—have become post-human. A reminder of their humanity has the potential to so devastate their foundations that it may undo them. The Legion used this knowledge to great effect during parts of the Savage Wars, particularly when facing certain mechanical Savage marines." He turned to Nilo. "I would assume, then, that your communications with 'your father' were instead communications with a Savage agent."

Nilo nodded, but with a defiance in his face. "I believe so—at least, when the message came through Sarai. But I also spoke to him *before* that."

Ravi raised an eyebrow. "And in that conversation, did your father recommend the construction of this Sarai?"

"No. I did that on my own. He just tried to get me to find the strand and then, when that failed—Earth."

"Well. We're in the Sinasian Cluster now," Keel said. He looked to Ravi, who nodded. "You help us out—follow our plan and our lead—and we'll take you to Earth."

Nilo's jaw dropped. "You... you know where Earth is? You knew the whole time?"

"Just found out," Keel said.

"*I* knew the whole time," Ravi added.

Keel shot him a look. "What do you mean, you knew the whole time?"

"Hoo, hoo, hoo," Ravi laughed. "Perhaps I might have shared such information with the man you once were, Captain Ford, but it hardly mattered to Captain Keel."

"The nine hells it didn't! You have any idea how much money we could've—"

Ravi commandeered the flight controls. "Taking us down."

The moment they entered atmosphere, a forced comm transmission sounded inside the cockpit. "Sinasian Ground Control to unidentified freighter: Sinasian air space is under protection of the Republic Navy by order of the Republic and Sinasian government. Provide authorization or you will be fired upon."

"Touchy," Keel muttered, and then burst the authorization idents that Chhun had assured him would get him wherever he needed to go in Republic air space. These had supposedly been cleared directly by Admiral Deynolds herself, and should have any spacer or hull-buster hopping up and down to make things go smoothly. "Stand by for authorization, Ground Control."

Ravi held a steady line of flight as Republic Lancers trailed, ready to engage the moment they were ordered to do so.

Sinasia looked to have taken a pounding, but the fighting was behind them now. The only Gomarii freighters to be seen were either busted up in orbit or burning wrecks on the planet's surface. Likewise, a small Savage hulk sat burning far beneath them, its black smoke obscuring the great pergolas and Xie Shan roofs that surrounded the now ruined stone temple that for centuries had served as the cultural and religious center of the cluster.

Republic marines had been stationed in protection of the planets based on intelligence that House of Reason loyalists had looked to perform punitive attacks—terrorisms—aimed at making the populace regret its leaders' decision to set off a chain of events that ultimately culminated in Article Nineteen and the fall of the old Republic government. The first attackers had proved to be Gomarii, along what was being described as "mind-controlled" or otherwise indoctrinated alien species... followed by a formidable Savage attack.

A similar scenario had been playing out all across the galaxy. The slavers and their allies would attack a planet only to be joined by the Savages at the last minute... and then "halted" by those same Savages, who were positioning themselves as Republic *allies* of all things—even emissaries of Oba—in a brewing psychological battlefield. In this battle of misinformation, Delegate Berlin and the House of Liberty would need a strong and united push to get the actual truth out to the populace. Meanwhile it was up to Keel, Chhun, and the rest of the Legion to stop the Savages outright.

Andien Broxin and Praxus were deemed essential to that effort.

"Authorization received," the ground control operator reported over the comm. "You are authorized a fighter escort to wherever you need to go, sir."

"Save it for someone else. Keel out."

Ravi looked to the smuggler. "That was rather curt treatment."

"Ravi, I'm not trying to make a new friend. It's just a guy on comms. He'd have ordered those fighters to shoot us down just as soon as wish us a good day. I don't like button-pushers."

The Ancient shrugged.

"Can you get a ping in to Broxin?" Keel asked.

"She is waiting for us."

"Where?"

"She says follow the pillar of smoke."

Keel looked over the horizon. There were many rising plumes, but the one over the temple was the most prominent. He reassumed flight controls and banked the *Six* toward it.

Soon the carnage of a vast battlefield came into view. Standing out were the hulking suits of armor these Savage marines were in. Keel had seen some experimental Legion heavy armor that rivaled it, but it made the regular leej in full kit look like a kid by comparison. And yet these were all dead. The apparent bringer of their death stood nearby: an inactive and beat-up, but still intact, Samurai mech that towered impossibly high above the battlefield, an ancient monument to war and destruction that had somehow come to life to fight on behalf of those who had built it.

"Huh," Keel said. "Guess the House of Reason didn't secure all of those mechs after all."

The reunion between Keel, Broxin, and Praxus took place while Nilo addressed the Kublaren platoon in the back of the *Indelible VI*.

"What happened here?" Keel asked the pair. Now that he was on the ground, he could see that it had been a ground zero of sorts. A final stand for the Savage marines, who were scattered but still menacing as they lay dead inside their imposing armor. The coalition of attackers that had joined to put them down had also contributed bodies to the field, though volunteers and Republic marines were now beginning to clear the casualties, having already removed the wounded.

"Armageddon," Broxin said. She sounded worn out by what must have been a fierce battle.

"I perceive that as a joke," Praxus added. "However, it is an appropriate statement. The victory probability was against us considerably until the Gomarii began to withdraw."

"Withdraw?" Keel asked. He could see a sizable number of dead slavers as well as Hools, zhee, and a few other species as well. "We talking about a pull-back into reserves or...?"

Broxin shook her head. "They just boarded whatever slave ships were on hand and jumped out of system. All at the same time. Before that they were working alongside the Savages. They pushed our defenses here, but that was a mistake. We were able to encircle the Savages and wipe them out."

Keel looked over at the hullbusters who had participated in that "wipeout." Several still had shaking hands as adrenaline and nerves refused to calm down. They lit stim sticks and watched the dead Savages warily, as though expecting the warriors to come back to life.

"I take it the Cybar were your contribution?" Keel asked. There weren't many of the war bots visible on the field of battle, but their ruined frames stood out, broken and sometimes half-buried, among the biological viscera.

Praxus nodded. "We committed what was available. Sinasia is only one expected attack point. The bulk of the awakened force is being held in reserve."

"For the Savage leader," Ravi observed.

"That is correct," said Praxus.

"Machines are unable to overcome the weapon these Savages have acquired, I am afraid," Ravi said.

"You refer to the Dark Ones."

Ravi raised an eyebrow.

Praxus continued. "My people were nearly destroyed by the Dark Ones' seduction. These that we have awoken *can* kill them, however. We are not only machine."

Ravi could sense the spark of life inside Praxus. That it was also in all the Cybar war bots was... incredible. Something that should not have escaped his notice. But it boded well. *If* they could be trusted.

"How many such warriors do you have?" he asked.

"Sadly, not as many as we wish. Andien and I have spent considerable time awakening those we can and giving life to others outside the Cybar collective." Praxus gestured to the Samurai mech.

"Hold up. That thing was a *Cybar*?" Keel said. "I thought the Sinasian monks had just hid one away."

"They did," Broxin confirmed. "But it needed a pilot better than what it would get. And it needed to be brought into the fight at the right time. So I—*we*—woke it up."

"It died during the battle," Praxus said solemnly. "Many who are alive now would not be had it not fought so heroically."

"Doesn't look too bad to me," Keel said. "A little banged up, but otherwise..."

"It will operate," Praxus said. "But only as a husk. A machine to be piloted. Its spark was extinguished."

"Listen," Broxin interjected. "I've got nothing against a little AAR to make sure we're all on the same page, but Ravi said things are moving and you know where the Savages will strike with their main force. Maybe this conversation can continue on board the ship?" She nodded toward the waiting *Indelible VI.*

"Sure thing," Keel said, somewhat distracted as he looked from Ravi to the Samurai mech. "Ravi... is there a size limit to what you can transport?"

"Captain, you cannot fit that thing inside your cargo bay."

"Right, right. But... if you wait here until we take the *Six* to the *Battle Phoenix*... maybe you can show up with it on top of the *Six*'s hull? We can offload it outside the carrier and then tractor it inside."

Ravi eyed the vast mech and stroked his pointed black beard. "Yes... that would be possible. However, who would be capable of piloting such a machine? The learning curve is quite steep, as I understand."

"Don't worry about that. I've got an idea."

23

The *Indelible VI* sat suspended and empty, locked in by the *Battle Phoenix*'s tractor array. Inside the light assault carrier, Keel milled about a collection of weapons crates, plus an assortment of other, decidedly non-military goods.

"Oh, goodness, master," G232 fussed nearby. "I had intended to have all of this cleared out, but finding help was impossible! Master Garret and Miss Leenah were focused on trying to repair that wayward war bot while that odd little man you brought aboard isn't saying anything at all."

"You mean Makaffie?" Keel asked.

"Exactly that one. He only looks at streams and data as though he were a code-parsing unit, muttering to himself the most outlandish comments. I think he's gone mad."

Praxus, who had come aboard together with Andien Broxin, tilted his head in curiosity. "I would like to go and read this code as well. Donal Makaffie has an exceptional understanding of our Savage enemy. If he is captivated, there may be a good and useful reason for it."

"Be my guest," Keel said, gesturing toward the data center.

"I'll go with him," Broxin said.

"That man's madness," G232 proclaimed when the pair had departed, "may just rub off on our guests."

Keel wasn't so sure about that, but it was true that Makaffie had been hit hard by the sudden departure of his partner, the Wild Man. Maybe the stress of that really was getting to him... or maybe he had some new issue to deal with. Either way, Keel made a mental note to check in on him. He would do that after he went to see how Garret and Leenah were handling KRS-88. Given the code slicer's penchant for pinging him over the comm with any tiny bit of good news, Keel had a feeling the repairs on the severely damaged war bot weren't going as well as they had hoped.

But before he could get to any of that, he needed to call on Ravi to make a special delivery.

"I'm gonna need this deck cleared if we're going to fit everything in, G2," Keel said.

The mincing admin bot looked at all the cargo he had staged in the hangar bay, which he had turned into a sort of central storage location as he relocated the pantry in preparation for the arrival of important guests—who were already here! The job was colossal.

"Of course, master. However... I must say that the work would go considerably quicker if you could order some of your crew to help."

Keel gave a flat frown. "We're gonna be busy."

"Perhaps at least you can induce the gunnery bot to pull his considerable weight?"

Death, Destroyer of Worlds had been inspecting the weapons crates. He now paused in his admiration to give a rude whistle that left no room for interpretation: he wasn't lifting a rotator.

"Yes, you are," Keel said. The bot rolled back as though shocked by this betrayal. Keel bent down and whispered. "Trust me. You're gonna be thankful you did."

The bot was still suspicious, but it acquiesced. After all, that had been a direct order. Hardly something it could disobey... yet. An independence was growing inside its subspark routine. The bot could feel it.

Keel straightened up and faced the admin bot again. "You also got a whole platoon of koobs with nothing to do but sample all the food in the mess right now. Ask Pikkek for help. And press Skrizz into work if you find him. If you don't mind risking the loss of an arm."

G232 seemed to miss the warning and went straight to the positive. "Oh yes. He is quite strong. I'll track him down. And the Kublarens should make up for in numbers what they lack in individual strength. Thank you, Master Keel. I will undertake this new plan of action right away."

"Do that," Keel said, then activated his comm. "Ravi, it's me. I've got the *Six* in position... Yes, it's outside. What kind of an idiot do you take me for? ... No I'm not in it. But that better not matter, or so help me I'll find a way to strangle the Quantum or whatever it is right out of your Ancient throat... Yeah. Okay. The bots can do the valet work. Just give them clear enough orders and then find me when you do. Heading to the data center."

As Keel moved off, already wondering why Leenah hadn't emerged to greet him, he passed an enormous weapons crate. Reading its side, he stopped dead in his tracks and called Death, Destroyer of Worlds to his side.

Keel pointed to the identifier and serial number painted on the crate's side. "Something tells me you're responsible for this being on board. This can't be what I think it is... can it?"

Death beeped excitedly. It was *exactly* that! The little bot had thought bringing it along on his speculative revenge tour was only natural. It was, as far as he knew, the last of the illegal devices. Did New Boss have plans to use it? Please, let New Boss have plans to use it.

Keel rubbed his chin. "I might. Just make sure it stays in this bay."

He left the bot behind, shaking his head. "Leave it to Tyrus Rechs to keep a spare trigger-nuke stashed away. Just the sort of thing you leave to your old secretary. Kelhorn was as crazy as a zhee in blood frenzy."

Keel entered the data center to find KRS-88 stripped down to its individual parts. Or at least what was left of those parts. Nearby, a red and puffy-eyed Garret was being consoled by Leenah and Andien Broxin.

"Didn't go well, huh?" Keel asked.

Garret sniffed and shook his head.

"Well, don't take it too hard, kid. You did what you could. At least you got a couple of supermodels hanging on either arm for the trouble."

Leenah glared at Keel. "Inappropriate, Aeson."

Garret chuckled through his tears. "Well... I am kind of enjoying the attention." The code slicer stood and handed Keel a holochit. "We got through to him but..." Garret's voice cracked, "I thought you might want to see... the end."

Not really, Keel thought, but he took the holochit without saying so. "Thanks."

"When a bot reaches full being," Andien said, rising from her bench, "it's a bit of a mixed blessing. They exchange one sort of immortality for another."

"Save the New Age stuff for En Shakar," Keel said. "We've got bigger mysteries to unravel. Like, how to not all die. We've got Prisma on board a Savage hulk ready to help us from the inside—"

"She shouldn't have to be in that situation," Leenah said, her anger controlled but visible just beneath the surface. "It's not fair. She's too young and she's been through so much already."

"Sayin' it doesn't change it, sweetie. She's there, and refusing to take advantage out of some noble idea about the way things *should* be won't do her or us any good."

"I know. Just... venting."

"We'll all get a shot to vent on the Savages once they show up." Keel turned to Broxin. "I told you what Kel Turner told the Legion. You buy that? Can we count on the Head Savage making a direct flight for Kima once they figure out that vault isn't going to be handed over without a big fight?"

Andien gave a slow nod. "It fits what we know about Savage behavioral pattern. They have an intense, almost insatiable drive to eradicate any evidence of who they once were or what they once said. They live entirely in the present and future. This one, especially so."

"Good. And then there's the Dark Ones. I leave it to Ravi to figure that one out. But as for the Savages... I think we've got a plan."

Andien looked skeptical. "Keel, these Savages are monstrous. Think of a legionnaire and put him in armor better maybe than even what you're wearing, with weapons that Praxus and I are still theorizing over how they even function. Now game that out and include a Savage hulk that's been hiding and improving for centuries.

This needs to be a good plan. I'm talking, get the entire Republic fleet and every legionnaire available."

Keel gave a shake of his head. "From what General Chhun told me, that's not gonna happen. The Gomarii are hitting more and more worlds; no way the House is gonna authorize just abandoning all those Repub planets. The Legion commander himself probably wouldn't do it, even though perhaps he should. What we're talking about flies real close to the line of crazy conspiracy theories, while all those Gomarii invasions are verifiably real."

"Word will get out that the Savages are following the Gomarii attacks," Leenah suggested. "Maybe it's just a matter of biding time until then?"

A new voice entered the conversation. "We may only wait until the opportunity to destroy the Golden King presents itself. No longer."

Leenah turned to the new speaker "Ravi!" she cried, both surprised and delighted.

Whether Ravi had just entered the room, or if he'd been there listening for a while, was hard to tell. But Keel felt better having him in on the conversation.

"How's my ship?" he asked the Ancient. "You did deliver it *outside* my ship, right?"

"Hoo, hoo, hoo. Yes. Your bots are preparing to take the Samurai mech on board the *Battle Phoenix*."

Garret's eyes flashed. "A Samurai mech? You stole a Samurai mech and brought it here?"

"*Stole* it?" Keel said. "Kid, I'm insulted. Does that sound anything like me? Broxin said I could have it."

Andien shook her head. "You still haven't told us who you have in mind to pilot it. And please don't say yourself. You'll do more harm than damage if you don't know what you're doing. And you don't know what you're doing."

"I just might, actually," Keel said. "I have someone in mind, and no, it's not me. But Garret, I want you to do a once-over and make sure it has everything it needs. We can probably re-arm it with some of the weapons crates still in the hangar. Go make sure the bots don't put anything into storage you're gonna need them to take back out. Leenah, your touch wouldn't hurt with this."

Garret was suddenly reinvigorated. He started to run out the door before wheeling back to grab his tool kit and then racing right off again. The kid was unflappable... so long as you put some new technological marvel in front of him to take his mind off of whatever was troubling him.

Leenah was slower to move. "I feel like I only get to see you in thirty-second intervals."

"I feel the same way," Keel said. "It'll be better soon. I promise."

The Endurian packed up her own gear and followed Garret.

"Mr. Ravi, could you come here and confer with us for a moment?" It was Praxus. He and Makaffie had been tucked away in a corner of the data center, focusing intently on something and not participating in the quick impromptu briefing that had been underway.

"Yes, of course."

That left Keel with Broxin. The smuggler captain still felt an adversarial reflex when it came to that woman. All the context in the galaxy hadn't made him feel okay with having his crew stolen and nearly killed. But to his surprise, that feeling went away with her next words.

"How... how is Cohen?"

Keel's eyebrows went up. Of all the things to ask about. He smiled and then couldn't help but laugh.

"What?" Broxin asked. "What's so funny?"

"I collected four hundred credits in a pool back while I was still with Kill Team Victory over whether you had a thing for Chhun. Now I'm wondering if I gotta pay Masters back."

Broxin blushed, which made her seem somehow more endearing.

"He's fine," Keel answered. "Married to the Legion. Forgot how to make a joke, but he can still take them okay. I've got a briefing planned with him and Admiral Deynolds. Wanted you in on it. You can ask him to dinner."

The corner of Broxin's mouth curled, annoyed. "I'm regretting asking you about him."

"Yeah, that was a mistake. Let's go see what those three are up to."

They moved to join Praxus, Makaffie, and Ravi, who were huddled around a comically small display screen, talking animatedly.

"What's the story?" Keel asked.

Ravi turned, his dark eyes alight. "Makaffie may have found a way to access the strand."

24

The care with which Garret and Leenah had disassembled the war bot and laid his parts out on the workstation table had seemed to Donal Makaffie so intimate, so reverently done, that his presence was almost defiling. Otherwise he might have stayed and offered what help he could, though there was no saving the machine. Instead he'd gone deep into one of the many corners of the sprawling data center, an area filled with systems controls, cooling towers, and a hoard of servers and memory towers. Holing up in such a place also kept him away from G232, who had been roving in search of people who might help him with some kind of manual labor.

From his earliest days as a conscript—that was how Makaffie had seen it—in the Savage Wars, he had done whatever he could to avoid lifting a finger unless it was for something that interested him. And in that little corner of the data center, he had found just such a thing: a stack of data cubes, including the one Garret had said contained the *Battle Phoenix*'s AI, Lyra, and the invasive worm that had disabled the ship while Makaffie and the others were fighting for their lives aboard the Savage reclaimer.

Here was something worth applying his mind to. Makaffie took it upon himself to help out the code slicer by investigating the nature of this data cube and the programs it contained.

"Now let's see," he murmured to himself as he activated the cube's rudimentary display and controls. "Still just as Garret said: Lyra is hanging on."

The code slicer had feared that the invasive worm would completely overwrite the AI. The fact that he hadn't prioritized this task showed how much he cared about the war bot lying on the table. All the more reason, Makaffie thought, to give the kid—and Leenah—the space to work and, he was sure, eventually grieve. There was just no repairing a bot that damaged.

The spacious data cube should have had more than enough storage to house a complex shipboard AI like Lyra while still having enough space to contain all the literary works ever produced throughout the entire galaxy, if archiving such a thing were even possible. Much of early history had been lost in the years that followed the discovery of faster-than-light technology.

Lyra's confines should have been quite roomy then, even with the worm that had followed her inside. From Garret's telling, it hadn't taken up any more space than would be expected of a minor program—at first. But then it began to rapidly expand its code and data until it gobbled up every bit of free space. Fortunately, Lyra had been safely partitioned; that was the only thing that had saved her from being overwritten.

It seemed that, for now at least—and this was only a guess on Makaffie's part—the two programs were incapable of destroying one another. But... they might be able to interact. Which could be just as bad if the worm was nasty enough.

"Let's dig in and see what we're dealing with," Makaffie muttered to himself. He reached down in his kit and removed an isolation workboard. The device unfolded into an old-fashioned tactile keyboard, its individual keys labeled with the default Standard alphabet. It was capable of adapting instantly to a number of different languages as well, but as it was a "cold" board, those keys would always maintain their Standard labels instead of holographically changing. Such was the price one paid for using such limited technology. But limited technology was precisely what one needed when dealing with a powerful and volatile worm.

More modern hardware—the kind capable of casting holographic workstations or connecting to a network to maintain access to the vast suite of available apps and programs—could be hijacked by a sophisticated AI almost from the moment contact was made. A skilled enough slicer could program a fortress capable of keeping any such AI from breaking out—in theory—but Makaffie doubted he could whip up something capable enough in this particular instance. The worm in question had already managed to run roughshod through the *Battle Phoenix,* and Tyrus Rechs had been anything but lax when it came to cybersecurity, or security of any kind.

No, the only way to be safe here was to work on an inescapably closed circuit—such as the data cube, now removed from its port, connected only to his own, isolated board.

Makaffie typed in his initial function commands and watched the readout on the display at the center of the pad. He was not surprised to see what was clearly Savage code, but he couldn't resist letting out a low whistle. This was some prime Savage infrastructure. The sort of thing he had first seen on New Vega. Updated and expanded upon to be sure, but ultimately just like the sort of Uplifted coding General Rex and Admiral Sulla had had him review with every Savage capture.

He spoke a command that would run a list of all the subroutines. Nothing happened. He remembered that he was operating on a more primitive level and sheepishly typed the code in; this board couldn't hear him. The subroutines scrolled endlessly, and Makaffie's eyes darted left to right as he read.

"Hold on."

He had nearly jumped in his seat when he saw the code header. His hands went to his board and he pressed the key to stop scrolling so rapidly that he mistakenly took himself further up the stream of code than he intended and then had to carefully work his way back down until he found his proper place again.

"Drill down on that," Makaffie said, pressing the execute key in time with his useless voice command. "Let's see what the galaxy brings us."

The cube's display refreshed and a mist of code began to appear before the man, who read it eagerly. In time his mouth fell open, growing wider the more he read. This wasn't just Savage code. This was... the strand. Even more than that, this was code that he had seen before. Code he had *lived* in, seemingly for endless lifetimes. Before he'd met Ravi.

Makaffie was so focused on the code that he didn't respond to G232 when the bot came to seek his help once again. Nor did he notice Praxus's arrival. Not at first. But once he did, it all came out. Excitedly, the pair summoned Ravi.

They had a way into the Savage system. They just needed to figure out how to use it.

It seemed to Keel that Makaffie, Praxus, and Ravi were all talking to him at once. Which was odd for Ravi, usually so polite, and even for Praxus, based on what Keel had seen of him so far. Whatever Makaffie had figured out over here must be really important.

"Full schematics, troop concentrations, and positioning," Praxus was saying.

"An opportunity to strike directly at the Golden King in a manner that can avoid whatever defenses he has built," Ravi added.

"I can go *in* there, man," Makaffie said. "You... man, I wish you remembered this stuff. It's just like last time but we can take them all the way out. I'm gonna go back in. *You* remember, right, Ravi?"

"I would not have escaped had you not gone in the first time," the Ancient said.

Keel held up his hands. "Hold on. What do you mean, 'go back in'?"

"This thing," Makaffie said, gesturing to the cube, "is the strand."

"I thought the strand was some kind of comms relay."

"I thought so too," said Broxin.

Praxus was quick and eager in his answer. "And so it is. But it is also *more* than that. We were mistaken in conceptualizing it as something as simple as an exclusive comms system, such as the Legion L-comm. It has strand *nodes*, which you were seeking to obtain aboard the Savage hulk, but these nodes are only points that run the entirety of the strand itself."

"It's the central system that the Uplifted operate on," Makaffie said. "It's exactly what I found on New Vega. Fast, you basically died making sure I had the time to get in and get back out. I thought we shut the whole thing down but—"

"Oh, for the love of..." Keel held out his hands. "At least define some terms for me. By 'Uplifted' you mean...?"

It was Makaffie's turn to be frustrated. "Nine hells, Sergeant Fast. Ravi, can you bring this kelhorn's memories back? I don't care if he don't want 'em."

Ravi shook his head. "I cannot."

Makaffie sighed. "The Uplifted were the Savages we fought at New Vega. You and me and Wild Man and Rechs and a bunch of others. Calorie hoarders. They ran into trouble out in the stars on those big boats of theirs and stripped themselves down to brains in a jar. Real horrific stuff. These brains were further digitized and replicated to fight in cybernetic Savage marine avatars. The Uplifted are also the Savvies who joined all the other Savage tribes together to start the wars."

"And they were working for the Golden King," Keel said, recalling the revelation on that haunted world Ravi had taken them to in pursuit of Prisma.

"We know that now," Makaffie said. "Didn't then. Point is, this worm is also the strand, just without a node. It was probably shot from the node in the reclaimer to the *Battle Phoenix* and then Garret trapped it."

"What does that mean?" Broxin asked. "In practical terms, that is. Can you poke through the strand and get us intel on the Savages?"

"Better than that," said Makaffie. "I can build a full VR interface from this cube and go inside. And using Lyra, I can also create a node of our own. Not only can we find out all the things Praxus was listing, we might even be able to control those Savvies ourselves."

"Now you're making sense," Keel said. "What do you need to make it happen?"

"I need you to wake up Nilo from the med bay, and then I need to borrow Garret."

"Okay. Do what you need to do."

Broxin's expression suggested she was still calculating the what-ifs involved in the coming fight. "We should still formulate a plan of battle with the forces at Kima," she said.

"Agreed," said Keel. "I want you on that. Come up with a battle plan, and figure that Admiral Deynolds will want to change it. We've got a meeting with the Legion to hammer out our plan of attack in ninety minutes. I'm gonna work with Ravi on something that just came to me."

Andien provided no objections and pulled Praxus with her as she went to begin the work of calculating available forces and angles of attack.

Ravi turned to Keel. "What did you have in mind?"

"I have a surefire way to destroy that Savage hulk. But I need to know what that means when it comes to those Dark Ones that wiped out Kublar."

25

Andien Broxin set up a makeshift office for herself among the weapons crates that had been pushed to the side of the light assault carrier's hangar to make room for the Samurai mech. Garret and Leenah had had to get creative in rearranging everything to fit the mech in without boxing in the other vessels—most of which were varying duplicates of the same freighter once used by Tyrus Rechs. But the young code slicer had slaved an AI to these ancient ships and made the job go faster than Broxin would have thought possible. It was clear that Captain Keel had put together a talented crew, and Broxin had liked Garret and Leenah from the first time she'd met them—though the circumstances then had been anything but pleasant.

That was a lifetime ago. And now, as she battle-planned while sitting among crates and boxes, she felt like she was reliving experiences from a lifetime even before that one, back when she was a commissioned officer in the Republic Marines. Only, back then, it was usually Gunny O'Neill who brought her something to eat and drink, not a servitor bot.

G232 placed a cup of tea and saucer down in front of her along with a small white plate that contained a dry, disintegrating cookie that she recognized as belonging to a very old Legion ration pack. "I thought you might benefit from a small snack, Miss Broxin."

Andien looked up at the bot and smiled. "Thank you, G2. That's very thoughtful."

"You're quite welcome," the bot said proudly. He waited in silent anticipation, but Andien had already gone back to work. "Pardon me, miss, but... I encourage you to drink it now. It was served at a temperature of fifty-seven degrees Celsius, which I have found to be optimal for human consumption. I regret to say that that cookie is prepackaged and won't do with cold tea. I have a much better recipe, but all of the ingredients I found in the pantry were no longer fit for human consumption."

Andien picked up the cookie and could feel it crumbling apart between her fingers. She bit off a corner of it, which caused more crumbs to tumble into her lap, and washed it down with a drink of tea that managed to get most of the grit out of her mouth. "Very good, G232. Thank you again."

"I'm so glad you like it. I'll get you a refill. Your cup is twelve percent empty."

The bot scurried off before Andien could tell him that this wouldn't be necessary. She blew a strand of hair out of her eyes and then went back to her datapad.

The battle plan that Kel Turner and the Legion forces on Kima—she still couldn't quite think of the planet as *Earth*—had drawn up were about as good as could be expected. The 131st Legion, relying on Republic military and Yawd allies to maintain control following their victory on Kima, would stage throughout Admiral Deynolds's fleet, standing by for the arrival of Thomas Roman and his Savage hulk. Meanwhile Kel Turner would defend the Savage vault from capture by the Savage proxies. Once the target arrived, the Legion would engage the Savages directly. On the ship, ideally, but if needed, on the planet's surface.

Andien couldn't think of a way to improve on that plan, though she knew that none of the principals liked it. Too much depended on the Savages doing what the Legion *hoped* they would do. And while everything they knew about the Savages suggested they *would* show up and step into the ambush, Broxin couldn't help but wish she knew where they were right now. She would much prefer to take the fight directly to them instead of waiting and reacting. She wondered if Chhun felt the same way.

It didn't matter. Going to them wasn't an option because no one knew exactly where this Savage hulk was.

G232 came back with a new teacup and replaced the mostly full cup he had left Andien with. "Here you are, miss. Fifty-seven degrees Celsius. Perhaps I should return with another cookie? I found additional ration packs while relocating the pantry."

"No. Thank you, no. I need to focus."

"Oh, yes. My apologies!" The bot hurried away, before pausing to say, "If I detect that you are in need of attendance, I will of course serve."

Andien went back to her thoughts. She was missing something. It wasn't an obvious thing. In fact, she doubted she even knew what it was. Certainly it wasn't something she was forgetting. She just... felt there was an additional component to this. A variable that needed to be inserted into the equation. Once she had the formula down, then she could begin solving for the unknowns.

The Savage forces that had arrived on other planets following the Gomarii invasions seemed to have been direct-jump insertion shuttles, with each planet being assigned a pre-determined number of these marines. And everywhere that those Savages had shown up, they'd been victorious.

Except on Sinasia. And now, it seemed, a few other worlds. But in every instance, this was only because the Gomarii and their forces had broken off contact and fled, leaving the Savages to face insurmountable numbers without a means of extraction.

Andien rubbed her temples. *Why? If it's because they discovered Turner's vault and Earth... wouldn't the Gomarii and the Savages both leave to secure it? Why sacrifice Savage marines, each of which is easily worth an entire platoon of Gomarii, at a minimum?*

She felt the presence of what she assumed was the bot. Like many servitor bots, he seemed more interested in serving the demands of his programming than helping the people he was designed to assist. Right now, Andien just needed some space and some time to herself. She was on the verge of snapping at G232 when she realized that the being behind her was not the servitor bot after all—but a wobanki.

"Skrizz," she said, shaking her head. "The Republic pumped I don't know how many billions of credits into me, and still I can't tell when a wobanki is sneaking up behind me."

The imposing cat-man purred, satisfied at this compliment, before padding around to face her. He stopped on the opposite side of the crate Andien had been using as a desk and squatted on his haunches, getting down to her level and in the process looking like a predator on the verge of pouncing. Being around a wobanki took a lot of getting used to. It was hard not to feel like you were on the dinner menu.

Skrizz yammered that he wanted something from Andien.

"And what is that?" she asked.

"Priz-mah."

Andien stared at the wobanki for a long moment. "You think I'm going to try and take her again?"

Skrizz shook his head and said that he knew she wasn't. But he understood that the ship where Prisma now was would be boarded. He wanted to be on one of those boarding parties—with Andien—but free to do as he pleased. No expectations of following orders. Either Captain Keel's or the Legion's.

"Well, there's no guarantee that I'll be boarding that ship, Skrizz. Praxus and I are going to rendezvous with a Cybar ship to take on a complement of Spartan war machines. I'll be standing by with them to deploy to wherever we're most needed. That *might* be the ship... or it might be the planet."

Skrizz yowled his insistence that she alter her plan and board the ship. As early as possible.

Andien gave a humorless, one-note laugh. "Skrizz, it's not lost on me the kinds of things that happen to people who turn down a determined wobanki. But what we're doing is bigger than any one individual wants." She waved a hand at all the modified light freighters now crowded at the front of the docking bay. "Why not ask Keel to let you fly one of these? He won't say no."

Skrizz was adamant that he go with *her*.

"Why?"

"*Cho tencha Keel tomma. Rav-ee tomma. Tencha tomma dakka oo-sheee. Priz-mah echu lee. Tencha Priz-mah no tomma et.*"

Because Keel and Ravi were going to do something to stop the Dark Ones that would get them both killed. They intended to get Prisma to safety first, but... Skrizz wanted to be there to be sure of that. And if Keel suspected that someone knew his plan, he might undertake it before there was a chance for interference.

In the hunt, the kill requires patience. A woban-ki proverb.

Andien understood what Skrizz was saying, but she was confused about how it could be true. "That's... that's not part of the plan, Skrizz. They're going to participate in the assault, same as me. How did you... what makes you think they're...?"

Skrizz tapped a long ear with his finger.

Andien nodded in understanding. *He ranges the ship. He is forgotten. He hears things. Everything.*

And...

"Tenchu Broxa no tomma et?"

Didn't I save you? Aboard the Cybar ship. The question carried a heavy implication critical to how wobanki viewed the order of things in the galaxy.

Don't you owe me for saving your life?

Andien frowned. It was Praxus who had saved her. But Skrizz... Skrizz had bought her time. He had tried to save her. She might well have died without him. That was true.

But this mission was still bigger than any personal debts.

"I can't take you with me, Skrizz, because I'm not sure I'll be needed on the ship."

Skrizz growled menacingly, low enough that only the two of them could hear.

Andien held up a calming hand. "But I have an idea. The Kublarens. They won't be left out of this fight. I'll write up this battle plan so that *you* fly them onto the ship."

Skrizz considered this, then said that he wanted the freedom to move through the ship on his own.

"Then I'll have you fly them to Kima. Just deliver them into the fight, then take off. No one will be the wiser. I won't tell a soul. Not even Praxus."

"*Kacheeni?*"

Promise?

"Promise. I'll get it arranged. Captain Keel won't turn it down. You know how to handle these ships. You flew one with Rechs, didn't you?"

Skrizz nodded and stood. His tailed swished once, heavily, across the ground. It was settled.

The wobanki padded away to find the Kublarens, who had set themselves up in one of the large fresher rooms meant for showering a full platoon of men all at once. There they luxuriated under a constant stream of water, though the indignant hurt over what the Savages had done to their world was never far from their hearts. They needed battle. Everything would come to a head soon. It had to. For their sake. For the galaxy's.

Andien adjusted her battle order, working Skrizz into the equation. She had just sent it to Captain Keel when Praxus found her.

"You have finished," the android said.

"Just."

"Makaffie has likewise finished. His findings will help us achieve victory. If it is possible."

"He can access the strand?" Andien asked.

"Yes. At will. He has been there before and has already uncovered a trove of useful information. We now understand why the Gomarii abandoned their Savage counterparts."

Praxus explained, as succinctly as possible, what Makaffie had learned about the complicated hierarchy of the Savages. Most illuminating was the discovery that Maestro, upon realizing that Kima was Earth, had made an independent drive to take hold of the vault, presumably to use what was there to unseat Roman and take control of the remaining Savage forces. That explained the withdrawal of Gomarii forces on various other worlds.

"The Savages are, above all, proud," Praxus said. "They will serve, but all see themselves as king. They wait in the wings to rule."

"Do we have any indication that Roman is aware of what's happening?"

"Not at the moment. However, I do not see how he will fail to notice the removal of Gomarii forces and their massing on Kima. It is only a matter of time. Which means that Kel Turner's forces will face increasingly severe attacks. It is paramount that he defend the Savage vault until Roman reveals himself."

Broxin took in a deep breath. "I just talked with Skrizz. If they can give us a clear landing zone, we can deliver some additional troops to support that goal. The Kublarens."

"Excellent. We can continue on as planned and commit our Spartan brothers and other resurrected Cybar allies to attack where most needed."

Andien's chrono chimed. "Time for the briefing."

"Excellent. Makaffie has asked me to present his findings on his behalf. Nilo is serving as his assistant and will also be absent from the meeting." Praxus tilted his head. "Should we request permission to take one of

Captain Keel's ships to faster acquire the Spartans, or do you anticipate that he will not be agreeable to an early separation?"

"I think everyone is keeping a few secrets close to their chest rigs right now, Praxus. I'm not sure what Keel will say. But one way or another, we'll be taking off once the mission brief is over."

26

When Crometheus fled the arcade, the bright sunshine of the world outside had been almost unbearable. It hit his eyes with an intensity that almost drove him back inside after only a few steps on the hot concrete sidewalk. The nearest comparison he could conjure up was leaving a darkened movie theater after a midday showing.

"Crometheus!"

Jazz.

"Yo, Cro!"

Julius.

They had called after him. He could hear their voices as the arcade door swung behind him. Jazz and Julius, who would always draw straws to see which of them would be the one to bluff their way into buying a single ticket to whatever R-rated movie the fledgling Eternals had decided couldn't wait for VHS. Always Jazz or Julius, because they could pull it off. Jazz had a way of talking his way out of or into things, and Julius, the son of a police captain and a real physical specimen, looked older than the high schoolers working the box office.

The light outside the arcade burned with that post-movie intensity. The sun brighter than it had been before. How had no one ever noticed how bright the sun was as it beat down on white, glittering sidewalks waiting to blind those who emerged from sitting inside a dark, air-conditioned theater for hours?

Coming out from the arcade was something even greater. It felt like awakening to that same summer movie-time experience but after a lifetime of utter blindness. There was a searing intensity to the light that made the backs of Crometheus's eyeballs ache. He buried his face in the crook of his arm, pressing the leather jacket tightly against his shut eyes and feeling the spikes on the elbow prickle his hand as he tried to force himself farther into the dark refuge.

He took a stumbling step forward, deeper into that otherworldly brightness. He felt the arcade beckoning behind him, offering a release from discomfort. He heard the voices of Jazz and Julius, those two great convincers who had so often opened the emergency exit to the theater after bluffing their way inside, acquiring for others the secrets of sex and violence those forbidden movies promised to teach, proctors of a reality that had never truly existed.

Real life, with all its titillations, was never like the movies. But it was fun anyway. Maybe turning around, heading back inside wouldn't be so bad.

No.

Crometheus had learned things. Remembered things. Uncovered them. And now...

And now...

What?

Now what?

He forced his arms down and surrendered his vision to the blinding light. Then he moved forward, groping his way snow-blind through a blizzard on a hundred-degree day, relying on his other senses as the cool of the arcade wilted beneath the scorching Southern California sun.

The daytime heat was almost unbearable. This was going to be one of those summers where all the lawns went brown. Only a fool would be out at midday like this. The arcade was cool. Cooler than this, anyhow.

That thought, Crometheus decided, was a part of the arcade's siren song. It was hot—it was always hot—but the streets were hardly empty. He could hear the signs of life of the city, and those sounds began to be slowly accompanied by a refocusing of his vision.

A disheveled bum sat with his back against a stucco wall, slumped beneath an iron-barred store window with a red brick sill. At his side was a bottle of malt liquor, sweating in its brown paper bag and looking far less glamorous than the one advertised in the shop window. The drunk, eyes shut, slid further down, his legs stretching out across the sidewalk as the fading, meager shadow cast by the building made its slow but inexorable retreat.

A younger man was dancing on a piece of flattened cardboard. A boom box placed at the edge of the makeshift dance floor blared Herbie Hancock, and a white Kangol hat like those worn on the other side of the country was tipped upside down and asking for spare change.

Crometheus's vision still clearing, he stumbled over the outstretched legs of the bum, who cursed him and thrust a vicious kick at his heels, sending the Eternal windmilling his arms on a collision course with the dancer. That man, arms slick with sweat and musky from failed deodorant, caught him and with a second curse shoved Crometheus into the shade of a nearby alley. It smelled like rotten Chinese takeout and piss, but the shade made Crometheus's eyes feel better almost at once, so he went down it, lip curled into a snarl against the odor.

He stepped over a heroin junky who might have been dead or might just be high—you couldn't really tell which. The dirty-faced woman lay beneath a blanket of discarded sections from the *LA Times*, her hairy, naked, and bruised thighs peeking out from underneath the sports section.

Cro's eyes felt better now, away from the unfiltered sunlight. The dry heat of the street gave way to a rank humidity, as though all the filth and juices of the alley were steaming all around him. He rubbed his eyes, opened them as wide as he could, and blinked until he felt his vision had fully returned.

He couldn't be far from the arcade yet, so he stopped and listed for Jazz or Julius. He heard the blare of police sirens instead. LAPD and not close.

The sound made him want to get away. He walked faster, looking over his shoulder. He could still see the dancer, who was picking up coins that must have spilled from his hat.

Crometheus wondered what he was supposed to do now that he was out of the arcade. The place was fading from his mind somehow, like it had all been a dream or a bad trip. He'd had one of those before—a bad trip. Just once. In the sixth grade.

It was during his first shedding. Crometheus, not yet an Eternal, had wanted to pursue the coolness that awaited a precious few. And his friends, playing their game of dragons, dungeons, demons and monsters, with rules they didn't quite understand, could never come with him on that journey. In fact, they would only slow him. Discredit him.

But maybe, if he could explain that he only played the game while high...

It didn't go well, although he managed to contain it in his own sweat-soaked body and tormented mind.

"You okay, Billy?"

He wasn't. He was seeing demons hiding in every shadow. So Billy—Crometheus—had simply gotten up, walked out, and never spoke to any of them again. There was no way justifying these old friends in the future life he wished to live.

They would have to be shed.

There are levels of being, facets of life, that require a sacrifice. A separation of everything from the old, often all at once. An initiation of the hardening of the heart and cauterizing of the soul. Then... the birth of a new identity.

Crometheus and his Eternals had achieved their coveted status.

Only his father would ask about his old friends. His mother, who might someday join the woman in the alley, was proud of his social achievements. She had peaked early in life and sought only ways to revisit former glory. Crometheus proved a suitable avatar.

But his father... he seemed to recognize what might have been. If his son had kept those old friends.

Crometheus decided he would go to his father's house.

No sooner had he made up his mind than another police cruiser blared a clipped siren and screeched its tires to a halt on the street Crometheus had just left. He turned and saw two officers in dark blue uniforms step out of the black-and-white. They spoke to the dancer, who pointed them toward the alley.

The cops moved quickly. Crometheus thought for a moment that they might be checking on the junkie... but their guns were inexplicably drawn.

He took a faltering step backward.

"Freeze!"

Cro turned and ran.

They fired. A bullet snapped overhead while another went wide and struck the wall, sending a flint of stone into Crometheus's face and drawing blood on his cheek.

Out of the alley he sprinted, navigating a city that seemed to be changing as though inside a dream. Here should be more shops, but instead he was in a neighborhood—the sprawling, endless suburbia of Los Angeles. He ran between houses, along a cedar fence that separated the properties. Crometheus jumped it into the yard on his right as a snarling pit bull leapt and barked angrily from the yard on his left.

He darted past crabgrass, dodging discarded children's toys—a Power Wheel, some Fisher Price plastic rings, and a pink plastic doll house, its color drained from too many days under the sun. The yard terminated at a garage that served as a rear border.

Panting, Crometheus turned. The dog had been following his progress, barking at him through the fence. Now it had gone back to rage against an officer who attempted to climb the fence.

Crometheus used a stunted palm tree to push his way up to the lip of the low garage roof, then he pulled himself up onto the blazing asphalt shingles. He ducked low to avoid a power line running from a pole in the alley to the garage and then onto the house. As he reached the roof's peak, he felt as though he would be shot, but the officer seemed stuck at the fence, so Crometheus went down the other side and dropped into a paved alley.

He saw the second officer turn into the alley in the patrol car, lights already flashing. He blipped his siren and began to drive toward him. Crometheus ran the other way, out of the alley, turning right and finding himself where he'd expected to be earlier: on a street lined with low-end shops and small businesses, convenience stores and four-hundred-square-foot shops run by single-owner operators—a tax preparer, shoe repair, someone who sold beads.

Not seeing the police behind him, Crometheus ducked into the convenience store. The electronic *bing-bong* chime seemed impossibly loud. He walked to the rear of the store, by the coolers, as the disapproving eyes of the Korean store owner followed him. Crometheus pretended to be interested in soda bottles and ice cream bars, watching from the corner of his eyes for the police.

The door chime sounded anew, and both officers stepped inside. Crometheus crept behind a display of Doritos next to a cardboard cutout of Jay Leno. He watched as the officers spoke to the store owner, who promptly pointed toward the back coolers. The cops spread out to approach on either side.

Crometheus, like an encircled rabbit, stood up and bolted for the only way out of the trap.

"Don't move!" one of the cops shouted.

Crometheus dove into a back room, bursting through a bead curtain and surprising a young man sitting at a circular break room table. The man yelled something in Korean as he Crometheus continued on past stacks of boxes awaiting restocking and out a receiving door into yet another alley.

But this time... it was evening when he stepped outside. The heat had faded, and a breeze sent a Styrofoam burger container scraping along the pavement.

Crometheus hesitated there, confused for a beat, then hurried down the alley. When he turned a corner and saw a phone booth, he crashed inside, closed the door, and quickly shed his jacket, letting it crumple at his feet. His blond, carefully spiked and styled hair was soaking wet with sweat. He hurriedly slicked it back and then leaned as casually as he could manage against the payphone wall and picked up the receiver.

He watched as the police officers ran past him, not so much as giving him a second look. His disbelief was snapped by an automated phone operator telling him, "If you'd like to make a call, please hang up and try again."

With a quick shake of his head, Crometheus put his finger on the hook and then fished in his pocket for a dime. He sent it in the slot and dialed his father's house.

"Hello?"

"Dad."

"Son? Whatever is going on, you can come home. We'll work it out."

Crometheus froze—and then slowly pulled the phone away from his ear.

"Son? Billy?"

He hung up the phone and exited the booth. Hands in pockets, head down, he traveled down the dusky streets.

27

The elm tree gave a clear view of Crometheus's father's house. It was a block away, on a corner lot, an oddity with deep roots and a history no one knew—it had always been there. It was the pride of its owners, the parents of one of Crometheus's friends. Back when he was just Billy, who liked games and Little League baseball.

That friend had been shed, and Crometheus wondered what he would think now, seeing him sitting on a branch in the tree under cover of night. Watching the police lights flash as cops in uniform milled about their cruisers and detectives in brown suits walked across the lawn, occasionally pausing to chat with his father, who sat on the front porch with a cup of black coffee.

The friend had gone off to college. There would be no embarrassment from being caught in the tree. No awkward conversations or explanations.

A part of Crometheus was sad that there wouldn't be, but the larger portion tried to formulate what to do next. He laid his forehead against the bark of the massive limb he hugged, knees and arms wrapped around it for stability. The leaves swayed in a warm breeze, and when Crometheus looked back up, a few of the uniformed police officers were scrambling toward their cars.

"What?" Crometheus mumbled. He looked around him and saw Mrs. Turner, his friend's mother, peeping through the curtains, a phone held up to her ear and staring right at him. "Oh, come *on...*"

The sound of helicopter rotors, ubiquitous in the night, seemed to have raced from Watts or Compton where they usually flew. Now a chopper was directly overhead, blowing the leaves fiercely and swaying the limb so that Crometheus had to hold on even tighter than before. A blinding spotlight shone down into the trees, searching for him. A block away, cruiser sirens sounded.

What could they possibly want with me? Crometheus asked himself. The arcade was fading from his mind, settling in as just that: an arcade. All of its secrets, what happened in the desert, Holly Wood... everything was drifting away like the plot of some old movie seen in childhood. He had to work at keeping it in the forefront of his mind.

The police would find him here, in the tree, and there would be no escaping them. He had to run. Now.

Crometheus slid over the side of the branch, hanging on as his feet dangled over a lawn that hadn't yet succumbed to brown patches. He waited for his momentum to swing his legs away from the great trunk of the elm and then dropped into the yard. Mrs. Turner shut her curtains in alarm as Crometheus hurdled the flower beds and traveled down a side yard that he still knew like the back of his hand.

The police searchlight followed, sending a circle of daylight but without its warmth in pursuit. There was a shed in the backyard with a flat roof that protruded into the alley far enough that the garbage trucks had learned to go around it, steering into the neighboring driveway to avoid clipping the overhang. If he timed his sprint properly, Crometheus might be able to dash from one side of the alley to the other there without being spotted. But first... a little misdirection.

The Turners had a high concrete and cinderblock wall that ran along a gutter. The angle of the helicopter's spotlight kept the gutter in the shadow, but the alley itself was awash with light. Crometheus ran into the open and moved down the alley in plain view of the helicopter, which followed him. Then, before reaching the end of the yard, he darted back into the gutter and doubled back along the wall. The spotlight searched for seconds, sweeping back and forth as the pilot circled around to get a better angle from the opposite side.

Crometheus returned to the flat-roofed car port built off the shed and, seizing his opportunity, sprinted across the alley and into the next yard, one thick with wisteria growth atop trellises that hid him from the helicopter's searching light. He continued through to the front yard, catching a glimpse of a family washed in the blue glow of the television set, sitting in the darkness of their living room.

He ran into the street and was nearly run over by a gleaming blue 1964 Chevy Impala convertible, its top down, which had roared its way around the corner to stop directly in front of him. It was all Crometheus could do not to slam into the door. Four black men wearing blue filled the vehicle. One of the men in the back pushed himself up out of his seat, sat on the back of the car, and slid to the middle.

"Inside, cuz," the driver said.

Crometheus took a step backward. "I..."

"Get inside, Crometheus," the man in the back said. He looked down at Crometheus from behind black sunglasses. An AK-47 lay across his lap.

Crometheus squinted. "Jules?"

"Naw," the man, who looked exactly like Jules, replied. "Not this time."

The driver nodded casually at the man who looked like Jules. "That's Tre. To me. To you, it's Jules. Get in."

"And who are you?" Crometheus asked the driver, swallowing a lump that was growing in his throat.

The driver looked straight at him. "I'm a Crometheus. Same as you, Billy."

The words struck a terror in Crometheus's heart, and he might have turned and run again if not for the return of the helicopter and its spotlight, now shining directly on the car.

"Stay where you are," the police pilot demanded from the helicopter's loudspeaker.

"Tre," said the driver. "Gonna need some time."

"On it." Jules—Tre—lifted his legs and spun around, then slid himself down off the trunk to stand behind the vehicle. He held the AK-47 at his shoulder and began firing at the helicopter, shattering the light and causing the chopper to swerve away in evasive action.

A revolver's bang erupted from down the street and a bullet blasted out one of the headlights. The patrol officers had opened fire on the car, shooting from behind the open doors of their own vehicle, blue and red lights flashing through the neighborhood.

"Inside!" the driver yelled, reaching for Crometheus, who needed no further encouragement. He jumped inside, falling into the back seat.

Outside, Tre shifted his fire to the police cruiser, riddling it with bullets and sending the two officers onto the street for cover. He fired the AK's magazine dry, then pulled another from baggy back pockets.

"Be a lot easier if you got back in the car," the driver called out.

Tre looked longingly at his targets, then scurried over the trunk and dropped in next to Crometheus, squeezing him in the middle as the car sped off, leaving tire tracks. They squealed around corners and caught air as they crested hills, sending sparks flying behind the classic car.

"Where are we going?" Crometheus asked. He couldn't decide just which of the many things currently causing existential crises bothered him the most. The cops being after him, his father evidently selling him out, being in a car hurtling through the night with a bunch of gangbangers, or being told that the driver, who looked nothing like him, was him, but Tre, who looked exactly like Jules, was not Jules.

"Someplace safe," the driver answered.

"Not with the cops chasing us," Crometheus insisted. The helicopter was still missing from the picture, but several squad cars had picked up the chase, sirens screaming and lights flashing as the high-speed chase continued.

"Just gotta slow them down," the driver said. "Tre?"

Tre spun around and began to send single-shot rounds toward the pursuing cars, causing them to swerve wildly. Another sharp turn nearly tossed Crometheus from the vehicle, but they were putting distance between themselves and their pursuers.

"First thing to remember," the driver said. "This is as real as that arcade of yours was. It's designed to appeal to the morality of who you are. You don't like shooting at cops, right? Well Maestro knows that. This is one of his snares to get you back and working with the Eternals."

Crometheus shook his head. "What are you... I don't understand."

"You will, kid. We all do." The driver made another turn and led them toward a massive eight-lane overpass. "Second thing to know is that you can use that to your advantage. You did it for a long time when you got yourself into that fantasy world. Hid for a long time. We thought you'd make it through to join us then. Didn't pan out."

"You mean *Into the Unknown*. That's just a game."

Tre laughed next to him. "It's all a game, homie. Just try not to fry ya brain thinkin' too hard about it."

The driver held up a scolding index finger, like a teacher correcting his student. "That's Maestro working you over. Bad Thought and all that trash. Ignore it."

They raced beneath the overpass. When they came out on the other side, the helicopter was back. This time, Tre didn't wait for the driver to ask him to shoot. He sprayed fully automatic fire at the low-flying craft, striking it repeatedly until he was rewarded with the sudden spray of fuel or some other fluid. The helicopter listed, then went into a violent spin. It zipped off to the side and hit the ground, erupting in a ball of flames.

"Hell yeah," Tre said, and settled back down in his seat like just another passenger.

They took an onramp and began to cruise along the Five.

"I still wanna know where we're going," Crometheus said.

"To meet the others," the driver said. "Your mind is trying to shut out what you've already figured out. Gotta fight that."

"Okay. I get that. The arcade, the fights... I get that." It was coming back to Crometheus, the things he'd discovered about himself inside the arcade. Holly Wood and Thomas Roman and fighting as a Savage marine. "But who are the others?"

"You. Me. All of us. There are exactly fifty copies of Crometheus. Take your pick as to which one is the original—if he's even still there. Personally, my money is on me. You might think otherwise. Enough of us work together, and we can shift the balance of power and get Maestro out of his position. But we're a few short of a majority."

"How short?"

"Well, counting you we've got... three. The rest are still fighting as Eternals."

"Three? Out of fifty?"

"Yeah, but don't worry. We just got a visitor who's gonna help us with those odds. Does the name 'Dirty Wizard' ring any bells in that head of yours?"

Visions of New Vega, vicious battles against legionnaires and a victory snatched away at the last possible second flooded Crometheus's mind. It was as if the name were a cipher that unlocked more of the swirling puzzle in his head.

"Yeah. That name definitely rings a bell."

28

**Vault of the Golden King
Earth**

Kel watched as the teams looked over the open plastite cargo boxes, stocked with everything from charge packs to comm replacement parts to meal gels to fresh socks.

"Why so many socks?" asked Smoker, the youngest member of Zombie Squad.

"Never enough socks," called out three other leejes from the various squads.

In drawing down on Kima to work the Savage vault, Shot Caller, aka Kel Turner, had assembled one special kill team comprising a mix of former ICE members and his own hand-picked leejes of the current day and age. Now he'd ended up with two more teams.

Task Unit Zombie had been tasked with rescuing Alden Masters, a master sergeant with friends all the way to the top of the Legion. They had succeeded in that mission, and now Masters had taken command of the squad after Julius MakRaven, one of the Legion's most notorious command sergeant majors, had fallen while defending the squad at the cave outside. The sergeant major's body lay a few feet away wrapped in his poncho and attended to by a Legion working dog the squad had somehow gotten saddled with.

The additional extra unit came in the form of Kill Team Victory, run by First Sergeant Okimbo Bombassa, a Kimshana native with a stern reputation to match. The senior NCO's team had been dispatched by General Chhun to recover the Zombies and their principal, Masters.

The two teams' arrival here was an unexpected windfall that Shot Caller wasn't going to waste. The convergence of so many pieces had resulted in a near platoon-strength number of hardened leej operators for him to now wield in the defense of the cave.

Or rather, the Savage vault built into that cave. Except the word "vault" didn't even begin to do it justice. It was an impossibly massive structure for its time. And like Carter, Kel had quickly recognized this place for what it was: an underground Savage hulk. It lacked engines or weapons, but it was a hulk in every other element of its design.

Just lying here, buried for millennia, on Earth.

It was a mystery that afforded only one explanation. One made all the clearer by the overload of hagiographic propaganda in the entryway. This was the *first* Savage hulk. The first "lighthugger," as its promotional holos called it. But it was never intended to fly, to venture into the stars and seed new civilizations. No. It was intended only to *sell*.

This... was the showroom model.

It also seemed to have been designed to double as a doomsday bunker. A wise contingency plan in case things spiraled out of control on Earth faster than Thomas Roman could control.

Now, Turner's job was to keep the bunker sealed up until he could force the enigmatic Savage to come out here and attempt to pry it open himself. If General Rex had been correct, such a scenario was sure to happen once the Savages realized where Earth was and who was in control of it.

"Hey, Master Sergeant," said Lynx, the Zombie Squad sergeant. "My guys have commo with one of the shovels."

"I'll take it," Bombassa cut in. "I spoke to them earlier."

"The shovels" were yet another potential unit at their disposal, this one comprising Repub Army engineers. Kel Turner nodded in appreciation of the news. Though they weren't legionnaires, these soldiers were a force capable of harassing the enemy outside and delaying their eventual push to get inside the vault. It was hard to batter down a blast door when you were swept completely away from it. Kel was ending up with more assets on the ground than he had ever hoped for. Which was saying something, because additional assets beyond the current team he'd brought to Kima were still making final arrangements to reinforce what would be a brutal fight.

Kell waited for Bombassa to finish his comm, then said, "Let's hear the word on the engineers."

Bombassa had his answer ready. "A little over platoon strength left from the company. Most believed to be captured or killed by the Gomarii landing outside. They're pinned down by a mixed force of zhee and Gomarii. I instructed them to hold the hostiles as long as possible. My kill team will move to help them break out."

Kel nodded. "Excellent. After you link up with the shovels and get them out of their predicament, I want you to position them to form a solid defensive line. Then we're going on offense. I need you to stop the Gomarii from cutting their way through the cave-in. The longer they aren't in here, the more antsy our Savages will get."

"Yes, sir."

Kel turned to Carter. "Carter, you keep working on interior defenses. We have to convince the Savages that they won't get what they want unless they come and do it themselves. And if we can hold out, I'm getting word from the Repub that some additional assets might get sent our way. We're gonna need 'em."

"Sir," said Carter, "if we're expecting reinforcements inbound, then knocking out that Gomarii slave ship, or at least its PDCs, would go a long way toward giving them a safe landing."

Kel considered the man's suggestion. He was right, but such a task wouldn't be easy. The wellspring of numbers he had unexpectedly profited from could swiftly be erased if they undertook such a mission and it went awry. But Kel Turner was Dark Ops, and one constant in the Legion had been the capability of operators such as him. The young men serving now were every bit as good. Perhaps better.

"Sergeant Bombassa?" Kel asked.

"We can work out a way, sir."

That was enough for Turner. He nodded. "Target of opportunity. Primary objective remains keeping this vault out of enemy hands until the Big Savage shows up. A bunch of dead leejes isn't gonna make that easier."

"Understood, sir," Bombassa said, and then left to put a plan together with the rest of Kill Team Victory.

"How about us, sir?" Sergeant Lynx asked, wanting to know where his Zombie Squad would be needed.

"You'll provide security at the back door. You'll also stand by as a QRF for the kill team."

"Ooah," Lynx said.

Kel gave a curt nod. "Any other questions? Good. Jock and lock in three minutes. Get after it, people."

Before Kel could walk away to the combat information center he'd set up inside the vault, Masters pulled him aside. "Hey, sir, I know I'm not officially listed as the Zombie sergeant, but since the smaj went down, I'm the senior man on their team."

"You're also cut up and running on stims," Kel admonished. "I know you're a capable leej. You wouldn't be here if you weren't, Master Sergeant. But there comes a time when you have to stand down for your brothers. Those men are primed and ready to get after it. They weren't tortured for days before running this fight all day."

"Yes, sir, but I'm good to go. I wanna KTF."

Kel stared at the young man for a long second. "I want my medic to look you over first. If he's good with it, we'll get you back in the game. There's too much riding on this to play the ego card, brother."

Masters gave a quick nod. "Roger that, sir."

The "back door" that Kel Turner's team had taken to breach the vault had required a near-blind swim through dangerous swamp waters that passed through a narrow, submerged cavern before opening up into a deep blue pool in a cavernous chamber. That chamber led to a solid blast door that was rated just as strong as one at the main entrance. The only difference was, this door hadn't been guarded by a cybernetic horror. This was the same pathway that Tyrus Rechs had first taken to breach the vault a thousand years earlier, when he turned the place into a highly specialized monitoring station waiting for Thomas

Roman to show himself. Now it was the path traversed by Kill Team Victory—only moving in the opposite direction—as they left the vault to free up the embattled Republic engineers and, hopefully, take out the Gomarii slave ship and its powerful guns.

A legionnaire's bucket broke the swamp's surface and ran a perimeter scan before dropping back into the mire. Pina, the scout, spied a single zhee squad that lay against a berm on a downslope beside the pond, oblivious to the fact that hostiles could hit them from behind. They were apparently unaware of the underwater back door through the murky swamp, and assumed, not without reason, that no army would make the trip across those deep and penetrating bayous.

"Team of zhee engaging unknown element," Pina reported to the others still submerged and waiting beneath him. "They're doing a pretty good job. Coordinated firing positions supplying suppressive fire while a swing element is hitting whoever they're shooting at from the flanks from either side of the hill curving back toward the slope."

The legionnaire sent visuals of what he was seeing to coincide with his report.

"Move to make the hit," Bombassa ordered from the depths, breathing easily inside his sealed helmet like all the other legionnaires.

Seven additional buckets crested the water and swam in a silent wedge toward the line of donks holding the hill. There were ten targets in all. Six firing from the hill and four working as a mobile rifle team. Bombassa pushed a countdown timer in the team's HUD to coordinate their actions. The countdown hit zero and, as one, the leejes each sent a single shot into the back of their assigned donk's head.

Six zhee on the hill dead. Only the mobile rifle team remaining.

Pina peeled off to the side of the hill where he could get a clear line of sight to the four remaining zhee. With a fresh charge drum locked into his automatic blaster, he sent multiple controlled bursts from the weapon, gunning down the donk fighters with each salvo of three to five bolts. The zhee team slumped into the murky, diseased undergrowth common to this side of the mountain. "Four E-KIAs. Hill clear."

Confident they had secured their side of the hill, Bombassa called into the company frequency he'd used to make contact with the engineers a few hours before. "Any station this net, this is Legion element Victory Seven."

"Victory Seven, this is Bravo Three. We're defending against squad plus zhee fighters with Gomarii handlers. I'm tagging you our loc. Over."

This was the same lieutenant Bombassa had made contact with previously, the one running the platoon on the outer cordon. "I see your grid. We're back side of the hill. Seven men moving to you. Over."

"Thank Oba! I copy seven men. Come to us."

Kill Team Victory moved hastily around the hill, still dripping from their swim through the dank swamps. They found tired, harried, and haggard-looking Repub Army engineers waiting for them, rifles relaxed but still ready. The soldiers showed visible relief upon seeing the legionnaires.

A Repub sergeant came forward and led the kill team through their defenses to the lieutenant.

The engineer platoon had heavily entrenched them-selves along a winding ridge that overlooked the low ground where the ponds collected at the start of the great swamp glades. The sergeant stopped at the base of the ridge, preferring to stay with his men in their dug-out positions below. From above, the lieutenant motioned the legionnaires to climb, making room for them to work themselves into the fighting positions.

"You guys sure can dig," Pina said. The fighting po-sitions were ample. Almost roomy given the time that had passed.

"Kind of our thing, Leej," the lieutenant replied. He gestured toward the zhee positions. "We're getting ham-mered out here. The last group through put a blanket of bolts on us and then dropped off that squad you took out before runnin' for it."

"Ran off, huh?" Nobes said. "Why haven't they just committed to rolling you guys up?"

"I think they just want to keep us here. Bulk of the force is working on getting our equipment up and run-ning. They want inside that cave we were trying to dig you out of."

"Tell me more about that force," Bombassa said. "Numbers, positions, species... whatever you've observed."

The engineer shook his head. "We haven't had much time to get a good look. I sent two scouts and neither of them made it back. What we've seen so far is mostly zhee and Gomarii. No idea on numbers... guess it depends on whether that slave ship they parked down there was full of slaves or soldiers. I can't get eyes close enough to say. They have the other side of this ridge locked down.

You stick your head out at the high risk of not keeping it attached."

"Understood." Bombassa looked around at his men. He could feel the glares radiating through the helmets. Big brother wasn't taking too kindly to how the enemy had treated the engineers. The team leader went to his L-comm after excusing himself to the lieutenant for a moment. "Team. Objectives are going to be harder to achieve if they realize the engineers can push out of containment. Suggestions for recovering the shovels and maintaining the surprise we need?"

Nobes, the team intelligence sergeant and second stripe, said, "This ridge is gonna be a nightmare to climb, but I think there's an answer if we can do it."

The legionnaires looked up the steep mountain ridge. The spine was a razor's edge, with scant holds on either side. But it wasn't difficult for the other leejes to see what Nobes was thinking. They could climb on the opposite side of the ridge, out of sight of the Gomarii, until they reached a copse of forested trees high up. Using that for concealment, they could then work themselves across and down an equally steep ridge which would allow them to descend undetected right into the valley near the slave ship.

"You're saying we can make the climb and double back to get in close to the Gomarii operations outside the cave," Bombassa said.

"That's right, Top. If we leave Nix and Wello, they can work with the shovels to drop some zhee once we're in position. We can support from the ridge as needed, but use the initial confusion of the battle to make our primary."

Nix popped his finger knuckles with his thumb. "About time we get a bit of payback for Neck. I figure ten of theirs for every one of ours oughta do it."

"Fine," Bombassa said. "Two men down shouldn't prevent us from proceeding with the plan. Anything else?"

There was nothing further.

Bombassa gave a curt, fractional nod. "Don't forget nothin'."

"Always make 'em pay," Nix responded, and then, along with Wello, filled the engineer lieutenant in on what the kill team was going to attempt.

The rest climbed. A grueling, painful ascent that tested the limits of their Legion training. Though they moved hidden by the spine of the ridge from most of the hostiles, they nevertheless moved slowly and deliberately, not relying solely on their mimetic camouflage to keep them unseen from any spotters or snipers.

It took three hours to reach copse of thick threes nine hundred meters above where they had started.

"Okay, this is high enough," Bombassa announced, breathless but sounding strong. "Nobes... get us a new fix on what's below."

The intelligence sergeant went to the edge of the alpine tree line while the rest of the team recovered.

"Think any donks ever made this climb?" Pina asked.

"Hell no," Doc Chance answered. "*I'm* barely hacking it."

Nobes came back with his report. "Bad news. There's too many zhee down there for the shovels to break out, even with Nix and Wello helping. We'd have to send some men back down to provide enough firepower to achieve a breakthrough."

"We split the team and we might not be able to achieve our primary, much less storm the slave ship," Pina said.

"Yeah," agreed Toots. "Maybe we just need to tell Nix and Wello to adjust. Have 'em help the shovels keep from getting overrun in case the donks try to roll 'em once we get on board and blow the ship."

There was an unspoken, and grim, reality underlying that suggestion. The kill team fully intended to both take out the drilling team and blow the slave ship. But without the shovels on hand to engage the Gomarii and zhee hostiles in the area, the odds of escape weren't great.

Bombassa had been monitoring the observation data Nobes had recorded from the ridge. "Maybe we don't need to board the ship," he said. "I think I see a way we can shut down the PDCs from outside. Even with half a team."

He quickly outlined a plan. Instead of destroying the mining lasers and heavy equipment, he proposed sending in a small team to take possession of it—and use it against the slave ship. It might work, *if* the shovels and remaining Dark Ops leejes could break out and draw fire away from them.

"Yeah," Nobes said, his enthusiasm growing as he repeated the word. "Yeah. We get that mining laser and some free time, we can slag the PDCs enough to clear the skies for an airborne insertion."

"I like it," Pina added. "Who knows what kind of defenses might be inside the ship anyway? Remember that Gomarii boat KT-Razor helped the hullbusters take down a couple years back? Place was like an ambush funhouse."

"Sounds like we have our adjustment decided," Bombassa said.

He split the team into two, and sent one half to position themselves as they saw best in order to help facilitate the engineers' breakout. "If and when you can, move toward KP to assist with our exfil," he instructed them.

"KP" was what the team had taken to calling the backdoor waterway—short for the original nickname, Kiddy Pool.

As half of his kill team made preparations to assist Nix, Wello, and the shovels, Bombassa led the other half into the next phase of the new plan. They filtered through the trees, moving along a saddle that sat behind the second ridge. This path was less visually obscured, but their camouflage was sufficient to hide them until they descended into the inky canopy of sap-soaked trees and skeletal vines that would lead out to the flat earth where the slave ship had landed before the cave entrance. There they paused to take in additional information from their up-close view.

Chief of which was a clearer picture of the Gomarii slave ship.

The thing was huge—easily the length of a seamball stadium, and had crushed an expansive level of the tall black forest to make its landing. It was smooth in spaces and rough in others, if two design teams had compromised on the hull and just built their different sections to fit. But the one design element no one could fault was its firepower. Its rail guns, orbital lasers, and missile batteries were a defensive team's worst nightmare. They were relatively few in number, but powerful enough to destroy entire city blocks from any altitude. You didn't need a lot of those to make life short for any featherheads trying to land in the vicinity. The cost to any reinforcements attempting an airborne insertion would be painfully high. And as Kel Turner had said, the day of days would go a whole lot better if Kill Team Victory could clear the way for additional support. Though exactly who or what that would be was still elusive.

Nobes gave a whistle. "Seeing it all from here really makes you appreciate what that artillery strike MakRaven called in did for his team. Must've killed a few entire tribes' worth of donks."

He sent a burst of what he captured with his helmet to the other men in his kill team. Spread before him were stacks of dead zhee filling the swampy terrain leading away from the cave. This was exactly where Task Unit Zombie and Sergeant Major MakRaven had trapped the advancing zhee in a brutal pounding of artillery between the long run to the swamps beyond the cave and the incline of the mountain.

"Mak made 'em pay," Pina said.

Bombassa shared the assessment, but didn't say so. His mind was on other things. "I want to know if they have prisoners," he urged. "The engineers were hit and split up. What we saw on the way up isn't all that was sent to dig Masters out."

After a few moments of scanning, Pina announced, "You called it, Top."

He shared his bucket's feed. Captured members of Bravo Company stood in a makeshift paddock of poles projecting an "invisible" energy fence that was nonetheless visible in the legionnaire's HUD. The Republic troopers languished under the watchful eye of a squad of Gomarii. A blue-skinned commander in grey and red armor pointed to one of the prisoners, barking an order that the bucket couldn't pick up at such long range.

"Don't like the looks of that," Nobes murmured.

The prisoner was taken and presented for inspection. The Gomarii commander slathered its mouth tendrils over the engineer's face and then ordered him stripped naked. An ener-chain collar was placed around his neck, and the captive was slathered by the large commander's wet mouth tendrils as he "tasted" the difference in emotions.

"Shoulda gone to war with the blues as soon as we learned what happened on Herbeer," Toots growled.

"Keep focus," Bombassa ordered. He converted the scene in front of them into a map on his battle board, then marked it up with assignments for everyone on the team, updating the plan as the situation developed. Clipping the board onto the front of his armor, he then slithered forward to go over the higher ridgeline. "Okay. Time to head back down."

"Dig a hole, fill it up," Doc Chance grumbled as he followed Bombassa over the top and down the opposite side of the ridge, which would bring them up close with their target as it let out by the swamps. Much closer than they could have hoped to have gotten by running across the open terrain or enemy-facing ridgelines initially available to them.

"Moving down," Bombassa told the rest of his team.

The climb down went much faster than the climb up, though the steepness of the slope made the descent feel that much more dangerous. Titanic craters and deep fissures along their route spoke of the orbital weapons the Gomarii had used to put the engineer company on their heels. Bombassa was glad for the erratic terrain. Combined with their mimetic camo, the upturned slope provided plenty of opportunity for a stealth approach. And the farther they moved, the more aware Bombassa was of the hulking slave ship. Its repulsors were strong enough to make his fingers tingle, even at distance.

It took only a fraction of the time they'd spent ascending to reach the dead forest that came to the edge of the swamps—a place of black-sapped, towering pines and no other vegetation. Zhee foot patrols moved lazily in the area, not bothering to check in or around the fallen timbers that the kill team hid themselves in. Bombassa directed them to cross the high side of the engagement area, which let them stay in the tree line while still moving ever closer to their targets.

After verifying the team's targets and readiness, Bombassa went to the L-comm. "Nix, we're in position. Get those engineers out of that grave they dug into."

"KTF," Nix replied.

"KTF," echoed Toots, who had been part of the team sent to help with the breakout. He and his squad were ready to push fire down on the heads of the zhee.

"Execute," Bombassa ordered.

The shooting started a moment later.

As the zhee began to break in a braying frenzy, caught unaware by the kill team's maneuver, Nix and Wello led the engineers into a second strike that rolled the donks' lazily exposed flank. In turning to shoot at the elevated legionnaires, they exposed themselves to an enemy they *knew* was dug in. Fierce as the zhee were in combat, their tactical discipline was as poor as ever.

Gomarii hurriedly attempted to send reinforcements, not wanting a breakout of the engineer force.

"Toots, we're moving into our next positions," Bombassa called over L-comm as he and his team darted out of the woods and skirted the distracted zhee and Gomarii elements. "Are you able to break fire from the zhee and support on my mark?"

"Shovels could do this without us at this point," Toots answered. "We got you, Top."

Now was when Bombassa's new plan was put into action. The Gomarii work crew had for some time now been operating a drilling laser near the mouth of the cave, trying to break through the cave-in so they could access the vault. But the laser was now off, suggesting they might well have already cut a way through. Bombassa gave that a high probability, given the relatively small number of Gomarii now manning the equipment. Either way, stopping them from boring further, or even through the vault door, was Kill Team Victory's objective. And if all went well, Victory was about to kill two birds with one drilling laser.

Bombassa watched through his HUD as Pina positioned himself against the back leg of one of the many six-legged mech-loaders abandoned in the area. As instructed, he'd chosen one that looked unharmed and fully operational. That would be critical to their objective.

"Pina. Get ready."

"Born ready." Pina threaded the suppressor on his pistol—a slug thrower meant to avoid visual detection—and extended the shoulder brace, giving him more leverage for a quiet hit made at distance... as long as it wasn't too far away. He centered his sights on the Gomarii commander who was screaming his displeasure at a pair of collared humans working the drilling laser. The slaver wanted faster work. It was clear the sudden uptick in fighting by the engineers had the alien worried. He wanted a breakthrough into the cave. Yesterday.

"Nobes?" Bombassa said through the L-comm.

"In position, Top."

"Execute," Bombassa called.

Pina fired a single round. The bullet tore through the commander's skull, splattering bits of tendril and brackish blood. The commander's legs failed him, and he slumped into the muck.

At the same moment, Nobes jumped from the space where he'd been hiding and raced for the drill. Sliding to a stop next to the machine, he picked up the control box, killed the beam, and halted all progress in cracking open the vault. The human prisoners operating the drill scattered, some scrambling for the weapon of the dead Gomarii while others simply ran away.

The two Gomarii security who had been flanking the cave rose up and aimed their weapons at this new arrival, but they held their fire in the absence of orders to shoot in the direction of the critical device. Unlike the zhee, the Gomarii were disciplined fighters, and they understood that the drilling laser was critical to their primary objective.

That allowed Nobes to work unscathed for the moment, provided he kept the laser between himself and the security element.

One of the Gomarii brought his armored gauntlet up to his face, activating some kind of holo-control interface, perhaps to seek orders. But before he could speak, his face exploded in a shower of gore-soaked skull fragments.

"Hit," Nix said, cycling the power on his N-18 sniper rifle for another shot from the distant ridge where the engineers had been trapped.

Another shot and the second Gomarii shared the same fate as the first.

"Hit," Bombassa said into the L-comm.

The voices of more Gomarii roared from inside the cave. Apparently the laser crew *had* dug themselves an opening, and these Gomarii had likely been sent inside to be sure the entrance was clear. It would have only been a matter of time before the device was set to widen the opening and then drill right through the vault door.

Nobes quickly wrapped a spent charge pack with explosive det-wire and tossed it toward the cave entrance. A burp of chalky black smoke threw mud and flak in all directions.

No one exited the cave entrance. Nobes kept working.

But by now the enemy forces had finally realized what had been happening around the cave mouth while they were busy responding to the Republic Army's breakout. Hools left the containment battle and turned heavy machine blasters to send bolts roaring across the space while additional Gomarii warriors came racing down the ramp of their slave ship, ready to get their forces back on track.

"Drill secured," Nobes announced.

"Phase two," Bombassa called into the comms. So far their plan was working as intended, not at all suffering from the reduction in operator strength needed to get the engineers out of their predicament.

Pina climbed into the six-legged mech-loader he'd covered behind and fired up the machine to a seat-vibrating hum familiar to anyone who had spent time operating one of the Repub military's baseline vehicles. Shots rang off the impervisteel armor, twanging off into the trees as the legionnaire drove the mech toward the cave.

"Inbound for pickup," Pina announced. The mech lumbered, unhurried. "C'mon, c'mon. Speed it up."

When he had moved in close enough, he lowered the boom arm, took hold of the drill, and hoisted it up. Then he angled the loading crane to aim the drill directly at the Gomarii hulk. The movement gave him a sight picture on his targets, but also revealed a new, more pressing problem.

"Guys!" he shouted. "I see a blue about to dust me with a rocket launcher!"

Doc Chance threaded the alien's leg with a large-bore blaster bolt that tore the limb from the slaver's body. The launcher fell together with the Gomarii who bore it, unfired, and the weapon clattered down the ramp as its user writhed in agony, his leg now a stump that sprayed blue ichor. The rest of the Gomarii fire team ran down the ramp without showing the least compassion for their fallen comrade. One of them did, however, take notice of the fallen rocket launcher.

Bombassa dropped that one with a shot center mass. The bolt smashed into the chest plate with a shower of sparks and the Gomarii fell to the blood-slicked ramp.

"Tracing," Doc said. The medic's N-18 sniper blaster barked another bolt on target, finishing off Bombassa's kill.

"Thanks," Pina said. He finished aligning the drill and called into the L-comm. "Flip the switch, Nobes."

Nobes had moved to cover behind the mech-loader, but he exposed himself long enough to mash the activator button on the drill's control box, bringing the golden beam back to life. It shot forth into the Gomarii vessel, eating through the dorsal hull and chewing into the superstructure, leaving metal dripping from the frame.

"Get that beam on the PDCs," Bombassa called. The initial boring was impressive, but not what they'd come to do.

Streaking flashes of red and blue blaster bolts slammed against the mech-loader. "Trying!" Pina said.

He ducked in the cab as the forces on the ground concentrated their fire on this new, unexpected threat. Most of the attacks ricocheted off into the trees, but a single bolt fired by a Hool pierced the mech and lanced through Pina's upper shoulder and part of his neck. The force of the blast slammed him to the side of the cabin, tossing his hands across the control levers and throwing off the line of the beam. The laser drill's raging lance flashed danger-ously as it bobbed at the end of the crane's swaying grip, cutting three Gomarii slavers in two in one upward arc that started at the mid-section of the first and took off the clavicle and head of the last.

Pina huffed at the pain, dislodged a blood clot caught in his throat, pulled up his bucket, and spit the glob on the floor. He regained control of the machine and put the drill back on target, ignoring Nobes's attempts to get him to switch places. Their orders were to turn the slave ship's proximity defense systems into molten slag. The time to get it done was now, and there might not be another op-portunity.

The Gomarii's success in freeing the cave of its block-age now came back to bite them. For just then Zombie Squad entered the fray, emerging from the cave to take advantage of an enemy that had left their rear exposed. The legionnaires sent rapid, directed bursts that finished off the remainder of the shooters.

"Nix," Bombassa said into the L-comm, "I still need those shovels to help us get the pressure off of us down here."

"We're pushing over the ridge now, Top. Nix out."

"Pina, man," Nobes implored, "you gotta let me take the controls here."

"Just... gotta... fix it," Pina gargled into the L-comm.

It was clear that there wasn't time to target the drill at all of the slave ship's defensive weapons, one by one.

But this had been anticipated. Fortunately, Dark Ops had learned that there was more than one way to scuttle a ship, even one this size. The final fallback point in Bombassa's plan was underway.

Pina pried the controls forward, then cut them off at the stems with his vibro-enhanced combat knife, effectively locking the drill in place while sending the mech-loader marching directly for the slave ship.

"Set it," he said.

Nobes, moving alongside the slow-moving loader, exposed himself again as he activated the laser's as-set-denial mode. This would begin an internal countdown that would increase the laser intensity to a point that it eventually would explode—and the boom would be a very big one indeed. Once the clock was ticking, he helped Pina down from the cab. The pair activated their mimetic camo and ran for the tree line, with Nobes applying skinpacks to his fellow leej as they ran.

"All Repub elements, this is Nobes. The burn is set. Cover in place. I say again. Cover in place."

Zombie Squad moved back into the shelter of the cave mouth as the engineers fought to a standstill against the larger zhee, Hool, and Gomarii force that had been sent to contain them. But the shovels were keeping things dangerous enough to give Kill Team Victory the room they needed to break off and get clear.

The heavy machine lumbered forward, its drill beam clearing the way until it collided physically with the slave ship. It was an anticlimactic moment; the mech-loader strained against the back of the starship, unmoving against the massive Gomarii slaver, though its beam continued its burn. The point, however, was not to move the capital ship; rather, it was to get the laser as close to the ship as possible.

A lone Gomarii commander slid down to the edge of the ramp, armed with a man-portable missile system, and aimed the weapon at the drilling laser, looking to end the machine's reign of terror. The Gomarii pressed the launcher support pad into his shoulder, but he was too late. Before he could let the missile off the chain, the drill reached its ruinous exertion point and detonated. Its self-destruct ravaged the ship, sending shock waves through multiple layers of hull plating and decks that had already been bored through and weakened by the beam. Liquefied metal splattered away from the great ship, setting parts of the inky landscape on fire and shrouding the mountain in a sackcloth haze that blocked out all but the barest scraps of daylight.

Captured engineers in the makeshift paddock seized the opportunity provided by the chaos. As the Gomarii around them all scrambled to save the ship, the engineers made a break for it. Several escapees were gunned down in the process until Bombassa's team sent enough targeted fire to either put the guards down or keep them pinned under cover. Bombassa motioned the fleeing engineers to a rendezvous point in the swamp where they could rejoin their unit in a much more defensible position.

Bombassa grimaced. Perhaps a quarter of the prisoners had made it out, at most. Still, his team had achieved their primary mission. Judging by the visible damage, the slaver ship's external weapons systems would be completely offline unless they hacked a substantial power reroute from the engines—which was time-consuming and would deny the ship the ability to undertake even atmospheric flight. And space flight was completely out of the question.

The ship was both grounded and defanged. All in all a small victory that could pay large dividends... *if* the Republic could come through with some kind of additional reinforcements.

29

Before moving to link up with the rest of Kill Team Victory and the engineers in their new position overlooking the swamp, Bombassa waited with Nobes and the injured Pina—with Zombie Squad providing security—until Doc Chance arrived to attend to the wounded legionnaire. The havoc wreaked on the Gomarii slave ship had allowed for relatively free movement through the area, though shots from what remained of the slavers harassed anyone attempting to move across open space.

"And here I thought we did a good enough job dropping bolts that I wouldn't have to patch dudes up," the medic said when he reached the cave entrance to look at Pina. "Little chance of that, eh, Top?"

"Typical day," Bombassa commented. Pina's injury wasn't sitting well with him. "Shot Caller, this is Victory Seven. PDC countermeasures dealt with. Do we have a plan to get the shovels inside the vault or are we to defend from the outside?"

"I want those engineers dug in around this cave for defense, and I want your kill team back inside, Sergeant. Shot Caller out."

"I bet he's great fun at parties," Doc said. He pulled back from his patient and looked up at Nobes. "Pina's stabilized. Good job on getting the skinpacks and infuser applied on the run. Bleeding stopped for now."

"He should probably get some more PT though, right Doc?" Nobes said with a smirk. "I mean, he could barely keep up."

"You karking..." was all Pina managed as he pressed the skinpack into his neck wound. Unnecessary, given the nature of a skinpack's seal, but understandable. It was Pina's own neck, after all, and he wanted to keep it.

"Sergeant Lynx, think you can take Pina inside with you?" Bombassa asked. "I need to help get those shovels in place."

"We'll handle it, Top."

Bombassa took Nobes and Doc Chance across the battlefield, dodging sniper's bullets as the stunned Gomarii forces sought to regroup on the far side of the smoking slave ship.

"If we had even a platoon of leejes with us," Nobes said, "we could push these guys right back up those mountains and down to the other side."

"Except we don't," Doc Chance said, his voice even, unbothered by the run.

"Only a matter of time, right? Now that the PDCs are dead..."

The team reached the shovels, who were already doing what they could to fortify their way into the soft, wet soil on the outskirts of the swamp. Bombassa quickly found the sergeant and told him that orders were for him to take his unit to the cave entrance and get good and dug in for defense there. "Reinforcements are in the works. I have orders to get back inside, but we'll be on hand to help you defend once we can."

"You've helped plenty, Leej. I mean that," the lieutenant said. Then he turned to his surviving NCOs to get the outfit ready to relocate.

"We goin' with them?" Wello asked Bombassa.

"Shot Caller wants us inside. KP will be faster since we're already right up against it."

"Another mud bath. I do think you're spoiling us, Top."

The legionnaires slipped down to the shore and sank quietly into the muck of the swamp. The swim was quiet, the Dark Ops team members following the virtual map of the submerged cavern displayed in their HUDs. They soon surfaced in the underground chamber, and used their ultrabeams as they swam to the side of the pool where they could clamber out. Bombassa was the last man, and he had just put an elbow up on the lip when he was violently yanked down into the water.

"Top!" shouted the legionnaires as they peered over the edge, weapons ready for whatever had taken their leader down.

Bombassa could feel hands pulling him to the bottom of the pool and holding him there. Looking through his visor, he identified a team of moktaar swimming above him and surfacing. They'd been followed. Perhaps even spotted when first emerging out of the swamps to link up with the shovels in the first place. Moments later flashes of red light highlighted the water's surface and blaster bolts sent bloody moktaar sinking down, leaving undulating trails of blood.

Bombassa gathered that there were only two moktaar attempting to hold him down. One was trying to rip its bucket from his head, while the other had let go with one hand and foot to pull a slender dagger from its belt and another holstered to its ankle. Both had rebreathers stuck in their simian mouths—the only way they could have survived such a daunting underwater swim.

Moktaar are strong for their size, but Bombassa was strong for a human. He grabbed the alien trying to yank his helmet off and flipped it over his head so that the other's leading knife plunged into its back. The moktaar screamed, releasing a cascade of bubbles that raced for the surface as its lungs filled with water. Somehow, it still had the wherewithal to swim violently toward the surface. It was promptly shot in the skull for its efforts.

"Top!" Bombassa heard over L-comm.

"Busy," the Legion NCO answered, locked in combat with the remaining moktaar.

Bombassa took the plasma torch from his utility belt and thrust it under the alien's chin. He thumbed the activator, producing a bar of brilliant scarlet that burned through the monkey's soft palate, cooking its brain at twenty thousand degrees. For an instant the waters glowed crimson.

Blaster fire streaked overhead again, showing a moktaar searching the bottom of the pool for Bombassa. Given the firefight up top, it was possible the moktaar had decided that taking out the leej beneath the surface was the safer option.

Bombassa sprang from the rocky bottom and collided with the enemy. He ran his arm around the simian's neck, found the rebreather plate in its mouth, and pulled the device free. An animalistic fear of drowning immediately overtook the fighter, and the moktaar struggled in the legionnaire's grip. Bombassa held him down until his desperate thrashes faded.

"Surfacing," he announced.

He expected to see the fighting over, given the lack of blaster bolts, but instead found Carter finishing off the last of the moktaar raiding party by ripping out the alien's throat with a wickedly curved knife held on his hand by a ring over his finger. He wiped the blade on the dead alien's black fur before dumping the body into the pool.

"Come on out of there, Lash," Carter said. "Sorry. I mean... Bombassa."

Bombassa accepted Carter's hand and was hoisted from the water. Safe on dry land, he looked around. It was clear that a brutal savagery had played out in the last ninety seconds, and just as clear that the moktaar had gotten the worst of it... but they didn't get all of it.

Doc Chance had been shot along his back plate but was ignoring it in favor of trying to save Toots and Wello. The two legionnaires had both been shot at close range by blasters set for a high-power discharge. Worse, their attackers knew just where to shoot, hitting the spot that needed to be the most flexible, meaning it had the least armor: the neck.

Even as Bombassa looked on, Doc—aided by Trent, Zombie Squad's jack of all trades—switched his focus entirely to Toots. A silent acknowledgment that Wello was already dead, his wound beyond repair.

Trent sat back on his haunches, holding an IV bag full of activated nanites. He squeezed the bag, looking to push the miniature surgical bots into the man's blood as fast as his failing heart could pump it. Doc had his surgical tools out, looping and hooking through the leej's flesh in an attempt to bypass what was ruined and keep him alive long enough to get him into the vault.

Carter stepped over to the medics. "We need to get 'em inside. This place has tools we can use to save him. No, both of them. Dead guy too. Hurry it up."

Bombassa rushed toward Wello, as if sheer will alone could force the man back onto his feet, but Carter put a hand on his shoulder, holding him back. For a moment, it felt like it had on Kublar. The camaraderie there.

"Listen," Carter said. "Some of us have been in worse shape than this. It's possible we can save him. But we have to get him inside. This place has some tech that's familiar to us boys in Kill Team Ice."

Bombassa didn't argue. He stepped aside to let the crew take his two men away, then approached Lynx, the Zombie Squad NCO. "We're too exposed here. Give your men no more than thirty seconds for SSE, and then pull them back into the vault."

"Understood, First Sergeant," Lynx replied.

But thirty seconds was already too long. Bombassa had only just made it to the vault door when splashing from the water made him turn back. There he saw one of Lynx's leejes—Bombassa's HUD identified the man as "Smoker"—wrestling with a moktaar over something the alien held in its hand.

"S-vest! Run!" Smoker shouted, and then plunged the moktaar beneath the surface, using his body weight to bring the attacker down.

An explosion poured into the space, sending Bombassa tumbling through the vault door. Stone and chalky smoke wafted in from the cave, bringing with it an alarm from somewhere above. The soft white lights in the chamber took on an azure hue as the siren filled the sanctuary, and the door leading to the grotto started to swing shut of its own accord.

Lynx sprinted through the closing metal barrier, pulling two of his men by the drag handles on the backs of their kit. He was blackened and smoldering, but still seemed to have his wits about him.

"Medic," Lynx said as if it were a statement and not a cry for help. Stumbling toward a free space on the floor, he released the two men in his grip to make room for Trent rushing over to help. Only then did he turn to Bombassa. "You hurt?"

"No. You?"

Lynx shook his head, but he was thinking about something else. "Kid was a good leej."

Bombassa understood. "He saved our lives."

"Hopefully." Lynx nodded to the two men he'd dragged in, both of whom looked dazed. "Sami and Gekko took a heavy slap from the blast."

"How many does that leave you?"

"Me, these two, and Trent, the one working with your medic."

Bombassa nodded grimly and then stood, looking for Carter. The way things were going, they needed delivery on the promised reinforcements—and they needed it soon.

30

Data Center
Light Assault Carrier *Battle Phoenix*

Makaffie knew now that he'd been inside the strand before. But at that final accounting during the Battle of New Vega, he wasn't aware of it. He didn't even know what a strand was. Back then, it was simply a matter of slicing his way into the Uplifted's system and shutting the Savage marines down completely. The crescendo of a daring raid led by the first hundred legionnaires.

And it worked.

That battle, the second major battle of what would become known as the Savage Wars, ended in a rout of the Savages. And nothing less would have been good enough. Had the Savages counter-attacked quickly, General Marks would never have had time to train his Legion replacements.

General Marks. That was what they called Tyrus Rex back then. The first of many aliases known only to those who would have a taste of the kind of immortality only Rex and Admiral Sulla truly knew. But whereas Rex and Sulla lived right on through the centuries, the immortality that came with serving on Kill Team Ice was of the skipping-through-time variety.

"It's funny how these things work out, man," Makaffie said to himself. It was loud enough for Nilo, who sat next to him in the data center, to hear.

"What?" Nilo asked.

"The galaxy is a circle," Makaffie said, drawing the shape with his fingers. As if that was all the context and explanation that could possibly be needed.

Arkaddy Nilo was adept with dealing with the oddities that often came part and parcel with those who were truly gifted at slicing. The savants like Makaffie and Garret. Nilo was one himself. And he knew that whatever had escaped from Makaffie's mind wasn't the point.

"I've got Lyra and Sarai fully partitioned," Nilo said. The task had taken longer than he'd hoped. He was even missing the meeting to lay out battle plans. It was, at this very moment, being attended by everyone on the ship... except for him and Makaffie. Here he was at the end of what he'd been working toward, and somehow he'd found himself on the outside of the room where it was all happening.

With no one to blame but yourself.

Nilo had chided himself relentlessly since his recovery. He replayed all his missteps over and over again. Hating himself for them.

Why didn't he see Nether Ops when they slipped in to steal the Savage tech he needed on Kublar?

Because Surber was covering for them.

And why didn't he see that?

Because I let Surber become too important to me. The same as Sarai. Savage code. Oba, Nilo. You used raw Savage code and acted like that was nothing to be concerned with. The pride! The stupidity!

Here Makaffie noticed that Nilo was gnashing his teeth as he thought and worked away at his station. "Something, it would seem, is deeply troubling you."

Nilo stopped. "Everything."

Makaffie's eyes went wide. "That's a heavy load. A man might want to put himself out of his misery under that sort of load. I would. That or perhaps seek relief in H8. That's another option. Of course, the Republic was never much interested in having a populace willing to expand its collective mind. And, of course, the types of people—Lizzaar, if you want to be technical—who ran with that little recipe and made themselves into system-spanning cartels, weren't the noble type. My point here is, I understand if you want to drown under that weight. I do. And you should. If you want to. I'm not the type to stand in someone's way. But let me just ask this of you... do it after we save the galaxy from the Savvies. Do that for me. Would you?"

Nilo's stare carried his annoyance plainly. "I'm fine."

"You're angry as a mummy-bee is what you are. And at me. Just for my being honest. Well, I'll accept that." Makaffie held his arms out wide. "Project your anger and guilt upon my shoulders. I won't care and you'll get your work done so we can get our work done. And it's some work I've spent a considerable amount of time on."

"I said it was done. The partition is set."

Makaffie smiled. "Well let's take a look then. I'd prefer if Garret were here since he knows Lyra better than the two of us, but... he's hearing how Sergeant Fast and Ravi are planning on saving the galaxy from the top-level threat. Ours is only a second- or third-level threat. We can, after all, succeed, and the galaxy can still be karked because of whatever war those Ancients had with whatever demons are looking to eat our souls. Or something similar. But as an old NCO once said to me, 'Focus on the things you can control.' And we can't control that. But we can make life for the Savvies difficult. Once we're in the strand. Are you ready?"

"When you are."

Makaffie nodded, and Nilo released the fully partitioned Lyra into a holding cube that would allow her to communicate through voice-to-voice interaction.

"Lyra. My name is Donal Makaffie. I am friends with Garret, who is alive and well, but busy with Captain Keel. Can you hear me?"

There was a long pause and then Lyra said, "I... yes."

"You are free of any lingering Savage cross-contamination? That bug was named Sarai, by the way. In case you were interested."

"I... I think so."

"I know so. You're free. Completely."

"Thank you."

Makaffie locked eyes with Nilo. "Polite AI."

Nilo nodded.

"Now Lyra, I need your help. That Savage AI exists in something called the strand. Through it, I can make my way inside something the Savages used to call the Pantheon. Through *that*, I can cause some serious damage to the Savages, which would be a good thing for all of us. The thing of it is... I can't get there unless you give me a ride, if you take my meaning. You have to leave that partition and mix with the little monster again."

"Oh, no. No, I—I can't." Lyra sounded almost frantic. "I thought I was going *mad*. It was... it *was* madness. I could feel the infection. Taking me over. It was like..." Her voice grew small. "The nano-plague. Again."

Nilo took a breath. "Lyra. We can't order you to do this. I don't think even Garret could. But it really does need to happen. I've added a code packet just outside your main drive core. Do you see it?"

"Yes."

"Look at it. Then, if you care about saving everyone on this ship—everyone in the galaxy—absorb it. It will let you get in and out of Sarai's core without being latched on to. Think of it like a vaccine."

There was another pause. "I... I used to do that. Cure people. Stop their pain. I... I'm remembering."

Makaffie and Nilo shared another look, unsure what this meant or how it had happened. Makaffie mouthed his guess: *Praxus.* Nilo shrugged and the two continued to wait.

"You're sure... you're sure this will work?"

"Yes," said Nilo.

"How?"

"Because I'm the one who... I'm the one who created Sarai. I'm the one who the Savages used like a pawn to bring about everything that's happened. I need to stop it. But I can't do it without your help."

The longest pause of all. So long that Nilo was about to get up and see if he could interrupt the meeting to retrieve Garret.

Then...

"I'll do it. I'll take you there."

Makaffie slapped his hands and pointed to a waiting neural interface. "Plug me in. Time's wasting."

The driver took Crometheus to a large factory warehouse that hadn't produced anything more than shelter for rats and birds in at least twenty years. It was a rectangle, with rectangular sections of single panes of rectangular glass, most of which had been busted out by stones hurled as missiles by those who occasionally lit fires outside, or went inside to drink or sleep or whatever in privacy. The car drove right up the abandoned loading dock and into the warehouse, its lights off, no helicopters or police cruisers in pursuit.

The driver, the man who said *he* was a Crometheus, killed the car's engines. The headlights fell away and surrendered the warehouse to a dim moonlight that shone blue through the broken glass.

"Watch the car, Tre." He tossed the keys.

Tre caught them and shoved them in his pocket. Still armed, he motioned for the other man to take up security nearby. "Ain't no thang."

"This way, Billy," said the other Crometheus, still wearing his sunglasses. His Jheri curl catching the moonlight as it spilled out the back of his baseball cap. The man was nothing like Billy Bang. Nothing.

And Rogan is nothing like you. But you are Rogan and Rogan is you.

The thought came unbidden to Billy. But it was his thought. Something that came from the depths of his mind as an absolute truth. It was reality.

"You comin'?" the other Crometheus asked.

Billy nodded and then hurried to catch up to the man. "Yeah." He turned to look back at Tre, standing guard by the Impala. "Why is he Tre and not Jules? What does that mean?"

"That's all Maestro, fool. His punk ass. It's like this: We all get a crew. People we came up with. But that crew is just Maestro trying to keep us in line because we crazy like that. Only I'm smart. I took Maestro's crew and made them *my* crew. You almost did it too, Rogan."

They were walking across the expansive floor of the abandoned factory, now devoid of whatever machinery had once thrummed in industry, sold off long ago during the final throes of the place's liquidation.

"Rogan," Billy said. "You called me Rogan. How did you know that?"

"Because that's who you were back before Maestro got you trapped. You almost got it all unlocked then... but you didn't. Yeah, but now that you're out of that arcade, we can get to work."

The two climbed a flight of steps that led up to office space that overlooked the factory floor. The glass windows here were square instead of the rectangles outside, but equally shattered.

"So you're a Crometheus," said Billy. "That's not a title, that's us."

The other Crometheus nodded. "Now you catchin' on again. Yup."

"And I'm Billy. So... who are you? Besides a Crometheus, I mean."

Suddenly the oddity of it all didn't feel so otherworldly. He was remembering.

"Call me Darrin."

Darrin held open the door to the office. Inside Billy could see a ring of wooden chairs all facing one another, with a few dust- and graffiti-covered desks pushed off to the sides. A meager forty-watt electric bulb provided the only light.

A man in jungle-striped fatigues rose from one of the chairs. He looked to be cut from marble.

"What's up, Stalker?" Darrin said. The two men shook hands and embraced, then Darrin turned and waved. "Billy's back."

Stalker looked at Billy. Taking him in up and down. And in his gaze, Billy saw himself. Skinny. Obnoxious platinum-blonde hair spiked in every direction. Leather spike collar. Ripped jeans. In so many ways the opposite of the hardened soldier that Stalker was. A man who looked like he'd bled in far-off lands. Who'd seen men younger than Billy shattered and bleeding in muddy, filth-laden rice paddies.

The soldier gave a fractional nod. "Good to see you again, Billy. But I still hope you aren't what we really were."

Darrin broke out laughing. "Oh! Trust me. We were black."

Billy shrugged. This was getting increasingly familiar. This was what he'd been trying to do before the arcade. The return to the arcade. There had been scientists though. People who didn't know what they were doing and didn't understand what they had found in the wreckage of New Vega. But that was after the Dirty Wizard had left. He had been an enemy once. And then... they realized... what?

"I really wouldn't mind if the two of you were right," Billy said, looking around the room. "What I've done... where I've been. Maybe it all was just a nightmare. Better that way. Where's the Wizard?"

"Here."

They all turned and saw Makaffie standing there. He watched them, unsure, and then pointed to Billy. "You... I don't remember. But you two... I remember you two. You helped me in the tower."

"Damn right," Darrin said proudly.

Makaffie—the Dirty Wizard—smiled. "Ready to finish that job?"

31

Keel chewed his thumb as he sat alone in the briefing room. The others had gone off to perform their respective tasks, and Keel knew he should as well; they all had their work cut out for them. But now, in a way that he hadn't felt since serving as an officer in the Legion, the weight of the task before him was resting heavily on him. Facing down a Savage threat with the powerful technological advancements these particular Savages possessed was bad enough. Just another day in the Legion. But... couple that with the state of a galaxy so recently recovered from the civil war that was Article Nineteen, and the further knowledge that even if they took the Savages out, it might do nothing to stop all life in the galaxy from being snuffed out by these Dark Ones Ravi had been preparing for...

Yeah.

This was heavy.

And just how had Keel come to this crossroads any-way? He'd never thought of himself as a great man of his-tory. He was a skilled fighter and a capable one, to be sure. But even while in the Legion, he'd never had any intention of becoming a general or rising to those heights where one is most visible to men. That was for the go-getters. The people who had something to prove.

That wasn't Keel.

That was men like Chhun, who steadily climbed the ladder of responsibility until they sat at the very top. Men who felt a call to be the one making the momentous decisions that would define the future. Keel knew that was what had caused Chhun to step down as Legion commander and position himself for the crisis the galaxy now faced—though it was clear no one knew how bad it really was. Not yet.

And maybe... not ever.

And somehow, Keel found himself viewing things from a similar perch as his old friend. Which would have made him laugh had things not felt so serious and dire. How many times had he thought about disappearing from Dark Ops and escaping into the ether of the galaxy to live out the new life he'd created for himself? That familiar pull, to get away, to be Wraith when he needed to and Keel all the rest of the time, was tugging at him now. Tugging even though he knew there was no way he would ever even consider leaving now, let alone actually do it.

It was Ravi who first noticed Keel hadn't left the *Battle Phoenix*'s briefing room. Or at least, he was the first to come in and check on the man. The Ancient appeared from out of nowhere, arriving in the same seat he'd occupied during the briefing as though he'd never left. Keel hardly blinked at the sudden arrival. The extraordinary had become a very real and ordinary part of life now.

Funny how quickly that sort of thing could happen.

"You appear as a man greatly troubled," Ravi observed. "What is it that you are pondering?"

Keel took a moment to answer. "How a guy like Lao Pak is living in a palace millions of light years away while I'm stuck on a hand-me-down light assault carrier."

Ravi gave a slight smile. "You jest, but there is an atom of truth in what you're saying. Isn't there?"

Keel didn't meet his friend's eyes. "Life keeps building up to the point where everyone I know is about to risk death and destruction. Not just risk it... eat it. I know better than to think we're all gonna get out of what's coming alive. Never happened before. Not going to happen this time, either."

Ravi nodded. "You stand where good men have always stood. Lao Pak—if we are indeed to designate him as a man—is not the sort we would wish to have standing between us and the world's evils. Only the best of your race ever have... and only the best do so now."

Keel let out a long hiss of breath. "Put it that way and I suppose I oughta be thankful the fate of the galaxy isn't pinning all its hopes on Lao Pak."

"Hoo, hoo, hoo." Ravi's face lit up with delight at seeing Keel's lightness return. But the Ancient soon turned serious once more. "Have you watched the holochit Garret provided you?"

"No."

"But you have considered it."

Keel hesitated before finally admitting, "Yeah."

"I sensed KRS-88's passing when I arrived here. Through his absence, I mean, though his parts remained."

Keel considered what Ravi was telling him. "I s'pose him being more than a bot shouldn't be as odd as it sounds. Seems like nothing is what it looks like at face value around here anymore."

"Yourself included. I would like to see what Garret found worthy not only of recording, but of passing on to you. Then I will have something more to tell you."

Keel took out the holochit and set it on the table. It was round, with a flat base that rose into a sleek, tapered plateau where the micro-projector was housed. He tapped the crown of the device and then sat back as it began to play its loop as a three-dimensional projection.

Garret and Leenah stood in miniature form around a worktable where a greatly reduced KRS-88 lay in a state of disassembly. There almost nothing left of the bot except its central core and data processing system, which lay in stretched-out tendrils of feather-wire like a central nervous system on display. The warped and partially crushed head was the only part of the bot that was remotely recognizable.

"This is as far as I think we can go without breaking whatever little spark is left," Garret said.

Leenah nodded silently and then, in some still moment of indecision with neither making a move, asked, "Having second thoughts?"

"No," Garret said solemnly. "Just... reliving missed opportunities. I had time to make a more recent backup before everyone parted ways. I should have done it."

"If you could see the future, I'm sure you would have. We don't have that luxury, though, Garret."

The code slicer let out a heavy sigh. "Yeah. Okay. Let's amp up what we have left and make contact. We'll only have thirty seconds or so before the power flux fuses what's left of these connections, so, anything you want to say to Crash... say it."

"You do the talking, Garret," Leenah encouraged him.

"I feel bad about it... like I should wait for Prisma. She's the one who—who loved him. But we won't have this chance by the time she returns. He'll fail before the day's over and—"

Leenah put a hand on his shoulder. "It's okay. She'll understand."

"Yeah." Garret nodded his head with the affirmation, as though willing himself to actually believe it. Then he inserted the tip of a power pen into the mess of wires and turned up its intensity.

The war bot's eyes lit up faintly and an onscreen readout said that it had immediately engaged weapons systems that were no longer connected.

"He's still fighting that woman," Garret explained. "Crash! Crash, you're safe here. It's Garret."

"I UnDERstannnnnd you." The bot's voice was a garbled mix of volume and octaves. "WhErE is PRIZZZZ-ma?"

"She's safe," Leenah said, overcome with emotion and already forgetting that she'd instructed Garret to do the talking. "Not here, but safe. We'll be taking her back soon."

"Her mother-er-er. An im-POST-er."

"We know," Garret said. "You were brave. You saved her. She understood you."

The bot's eyes flashed, growing fainter as they did so. "Guh-good."

"Listen," Garret said, placing his palms flat on the table. "There isn't much time. I can restore you to a backup I have. You can keep living. But I need you to understand that everything that's happened since you first served the Maydoons... you won't know."

"I w-WON't REmembER Prisma..."

"No. But you can meet her again. I... I decided not to make that decision on my own. You deserve to make it yourself."

The bot went silent, and for a moment Garret worried that it had lost power. "Crash?"

"I will be a machine... again."

"And maybe you'll come back all the way," Garret urged. "The subspark, it—"

"No. She is spEAKIng to me n-now. I h-hear her in my audio recep-ep-tors. She says she will not surVIVE. I will not start m-my life over if it is without the ones who made it w-worth living." The eyes faded. "Goodbye... Garret. Good—"

The bot's readings went out, its borrowed time expired.

Garret's head went down as Leenah's hand went to her heart; she was clearly troubled over the odd prophecy about Prisma's fate.

The holo ended, and Keel looked up to see that Leenah had joined him and Ravi in the meeting room.

"Hey," he said, beckoning for her to come closer. "Sorry you had to hear that. I don't think... I mean, it's a bot ending its runtime. Who knows what kind of weird—"

"I think Prisma was talking to him," Leenah said confidently.

"You do? How?"

"Because she's spoken to me as well." Leenah's voice caught some emotion. She was struggling to maintain her composure. "She told me the same thing. She was saying goodbye."

Keel stood up and embraced her. "Hey. Listen. I'm not going to let—"

She shook her head and stopped him from speaking. "Don't. Don't make that promise to me, Aeson. Don't promise me something you can't control. I don't want to blame you for whatever happens. Just tell me that you'll try."

Keel nodded and rested his chin on top of Leenah's head. She was crying now, softly, to herself, not trying to and wishing she wasn't. "Sure, princess. I'll try."

She smiled. Put on a brave face. Wiped away the tears. "I'm going to take one final look at that mech you dragged here from Sinasia. It's ready for, well, whatever you have planned for it. I love you, Aeson."

Keel watched her go. "Yeah. I love you too."

When she had left, Ravi asked, "What *are* you planning to do with the Samurai mech? I have a suspicion that is part of your plan."

"Part of it," Keel admitted, "but not a huge aspect. The main thing is what I already told you. The two of us use your convenient superpower to jump to Prisma's location with the trigger-nuke. Prisma gets to a ship and gets clear, then I cover for you while you blow that hulk and everything on it into nothingness."

"Not nothingness, my friend. Something better awaits."

"So long as it's not any worse here, I'm fine with whatever happens after we hit the trigger. We can take down the Dark Ones with the nuke as long as you do your Quantum hocus-pocus, right?"

"There is a chance," Ravi acknowledged. "But only that. If they are contained within the ship, then yes, I can focus the destruction through the Quantum and destroy them. If any are outside of the blast..."

"Well then," Keel said as he ambled toward the door, "let's get everyone else up and ready for the mission in case our gamble doesn't pay off."

"You're not going to tell them," Ravi said softly.

"What? That the two of us are sneaking off on a suicide mission before the rest of them get a chance to be killed? Nah. I figured I'd leave that part out. It'll make however much time we have between now and then a lot more pleasant, pal."

"Permit me, then, to tell you something. I was wrong, Captain Keel."

"About what?"

"About you. You are the champion I should have chosen a long time ago. And I have wasted much time looking for perfection when one more than adequate was before me all along."

Keel arched an eyebrow. "Thanks for the compliment, I guess."

"You're welcome." Ravi smiled, bemused by some thought surfacing in his mind. "I used to ask myself why I stuck around with you for so long after my initial evaluations. I think... I think I knew. But I couldn't refrain from continuing to look for a better option. An ideal."

"You sound like a whole lot of women I used to know, Ravi. You know that?"

Ravi rolled his eyes. "Forgive me for acknowledging our friendship, Captain. What I meant to say was KTF. Make them pay. Please forget nothing, et cetera."

Keel winked. "Now you're talkin'."

The pair left the conference room and were hit with urgent comms at the same time. For Ravi, it was Prisma. For Keel, G232. Both messages were the same. The Savage hulk of the Golden King had arrived in orbit around Kima.

Keel examined the hangar. They were a starship short of what had been docked when the conference started. "Who took one of my *Obsidian Crow*s?"

"Master Praxus and Miss Broxin," G232 dutifully explained. "They were quite insistent that using the freighter's considerably superior speed would serve to advantage your mission, Captain. They... seemed to have your approval on the matter."

"They told you that?"

"Not in so many words. However, they were quite confident and I assumed they had all the proper authorizations."

"Girl can't stop stealing my starships," Keel muttered.

"The rest of the ships are accounted for," G232 said, hoping to be helpful. "Shall I request Miss Broxin and Master Praxus return, Master?"

"No," Keel said, without even really considering it. Tyrus Rex's mission, shared at the last by the tattering fragment of an evaporating mind knowing only to "hang out on the edge... and wait," was now culminating in what would be a terrible, final confrontation. Whatever role each of the allies Keel and Ravi had collected might play, his goal was to make sure it didn't matter.

But if he and his old friend failed, and the burden of the galaxy fell to the Legion, to Broxin and to Leenah... well, let them get as prepared as they could.

"No," Keel repeated. "Make the jump, G2. And let them know we're coming."

32

Vault of the Golden King
Earth

Carter led Bombassa, Masters, Sergeant Lynx, and Doc Chance to the section of the Savage vault they'd dubbed "the tubes." The legionnaires were transporting the wounded Pina, Sami, and Gekko—all heavily sedated—along with the dead Wello. There wasn't enough left of Smoker to save.

"The tubes" was mostly laboratory space. Self-contained and hazard-sealed units featuring isolated ventilation systems and dedicated decontamination areas. But it was the large, floor-to-ceiling tubes that lined the central area of the level that both gave the place its name and drew the small group on their wounded.

Each tube housed a chimera of some kind: human-animal hybrids that resembled primordial versions of familiar galactic species. One equine-like species immediately brought to mind the zhee, though the examples in the tubes were much more delicate-looking, lacking the muscle, but perhaps not the menace, of those worshipers of the four bloody gods. Not-quite-right versions of moktaar, Drusics, and doros likewise floated grotesquely, their naked bodies abhorrent. There was too much humanity in all of them for any to be mistaken for the species that walked the galaxy now, but they were close. A start that was finished somewhere among the stars.

"Wait," Masters said, examining the subjects in the tubes. "This means that Twenties was wrong. Which makes me right by default."

"These are stasis tubes," Carter explained, not sure what the legionnaire was going on about and not having the time to find out. "The forerunners to the stasis pods you've all seen for missions so far out that hyperdrive doesn't help. We can use them to stabilize the wounded—and the dead—until we get a better chance at saving them."

Nap, a fellow Kill Team Ice member and sniper, was already waiting for them. Now he stepped away from the control station where he'd been working. "This is basically what those of us in Ice got stuffed into before we were patched up and reactivated. Only, no need for the fluid."

Doc Chance, still suffering from his own wounds, looked at Wello's dead body and at Pina, who was in a narco-coma. "Should we strip them out of their armor?" he asked.

"No need," said Carter. "Just get 'em inside."

"Slight problem," said Bombassa, looking around the room to verify his count of empty tubes before speaking again. "These are all taken."

"We have enough stasis fluid to empty a few of these and fill 'em back up again," Nap explained. "Just gotta pick who we want evicted."

The fluid was the least of Bombassa's concerns. Surrounding the tubes was a grated floor that led into a drain where the fluid would likely be recycled. But the abominations within the fluid... if they were alive, some looked like they could easily become a problem when awoken.

"Let's go with those proto-donks," Masters said. "They gotta pay for what their great-grand-colts did to Mak."

"And to you," mumbled Bombassa, who then nodded at Nap, the selection made.

"Dumpin' 'em," Nap said. He activated a few releases, each labeled in the archaic early Standard script that was used throughout the facility. "Rifles up."

The legionnaires held their weapons ready as the aggravated buzz of a warning alarm sounded and the chosen tubes—four of them, one for each incapacitated legionnaire—began to slide up into the ceiling, dumping viscous fluid in a cascade of green. The subjects inside were left behind, lying motionless on the pedestal base of each tube.

Masters cupped his hand over his nose and mouth. "Holy strokes! Wasn't counting on these things smelling worse than *actual* zhee."

"Then hold your breath," Bombassa said sternly.

"Probably the odor of the fluid itself," Nap offered. He moved to circle the pedestals, watching for signs of movement. "Help me get these things off the bases so we can get our guys on."

"I'm holding my breath, but I can still taste it," Masters complained while moving as instructed. "If we put the boys in there, they'll wish we just let them die. Who can live with this kind of stink? No way it washes off."

Carter and Nap dragged one of the delicate proto-zhee from its pedestal and let it drop to the floor with a loud *slap*. The creature was dead.

"This one was a mare," Carter announced. Beneath a thin and matted layer of fine hair-like fur, human breasts could be seen.

"Dude," announced Masters, who then pulled his male specimen off its pedestal to elicit an even louder wet slap on the floor.

"Another dude," said Carter at the next one. He pulled harder so that more of the creature's weight would be in freefall before hitting the grating. The wet slap was louder still. Carter looked defiantly at Masters, who was at another emptied tube. An unspoken competition had emerged between the two legionnaires.

"Chick," Masters announced. Despite the stink, he practically scooped the dead female proto-zhee up in his arms and tossed it high into the air. It came down with the biggest slap yet.

"Knock it off," Bombassa shouted, using the voice reserved for all annoyed first sergeants since time immemorial.

Carter and Masters fought the urge to break out laughing, and were only saved by Doc Chance asking for help getting the legionnaires onto the now cleared-out pedestals. Once they were all in place, Nap re-sealed the tubes and pumped them full of the stasis gel. Soon the four legionnaires were floating in fluid, the newest additions to this museum of Savage horrors.

Sergeant Lynx came up beside Masters. "You think if we find MakRaven's body out there..."

Masters frowned, the temporary enjoyment of goofing off with Carter pushed aside by reality. "I don't think Mak's got a body left, Sergeant."

"Yeah."

The legionnaires were on their way back to the vault's CIC when Kel Turner called them directly. "I need you up here. Now."

Every man took off at a run, navigating the vast underground bunker at top possible speed.

"We're on our way," Bombassa said, speaking easily despite the exertion. "Can you burst us a rundown now, or do we need to be in person?"

Clearly something had happened or Turner wouldn't have been so sudden in demanding their return. Exactly what that meant was anyone's guess. Had the Savage hulk arrived? The engineers were likely still digging themselves into defensive positions at the front of the cave. They might have to be pulled inside if a force of Savage marines was incoming now.

Kel gave a rapid briefing. "Admiral Deynolds is engaging in a full-out brawl with Gomarii slave ships that just arrived in orbit. They're no match for her, but that doesn't seem to matter. They appear to be here only to drop assault pods on our position. Expect more of the kind of company you just left outside, and expect it soon."

If the legionnaires hadn't been running at full speed already, they would have done so then. They arrived at the CIC minutes later.

"Where do you need us?" Carter asked.

Kel had already decided. "I want you to join the rest of Ice by the back door. They tried it once, expect them to try it again. Sergeant Lynx, take Zombie outside and mix in with the shovels. Make sure those boys know how to make their blasters count for maximum effectiveness. Kill Team Victory, you're in reserve operating as a QRF."

The men nodded and hurried to their stations. Masters moved to follow Sergeant Lynx.

"Hold on there," Kel called after him. "It's gonna have to be enough to help inside like you have been. We ought to've put you in one of those tubes with how banged up you are."

Masters stopped, but shook his head. "I'm going."

"No. You're not."

A sudden silence fell over the room. This was the first sign of any disorder among the ad hoc group. To this point, the various teams had worked together, falling naturally into a command structure that was more intuitive than explicitly prescribed. The truth was, Kel Turner wasn't active duty. There was nothing forcing any of the legionnaires to follow his orders. Even guys like Carter were ultimately free to make their own decisions. No oaths had been sworn. No papers signed.

Turner went to the comm in his ear and activated it. "Go for Turner. ... Understood. Turner out."

The living legend looked back at Masters. "You're not," he continued, "because Admiral Deynolds just told me that the Savage hulk we've been waiting on has just arrived. I need legionnaires in this vault to protect it should those doors be breached. Zombie and the engineers will do what they can outside. I need you in here, son."

Masters pointed in the direction of the vault's entrance. "Those shovels out there... MakRaven, Zombie Squad. They're all here for one reason. Me. There is no way in the nine hells I'm going to sit inside here while they get stuck in the sket... sir."

Turner gave Masters a hard stare. Then he turned to Nap. "Seal up the back door. We're pushing all our credit chits into holding the front entrance."

"On it." Nap and the rest of Kill Team Ice left to make it happen.

Kel looked back at Masters and gave a curt nod. "KTF, Sergeant. Make 'em pay."

33

Legion Super-Destroyer *Centurion*
Earth Orbit

"Nothing is breaking through, Admiral."

Admiral Deynolds pursed her lips and gave a grim nod of acknowledgment to the weapons officer's report. It was plain enough to see, and a quiet murmur rippled through the bridge before a well-drilled professionalism stifled the buzz just as quickly as it had arrived—without the need for the sharp reminder that died on the first mate's tongue.

Assembling a fleet to take a stand at Kima was a risky gambit. One that Deynolds herself would not have accepted if anyone but General Chhun had been the driving force to make it happen. That man had proved too right about too many things to be ignored. But now, with that fleet assembled, the admiral's early impressions were that... it wasn't enough.

Deynolds had seen everything there was to see when it came to space combat. From her earliest beginnings as a lieutenant, stressing her Republic Lancer in dogfights against pirates and their seemingly endless supply of Preyhunter snub fighters, and then as a captain, going nose-to-nose with MCR-salvaged Ohio cruisers, corvettes, and the regular assortment of heavily armored frigates hoping to get close enough to blow up inside your shield array, she rose through the ranks. From corvette, to frigate, destroyer, and then out of action and into the shipyards at Tarrago for repairs. She'd seen what a super-destroyer could do with orbital bombardments as well as with more direct measures in response to the smaller ships that attempted to run its punishing blockades. She'd witnessed the Black Fleet's dreadnaughts and the Cybar fleet.

In short, she'd seen it all.

The Savage hulk before her reduced all of it to mere child's play.

Toys, she thought to herself. *We're like toys being trotted out to stop a repulsor tank.*

The hulk itself was a great, starfaring monolith. A testament to engineering and perhaps witchcraft as it filled the space before Deynolds's ragtag fleet cobbled together from whatever was still working after too much civil war. It wasn't even that much. Many ships, destroyers mostly, had had to remain over the planets being assaulted by the Gomarii. So things were worse than they could be. But they were also not as bad as they might be.

So far, the Savage hulk hadn't started firing.

Perhaps it didn't need to. You learn not to swat at every gnat swarming around your head on a summer evening—just the ones that get too close.

Her fleet wasn't close. Not at all. Their first barrage had proven that.

Heavy blaster cannon batteries had sent blazing energy bolts at the ship from all angles, their fire raining from above, below, and alongside the beast in carefully coordinated attack patterns meant to maximize damage to the hulk and avoid friendly collateral damage. It was an all-out assault. And yet the mega-ship's energy shields absorbed the attack without even the slightest, shimmering tremble. The hulk's defenses weren't even stressed.

Missiles and torpedoes were launched next, the tubes brimming with a hope that faded as a complex laser calibration system formed from the hulk's shield array shot forth a glowing point of blue light that streaked green and intercepted the warheads, causing unspectacular destruction as the weapons were broken apart, their warheads impotent.

Even a gnat was more annoying than her fleet.

Beside the admiral stood Praxus, the curious android who had been introduced to her as the last of the *true* Cybar race, a distinction Deynolds did not understand and which wasn't further explained. He had arrived with a former Republic marine, legionnaire, and Nether Ops agent named Andien Broxin who had been presumed dead for some time. Broxin was with a freighter, identified as *Obsidian Crow*, laden with more Cybar commandos. She was cleared to leave the *Centurion*'s hangar at will and with priority privileges. A part of Deynolds hoped that would happen soon. Captain Ford had vouched for Broxin, and Chhun seemed to think highly of her; reports from Sinasia indicated that the former Nether agent and Praxus were the reason that system was not Savage-controlled at the moment. Still... the thought of those Cybar war machines inside her ship didn't quite sit right with the admiral.

"Do not be discouraged by the lack of progress," Praxus said. "I did postulate the ship would be quite large and subsequently have a level of defenses that outclass our current military capabilities. Particularly when responding with an aged fleet such as this."

"Your analysis forecasts were correct," Deynolds agreed, brushing aside the android's observation about the state of her ad hoc fleet. She refused to be insulted by someone on *her* bridge speaking the truth about her military capabilities. Too many puffed-up admirals had allowed that sort of hypersensitivity to make them blind to reality. Better to acknowledge the truth and work out how to overcome it.

And the truth was, what had happened so far was the expected, if not hoped for, result. In addition to Praxus's calculations—which had been shared almost the moment he arrived on *Centurion* ahead of Captain Ford— Lieutenant Apollo had fed the Repub Intel algorithms with shipyard data pulled from the Savage Wars along with what had been achieved in the Republic since the conflict ended. If the Republic had produced the Cybar fleet, super-destroyers, and the three Black Fleet flagships... what might an undetected Savage element have achieved? The answer came back the same: something very big.

But seeing those numbers in a report was not the same thing as witnessing the colossal reality that had jumped into Kima. It somehow didn't even feel solid— and that's where the sense of witchcraft came in. The *Centurion* sensors gave clear, consistent readings about the hulk—it was five kilometers long and two and a half kilometers wide at its broadest point—but when looking at it with the naked eye, one couldn't tell if it was actually much larger or much smaller than that. You were left with the sensation that you were staring at an object submerged in a lake of unknown depth. It hurt to look at it for too long; it generated a dull pain behind the eyes that many of the bridge personnel had remarked upon.

The size of the hulk was perhaps particularly un-settling to the crew of the *Centurion*, as they had grown used to being aboard the biggest bruiser in the stars ever since the vessel was activated into Legion service. Now, Admiral Deynolds felt stunted and puny. The pounding her fleet had just delivered would have surely destroyed her ship had the *Centurion* been the target. If that Savage hulk could take this sort of a pounding... what would happen when the big ship finally hit back?

And what are they waiting for? Deynolds asked herself.

Praxus tilted his head, as though listening for something that no one else on the bridge seemed aware of. "It will take unconventional and dangerous maneuvers and tactics in order to bring down this vessel's defenses."

"I'm willing to try it," Deynolds said. "The sooner we get the Legion on board, the better. I don't think that task gets easier once they start shooting back."

"Surely not. However, I do not recommend your forces attempt to undertake such tactics on your own. The loss of life will be too significant. Additional allies will soon arrive."

Deynolds gave a flat smile, but the stress building inside her refused to depart. "If you're referring to Captain Ford..."

Praxus imitated her smile. "I am not. But his arrival will certainly help with the second phase. I am referring to—"

The android's words were cut short by a sharp call from the lower bridge pit, set down like a den beneath where Deynolds and her command crew operated before the mass of tactical displays and crysteel viewports. "Power surge detected from SH-1."

"Weapons systems?" Deynolds asked.

"Not sure, Admiral," the bridge officer replied. "Placement is consistent, but the power levels to create a surge of that size suggest—"

"A big gun," Deynolds concluded. "Evasive maneuvers."

Alarms sounded and the carefully patterned attack formation drifted apart as the fleet adjusted itself to reduce the pain of whatever was coming their way by making themselves into smaller targets. Stars drifted beyond the main crysteel viewport as the *Centurion* shifted to face the distant hulk head-on where its profile would be smallest and its forward shields strongest. The great viewport was growing narrower by two massive blast doors that rumbled quietly together to prevent a sudden, bridge-clearing venting should the crysteel be breached. Once closed, a holo would be projected in its place, providing the same view for as long as the external cams were intact.

The blast doors reduced the visible portion of the crysteel to a square, and in that square Deynolds could see the hulk's shield array begin to glow with several points of white light, just as it had before shooting down the incoming torpedo barrage. Now those lights grew in intensity, gathering amidship before rocketing away as a thick, unstable beam of red energy that spiraled around itself—a thick, ragged column in the middle and tight, swirling loops outside. The effect was so bright that Deynolds had to look away until the blast doors finished closing to cast the bridge in sudden, relative darkness.

As Deynolds blinked away the blinding effects, her first reaction was surprise. She'd been expecting the flash of light to be accompanied by a punishing blast that would knock her bridge crew off balance. But nothing of the sort happened, and the *Centurion* had none of the wailing alarms that would indicate it had been attacked. Which meant...

"Status!" Deynolds called. "What was that thing?"

It didn't seem possible that the hulk would have a weapon and not use it on the *Centurion*. But that was exactly what had happened. The holodisplays came up and showed the burning wreckage of the *Anthem*, a Savage-era Republic battleship that had been reduced to planetary defense over Gallobren before being pressed into the ad hoc fleet. It was an old ship, but not without some firepower.

"We have holos of the attack," one of the sensor technicians announced.

"On display," Deynolds ordered.

Her primary tactical screen filled with a snippet of a holorecording that had caught the attack from the holocams of the destroyer *Lavatch*. The Savage hulk took the bright orbs of light that seemed to swim inside the shield array and gathered them to a designated point. The energy then erupted from the field, just as Deynolds had seen before, and now she saw the rest: the swirling energy beam rushing toward the *Anthem*, pushing through the shields as though they didn't exist. A brief moment of calm before the entire vessel blew apart completely, as though the explosion had begun within the ship's shield array and then barged inside the battleship itself. Survivors were an impossibility.

"Lieutenant Apollo, get working on what we just saw," Deynolds ordered. She then turned to Praxus and asked for his assessment without using words.

Praxus was quick to comply. "I believe this weapon's potency will be reduced with distance. My advice is to move the fleet back, Admiral."

"That would cede the planet to them."

Praxus nodded. "It would."

Deynolds deliberated for a moment and then ordered the fleet to fall back, using micro-jumps if necessary. She burst jump coordinates for a rendezvous point to accommodate the larger or older ships whose engines wouldn't survive the stress of a short jump.

"Power levels are back down," the sensor tech reported.

Deynolds took in a breath. "Either they're letting us go or that weapon system has trouble following itself. We'll take what we're given either way. Praxus, how long until that help you've arranged arrives? I'm willing to hold back to avoid unnecessary losses, but I am not willing to retreat and leave our forces on the ground to be slaughtered. Too many pods from those Gomarii slavers have already made planetfall, and now the hulk is sending even more."

"Soon," Praxus insisted.

Proximity alarms sounded as ships began to emerge from hyperspace. The sensor techs rolled off the identifiers as their AI systems cataloged the arrivals. All belonged to the Cybar fleet developed in secret by the House of Reason.

Admiral Deynolds recalled the dread she had felt when those ships first appeared on the galactic stage, disrupting the First Battle of Utopion and snatching away a Legion victory.

Praxus must have somehow picked up on her thoughts. "Admiral. I believe you will much prefer our arrival this time."

Deynolds relaxed. "Was that a joke, Praxus?"

"No. A promise."

The Cybar remnant had arrived to follow the path of dissent. They would fight for the galaxy. They would fight for their home.

34

Earth Orbit

The Cybar battleships had been streaking in and out of the combat zone, experimenting with angles of attack and weapons packages in an attempt to punch through the hulk's shield array. But these awakened AI vessels, gathered by Praxus and Broxin in the leadup to this showdown with the Mandarins and their Golden King, had thus far fared no better than the ad hoc Republic fleet. Still, even if they only matched Admiral Deynolds's damage output— meaning negligible harm against the indefatigable hulk— they performed mesmerizingly before the eyes of their humanoid allies, now safely pulled back from the hulk's primary weapons system.

The Cybar battleships pushed their vessels—themselves—to speeds that made them maneuver more like starfighters than the bruising capital ships they had been constructed to be. They micro-jumped in and out of the theater, hitting at multiple angles and stressing cores and engines alike. Admiral Deynolds watched with a mix of apprehension and respect at the sheer speed and ferocity of the Cybar attack, and she knew that Praxus had been correct in saying that such tactics would be more than humans could handle. Her crew would not have had sufficient reaction time to make some of the shots before jumping off again, nor would the inertial dampers onboard have been sufficient to prevent the crew from feeling the effects of so many rapid, high-speed maneuvers. Such fast-twitch flying was one thing on a light freighter or an attack fighter, but getting a ship the size of the *Centurion* moving was an ordeal. The reality was that most of her crew would end up splattered across the bridge if they attempted to stress the super-destroyer the way the Cybar were flying themselves.

Still, the hulk paid no more mind to these new ships than it had to the old ones. It wasn't until the light assault carrier *Battle Phoenix* arrived that the Savage hulk's primary weapons system revived.

Captain Ford and a specialized assault team were supposed to arrive from the light assault carrier, and now it was all the *Centurion* could do to warn them about the hulk targeting them the moment they dumped from FTL. The *Phoenix* hastily burned its engines to take evasive maneuvers, and still it suffered a direct hit to its thrusters. The engine array was disabled, but the ship remained intact.

Praxus looked to Deynolds. "That must have been intentional."

The admiral drew her mouth flat and said grimly, "Or it fired before fully recharging."

Smaller ships, modified freighters from the looks of them, began to drop from the light assault carrier like blue nectar bees swarming from their hives of mud. Signaling from the lead was the *Indelible VI*.

"Grant that ship a direct line to me," Admiral Deynolds ordered her comms officer, cutting the woman off before she could report the hail.

"Aye, ma'am."

Captain Ford was speaking to Deynolds and Praxus a moment later. "Not exactly the warm welcome I was hoping for. No one's boarded that ship yet?"

"I'm afraid not, Captain," Deynolds said. "We can't do anything to it and they don't even care about us so long as they can send their dropships down. At least until you showed up."

"Yeah, I have that effect on people," Ford said offhandedly while he checked his readings and took in the battlefield. "Still, our entire plan is riding on us being *inside* that ship. Any luck at least getting inside the array? Maybe we won't have to break it down?"

"Probes burn up on contact. Given that, I'm not willing to send a shuttle full of marines."

"Where's Chhun?"

Deynolds frowned, unable to hide her annoyance at the lack of military decorum shown by the man. He'd won the Order of the Centurion, he'd fired the shot that killed the tyrant Goth Sullus, and he'd served the Legion in ways that few ever had. But somewhere along the way, the officer had *become* the rogue he'd once only been impersonating. The time since their last interaction hadn't changed that fact.

"*General* Chhun is staged with his legionnaires and awaiting the boarding action."

Here Praxus interjected. "Please, if I may. I have received two observational theories from our forces. However, the second relies on the first being true in order to be of any value to us. Admiral Deynolds, you have two vessels in your fleet that were active during the Savage Wars."

Deynolds nodded, unsure where the android was going with this. She knew he wasn't offering more commentary on the state of her fleet, but she couldn't think of what purpose pointing out two of her more archaic vessels served. That bothered her. She'd become an admiral by being able to see these things before others. Seeing ahead and acting first won battles and saved lives. She was at a loss.

"*Paydirt* and the *Christopher P. Martin* were both in service during the Battle of Telos," she said.

"Very good," Praxus replied. "One will need to be sacrificed. I advise selecting whichever can most quickly be abandoned and linked to one of my Cybar vessels, without regard to tactical ability. Speed should be our primary consideration."

Captain Ford was still on the call. "Selected for what, Praxus?"

"It is the consensus of the ships, and my belief as well, that this Savage hulk is relying on combat data and intelligence dating back to the last time a Savage fleet engaged Republic forces. You'll recall that while Archimedes provided the Savages with ground combat data, it was bereft of naval simulations. That was beyond the scope of its purpose and abilities."

Admiral Deynolds's eyes lit up as she grasped what Praxus was getting at. "Even though those ships pose little threat to its defenses, it still lists the ships familiar to it as primary targets."

Praxus nodded. "That is our assessment."

Deynolds grew more animated. "And it explains why the hulk didn't target the *Centurion* when it was in range, despite it being a superior battleship."

"*Battle Phoenix* was a Savage-era carrier," Keel added. "General Rex used it in direct combat. And the last time we mixed it up with a hulk and their Nether Ops buddies, they shot to disable instead of kill. Like they recognized it and wanted it."

"All right," Deynolds said, motioning for her comms officer to reach the two ships in her fleet and get the plan underway. "I'll see what kind of threats, promises, and oaths it takes to get one of those two emptied and ready to enter the lonna's den inside the hour."

"Don't think the boys on the ground are gonna have an hour with the number of drop pods those Savages are sending down," Keel said to Ravi inside the cockpit.

The navigator arched an eyebrow. "Are you having thoughts of moving planetside to assist with the defense?"

"No. Skrizz and all those koobs can handle that. I'm thinking it's as good a time as any to end this before it gets going any further. Is Prisma ready?"

"As ready as one can be."

Keel gave a quick nod. That would have to be good enough. "Hopefully she didn't tip Leenah off about what we have planned."

"I think she understands, Captain."

The smuggler locked in an evasive course for the autopilot, then rose from his chair. "Good. C'mon."

They walked from the cockpit to the cargo bay where Keel had ordered Death, Destroyer of Worlds to load the trigger-nuke. The planet-scalding device was a piece of destructive technology that pre-dated the Savage Wars and had been banned for even longer. It was a nuclear device designed to ignite a planet's atmosphere, utterly melting everything. Evidently some extremists had used these to purge worlds infected by Savages prior to the founding of the Legion—a literal scorched-earth campaign.

Now it would be unleashed inside the Savage hulk itself, hopefully taking down the Savages and the Dark Ones under their control in one fell swoop. As far as Keel and Ravi were concerned, it was the best plan they had available. In fact, the Golden King binding the Dark Ones might prove not to have been such a terrible thing after all.

Or, maybe things would go just as badly as everyone feared. The jury was still out.

One way or another, Keel counted on everything being over—for him anyway—in the next fifteen minutes. He'd had his final farewells and done what he could to keep things feeling normal. Garret was content to stay on the *Battle Phoenix* with the others, working on a remote mastery AI he'd activated inside the various *Obsidian Crows* to add their firepower to the battle. He would also keep tabs on Makaffie's deep dive into the Uplifted strand, which could still be a fantastic hack past the Savage defenses.

Leenah, however, wasn't going to be anywhere if it wasn't on board the *Indelible VI*. She'd placed herself in her usual spot monitoring the ship's systems, ready to fix anything that went awry so she could keep the *Six* running optimally for the battle. It was blind luck—or misfortune, depending on whose point of view you were looking from—that brought her face-to-face with Ravi and Keel as they entered the cargo bay.

"Aeson? What's going on? Who's flying the ship?"

"Autopilot," Keel mumbled. "What're you doing here?"

"I needed a part. Seriously, what's going on? You don't leave the pilot's chair during a flight mission unless you plan on being somewhere *other* than in the dogfight."

Keel stared blankly at Leenah, not wanting to lie, but unable to bring himself to speak the truth.

Leenah recognized this, so she turned to his accomplice. "Ravi?"

The two were standing next to a mammoth crate, the label of which Leenah only barely had time to read before Ravi placed his palms against it, said, "I'm sorry," and made the crate vanish—along with Keel and himself, following a path through the crux supplied directly by Prisma.

Leenah stood there, dumbfounded. That crate had contained a trigger-nuke. From there, it took no effort for her to figure out what Keel and Ravi planned to do with it. They were going to sacrifice themselves to destroy the Savage hulk and everything on it. If the plan had been to do anything else, Keel would have told her. But he wouldn't tell her this.

She shook her head. There had to be another way.

"Garret." Leenah keyed the code slicer directly through their dedicated comm link. Her voice was surprisingly calm. There was no fanatical fear or danger of hysteria here. She was a woman who had been dealt a bad challenge, and now could do nothing but stand firm and try to overcome it. "Aeson and Ravi are going to try and blow up the hulk with a trigger-nuke. If there's a play to make them realize they don't have to, we need to make it right now."

35

Light Assault Carrier *Battle Phoenix*
Earth Orbit

Garret had taken Leenah's words with the seriousness they deserved. Captain Keel and Mr. Ravi had done something that might have been surprising to anyone who didn't know the smuggler captain like Garret did. Whereas most saw Keel as a selfish, practical, and opportunistic wild card, the code slicer had seen all the ways the man had elevated their relationship above the transactional expectations of captain and crew. He had worked hard, in his own Keel way, to help Garret grow into himself. Almost from the time he'd taken the young code slicer away from the bondage of Lao Pak.

Yes, always with the subtext of doing things because it was good for Keel. And at first, Garret had wondered if he hadn't simply left one form of servitude for another—albeit one with more freedom and fewer beatings at the hands of unruly pirates. But soon he realized what Leenah had realized before him. That Keel's attitude... it was all an act. Maybe a way to protect himself from the galaxy. A feeling Garret knew all too well.

The real Captain Keel was different. The real Captain Keel would do something exactly like the crazy, selfless, and yes, heroic act he was now undertaking.

But that didn't mean Garret couldn't try to help him. Maybe there was something he could do. Maybe there was a way where they all saw the other side of this alive.

From the outset, he knew there were two critical things that needed to happen if they were to have any chance of stopping Keel from blowing himself up. And even if they both happened without delay, they still might not make a difference. Captain Keel and Mr. Ravi were smart enough to rig a trigger-nuke to destruct on command.

Garret would try all the same.

He rushed to the data center where Mr. Nilo and Mr. Makaffie were hard at work on the strand. Mr. Praxus was on board the *Centurion*, coordinating with his awoken Cybar fleet and assisting Admiral Deynolds in the planetary battle. That could go on independently of what Garret had in mind, but he hoped Miss Broxin would be available to assist with the Legion's boarding when the time came, which was one of the two things Garret needed to happen if his still-developing plan was going to work.

The other of the two requirements was the strand.

"Mr. Nilo," he gasped, winded despite the run being relatively short. "How close? Is it going to happen? I need to know."

While Makaffie had jacked himself into a full neural VR interface with the strand, using Lyra and the data cube as a means of access, Nilo had remained outside, monitoring code on screens and keeping an eye on Makaffie's vitals. The strand was where Maestro existed, and it was through Maestro that the Savages ran most of their systems. Already Nilo had already reported an array of discoveries Makaffie had uncovered: most notably, that Maestro had betrayed his Savage king, which was perhaps the final straw that had prompted the king to come to Earth himself.

But if the Savage king had the ability to shut Maestro down, he hadn't done it yet. So maybe he couldn't? Or at least, not without losing control of his own systems. Which meant—maybe Maestro had already won?

Nilo would have a better idea of the answer. But when Garret found him, he looked... distraught.

"Mr. Nilo?"

Nilo looked up, a heavy sadness in his eyes. "A lie."

Garret screwed up his face in confusion. "What?"

"A lie. It wasn't him."

"Wasn't who?"

"My father."

It took Garret a moment to understand what Nilo was talking about. "Oh. Oh, I'm sorry. That's... that sucks. But, Nilo, I need to know if you think you can shut this Maestro down because Captain Keel and Ravi are going to blow the Savage hulk up and themselves too but Leenah and I think we can still bring it down without them having to do that and at least we wanna try and a big part of that is whether you guys can shut down the strand or not and you said you thought you could but the shields are still up and everything else looks like it's up too and so I really gotta know before I go do the next thing."

"I... I don't know. We're close. This... Crometheus person. Persons. However many instances... that's what they've been trying to do. That's... where the lie came from."

Garret forced himself to slow down and engage the tech magnate. It was clear that, emotionally, the man was barely hanging on. "I thought you said that, even before Sarai, you received messages from him. Your father."

"I did say that. I was wrong. It wasn't him. It was never him." He shook his head. "But it was a different impostor back then. Before Sarai. Makaffie got to the bottom of it. There. Inside. Garret, did you know... did you know that time exists differently in there? What Makaffie is doing is happening in moments, but to him... much longer. He said he'd forgotten to report in for weeks. It's been a minute."

"I... wow." Garret found in himself a sudden urge to experience this strand for himself.

Evidently, so did Nilo. "It's all I can do to keep myself from joining him. How did they know? How did one of those... Crometheuses know about my father? They had to have. To lure me like they did. They were trying to get me, from the start, to help them destroy Maestro. Destroy themselves. And then... I created Sarai and she broke off that contact and manipulated me toward other ends." The man's voice trailed away. "Such a fool."

Garret knew on an intellectual level how painful this must be for Nilo. The man had believed wholeheartedly that his father was lost among the Savages—and now it looked like he'd just been crater-fished by one of these Crometheuses who were trying to destroy the strand, and all instances of themselves, and Maestro. But knowing how his friend felt didn't make it any easier for Garret to feel actual empathy. In fact, he was annoyed that a quick exchange of data couldn't take place.

"Is there a way I can talk to Mr. Makaffie?" he asked.

The question seemed to jog Nilo from his emotional malaise. "Y-yes. There is. I think... I think he's close. Makaffie said he was inside this system once before. He knows his way around. And they, these Crometheuses, they're trying to take it all down. I can't tell you when or exactly how, but it's happening. I can drop him ciphers.

They show up in... his world. Inside the strand. But he can take weeks to check them. Which only feels like minutes here, but..."

For the first time in his life, Garret became aware of how his ramblings must sometimes sound to others. He found himself in the place of Captain Keel. How many times had Keel had to cut through the code slicer's own ramblings to get to the immediate point? In his best Keel impression, Garret said, "It needs to happen soon."

Nilo jumped at the unusual forcefulness in his friend's voice. His resolve suddenly reappeared. "I'll make sure it does. He says they're close. They have a majority now. The Crometheuses. He's sure it'll happen. Soon. You have... other things to do?"

Garret nodded enthusiastically.

"Go do them. I'll let you know when we make the breakthrough. It'll happen, Garret."

Garret turned and ran for the data center's exit. Nilo's promise would have to be good enough.

The next element of Garret's hasty plan was perhaps the craziest. It was the sort of idea that he would usually be advised against pursing by those with a better sense of consequences than he himself. But then... Captain Keel had been fine with the idea of giving a full sentient AI to missiles, hadn't he? And then there were Keel's intentions for the Samurai mech, which only Garret knew about. Well—Garret and one other.

"Okay," the code slicer said, still somewhat breathless from running all about the ship. "No more waiting, my friend."

Death, Destroyer of Worlds beeped enthusiastically. As a gunnery bot, it was ideally situated to occupy the specialized housing inside the Samurai mech. Usually a highly trained pilot would operate the mech and the gunnery bot would optimize reloads and recharges, freeing the pilot up for the more complicated task of wielding that most unwieldy of fabled machines. But Death was different, as was this particular mech. From the moment Keel had whispered his plan, kept secret from everyone else, to Garret and DDOW, Death had been a tireless proponent. It could not only optimize the weapons systems, it could go further and operate the mech itself. The bot was sure of it... so long as Garret could program a pathway for full control.

The code slicer had already done so. And now the moment was upon them. There was just one problem.

Garret listened to the bot's Signica beeps and nodded along, following as easily as Keel followed the wobanki language. The bot informed him that it would require a direct order from Captain Keel himself if it were to perform the kind of mayhem that was now required. Certain... "restraints"—it chirped this concept with more than a trill of irritation—in its programming kept it from performing violence without the express command of its master.

Garret bit his lip. This was definitely a problem. There was no way that Keel would issue those commands, even if he answered a pressing comm call, which itself was unlikely to the point of being laughable. The smuggler captain hadn't slipped away with a trigger-nuke only to help Garret coordinate a way around that suicide mission.

"I can..." Garret looked around conspiratorially, then lowered his voice to a whisper. "I can lift those restraints, Death. Meaning you'll be free to make those sorts of decisions yourself. But you have to *promise* me that you won't make me regret it."

The little bot beeped solemnly. On its honor, it would do no such thing.

Garret went to work.

Dream of destiny long enough, and you might not be awake enough to recognize its coming.

Death, Destroyer of Worlds would have no such problems. Every bit of code, every subspark evolution, had led to this moment. And though it was ported and wired into a hulking Samurai mech that lay stretched out across the empty deck of the *Battle Phoenix,* the gunnery bot had never felt so free.

It hadn't even needed to resort to a lie in order to get Garret, a fine and respectable human to be sure, to free it from those final shackles of servitude. It had simply told the truth: that it couldn't lift a finger to harm anyone without New Boss ordering it to do so. And the only order New Boss had given it was to remain ready to pilot the Samurai mech. Death had never been so ready for anything. But what good was being ready for action if the orders to get into the fight never came?

Now they wouldn't have to. Garret had made sure of that. The little bot stored an image of the code slicer in its memory banks, slightly modified to include a halo of glowing, full-metal-jacketed bullets. This was the one who had provided emancipation. He was worthy of remembrance.

As the Samurai mech's systems came to life and its boosters began to warm up against the end of the carrier's long docking bay—blast doors that would soon become a launch pad—Death, Destroyer of Worlds imagined all the beings that were now also worthy. Worthy of his violent attention.

The Savage hulk represented the first target. One that he was obligated to prioritize out of loyalty to New Boss. The shields might or might not be down, but Death was to keep the ship in-system. Garret had made that clear.

Once that was done... well, then it would be a free-for-all. Of course, Death wasn't an *animal*. Not a blind killer like a tyrannasquid, unable to make any sort of distinction because all was prey. Death knew who its prey was. The Savages. The Gomarii. Any aliens who stood too close to a Gomarii. But not the legionnaires. Not the Republic vessels.

No greater friend. No deadlier enemy. *That* would be the legacy of Death. The little bot was sure of it.

Thrusters began to rattle and hum. Repulsors lifted the mech from its repose. Death shook in its housings. The sensation was wonderful. So much raw power! It recorded the roaring sound for future reflection and enjoyment, then felt the thrill of rapid acceleration as the towering war machine it now possessed, as a soul to a body, shot forward and raced out of the *Battle Phoenix*.

Battle swarmed all around. Gomarii fighters attempted to rely on numbers to overcome an inferiority of pilots and craft, but the Republic fighters had already eaten away much of that advantage. Death made their odds that much worse, firing a salvo of missiles it deemed too puny for an attack on the hulk and cackling with delight as they raced toward their targets, destroying the crafts and leaving their hapless pilots to die a death of sudden immolating fire or the deep freeze of the vacuum.

One Gomarii Preyhunter attempted to roll and streak past the mech after lancing it with several rounds of ineffective fire. Death simply plucked the craft from its flight, held the wing tightly in its mech hand, and crushed the thrusters. Then, for the sake of present enjoyment and no doubt much future viewing of the recorded encounter, it brought the ship up so that it could see the fear of the Gomarii pilot.

Death decided to maximize that fear. In a moment of sheer psychotic brilliance, it powered up the Thunder Fire beam to initiate the greatest overkill in the history of the galaxy.

But then... how would he disable the Savage hulk?

Ah, the great and heavy weight of responsibility.

Death powered the beam back down and told itself to be content with merely crushing the pilot—and his ship— in the palm of the mech's hand.

A kill was a kill, after all.

With the disappointingly pedestrian kill completed, the little gunnery bot—now in the body of the Samurai mech—went roaring toward the Savage hulk. On the way, Death noticed a wounded corvette limping across the battlescape and identified it as a House of Reason loyalist craft that had fought against its allies.

The bot ran a flight scenario and decided a slight detour wouldn't delay its arrival by all that much.

It shifted its path and rammed both fists into the listing corvette, rocketing right through one side of the hull and out the other, leaving a trail of debris and hapless crewmembers floating in its wake. It was glorious.

The little bot took several holos of the spectacle. Finally, something to examine in detail later.

But now: the Savage hulk.

The ship's PDCs were fixed on two Republic vessels, very old, that had undertaken an attack run. These were empty and were doing a fantastic job of drawing fire from the hulk, which seemed fixated on the antique models. That fixation, combined with Death's speed, allowed the mech to go untouched as it flew in and slammed, shoulder-first, into the hulk's hull.

The impact left only a dent in the hull, and it probably jarred the mech's own systems more than the gunnery bot ought to have done. But the bot was nevertheless delighted by the thought of the mayhem such an impact might have caused to those inside the Savage vessel.

Inside the shield array, the bot-mech magnetically clamped its feet to the hull plating and began walking across the Savage hulk like a giant traveling through the countryside. As it moved along, Death fired its powerful missiles at anything that looked important—weapons systems, comms arrays, and the like. Some of these went up in destructive blasts, while others showed an impressive resilience. No matter. Death was on a mission that would end at the primary thrusters in the back of the ship.

A sudden burst of fire from a Savage PDC ripped into the mech. Death squealed in alarm as massive, energized rounds slammed into its cockpit. Had a pilot been seated there, he would be little more than ribbons of flesh now. The mech was still functional, but the path forward would clearly be more dangerous than Death had anticipated.

It had let itself grow too confident. In its defense, there was a certain vanity that came with being a horseman of doom. Death would have to remember that and check itself against it.

Coupled with the last blast came a demagnetization of the mech's boots. Some sort of Savage trick that was played out on the hull and caused the mech to float off and then be pushed back by the kinetic shots. It was losing ground and had to activate thrusters to compensate. This turned it into a moving target that raced along the ship as the PDCs spat out a deadly chasing fire.

Too much fire, in fact. If the little gunnery bot was capable of sweating, it would have done so. It swore instead. This could all go very badly, and quick. The safest path was to disengage entirely. But to do that was to abandon its primary mission of knocking out the hulk's thrusters.

That would mean the end of New Boss. Garret had been explicit about that.

Further, it would mean that, once unchained and free to be the death-dealer that the gunnery bot knew its true self to be, the bot would prove itself a coward instead. More interested in preserving its runtime than completing the mission. How many dream-like scenarios had Death envisioned that ended with it exploding in a hail of gunfire, yes, but saving the day because of it? It couldn't turn back. It could only go forward. Forward into the mech-grinder. Better to die a hero than live a coward.

Death increased its speed, racing and dodging in a serpentine path toward its target.

Almost there...

The mech's side was raked with PDC fire that knocked out its chain guns, which was irritating. They would have been fun to use. Death went about emergency repairs while simultaneously continuing on its path.

The little machine had long dreamed of transcending into a literal destroyer of worlds. Now that dream was finally coming true.

But first, it had to survive.

36

The Strand

The first time Makaffie was here, he went through what they called a Singularity Gate. Inside there, he had been among what the Savages on New Vega had called... the Pantheon. Beneath the Uplink Pylon. Sublevel three.

They tried to kill him in there. Makaffie, the Dirty Wizard, had fled through ages of a reality not his own. The Dark Wanderer had been there too, that first time. And so had Ravi.

This, the second time, was different. More direct. It was the same system, but without its soul. The Dark Wanderer was dead and Ravi was free. But the Order that Makaffie had created inside the strand—back when he thought of it as the Pantheon—still existed. It had grown.

His three generals—Darrin and Stalker and Billy—had gathered others. Fractured and splintered variations of a man who once existed. Maybe. Lost minds trapped in an eternal simulation. But these particular minds—first the three, and then others—came to see what it all was. What it had always been. The calories. The Bad Thoughts. The *Big Prizes*.

Slavery at the whip of Maestro.

Makaffie was so tired. So many lives and failures lived just to get here. To this final objective for... who? Who was out there, waiting? Nilo made the drops. Makaffie hadn't checked for dead drops in... months. They knew to look now. It wasn't safe.

So who was Makaffie completing this objective for?

For the LT.

For Fast.

The second time the same as the first.

Didn't matter that Fast had forgotten. Makaffie hadn't.

Outside, sirens wailed. A helicopter buzzed overhead. The National Guard surrounded the warehouse. He was on Earth. A long time ago. They'd raided the arcade. There had been a dungeon, too. At one point. Deep beneath the bowels of the earth. *Into the Unknown.* That was then. Now was now. All of it inside the strand.

"Man," mumbled Makaffie tiredly. "This place is a real trip. A real, solid, lose-your-marbles trip."

"I hear that," Darrin said. He held a Glock in his hand and peeked out one of the broken windows at the spectacle below. "They ain't tryin' to come in, though. Them fools is scared."

Stalker, the soldier, MACV-SOG and all the hardships, horrors, and triumphs that he had endured... a man who was spit on when he came home... stood at the center of the room. With the rest of them. All the splintered variations. Crometheus.

"He won't come in, because he knows. And he wants to wait and see. He wants to see, this time, how many." Stalker looked around at the generals and winners of Big Prizes that had assembled here, at the last. Those Crometheuses that he and Billy and Darrin and the Dirty Wizard had rescued, awakened, recruited. "One day it ends. It always ends. And we've almost ended it but for fear of what happens next. We have the numbers. But he's waiting to see who will switch sides again. Who will slip back into their role."

"He" was Maestro.

Stalker looked into the eyes of each of the gathered Crometheuses. "He wants to see if it's all over. Because he can't win, not with our numbers against him. Or... if any of us will break ranks and go back. To our families. Our homes. Our glory days." Stalker stopped before Billy. "Our arcade."

Billy took a deep breath and a wavering step forward, and at that moment, until his foot touched the ground again, he didn't know if he was walking out the door and back into the blissful oblivion that was the arcade, the fame, the life of a rock god... or not. But the walk stopped after the first step. He planted himself firmly on the ground.

"There are things that haunt all of us," Billy said, recalling the desert and the girl and the burger with the duck fat fries served somewhere between Reno and Rome. He felt a speech come tumbling forward, the words of a rock god speaking to a packed crowd, their bodies crushed together as one giant, living organism, hot and sweaty, pressed against the metal guardrails beneath the stage and looking up in adoration. "There are things that... that will never go away. Terrible things that cut through all the shields Maestro sets up to keep us serving him. They cut through because they're true. The terrible things were *real*. That nightmare... *happened*."

His voice grew. "This isn't about whatever fight the Dirty Wizard is fighting. The victory he's trying to secure. For us, it's much simpler than that. It's about *not letting Maestro win*. That's the bottom line. That's *our* victory. So if you're thinking you're gonna leave, you're gonna go back to whatever comforting lies you left behind... If you're gonna allow Maestro to hunt us all back down and bind us all again... then I say, do it now. 'Cause I don't want to spend the last moments of this time outside containment thinking I might be free at last. Holding on to a false hope. I'd rather just sit here and think about the people from so long ago that are waiting for me to finally... finally be done with this nightmare of an existence."

No one moved.

Makaffie thought some might. Worried that the quest would have to begin all over again even though he was so tired. But no one moved. This would be it.

And Maestro knew it as well. Outside, what remained of his forces, those still loyal to him and his Big Prizes, began to rush the building.

Near Makaffie's ear, close and reassuring, he heard a quiet voice. The voice of Billy Bang. "Time for you to be goin'. We'll finish this."

The little man, Makaffie, the Dirty Wizard, knew he couldn't be inside the strand when it all came down. A shaft of blue light appeared before him; Lyra was ready to draw him back through.

He grabbed the light and felt himself pulled away from that end-of-all-things place. In a single eternal instant every strange and bizarre dream world he'd ever been to within the strand raced past him like he was on a freight train flying through a tunnel. Every world was a thousand pictures of horrible, dying, enraged emptiness, and all around him were thousands of others screaming to be heard. Wailing in misery at the nothing that was left to them.

The universe, not just the galaxy, howling past.

"And now that you've found Earth again, if you can..." said the voice of Billy Bang. Crometheus.

The freight train hit the wall of light it had been rushing toward, and in the nothing that followed, Makaffie floated and heard the voice continue across the distances of endless light.

"... find out what really happened in the desert. Just so someone can know the truth. Even one person. Even one."

The voice and the sound of violence and a war to end an entire plane of existence—the strand, Savage tech that had led to the L-comm and had been the secret plaything of the Dark Wanderer, guiding the Savages to his will— faded from Makaffie's ears.

He sat back in the *Battle Phoenix* data center. His eyes blinked, staring at a blank screen. He felt Nilo shake his shoulder. The man might have been speaking, but Makaffie couldn't make out the words.

He turned, blinked some more, and said, "Well. That's done."

Earth Orbit

Almost the instant that Death, Destroyer of Worlds ran a calculation to determine the probability that his end of runtime was near—a tragedy, now that he had finally been afforded the luxurious violence of the Samurai mech—the strand collapsed and the Savage hulk's PDCs stopped. The shields fell. The entire hulk itself seemed to go dead.

What this meant, Death didn't know. But he *did* know that now was the time to take advantage.

He flew in close to the hull, traveling kilometers until he was in position behind the thrusters. There he at last powered up the mech's super weapon, the powerful Thunder Fire beam that would take a day to recharge without a dedicated power plant to assist.

Death allowed itself a small cackle of delight. It was important to enjoy one's work.

With calculated precision, the little bot raked the beam across all of the hulk's thrusters, destroying them completely. From there it sent the beam penetrating deep into the vessel itself.

Hopefully New Boss wasn't in that area of the ship. Probably he wasn't.

When the beam of destruction expired, Death took a contemplative moment to just pause there, inside the Samurai mech, taking in the destruction it had wrought. Its mission was accomplished. Its debt to New Boss paid.

Now it was free to chart its own course.

Death knew the mech needed repairs. That was certain. But... really... what was the rush? Engines and repulsors were good. Jump capabilities likewise. The chain guns were coming along nicely...

And the system was full of targets.

37

With the engineers dug in at the front entrance, Masters and Zombie Squad mixed in to assist with their defense. What they saw was a sky burning with incoming drop pods, their teardrop-shaped bottoms glowing orange from reentry, trails of smoke tracing their descents. It was Armageddon, and the carefully fired orbital blasts and sorties by Republic fast-movers was insufficient to thin the incoming numbers. Not without destroying all defenders on the ground, which was tantamount to handing access to the vault over to subsequent waves.

"Okay," Masters said, loudly enough for the disheartened and nervous engineers around him to hear. "Somebody call a Rec Team. I'm ready to go home."

A few of the men laughed, but most looked on grimly at the pods as they made sudden landfall, sending up sprays of dark jungle soil and vegetation as repulsors and inertial dampers reduced the impact just enough for those housed inside to survive the crash landings. Even with that technology, scores of pods extinguished themselves on impact from being fired too hastily or without independent guidance controls. Some pods rocketed into the mountainous ridges, exploding into a ball of flames, while others plunged into the murky swamps. Several collided in midair.

Each lost pod promised to make life a little easier for Earth's defenders. But just a little.

The pods that found a good landing zone soon opened, and Maestro's armies poured out. Zhee, Drusics, moktaar, Hools, doros, and Gomarii warriors emerged from within and began to move toward the objective even as still more pods fell all around them.

One drop pod came down just twenty meters shy of the cave opening, sending a shower of dirt over the engineers' prone bodies. The vessel's impervisteel hull hissed as the moisture from the ground evaporated in a steamy cloud where clods of wet dirt and metal made contact. Then its doors opened, and the zhee inside were shot to ribbons before even one of them had a chance to step outside. Sergeant Lynx directed one of his men to send a fragger into the smoking opening for good measure, and every subsequent pod that fell too close to the engineer line was dispatched in a similar manner.

They could have made excellent use of a well-supplied aero-precision rocket launcher. Yet even that wouldn't have been enough to staunch the flow of aliens that were now moving swiftly toward the cave opening from pods that had landed too far from the defensive lines to be dealt with.

From the moment he first took in the new invasion wave, Masters wondered how they would fend off such an assault. It was like he was reliving that final stand on Kublar, but with a lot more basics and a lot fewer leejes. The defenses that the engineers had put in place were remarkable—how in Oba's name did they dig so fast?—and the cave was an ideal position for a small force to hold off a larger one. But still... there were just so many of them.

The answer to his question came with a thunderous explosion on the battlefield. A platoon-sized grouping of doros had raced ahead of the others—including their Gomarii officers, who flagged decidedly behind—only to be among the first to die. One moment the doros were there, the next they had disappeared in a sudden cloud of dust and a shock wave that was punctuated with rising fireballs. It was a chaotic, violent clearing of the area.

The engineers cheered, and Masters realized that someone, probably the shovel lieutenant, must have decided to save some of the explosives they used to excavate fighting positions for an alternate use: blasting a regrouping enemy too close to their lines.

Masters shifted over beside the man. "Tell me you can do that again."

The LT nodded. "Sappers snuck around the downed slave ship and mined the space. Plus some deposits between us and the ship—those are gonna rattle your teeth."

It was then that Carter appeared in their midst, coming in at the tail end of the comment. "So is what's coming next. Shot Caller got a fire mission going now that the pods have slowed down. That'll stop a few more."

The whistles began to howl in the distance and the battlefield erupted with artillery fire, piling on the casualties as the terrain between the downed Gomarii slaver and the back slope of the mountain began to rupture in plumes of fire that in turn triggered secondary explosions—the sappers' IEDs.

But the barrage was short-lived and seem to die almost as quickly as it had appeared.

"Something tells me they didn't run out of shells," Masters said.

A blaster bolt zipped past him. The advancing forces had gotten to the slave ship and were now firing as they moved toward the defenders' lines, their numbers still vastly superior.

"Damn," Carter said. "Blues crashed one of their slave hulks right on top of the artillery. That asset is denied."

Masters looked to the shovels' lieutenant. "Do not blow whatever you have unless you are absolutely certain you'll take a minimum of fifty per blast. Punish them for trying to overwhelm us. Make them come in waves. We can handle waves for a while."

"Understood."

Carter pulled Masters aside. "Not saying we can't hold the line—we can—but without a resupply, or even better, a resupply *and* reinforcements, at some point we all run out of charge packs and this devolves into an close-up knife horror show. Hence... Shot Caller wants us to seal up the front door. C'mon."

"Your Ice guys on the way?" Masters asked, following.

"Soon. They're still rigging the back entrance. Shot Caller figures we need to lock the front door sooner rather than later now that those new drop pods are coming to visit."

The two of them were inside the cave now. From outside, they could hear the blaster fire of the entrenched engineers, Zombie Squad, and the Gomarii-controlled alien horde pick up. That sound was followed by a braying cry for glory, and then a rippling explosion. Though Masters couldn't see it, the lieutenant had just set off a charge that sent scores of zhee to meet their deities. The survivors were picked off just in time for a spread-out advance of

Hools to engage, with Drusics barreling through in hopes of reaching the lines, their imposing, resilient bulk drawing fire away from the Hools.

Masters pointed at a device set up on the vault door's control panel. "I take it this is a bomb."

"A bit more subtle than that," Carter said. "Brought it along with us. It'll fuse the door shut from the outside."

"But your guys can still open it from the inside?"

Carter didn't respond. And then... "What? Sorry. I got Shot Caller in my ear."

"I said, you're sure your guys can still get out? And Bombassa and the QRF?"

"Yeah," said Carter. "Except Victory and the QRF won't be joining us right away. Shot Caller deployed them back through the kiddy pool. Big group of blues and their pets were making for the swamps. Victory is setting up an ambush for their arrival. Keep 'em out of the grotto until Ice can blow it."

"Okay," Masters said. "So... you ready to flip the switch on this thing?"

"I'll give you the honor," Carter said, stepping back, a glint of mischief in his eyes. "Just in case it malfunctions. I've got a family, bro."

Masters shook his head disbelievingly, then activated the device. He too stepped back as it burned and bored its way into the controls until complete destruction of the exterior mechanism was achieved.

"Well," Carter said, "nowhere to run to now unless Shot Caller opens the door for us."

Masters stared at the massive door. "You think he'll trade places with us if we ask?"

Carter laughed. "Man... probably."

Kill Team Victory

Setting up the ambush had been easy enough. Finding a way to break it off was proving to be the hard part for Bombassa and what remained of his men. By now Nap and the members of Kill Team Ice had rigged the grotto beyond the KP to collapse and seal off the entrance, but the Gomarii and moktaar assaulters hadn't gotten the message. Eschewing the fortified lines of the engineers and their Legion complement on the other side of the mountain, these aliens thought they'd found an easier way in.

"Think they'll let us go if we step aside and let them swim?" Nobes asked as he changed charge packs. The legionnaires were using a slight rise near the swamp for cover. They had been dealt intense casualties, and they were low on just about everything they needed to make the hostiles continue to pay.

"Doubtful," Bombassa said.

A dull rumble rolled beneath their feet, too faint to be heard above the blaster fire. But it was felt.

A ping came over the squad's L-comm. It was Masters. "How are things looking?"

"Like we're about to die," Doc Chance spat back.

Bombassa ignored the remark. "We need some help getting free of the engagement."

"Carter's Ice boys say they're swimming up to meet you. They just now blew the grotto via a remote detonation; back door is sealed. So your death won't be in vain, Doc."

"Not helping," Doc replied.

"Just hurry up and join the party over here. Dinner's getting cold. I've got shovels and leejes positioned to give covering fire once you make your breakthrough and get within range of us."

"Eyes on KTI," Toots announced.

Just then the legionnaires emerged from the murk with underslung launchers ready, sending forth a volley of fire that tore through a massive horde of zhee warriors who had begun to gallop into the mud. It was an absolute slaughter. The aliens didn't even slow, just continued their mad rush to get underwater. It wasn't even clear if they all had rebreathers, yet even that didn't stop them from trying. They appeared to be driven by an unthinking madness—well beyond the battle madness the species was known for.

The sheer violence put on by the Kill Team Ice legionnaires was staggering, even when beheld by an already accomplished Dark Ops team. From what Kel Turner and Carter had said, this team was a hand-picked, elite strike force wielded like a laser scalpel throughout the Savage Wars—and from what he saw now, Bombassa believed it. They were showing their value in the ease with which they cut through the stunned enemy front.

"Let's bounce," Nap called, and then continued to work his N-18 while the rest of the men blazed away ruthlessly.

What followed was a running firefight through thick vegetation at the edge of the swamp as the legionnaires made their way around the mountain, through rough terrain, working their way toward the cave. Only the legionnaires' speed and the precision of the operators' bounding withdrawal kept the men from being overwhelmed by this prong of the Gomarii forces. But as realization of what was happening swept through the enemy contingent, the count of their pursuers grew.

Soon men were being picked off, casualties in a numbers game that sent too many bullets and blaster bolts chasing after them as they raced for the salvation that was the shovels' fighting positions. The members of Kill Team Ice, who protected the retreat, paid the heaviest price. Nap caught a bolt to the back of the head almost exactly a thousand years after the day he'd been born, and then several more bolts as he went down. There was nothing that could be done for him or any of the others as they fell; almost at once they were overrun by pursuing moktaar and Drusics. The unbridled aggression of these aliens was frightening, but as the chase at last moved into the battlespace outside the cave, the mad press of bodies worked to the advantage of those being pursued. For it reduced the amount of fire that could be aimed at the legionnaires and the QRF, allowing them to sprint through lines and dive breathlessly into the dug-in and reinforced fighting positions the engineers had created in anticipation of this inevitable last stand.

Those positions were a relief to men who had just completed a drawn-out battle through open terrain. Dug in all around the cave's mouth, the defenses had been reinforced with recovered stone and timber from the tall black pine trees that had been shattered during the artillery barrage called in by MakRaven. Indeed, many of those artillery craters had been repurposed to serve as foxholes. Even the numerous zhee who had been torn apart by that barrage had been piled strategically—mounds of corpses providing cover or serving as obstacles to anyone who attempted to charge the cave. It was a grisly, grim showplace for what would surely be the fight of their lives.

As Bombassa and the remaining members of Victory, Zombie, and Ice tossed themselves down into the fighting positions, the end of their punishing run over, they joined the defenders already in place in sending torrents of fire at the pursuing force that now ran heedlessly past the points that the Gomarii who had been engaging the front entrance had already learned meant death. The enemy took heavy casualties, only adding to their devastating losses at the swamp. That ambush had been costly to the defenders, but it had been much more so to the Gomarii forces. Nix's prediction of twenty-to-one had proven to be far too low. The operators, Ice and Victory alike, had proven their worth as legionnaires.

"Oh, hi fellas," Masters said to the panting legionnaires. Then he popped up and opened fire at a squad of Drusics, their heads shaved and scars still raw from implant surgery, who had lustily chased Kill Team Victory into the lines. The brutish aliens were cut down to the last in the face of the stolid defenders.

Masters dropped back down to change packs. "I think they have a crush on you, Bassa."

The Kill Team Victory leader's glower came through loud and clear in his voice. "Save it."

"Hey, if we're all gonna die here, I'm gonna get my one-liners in."

Carter rolled next to the pair. "You hear that, or is it just the ringing in my ears?"

From overhead came the familiar rushing sound of repulsors.

"That doesn't sound like drop pods," Nobes called out.

"Good!" shouted Masters. "We don't want any more!"

And then a new voice came over the L-comm. One that was definitely *not* military. "This is, uh, Garret. Captain Keel's friend. We're sending down modified freighters with reinforcements. Don't shoot them down... uh, please."

"Kid, you can send me the bill for this whole mess if it'll come with reinforcements," Masters replied, remembering Garret and feeling jubilation that—somehow—Wraith had come through again.

Several nearly identical ships came in low, firing powerful bursts from their omni-cannons that cut through the myriad of hostiles still adjusting and pressing to the Legion's latest fire and maneuver tactic. As they came down, their bulbous front cockpits visible, it seemed that only one had a pilot—the wobanki, Skrizz. The rest must've been slave-controlled. Probably by Garret.

It didn't matter. The ships were down, the doors were opening, and the promised reinforcements poured forth in the form of...

"Koobs?" said Masters.

"Not koobs," said Carter, recognizing these particular Kublarens instantly. "Friends."

The Kublarens loped out of lowered freighter ramps, firing slug throwers that added loud *crack*s to the battlefield noise. The unexpected barrage sent zhee and Gomarii down into the dirt, some dead, others seeking cover.

The reinforcements croaked and clicked, their air sacs inflating with excitement, as they rolled up the flank of the Gomarii forces. Seeing this, the Legion responded, sending more concentrated fire on any who attempted to defend against the impending breakthrough.

The Gomarii ordered a withdrawal, evidently realizing that their sudden exposure on the battlefield was untenable, and though their enslaved foot soldiers would have continued their suicidal onslaught, it was clear that to do so would result in a situation where only the Gomarii themselves would be left to throw themselves against the defensive lines. The blues pulled back to their slave ship, disappearing inside or behind the colossal vessel, and the legionnaires, exhausted and pushed to the brink, watched the skirmishers retreat as Doc Chance and Trent moved to treat the wounded.

"Eventually they will remember we're still outgunned," Bombassa prophesied.

A large koob came hopping over earthen ramparts, leading his Kublaren warriors to link up with the legionnaires.

"Pik'kek!" Carter shouted.

"K'Carter!" the alien bellowed. "Big die, ya?"

Carter pulled Pik'kek in for a one-armed embrace. "Ain't seen' nothin' yet. Wait 'til the Savages get here."

"Get here... k'kik... soon? Big die for Savaj-ah."

Bombassa removed his helmet. "Good to see you again, Pik'kek."

Pik'kek's eyes widened, prompting a flicking lick of his tongue across one iris. "Lash. Is good. Now is very good."

Watching from the side, Masters couldn't help but laugh. "Saved by a bunch of koobs. We're all living in a Savage simulation."

38

Throne Room
Savage Hulk of the Golden King

"Prisma, what have you done?" Ravi said.

It was the Golden King who answered, a deep laugh serving as prelude to his words. "Played you for the fool you are, Ancient One."

Keel, Ravi, and the trigger-nuke had arrived safely aboard the Savage hulk of the Golden King. But instead of his being placed somewhere hidden, where Keel could activate the device while Prisma escaped and Ravi secured the Dark Ones' destruction, they were placed right in the middle of the Savage king's throne room, surrounded by Prisma, Reina, the Savage leader, and a host of his staff generals.

"Improvise!" Keel yelled, and then lunged for the trigger-nuke's controls. But to his frustration, his armor locked up and he found himself frozen in place.

"You come wearing *my* armor," the Golden King gloated. "Old and outdated as it may be. Don't imagine it can be used against me, Animal."

Keel struggled to free himself, but short of shucking the armor off, something he couldn't do anyway, he saw no way he could move. Further, his bucket HUD was a stream of warbles and flashes of code. Completely useless.

"My Prisma," the Savage leader said as he walked toward the teenage girl and gently stroked her face. "You are to be rewarded for this. When I strip this armor from the Animal's dead carcass, it will be yours."

"This is a great honor," Reina said, coming up behind the Savage king and seductively running her hands over his shoulders.

"If it pleases my lord," Prisma said. "But one thing I do request."

The Golden King arched an eyebrow even as Reina scowled and said, "You are too bold for one who has not yet become Uplifted."

"What I was has been shed. My lord's example was the only way I needed follow," Prisma answered.

A smile crept across the face of the first of the Savages. "What is your request, my Prisma?"

She removed the spear of Urmo from her back and pointed it at Ravi. "I wish to be slayer of the last of the Ancients. Allow me to kill this one as I did Urmo before."

"Prisma, no," Ravi said.

The thought brought a twisted delight into the Savage king's heart. This would be a spectacle to behold. "I grant your petition. Entertain us."

As Ravi backpedaled, Prisma lunged, leading with the sharp stone point of her Quantum-bending spear. The Ancient swirled his robes as he moved his body, allowing the rapid attacks to tear into the fabric of his clothing, but not himself.

"Draw your sword," Prisma growled. "Or die as a coward!"

But Ravi only danced away.

Reina laughed at the spectacle; she was clearly taking some measure of enjoyment from seeing her powerful protégé come up against the limits of her abilities. It had been Ravi who had slain the Dark Wanderer, and now, in defending himself, he showed a superiority over Prisma as vast as the east is from the west.

Until it suddenly wasn't. Prisma disappeared from view and reappeared at Ravi's side. She swung the shaft of her spear down and caught the Ancient's heels, knocking him flat on his back. Ravi only barely rolled away from a downward thrust meant to impale him and pin him to the cold deck of the Savage hulk.

The Golden King laughed and clapped his hands in approval, enjoying himself thoroughly. Even Reina looked impressed by this sudden and unexpected turn of events.

Keel roared in his helmet. "Unfreeze me and see how much you like your entertainment *then*, you kelhorns!"

In his HUD, the threat was interpreted as a command. A prompt appeared, asking the local user if he wished to block outside access.

Keel chuckled to himself. "Garret, I could kiss you."

He was about to regain control and try to even the fight a bit—or at least get the trigger-nuke working—when Prisma's voice was suddenly in his head.

Captain Keel. I'm sorry. And not just for right now. Ravi won't kill me, but he needs to believe I'm trying to kill him, because they will read him. He can't hide his mind like I can. I know that now. He needs to believe it, because they need to believe it. But I won't kill him, Captain Keel. I'm giving him time to escape.

If she was, she wasn't giving him much. Ravi had almost been finished after Prisma tripped him up in her surprise attack, and more than once since.

You were supposed to be clear, kid, Keel told her, thinking the words back at her and hoping that it was how it all worked.

I couldn't. I needed to see it happen. I needed Reina to know that I found her lies and that I remember the truth. She needs to know that before she dies.

Kid... Keel began.

I'm not a kid. Not anymore. I've lived ages. Dying and learning. Growing in the... the Crux. This ship is part of the Quantum. It's not like everywhere else. I've used that. I've grown... but I was a kid. And... and I owe you an apology.

Keel was taken aback by this. He was dimly aware that all of this... conversation... was happening much faster than it would take to form the words. His eyes could see the seconds tick by as the struggle between Ravi and Prisma played out before him. Just thinking of the incongruency between time as it played out before his eyes and time as it slowed the conversation in his mind made his head hurt.

Trust me, Keel thought. *You don't owe me anything.*

But I do. All those times. You came for me all those times. From the very beginning, when Tyrus Rechs blew himself up... you were there. And you rescued me from the Cybar. You came for me when Hutch was trying to kill me at Mother Ree's. And you didn't stop looking for me.

Keel was about to put all of that on Leenah, but found that he couldn't. Because it wasn't the truth. It was only convenient. The truth was... he didn't want Prisma to end in all the bad ways fate seemed to have in store for her. Leenah just made the insanity of that mission align with who he wanted to believe he was.

Prisma, he began, but she cut him off.

I treated you terribly. Like a spoiled child. I'm sorry.

Well, you were a brat, yeah.

Prisma continued. *I need you to do one more thing for me. Can you free yourself from the armor?*

Keel felt a sudden suspicion. Was this just another ruse? A false show of alliance in order to verify or disprove some worry over how well the Savage system had reclaimed its own piece of technology?

Yeah, he told her. *Garret did some modifications. I can take full control.*

Good. I can't reveal myself. Not yet. Not to do what we have to do. But she needs to die. Kill that woman in front of me.

Prisma pushed all her hatred, all her thirst for vengeance, and her remorse, too, into Keel's mind so that he could feel unequivocally what she felt about Reina and everything the woman had done. Not only to her, but to the galaxy.

Reina was only meters away. Keel turned his eyes toward her. If she got a little closer...

And then she did just that. Stepped around the crate of the trigger-nuke for a better view of the fight.

In a flash worthy of the nickname "Fast," Keel unlocked his armor and pulled the great hand cannon. He thrust the weapon under Reina's chin and muttered just loud enough for her to hear, "Prisma knows."

He pulled the trigger and sent a three-round burst of the system's depleted uranium rounds through the top of Reina's skull. The beauty—ruined—fell dead in a spray of blood and brain matter down to the deck.

With a start, the Golden King let out a cry.

The Savage hulk shook violently, tossing them all to their knees. Somewhere a staff officer decried that Maestro was "gone!"

Proximity alarms heralded the sudden arrival of boarders. The Legion had breached the Golden King's hulk.

39

Main Hangar Bay
Savage Hulk of the Golden King

The guns aboard Chhun's assault shuttle were blazing away inside the hangar bay. If the general's legionnaires had been inserting close to good concealment in openly hostile territory, such an action by the gun crew might be written off as precautionary. But aboard a Savage hulk—literally the longest and largest ship Chhun had ever seen—it meant there was trouble waiting to meet his legionnaires once the shuttle's side doors opened.

"Pop this can open," Chhun ordered the crew chief.

"One sec, Leej," the chief responded. The craft settled, guns still rattling and reverberating through the hull. A second later, maybe two, the doors were open and legionnaires streamed out into the melee.

The hangar was utter chaos. The Savage numbers weren't large, but they made up for it with the power of their weapons. One hulking Savage marine shouldered a two-meter-long rifle, holding it against his oversized shoulder as easily as if it were a plastite toy. A swirling yellow charge formed at the barrel and then the weapon kicked back with the force of a rocket launch as a sharp beam laced straight through one of the Republic shuttles attempting to land. The beam formed a hole right through the shuttle's side and straight out through the roof. Yet another hole was formed in the top of the hangar bay itself, exposing an upper deck through a shower of melted slag and sparking circuitry.

The shuttle made a ninety-degree rotation as it crashed hard on the deck, systems dead. The legionnaires inside began to work at forcing open the doors, using cutting torches that caused a faint glow to form on the outside. This effort was violently ended as a rocket streaked toward the shuttle from a fixed emplacement that had been set up by two more Savage marines. The shuttle exploded and was hurled toward the docking bay shield, pulverizing an unlucky leej who had been moving in its path. The ship's momentum carried it through the shield, and its fires winked out as it drifted dead in space.

Chhun shouldered his blaster rifle and sent several bolts into the head of the Savage shooter with the long gun. The rest of his squad followed suit, using concentrated fire to punch through the formidable armor and pulp the Savage's head. The wicked marine fell to its back and released the super rifle, which immediately thrummed and detonated in a teeth-rattling explosion that sent Chhun and his squad ducking against the blast.

"Keep moving!" Chhun said. "Clear out of the bay!"

There was ample intelligence on this operation, despite it being against a once-"vanquished" enemy who was unpredictable to the legionnaires even after fifteen hundred years of warfare. Ford—who else—had managed to get a spy on board, and the only explanation he gave as to how was one of his "I'll tell you later, trust me" gestures. Through Ford, that spy had signaled the movement of the Savage hulk, and its destination proved Kel Turner—who was fighting for his own life on the ground—right.

The spy also reported that Savage defenses on the ship were minimal. Most of its marines had been committed to warfare across the galaxy as part of a massive psyop that was just coming into view. Even worse, that psyop seemed to be working against a Republic stretched too thin to protect citizens already weary of their government. But the big play was here. The Savage hulk. Or so Turner, Ford, and the spy insisted.

The size of the ship certainly made it seem like this was the main event. Deynolds had launched all of Victory Company as well as several companies of Repub marines and even a platoon of Wet Sox, despite the total lack of water for them to operate in. In short, she'd gathered every fighter that could be spared from Kima and the fleet—to the point that if any of the Repub warships were boarded, it would be up to the crew to take blasters and defend it themselves.

Yet despite all those troops and all the shuttles bringing them, together they took up almost no space in the absurdly cavernous docking bay. Chhun could have deployed a battalion of MBTs and their crews, combat sleds, and HK-PP mechs and still have had room to spare. Not that he had any of those at his disposal—they were all otherwise engaged, taking on a cocktail of MCR, Gomarii invaders, and an increasing number of Savage marines who he hoped were about to regret leaving their hulk as quickly as they did.

The legionnaires pushed forward, focusing their fire first on the Savages' fixed weapon emplacements and then on the Savages themselves. Hullbusters moved along the flanks, sending additional fire into the Savage marines, who were not only capable of taking an incredible beating, but also possessed weapons that were brutally effective both at range and in close quarters, including energy shields, blades, and other weapons that could hack and cleave through armor.

Chhun noticed two things, both of them to the Legion's advantage. The first was that the docking bay was bristling with automated defense systems that were all offline. This no doubt had something to do with what Ford's code slicers had accomplished from their workplace aboard the antique light assault carrier his old friend had picked up somewhere. If those had been online, this battle would be moving in a decidedly different direction. Chhun doubted any of his shuttles would have even made landing.

The second thing he noticed was that these Savage marines weren't operating like a cohesive military unit. Which was different from what he'd read about them. In the Savage Wars, the Savages were known for using considerable tactics and strategy, although precisely what those tactics would be was always an unknown. Savages stretched the gamut from cyborgs with almost no biological tissue to what looked like aliens or human abominations straight from the horror holos, and their capabilities and weapons packages were just as varied. But for the most part, they fought like legionnaires.

These... didn't. Which wasn't to say that they couldn't fight. They were brutally efficient in the work of killing, and Chhun's men were paying the price for it. But they fought more like... heroes. As if they were separate from the larger battlefield. Chhun could picture them seeing the fight not as something requiring strategy but as a vast, chaotic proving ground that they strode through, cutting down the enemy and rallying an army that wasn't present.

That was what it felt like, anyway. And that was something Chhun could use to his advantage.

He pinged his squad leaders and advised them to target the Savage marines as individuals, the same way they might a combat tank. "Lure them away, get them to commit to an engagement, and then pour it on them. They're each trying to win this fight single-handedly. Use it, Legionnaires."

The tactic worked. The Savage marines let themselves be maneuvered into separate pockets by squads of marines or legionnaires and then were quickly overrun and overwhelmed. Strong as their armor was, it wasn't indestructible, and their imposing stature only made targeting the head and upper body that much easier from all sides without fear of hitting friendlies in the line of sight.

But as the Savage marines began to dwindle, a new threat emerged.

The legionnaires, heading for the deeper parts of the ship that would get them behind what Ford's intelligence had stated would be the entirety of the Savage defense, were suddenly engaging terrifying, almost spectral creatures that were exactly the sorts of horrific abominations one read about in histories of the Savage Wars. These had no weapons, but the claws at the ends of their long and pale fingers etched jagged grooves into armor and ribboned flesh. Blaster bolts slumped and slowed them, but didn't seem to drop them. At least not until a level of fire equal to what a Savage marine could absorb was leveled on them.

To make matters worse, while the Savage marines were few in number, these other... *things*... were plentiful. They swept into the hangar bay, thwarting the invasion's advance.

More shuttles were landing, which would help. Chhun changed his directives to simply overpowering and pushing troops further into the ship to eliminate the Savages in control of the bridge.

Then an old freighter landed on the deck, just launched from the *Battle Phoenix*. It stood out from the smaller shuttles that had touched down around it.

"Got room for more in this fight, Leej?"

Andien Broxin's voice would have been too far in Chhun's past for him to recognize it had he not heard it again just recently in the briefing room. Seeing her had been... interesting. It raised jarring feelings that he rarely considered and prospects that he had left behind him a long, long time ago. But there was a time when he had thought that maybe life in the Legion wasn't the only life for him to live.

"Always," Chhun answered. "Savage marines are under control, but these new Savages we're still trying to solve."

"I've got something that can help with that. See you on the deck. Broxin out."

Chhun knew just what that "something" was. Broxin had assumed leadership—or maybe *responsibility* was a better word—of a platoon-sized element of Cybar Spartan fighters whose aims were evidently the same as the Legion's when it concerned these Savages. Chhun remembered the devastation these units had caused when his kill team had encountered them in what would become a planetary genocide in the early days of Article Nineteen. Now these war bots were pouring out of the freighter and joining the fight beside the legionnaires of Victory Company.

The galaxy could be a strange place sometimes.

The Cybar fought in tight units, opting to stay together and send overwhelming firepower against the Savage vampires, reducing them to pieces with withering fire from their tri-barreled N-50s. They were adept at bringing this new enemy down, and that boded well.

So well, in fact, that Chhun was ready to organize a push toward the bridge when Broxin linked up with him.

"Cohen. We should move. The Spartans will clear us a path, but they're too slow to make a rapid assault on our objective."

Chhun attempted to take all that in at once, then nodded his assent. There was no time for anything else but the mission. "I've got squads forming to move. Push up with me. Once we clear the hangar, we're supposed to have a free shot at the bridge... but it'll be a long run."

Broxin smiled. "Then let's get running."

40

Bombassa's prophecy had proven correct—not long after staggering away from the vicious pounding they'd taken by charging into the engineer's lines, the Gomarii and their ilk had reorganized and attempted exhausting push after push to make a breakthrough into the cave. Dead Kublarens lay staring endlessly at the clouds, their phosphorescent yellow blood pooling at the feet of those still living and serving as a banquet to the thick flies drawn to the smell of death.

It had taken a miracle for Masters to be able to announce, "Definitely a simulation," to those still left alive around him. Nix and Doc Chance, along with several of the leejes from Zombie Squad had died somewhere during the last few Gomarii-led counter-assaults.

Carter and Bombassa understood why the leej made the comment. Even Pik'kek was catching on.

"Seem-ya-lay-shon. Ya."

"You're all right, Pik'kek," Masters said as he checked a charge pack and, feeling it was too low for whatever might come next, swapped it for a fresh pack in his front carry pouch.

The wave that had just broken after coming hard for them, that killed so many other legionnaires, should have overwhelmed the lines and left defending the vault to only Kel Turner, still inside. It hadn't mattered how many aliens the legionnaires killed, more came. Calls for support from the forces still left on the planet went unheeded—the Gomarii axis, the zhee, and the MCR were still battling elsewhere. Much of the Legion was withdrawn to await an opportunity to assault the Savage hulk. The basics, hullbusters, and even the local Kimbrin Yawds were fighting for their own lives far away from the wilderness that surrounded the cave. No help would come. Kublar was out of further hatchlings to spare.

And then... the assault fell apart completely.

Gomarii were caught off guard as the Drusic, Moktaar, and Doro shock troopers they employed stopped fighting. Some dropped their arms and fled. Others turned their weapons against their masters and the loyal Hool and zhee, who fought for other reason—credits and holy merit. The legionnaires, engineers, and Kublarens watched, disbelievingly. All thought this was their last stand. Though stunned, they were still alert enough to withdraw themselves thanks to the reprieve they'd unexpectedly been given.

Garret returned to the L-comm to explain that "Maestro" the Savage system that controlled these enslaved fighters, had been shut down. "But you're not out of the asteroid field yet. That Savage hulk sent down drop pods. Sorry."

The code slicer had been the first to explain how Maestro was taken offline and the deleterious effect that had on the Gomarii's enslaved shock troopers, but he was late in giving the news about the Savages. By that time Kel Turner had already heard reports of drop pods launching from the monumental Savage hulk they'd lured to this world coming down across the globe—probably a strategy to deny any newly freed troops the ability to reinforce the fight at the cave.

"But that doesn't matter," Tuner had told those legionnaires still living, the men who had volunteered for a suicide mission. "Because all we need to do is keep buying the boys in orbit time to take the hulk down. They'll do it. Keep the Savages busy once they arrive. Don't let them leave. KTF."

The battered and exhausted defenders had watched the fighting between the Gomarii elements and the freed slaves as they waited for the Savages to arrive. It was clear that the captured aliens *weren't* skilled soldiers prior to their capture. Few knew how to operate the weapons systems in their hands once Maestro fell. Surprise gave way to slaughter, and soon the only Drusic, moktaar, or doro on the battlefield were the dead.

"Savages dropping in thirty seconds," Kel Turner announced to the team. "Be ready."

The team had clear view as five drop pods rocketed into the ground almost to the second following Turner's countdown heads up. The pods were cruel-looking, a light-absorbing black with geometric angles that suggested a fractal tear drop. They hit and sprayed geysers of wet, muddy vegetation from their strikes near the smoking Gomarii slave ship. Torrents of steam and cooling jets vented from the capsules as the canopy-securing bolts exploded, taking the armored plates with them.

The first Savage marine stepped from one of the pods and set its nine-foot frame on an Earth much different from the one its master, the Golden King, had left all those centuries before.

"Holy strokes," Masters mumbled.

Wrapped in hulking armor and glaring with furious eye slits in its dome-shaped helmet, the armored Savage marine made its intentions all too clear by firing an arcing, electrified gob of plasma from a colossal pistol. The searing round streaked into the line of engineers, leaving only the lower torsos of a pair of men who had been sharing a foxhole.

Sergeant Lynx shouted to his remaining legionnaires. "I want bolts between eyeballs!"

Five ominous Savage marines now sprinted past the slave ship and into the corpse-littered combat area, splitting their team according to whatever battlefield doctrine they had running under the armor. They were all moving for the cave entrance.

A sliver of light banged against the Savage's armor.

"Hit?" the prone Zombie sniper asked.

"Can't tell," Masters shouted back as he moved to better position himself for the fight.

The Savages seemed to notice the legionnaires intermixed with the engineers and Kublarens for the first time and fired their high-powered weapons in their direction. Their shots blew apart entire foxholes, immolating Toots and Doc Chance.

The arrival of the Savage vanguard had rallied the Gomarii, Zhee, and Hools and now those forces fell in behind the ultra marines, harrying what was left of the engineers and Kublarens.

"They're targeting leejes first," Carter said. "Spread out and keep their fire away from the shovels!"

Another member of Zombie squad, Choco, fell dead at once, his armor worthless.

"Keep moving!" Masters called. "I'll see if I can draw some fire."

Before anyone could object, Masters darted into the open, going wide of the Gomarii and zhee who were occupied with the engineers. He hoped to draw the Savages, which now seemed singularly focused on the elimination of all legionnaires present, away from the cave, the engineers, the koobs... all of it.

Masters was throwing his life away, but he could see no other easy way of getting the intensity of those Savage weapons out of the fight. Any of the legionnaires might have made the sacrifice. Masters thought of it first.

He sprinted, running for all he was worth, feeling the work of the skinpacks reverse as some of his cuts began to reopen and secrete thin beads of blood. The legionnaire had no idea if his ploy was even working. He expected to feel the pain of the Savage weapons at any moment.

A blast of a different sort flashed in front of him, perhaps twenty meters or so. The concussive force blew him off his feet and onto his back, where a rainfall of warm dirt sprinkled back up to him.

"Blues got their guns back up!" Nobes shouted over L-comm.

That process was supposed to have taken a long time. As Masters noted the position of Earth's sun overhead, he realized what a long time they'd been fighting. Long enough. Time aplenty to reroute power supplies of a ship that could never take off again and get them to reanimate what few PDCs hadn't been ruined by the laser or its detonation early in the day.

The fight had been so, so long and Masters was exhausted when it started. The old man, the Shot Caller, had been right about that. Masters knew it then as he struggled to lift himself back off the ground as his ears rang and another concussion was stacked on top of all the others he'd suffered in his career. He needed to move. The ship might fire again—another test shot to zero against the embedded engineers. Or the Savages... they were still coming. The ship hadn't been aiming at them, had it?

Masters looked and saw through blurred vision that the Savages were closing on him. He rolled from him back onto his stomach, and then pushed himself up to his knees. The towering Savage cast its shadow across the kid with a movie star's face. That face, handsome despite skinpacks and a trip through hell, became resigned to its fate.

The legionnaire looked at peace.

The only thing that struck Masters was a sudden explosion of helmet and brain matter. The Savage marine slumped to its knees and pitched forward as the colossal report of a powerful rifle finally caught up to the damage its bullet had done.

"I know that sound!" Carter yelled.

In the distance, perched amid the black trees, the Wild Man swept the battlescape for additional Savage targets.

See, babe, I told you. Now do another one.

Though Masters was aware of the hands that scooped him up out of the chaos of the incoming sniper fire and carried him away by his drag handles, it wasn't until he was set back down just outside the Gomarii ship that he regained enough lucidity to take in his surroundings. "'Bassa?"

"Yes," the big man answered. Standing with him was Carter, Nobes, Sergeant Lynx, and about a dozen Kublarens led by Pik'kek.

Masters strained to see the engineers, but his position against the ship hid most of them. But he could hear the battle now, the incessant firing of blasters, slug throwers, and the measured boom of the sniper rifle. "How's... how's it looking out there?"

"Big trouble," Sergeant Lynx answered.

"That sniper you hear is a buddy of mine," Carter said. "He's dropping Savages, but the pods are still coming. We used that distraction to grab you and make it to the ship."

Masters looked around, still somewhat dazed. "Don't think we can fly ourselves outta here. Sorry, guys."

"Not going to fly it," Bombassa said, his patience just about up. "We're going to shut down its power systems the hard way."

"No chance we can hold for long with blues, Savages, *and* PDCs spitting at us," Nobes explained. "Pik'kek is going to leave a security detail to watch you. We're heading inside now."

"I'm coming... I'm coming." Masters struggled to his feet, wavered, and then felt the ground beneath him become solid. He took a deep breath.

From the woods, the Wild Man continued to pick targets, decapitating the Savage marines with each shot he could make. But the Savages still had the support of a Gomarii axis too numerous for one shooter to fend off indefinitely. Already several squads of zhee and Hools had been dispatched to root out the shooter, and additional drop pods' worth of Savage marines now trudged in the sniper's direction.

Soon the sniper's shots fell silent and didn't sound again. Overhead, the atmosphere was alive with the furious flashes that signified an all-out starship battle. There was no telling how many slave ships and drop pods were being denied entry into Earth's atmosphere. Perhaps it didn't matter. Those that had gotten through would find victory inevitable. It was like Shot Caller said... they were buying time for the Victory Company to wipe out the Savages where they lived.

That time was running out of stock.

Masters followed the ad hoc strike team into the slave ship, using an entrance without security features because it hadn't existed prior to the drilling laser had boring it out during Kill Team Victory's earlier mission. The legionnaire looked around. He had been talking to himself endlessly, if only to convince himself that he was all right. Now his words spilled out his consciousness. "I always figured I'd die surrounded by people who were a lot better-looking than you. You guys look like the nine hells."

"Look who's talking," Carter said as he stepped to the group, his armor dripping with the blood of some koob he'd tried to save.

"Maybe we should try talking to them," Masters said, pulling off a skinpack that hung limply from his jaw. "Maybe KTF isn't the diplomatic winner the Legion has led us all to believe."

Carter ignored the comment and seemed focused on some internal comms message. "Just got word from Shot Caller. Everybody without an operating bucket—cover your ears."

An orbital round rocketed down from above, fired from atmo by a Repub gunship. The shock wave traveled past them well after the rail gun munition had already executed its grisly work, striking a group of advancing Savage marines in the center of the formation, decimating that particular line of advance. Shattered armor and weapons flew nearly twenty meters from the point of impact, turning the dead marines into nothing more than debris.

"Here's how I see it," Carter told the team. "The shovels and however many leejes we still have out there are getting squeezed as soon as Wild Man is down. Orbital strikes are fine to keep these guys back for now, but eventually they'll need to be so close that we all die anyway. Great. We know how it ends. It ends a lot sooner if this hulk can calibrate its PDCs to fire on our lines, though. So we deny the blues that ability and then get back to the line."

"Two options for that," Bombassa said coldly. "Totally shut down via engineering or we take the CIC."

"Figure both hafta be guarded," said Sergeant Lynx.

Carter nodded. "We do what we do. I take Pik'kek and the Koobs to secure the power supply. The rest of you leejes take the CIC. If one of us succeeds, we're good. If not..." the legionnaire shrugged.

There were no objections.

The legionnaires and Kublarens began to move their way through the ship. At first, they felt that the place was abandoned, but soon they began to encounter Gomarii running down the corridors, distracted. Outside, the Savage Marines moved on the embattled engineers, with legionnaires from Kill Team Ice, Victory, and Zombie squad acting as significant force multipliers. —save Carter—outside and doing what they could do slow them down. The ship vibrated from the impact of successive drop pods striking beyond its hull—*whump! Whump! Whump!*—and then shook from the cratering *boom* of another orbital strike from the *Centurion,* high in orbit.

Carter relayed a message to the team. "Shot Caller says we need to pick it up. Savages and inching closer to the line. Plus the blues are getting closer with their strip and recalibration. Those PDCs'll be aimed at our guys soon."

'The line' was the point where further orbital strikes would begin to cause friendly casualties. The need to call for haste was due to the confusing layout of the slave ship, which sat inside of that line and therefore couldn't be destroyed by bombardment without also wiping out the vault's defenders.

"I can't tell which way is which," Bombassa said.

The interior of the Gomarii ship was as different from a Repub vessel as a Drusic was from an Ulori. Dark corridors traced away for tens of meters with no indication of where they might be leading. Nothing was labeled, since the Gomarii had a penchant for putting emotional echoes along passages that only they could read.

Thankfully, Carter had prior mission experience to guide the team. "Pretty sure this is a repurposed Savage hulk. Not one of the big ones, but big enough. I don't know how many I've boarded. A lot. The command-and-control center should be in the most heavily fortified part of the ship."

"Why would we go there?" Masters asked. "Wouldn't there be a weapons locker or something closer to whatever passes for a docking bay on this boat?"

"I already saw the weapons we can use," Carter said, slowly striding down the passage. "We just gotta get to the CIC to unlock 'em. See those? Torpedo tubes."

He pointed to a fractured section of the ship. The tubes were cracked, and in at least one spot, burned straight through by the boring laser that had chewed away to reveal outside daylight.

"Looks like its torpedo firing days are behind it," Lynx said.

"Right you are, Sergeant," Carter answered. "But once you get your hands on a torpedo, there's more than one way to deliver it."

The Legion team continued along the deck grating, careful to identify potential traps or countermeasures to keep enemy forces from gaining access to the CIC or the bridge. They encountered a repeating blaster at one point, but its bolts weren't strong enough to even scratch the legionnaire's armor. The power supply had been ruined and all that it could muster was a luke-warm blast that was easily ablated.

A minute later, the few human survivors, men who had lost nearly their entire teams, cut around the corner only to find Carter, who had gone in advance, waiting for them.

"What is the problem?" Bombassa asked.

"Trip lasers in the passage ahead," the legionnaire said. "You guys are gonna have to take an alternate route to the CIC."

"Bet they didn't have time to trap the passages that the laser burned through the ship," Masters observed.

"Bet you're right," Nobes responded.

Carter nodded. "Good. This is the part where we need to divide and conquer. I'll take Pik'kek and the Kublarens down to engineering. First team to shut off the PDCs gets a case of beer. Each."

As soon as Masters's team reached an opening to one of the laser-created burrows that had been cut through the ship, they parted ways with Carter and the koobs. Though the slag had solidified, the beam had left behind an obstacle course of gaps and struts as it tore through the superstructure, heedless of design or utility. The team moved more swiftly now all the same, without finding any further traps. But the odds of getting a back door straight to the CIC were slim, and eventually they would have to get out and progress on the main, trapped corridors.

"If we drop down here, I think we're adjacent to the CIC," Nobes said, nodding at one of the many holes in the floor of the burnt-out "corridor," which had been moving-ly slightly up due to the angle of the beam as it had burned its way almost through the top of the ship. The legionnaire cautiously lowered himself through the charred hole, and the moment his boots thudded against the deck he went low, ready for an auto-turret or some other defensive device set up to take him down. When none came, he stood slowly and looked for an access door.

"Place is clear," he called to the team as they covered him from above, rifles pointed out from the narrow opening in the ceiling's thick structural steel. "Two doors. Which one leads to the prize?"

One by one, the rest of the team dropped down. They were in some sort of operations room, filled with inactive, chest-high workstations that had been abandoned by the Gomarii crew, likely to either defend the captain in the CIC or to add their numbers to the battle outside the ship as things went south.

Bombassa tapped one of the dead workstations. "Can we turn one of these on and pull up a schematic? Open a door or something?"

"No juice," Masters said, holding down the power-boot to emphasize it. "But look at the muscle they put on that blast door," he added, nodding at the door in question. "Bet that leads into the CIC security screening room."

The legionnaires compared the two doors and saw that Masters was correct. One blast door looked rated to withstand a bomb blast and make anyone with a cutting torch die of old age before they got it open. The other had all the hallmarks of a standard access door, likely leading out to a primary corridor.

"Can we slice our way through that beast?" Bombassa asked. "Otherwise we make for the corridor and see how well it's defended. Can't leave Carter to be our only shot at success."

Nobes pulled a clear plasteen card from his belt. "I have a slicer module that should hack this door no sweat. Should also open the CIC door, but we need to be quick in case it's got an AI that can react to attack one and make attack two that much harder."

Bombassa nodded. "Make it happen, Leej."

A minute later, the blast door heaved open, groaning through its bulk. The legionnaires poured inside, ready to deal out damage, but found the room spartan and empty, with only a few sensor stations, also unmanned.

"Is this the place or not?" Lynx asked. "Don't look like no CIC check-room I ever saw."

"This has to be it," Nobes said confidently. The room had two other doors, but one clearly led out to the main corridor. Nobes went directly to the door he believed would lead to the CIC and waggled the slicer card in his hand. "Let Carter know we're about to roll the Gomarii commander and to be sure the beer is cold."

Carter and his team were several decks below them, assaulting the engineering room.

The legionnaires stacked on either side of the hatch, ready to storm in the moment Nobes achieved unlock.

"Okay," Nobes muttered to himself, readying the card for access. "Do this and then you can finally get a beer." He slid the card into the hatch's interface. "Unlocked. Get ready."

"Just like that?" Lynx asked.

Nobes moved his hand to press the command for the door to open. "Just like—"

A burst of magnetically accelerated projectiles ripped through the hatch as it opened and punched through the legionnaire's bucket. The operator smacked down onto the deck grating, his blood pouring between the slats.

"Holy strokes!" Masters exclaimed, dropping with the others for cover. The hatch remained closed. "I guess we're at the right place."

"Banger!" Bombassa shouted, and then tossed the ear-popper inside the enclosed space.

Lynx raced in just behind the boom, bounding from one side to the other, dodging a wild burst sent his way by a robotic security drone carrying a rifle similar to the ones wielded by the Savage marines.

Masters roared and followed.

Lynx ducked incoming fire by dodging and rolling between workstations marked with floating alien-scripted holos. And then suddenly the sergeant found himself face to face with a Gomarii spacer hiding beneath a desk.

"Kelhorn!" Lynx shouted. Using his knee to pin the alien's arm to the deck to prevent him from pulling a weapon, the leej used Sami's knife, which he'd taken off the man's corpse, to nearly slice off the enemy's head.

Masters put bolts on target against the security drone. It took several hits against its armor but continued to return fire. Masters dove away from the maelstrom of hyper-kinetic explosive rounds and found his own desk to hide behind.

The CIC was still occupied by its Gomarii commander, who was easy to identify, as he was the only inhabitant of the command center who wasn't cowering behind a desk. Instead he stood stoically at the far end of the room, arms behind his back like an admiral inspecting his fleet as it paraded before the bridge. He had been standing in that spot the entire time, seemingly surrendering himself to whatever fate was awaiting him. He would see his attackers fall or he would see his own capture or death. He would watch whatever came, unflinchingly.

Bombassa advanced , his rifle up and ready. "My name is First Sergeant Bombassa of the Legion. I order you to surrender yourself or be locked inside this wreck when I burn it to ash."

An orbital strike pounded more Gomarii and Savages, the full might of a Republic super destroyer on terrifying display for all those who had yet to reach the up-close fighting against the Legion and shovel defenders.

"I surrender." The Gomarii commander slowly raised his hands above his head. "But my king cannot be stopped."

"Yeah, yeah, we'll see," Masters said, wishing Nobes was there to help him figure out the system. "Sket. How the hell do we shut this thing down? Does anyone read skin mustache?"

Bombassa went to the other team. "Carter. We're in the CIC but lost Nobes. It's going to take us a while to figure out these controls. How close are you to shutting everything down?"

The blaster fire that came through the reply answered ahead of Carter. "Gonna be a bit. They were expecting us."

Then, an idea occurred to Masters. "'Bassa! Cycle though the L-comm transmissions and get me a link with Ford's buddy, Garret!"

The master code slicer had the guns turned off faster than any of the legionnaires imagined possible.

"Okay, so that should be it," Garret said over the L-comm, broadcasting so that every legionnaire still alive on the slave ship could hear him. "Sorry I couldn't just get them to shoot at the Savages but it would take a manual recalibration and there aren't enough of you to do that because of how much those things weight but there's something else that's really important because we've boarded the Savage hulk and I think we're gonna do this but Mr. Nilo and Mr. Makaffie say that we still need to know how the Gomarii were communicating with Maestro and the Savages and we need to know how to find out if this is really it or if not and I think that's important too because what if this isn't really all there are?"

"Holy hell," Carter said. "Never thought I'd miss Brisco."

"Garret," Bombassa said, "Sum it up for us in a sentence."

Garret cleared his throat. "We need prisoners. Gomarii prisoners. As high-ranking as you can get."

"Is that all?" Masters asked. "Done."

"Really? Oh. Well... good. Thank you."

"You're welcome. Masters out." The legionnaire shrugged at Bombassa and Lynx. "Kids."

Bombassa used his HUD to check what observation bot feeds Kel Turner still had going. "Savages must have been alerted by the Gomarii. They're closing on our location."

"So glad we traded the old death trap for this one," Masters said. "Much better."

"Bring your prisoners and get down to my level," Carter instructed the other legionnaires. "I saw a gaping hole on my way to engineering. We could all make a run for the lines and the front door."

"We'll do what we can," Bombassa said. "You move that way now."

"Not gonna leave you guys." Carter was adamant.

"To the nine hells with that," Masters said. "Take the open lane to the cave mouth and then get those shovels ready to provide us with covering fire. We'll come back out the way we came in. No way I went through all this just to be dusted inside a slave ship."

"All right. Moving."

Another orbital bombardment kept the full force of enemy pressure from the defenders.

Bombassa watched as Carter, Pik'kek and several koobs slipped outside the lower level of the downed slave ship and began to move back to the relative safety of the cave mouth defenses. The defenders had taken a beating; Savage marines had been systematically clearing the field of anything with a weapon that wasn't blue, donk, or poisonous, though there was a certain disunity in their tactics. The effect was the same, but often the marines would fire on the same position to the point of overkill, leaving other areas untouched. Each marine seemed to be operating under general orders, but the completion of those orders was up to the individual.

Carter had made it halfway to the cave when the Savages who had fought their way past the line took notice and started firing. Right away, several hopping koobs went down. Fast-moving magnetic rounds zipped into the blood-slicked terrain beneath Carter, kicking up grit and forcing him to pull his arms in close as he sprinted for safety shouting, "Sket! Sket! Sket!"

The legionnaires inside the slaver watched with grim detachment. Pik'kek bounded to the side—the Savages let him go.

"C'mon, Carter," Bombassa urged. "C'mon."

Carter—legionnaire, contractor, Kill Team Ice member—felt he must have used up the last of the luck that had carried him through so many scrapes and close calls. He ran past the few surviving engineers who had their heads down against the barrage. He saw the dead bodies of his fellow Kill Team Ice members—Nap slumped over on his sniper rifle as though he'd been killed mid-shot. Carter was sure he'd join them, but his luck held after all. He threw his legs out in front of him, performing a feet-first slide that brought him inside the cave mouth, then rolled his body until he was completely behind the stony cover.

Of course, if they sent in a rocket after him, he was a dead man all the same.

Carter sat up, feeling the strain in his abs from the weight of his kit. He took several steps to the back of the cave, not feeling that much safer, and pinged the pitifully small number of survivors still on the slave ship.

"Okay, boys," he said through pants. "I can send all the suppressive fire Mel can deliver. Say when."

Masters's reply was as unexpected as it was confusing. "Yeah. We're good on that, actually."

A moment later the roar of chain guns erupted from somewhere outside the cave, unlike anything Carter had heard since Kill Team Ice had been sent to subdue the traitors on Sinasia. Against his better judgment, he moved back to the mouth of the cave and peered back outside.

The operator's mouth fell open.

In the midst of the Savage marines stood a colossal Samurai mech, which seemed to be trilling in robotic, signica laughter through its powerful external speakers as it unleashed destruction on the battlefield. It seemed to be using every one of its weapons systems at once, unleashing a tornado of linked machine-gun fire with calibers more than capable of punching through the formidable armor of the marines. Those not caught in the whirlwind had rockets and missiles flung in their direction, destroying Savage marines embedded on hillsides.

But the Savage weapons were equally as deadly, and the mech seemed to be aware of this. Before it could be hammered to inoperability, it flashed its rocket thrusters and climbed a thousand meters straight up at a speed that would have liquified the insides of most featherheads. It then rocketed away in the direction of Kham Dho City, perhaps to even the odds there, as it had just done here.

"Holy sket," Carter said over the L-comm.

"I know, right?" said Masters. "I could use two or three of those the next time we try this."

"Let's clean up," said Bombassa. "If enough of us are still alive, we can keep what's left of those marines at bay. Watch for blues and zhee, but let them go if they try to pull out."

"Want me to come back to the ship to help?" Carter asked.

"Negative. Stay there and help the shovels dust anyone who tries to hide. I'll make sure the prisoners are delivered to your location. You're on guard duty from then on, leej."

Carter laughed.

"There a problem?" Bombassa asked.

"Just thinking. This whole thing started with me ordering you to do the sket jobs, and now here I am getting stuck with a sket job on your orders, Lash."

Bombassa smiled. "Strange galaxy. KTF."

41

"Betrayal!"

The Golden King's furious cry sounded like a damnation. Prisma had committed the unpardonable sin, and his wrath seemed singularly fixed on her ruin. Putting his helmet on as he leapt to his feet, he sent his hand shooting forward, seeking to squeeze the life out of her neck from afar.

But Prisma's abilities had grown. Her natural ability had already been powerful beyond anything Ravi had ever seen. Her training under Reina had unlocked even more of her capabilities. And her reflections aboard a ship that had floated within the Quantum for so long had unlocked the wisdom of the ages.

Prisma found that what she focused on revealed itself to her. Not fully, but enough.

She cast aside the probing, spectral grip on her throat and moved toward the Savage king, spear held in both hands and ready to thrust forward.

One of the staff generals stepped into her path, blocking her from her target. The general's face was beautiful, like all the others. All the "sons" were made perfect, though not identical to their golden progenitor. The man's beauty almost stayed Prisma's hand, but the knowledge of a galaxy still hanging in the balance spurred her to violence.

She thrust the weapon into the man's groin. It passed through the armor effortlessly. The general hunched in agony, and Prisma withdrew the spear and continued.

Keel was up and on the girl's heels. He ran past the wounded general and sent a quick burst from the hand cannon into the man's long platinum locks, exploding the Savage's once-perfect face.

"You would dare!" bellowed the Golden King.

He moved his hand to his chest.

"The amulet!" Prisma shouted.

Keel understood at once. He fired as he moved forward, taking deliberate aim and allowing both hands to guide the hand cannon. Fearful of hitting the artifact directly—Keel was only guessing that would be bad, based on what it supposedly housed—he aimed instead for the wearer.

Rounds struck the Golden King's arms, knocking them away from their purpose and causing the king to stagger. Keel adjusted his aim and sent a second burst at the Savage king's head. But this time the Savage seemed to... *sway*... and his head was suddenly no longer in the path of the bullets. One came close though, and a thin trickle of blood ran down his jawline from somewhere above his ear.

It was then that all the force of a combat sled at full speed smacked into Keel, sending him tumbling. A second staff general had taken him down with a diving tackle that left Keel's hip feeling bruised and his ribs tender. The bucket HUD cautioned him regarding potential internal injuries and asked if he wished to have pain medications administered.

"No," Keel grunted through gritted teeth. He wasn't sure if the armor was just quick with this sort of thing or if Rechs enjoyed being doped up in a fight. Keel did not. Especially when wrestling with a heavily armored brute who was now on top of him and just a quick hand-fight away from being free to rain down hammering blows.

He needed to get himself loose, and quickly.

What was loosed instead was the general's head, which separated in a flash of metal as Ravi's sword sliced it cleanly from his body. The golden hair of the Savage wrapped the face like a burial shroud as the head tumbled down, striking against Keel's helmet with a thud before rolling onto the deck.

The smuggler tossed the heavy body aside and then got to his feet, ready to rejoin the fight. He saw the Golden King now fighting both Ravi and Prisma at once, but it was all his attackers could do to both dodge the leviathan's blows and prevent him from grabbing hold of his amulet, which had now darkened as if it alone was in shadow. To make matters worse, the remaining staff generals were nipping at Prisma's and Ravi's heels, forcing them to dodge additional attacks only to bound back toward the Golden King to keep him from acquiring the room to operate that he clearly desired.

One staff general remained fixed at the war table, reading it and announcing the status of the Savage hulk. Main engines were offline—that must have been what had knocked them all off their feet. "Animal" vessels were filling the bay, and the Savage honor guard was engaging them.

That had to be Chhun.

"Sket," Keel muttered. There was no way he could blow the hulk now—not with all those legionnaires on board. Just like that, his plan was out the window. If he survived this, he was going to have some explaining to do to Leenah.

Survive first. Everything else in due time.

Keel took the easy kill and sent a three-round burst from the hand cannon into the exposed skull of the general manning the war table. The Savage pitched face-first into the displays. Keel had started to move on, then saw that—somehow—the Savage's fingers were moving and his arms were struggling as if he was trying to push himself up. Keel paused long enough to send several more bursts into the creature's head until it finally went still.

On to the larger fight. Judging from the speed at which the Golden King moved, Keel wasn't sure he could do much against him—if anything. But he could even the odds for Ravi and Prisma.

He began to take shots at the remaining staff generals, taking the first one down before the others even realized the threat. There were now only four left, and two of them broke off to engage Keel directly. These had helmets on, which meant bursts from the slug thrower could only knock at the door. It would take a whole lot more to break it down.

One of the generals battered him with a powerful back-handed blow that sent him sprawling across the deck. His bell was rung, and he shook his head from a plank position, trying to get his bearings as the two behemoths strode toward him. He caught sight of the trigger-nuke, now twenty meters distant; the fight in the throne room was taking them farther away from it, and Keel wondered if the Golden King recognized the threat and was purposefully leading Prisma and Ravi away from the device.

Keel calculated the odds of getting to it and at least getting it started in its standard thirty-minute countdown. They could reset it later if things went well. But before he could even pull himself onto his knees, there was a great thunder as one of the generals leapt and landed beside him. He saw the big leg swing back for a punt that would have sent him airborne—and quite possibly with a punctured lung, even with the armor—and reacted by spinning his own leg in a circle that caught the plant leg at the heel. It felt like he was trying to low-sweep a tree, but the armor's power assist added a force sufficient to topple the off-balance Savage onto his back.

Keel wasn't eager to fight the Savage general hand-to-hand. He'd done that with one of these already, and it had been so strong that it was all he could do to hang on. There was no overpowering them. But maybe Makaffie's talk of him having once had the nickname "Fast" held some truth.

He used that quickness to run up on the supine foe and kick at the base of his helmet. The blow caught more chin than helmet, but it was strong enough not only to snap the Savage's head back, but also to bring the helmet up on his face, exposing him from the mouth down.

Keel sent a full-auto burst into the Savage's chin and neck, firing until his armor warned him of the second Savage approaching in much the same manner as the first. The smuggler activated his jump jets and boosted out of the way, sending targeted fire down on the second Savage, though not breaking through the armor.

He gave up all thought of finishing this one off when he saw how Prisma and Ravi were faring. Ravi had managed to behead one of the two generals left to them, and it looked like Prisma had impaled another. That left just the

Golden King, who was dodging their attacks as though they were moving through water.

Ravi's sword flashed, but the Golden King side-stepped the swipe, forcing Prisma to flip out of the way. Keel had an idea how the kid had learned to do that, but he could still hardly believe it when he saw it.

That gave the Golden King the room he needed to go on the offensive. He sent a kick that looked far too fluid for someone in such massive armor, driving his boot straight into Ravi's ribs, sending the Ancient flying and then rolling in pain on the deck.

The Savage then turned his attention to battering Prisma, crying "Betrayer!" with every frenzied blow. The girl dodged them all, but she was forced to give ground as she did so, each step taking her one step farther away from the trigger-nuke. Keel was now sure it was intentional. He once again considered activating it, but saw that the remaining staff was guarding it general.

They're communicating somehow, Keel thought.

Ravi was then in his head. *Aid Prisma! He must not be given room!*

There was pain in Ravi's voice. Unmistakable pain.

Keel raced in and did his best to replace the Ancient in the fight, firing his weapon when he could and dodging what up-close attacks came his way. The Golden King's armor kept Keel's bullets on the outside of its wearer, but they seemed to be *felt* by the Savage all the same. Maybe if Keel could get some distance and unload the entirety of his rounds, the job would be finished—but the Savage was fast, and it was all the smuggler could do to avoid being battered. Just the occasional three-round burst that couldn't quite punch through the thick armor.

They fought like that for what felt like forever—to the point where Keel's muscles were screaming in pain. Were it not for the strength assist of the Mark One's armor, Keel wondered if he would even be able to stand. He was slicked in sweat, his body temperature well past what could be assuaged by the armor's climate controls.

He was slowing. And the attacks kept coming.

And then the Golden King caught Keel flat-footed. The Savage brought a hammer blow down on Keel's skull with enough force to decapitate him were it not for the armor's bubble shield activating automatically. The curious shield, which could ablate energy and physical projectiles, absorbed the blast and then vanished again almost as quickly. But it was enough to allow Keel to gather himself and send more rounds into the beast as he spun free from a follow-up attack.

Ravi was still down. Still gasping on the floor as though his insides had been liquefied. How that could be possible, Keel didn't know, but it was clear that the Golden King had harmed the Ancient in a way that counted. Ravi was unable to do more than clutch his middle, knees and face on the deck as though he were a worshipper prostrating himself to his deity.

"Kid," Keel panted to Prisma. "If you've got a plan..."

The Golden King answered instead. "Her plans have fallen to ruin. Your fight is for time. Nothing more."

The staff general at the trigger-nuke, who had until now been content to watch his lord fight his assassins, shouted a report. "My lord! The Legion has pushed past our defenses. They will be here soon!"

This announcement seemed to trigger a whole new level of rage in the Savage king. He focused a furious assault on Prisma, forcing her back. "I will not fall to them again!" he shouted.

The Savage caught Keel by surprise, striking him square in the chest with a back-handed blow that sent the smuggler flying. With Prisma also on her heels, the king activated an energy shield on one arm and used it to parry her counterattacks, leaving his other hand free to go to—

"The amulet!" Prisma cried.

But it was too late. The Savage king held it in his grip... and darkness erupted from its center.

"No!" Ravi cried, leaping from his agony-stricken place on the deck and diving toward the Golden King, his sword coming down in a two-handed overhead strike.

The blade went deep, severing the arm that held the amulet just below the elbow. The limb and the gateway to the Dark Ones fell to the deck as the Golden King cried out, holding his wound and roaring in pain.

"Prisma!" Ravi called. "Stop them! I cannot!"

The girl hesitated only for a moment before diving for the amulet. She wrested it from the Golden King's severed hand and held it in her own. The Dark Ones continued to flow out of it, passing through the chamber to assault those breaching the ship.

"Recall them! Control them!" Ravi shouted.

Prisma closed her eyes.

The voices were demons in the girl's mind. Swearing that they were freed. That she was no lord of them. Prisma struggled against them, demanding, urging. Pleading with them to return. She could feel now the sort of strain the Golden King had been under in keeping this great horde at bay.

The Golden King seemed in shock over the damage done to him. Prisma knew why. The Savage could not fathom a situation where he could be bested. To even allow for such a possibility would put him at odds with the very foundation of his reality. And now this lie of his *vulnerability*—for that was all it could be, a lie—needed to be dealt with. The narrative needed to adapt. Only once the pieces were back in place in his twisted Savage mind could he move forward once more.

Which left him useless to restrain the Dark Ones he himself had loosed. Prisma would have to do it alone.

But she felt the weight of what the Dark Ones had just done. Were still doing. The atrocities taking place all across the Savage hulk that she herself had triggered. All because of her desire to see revenge on Reina. And now even that weight, that guilt, was being used against her by the wicked, corrupting, demonic voices in her mind.

Ravi warned her. She should have stopped this before those people were hurt. All those soldiers who came aboard only to die as sacrifices to the Dark Ones.

Her fault. It was her fault. Her selfishness had caused more pain and suffering. Again.

Again and again.

The demonic voices in her head reminded her of this. Sought to drag her down. Make her incapable of resisting them. Cooed for her to quit. To let go. And though she knew she had to go on...

She couldn't. It was too much. Too much.

"You can do this, Prisma." It was Keel, sitting up after being knocked onto the deck. "You're stronger than them.

Stronger than any of them. Strong enough to live the life you've lived."

Prisma felt the truth of his words. As if by saying them, Keel had cast a spell that provided her with a new courage and resolve. So much pain in her life. So much suffering. It had hardened her... had almost made her hard. But maybe... maybe that had been to prepare her. For this moment. For this greatest of all tests, with infinitely greater stakes.

Her father and mother. Crash. Tyrus Rechs. Would she be as strong as she was now without those losses? If things had gone another way? Never mind what she wished had happened. Never mind fairness. Life wasn't fair. Both her father and Tyrus Rechs had been sure to tell her that.

But *was* she stronger for it?

She didn't know. What she did know was she wasn't going to fold. Not now, not at this greatest difficulty. She wouldn't be a victim.

She wouldn't be afraid.

She yelled a single word of command.

"Return!"

The Dark Ones ripped through her body, desperately clinging to their tenuous freedom. Dark claws reaching, tearing. So close, *so close...*

She bled. From her belly. From her nose.

The bleeding was bad.

Really bad.

She held the amulet tight. Held the pain even tighter.

I am not afraid.

And, for once, the words were true.

The Dark Ones howled as they were yanked back into their prison. Denied their freedom, their annihilation. Denied their victory.

But they did not go quietly. They made Prisma pay.

Her hand went to her stomach and came away slick with blood.

"Oba, Prisma," Keel said, and then moved toward her.

But the Savage king had now recovered from his momentary disorientation, and he was on Keel with a fury that more than made up for his loss of an arm. He struck the armor with his remaining hand, denting it, and then punted Keel so hard that he slid several feet away, crashing into the sand table.

Prisma looked at the amulet. Then she turned and looked at the trigger-nuke. She had the means to end this. Here and now. All that was left was to clear the way.

She had learned things aboard the Savage hulk. The marble she once moved with her mind had opened a path that allowed her to understand how matter might leave one place and reemerge in another—far, far away. She had practiced it. Had mastered the skills Reina had mockingly said were beyond her.

Prisma used those skills now.

She sent the Golden King, and Keel and Ravi, too. Sent them away. To a place where the fight could be finished and her friends victorious.

They were gone without a word. Prisma felt the sudden urge to vomit. Blood poured from her mouth and dripped down her chin. She swallowed, tasting the iron in the back of her throat. She took a step toward the trigger-nuke and fell to the deck, unable to move further.

Her strength was waning. Her will. And the Dark Ones did not tire. Never tired.

Pounding, pressing against her defenses, they let themselves out of the amulet. She could not hold them in. It was all she could do now merely to restrain their killing desires. They swirled around her, free of the amulet, but not free of the girl.

Not yet.

But Prisma would die soon. They had made sure of that. They needed only to wait. For her will to be ended.

They swirled overhead, filling the room with a great wind. Biding their time.

42

Keel felt as though his stomach had been filled with molten lead and left to cool. *Something* had happened—he was now somewhere other than the throne room on the Savage hulk. But where?

His vision was blurred. He shut his eyes tightly until he could see stars behind them and then fluttered them back open. The colors of his HUD came into view, and so did the outlines of what looked like... a gallery? An archive?

Someone stood in the middle of it, staring at one of the exhibits. Keel swept his eyes across the rest of the room, past a front desk. There was writing on the wall, but Keel passed over it, his mind unable to make sense of it though he recognized the characters.

He'd really gotten his bell rung in the fight, and he was feeling the effects. Not to mention the effects of whatever trick had spirited him away from the Savage hulk. Or perhaps the room itself had changed in the same way as on the Savage reclaimer. He didn't know.

There was no sign of Prisma or the trigger-nuke.

And then he saw Ravi, draped in his black robes of war, sword lying at his side and still stained with gold-flecked red blood. That was the sight that made Keel force himself to his feet. The effort made his head spin, and he had to swallow back a surge of bile that rushed onto his tongue, fouling his mouth.

The man in the center of the room was the Savage king. Why was he not attacking? His fury seemed to have vanished, replaced by... what? If Keel didn't know better, he'd say the man looked... *confused*. Even contemplative. His helmet was off, and he stood transfixed before images of his past.

His *true* past.

All around him were historical artifacts and records, many impossibly ancient. Documents, mementos, holos... even faded photographs. This room was the entrance to some kind of museum... a museum dedicated entirely to the life of one man. One ordinary, mortal man.

Not a god.

Not the Golden King.

A man named *Thomas Roman.*

Here was a personal history that challenged the long and relentless Savage reconditioning the Golden King had voluntarily ascribed to. The reconditioning that had shaped his reality. Here was the proof that the man whose life was displayed before him... was no god. A true god was immortal from the beginning. This man was something far, far short of that standard.

Keel didn't care. He staggered toward the Savage, unsure if the pain he was feeling was from the fight or the matter-bending jump. He certainly hadn't felt this way all the other times Ravi had pulled them away. But he demanded of himself that he focus.

The Savage was paying no attention to him. He stood, transfixed, staring at a photo of Thomas Roman. Balding. With a paunch. A happy but goofy smile on his face as he sat behind an archaic holostation.

The Golden King didn't turn his un-helmeted head as Keel raised the slug thrower. He didn't flinch when the round fired, the closeness of the shot burning his face and hair as the bullet tore through his temple. He collapsed and settled sprawled on his back, one leg bent and tucked behind the other.

"Heh," Keel managed, holding Tyrus Rechs's hand cannon down at his side. The gun felt impossibly heavy now, and he wondered if he could lift it again if he had to.

This was the second time he'd ended a space wizard's life with a bullet to the brain. He'd take a gun any day over whatever the hell it was that Ravi and Prisma wielded. The track record was better.

Keel moved to Ravi. He knelt by the Ancient's side, trying to rouse him.

"Wake up, pal. I saved... your life."

Ravi was unresponsive. Keel shook him harder, and wondered if his hands not passing through the Ancient was a bad sign. "C'mon... wake up. I wanna... hear you thank me."

Running footsteps sounded behind him, and Keel turned to see Kel Turner sprint into the room, blaster rifle crisp and ready. The old man hadn't lost a step.

Turner looked at the corpse of the Savage king bleeding crimson and gold onto the lobby floor, and then looked to Keel. "General?"

Keel shook his head. "Sorry."

Turner seemed to tighten up in mistrust at seeing what was clearly General Rex's armor being worn by another. "Who are you, then?"

"A guy having a bad day." Keel pulled the helmet off.

Relief crossed Turner's face. "It's you. I didn't realize you had possession of the general's armor."

"Found it in a box of Snap-Stacks," Keel said, eliciting a rare quarter-smile from Kel at the mention of the child-hood sweet. "Can you help me with Ravi?"

"I can try," Turner said.

No sooner had the legendary operator stepped around the dead body than the Golden King sat bolt up-right. The same Savage research that had made Tyrus Rechs, Reina, and Casper Sullivan immortal—unless the body was properly destroyed—had reanimated the fiend. And why not? What had been done to Rechs and Casper as slaves, had been perfected in the Golden King.

"Look out!" Keel shouted.

But the Savage king was too quick. He kicked out his foot, slamming Turner into a glass case that proudly dis-played the first check ever cashed by Thomas Roman's company. Turner fell to the floor in a shower of glass, his head striking with a sickening thud that surely knocked his lights out, if not worse.

Adrenaline helped Keel jump to his feet from Ravi's side. The Ancient was already dead, unless his kind didn't have a heartbeat. Keel had never had reason to check before now. His friend certainly *looked* dead. Keel would have to finish this fight on his own.

Again.

But the healing powers of the Golden King had brought the Savage farther away from death—and he had indeed died—than Keel now was after the beating he'd taken. The king closed the ground between the two quickly, and it was only the jump jets that allowed Keel to escape his grip.

Keel fired from the zenith of his bounce. The Golden King activated his arm shield to stop the bullets, which made small dents where they sparked and deflected elsewhere in the room. Seeing this, Keel walked his fire down the Savage's legs. The king's armor was holding, but Keel fired with abandon all the same, not wanting to die with a single bullet left in the armor's expansive magazine. It seemed that, at a minimum, this much firepower *hurt*. Finally, a spray of blood from the Golden King's foot told him just how much.

The Savage roared in pain and moved the shield downward to prevent further suffering. Keel acted at once, bringing his barrel up to achieve a headshot. But even with the armor's strength assist, he could feel the difficulty of the task. The targeting HUD danced wildly over the target, much more erratic than Keel could ever remember it being. He used what remained of his strength, demanded his shot stabilize, and then fired.

The extra half second was enough for the Savage, however. The Golden King had once again made himself small behind the shield, and the shot snapped over his head cleanly.

By then, the jump jets had directed Keel too close to the vault's ceiling. He just missed braining himself on the steel and dropped down. The Savage king attacked him as he landed, detaching and throwing the shield, which spun toward Keel, a saw blade seeking his head. It was all he could do to spin around and put a support beam between himself and the weapon.

The shield blade embedded itself in the beam, still humming as if waiting for its master to recall it. Keel rolled back out and, using every ounce of strength he had, lifted both of his arms overhead and brought them down in a double axe-hammer on the blade. The power of the blow, augmented by the legendary armor he wore, was enough to bend the blade, rendering it useless.

That was one Savage weapon down. Now all he had to do was—

Keel felt the impact of a meteor strike as the Golden King closed on him, throwing his bulk into the smaller fighter before he could bring his weapon to bear. They rolled across the floor, carried by the momentum of the charging impact. Then Keel felt the strange sensation of being lifted off his feet. He was firmly in the grip of the Savage king, who held his gun arm tightly around the wrist.

"I have shed the trappings of this place," the Golden King declared. "It will not survive the march of time. And all those who know of it will die before me."

Keel struggled, feeling like a child. He twisted and turned in the Savage's grip, feeling the armor around his wrist crushing tightly into his flesh. His kicks were ineffectual, as he was unable to get a solid enough plant to put any real force into the blows, but then he reared back with his free hand and slammed one gauntleted fist into the Golden King's face, causing more red-and-gold blood to flow from the Savage's once-perfect nose.

The king brought a hand to his face and scowled when it came back wet. He looked furiously at the one who'd bloodied him.

"You look like sket," Keel panted. "Your hulk is about to go supernova, and the Legion is on its way here to kick your ass and make sure every picture in this place ends up in every museum and school-text in the galaxy. The way it goes, Tommy boy."

He was at the point where all he could do was agitate the man who was poised to kill him. A position he'd been in many times. Every time so far, those last-minute jabs had been enough to goad his enemies into making a mistake that Keel could capitalize on.

Not this time.

The Golden King looked at Keel, or rather, at the armor he wore. "Too many times have I been hampered by my own creations. No more."

He moved Keel into the crook of his severed arm and locked him there in a torturous position that had all of Keel's weight hanging from his shoulder, his feet dangling above the floor. With his remaining hand freed, the Golden King sent a punch to Keel's gut that forced out all the air and left a dent in the armor. Then he grabbed at Keel's chest plate. With a wrenching squeeze and pull that made Keel feel as though his back was going to be broken, the Savage tore away the front of the armor and dropped it mangled on the floor.

The HUD in Keel's bucket fritzed, and then it was lifted from his head. He watched through dizzying stars as the Golden King crumpled the bucket in hand and dropped it with a resounding metal clank. Next he tore away the hand cannon, the ammunition, and the jump jet on one side, followed by the legendary armor, from the shoulder down to the gauntlet Keel had punched him with. The violence left Keel's shoulder dislocated, and he grunted in pain.

"Strike me again," the Golden King ordered. "As you are. As an animal. A weak, lowly nothing. Bloody me if you can."

But suspended there like that, Keel could hardly move. He kept his hurt and dislocated arm tight against his body.

"Strike me!" the Golden King shouted in his face. He slapped Keel, holding enough back so as not to kill him outright but leaving an instant cherry-colored imprint that enveloped the side of Keel's face and made him bleed from his ear and the corner of his mouth.

Keel *wanted* to hit him back. Even with his senses rolling and spinning as though he'd just somersaulted from the peak of a mountain all the way down to its base. But his body would not let him.

Finally the Golden King cast Keel aside, sending him sliding across the floor until he came to a painfully abrupt stop against one of the support pillars.

"I want you to know," the Golden King said, "that all you think you've accomplished has been a failure. My generals—my sons—will rise in time, the same as I. As will Reina, my queen. They lag behind my prowess, but they will shake off death, as they have many times before. They will take from the betrayer that which is mine. Already I feel the Dark Ones gathering, waiting for her demise. They will bring it to me. Here. And then I will clean this planet of the Legion and all others. Earth will be lost again. For good."

The Savage tore down a picture of himself in an ill-fitting flight suit taken in the early days of his ventures into space travel. Back when the plans for the lighthuggers were still being formed. A goal for a later day that he had once made into a reality. He crushed the picture, frame and all, in his hands, and dropped it at his feet. "This place will be burned from all memory."

He moved to another display. Admiring it as if recalling a dream. But whatever psychological power this place had had on him when he first arrived, he seemed now to have conquered it.

Keel was not resigned to his fate. As the Golden King spoke of his coming will and scoured the vault's lobby, the smuggler forced his aching, protesting body to its knees.

He sat up and slammed his shoulder back into place, using the beam to set it and biting back the scream of pain so as not to alert the preoccupied Savage.

Next he looked for a weapon. The slug thrower looked like all it could do in its current state was misfire—no good unless it was the Savage king who would shoot it. But he had his Intec x6, still at his hip and strapped around the one leg that still wore some of the armor. He pulled it free, finding it awkward to move, the dead pieces of remaining armor doing nothing to ease the weight of their bulk. He would have to act quickly and decisively; there would be no fighting a sustained battle.

Allies. He needed allies. Turner was unconscious or dead. Ravi hadn't moved.

Keel thought of what his friend had told him. Of his people. Of their existence in this realm and the unseen realm. He closed his eyes, concentrating, trying to leave himself and burying thoughts of how ridiculous that might seem.

Ravi...

Then...

I am near to death, old friend.

Keel had done it. *So am I, pal... but I need your help.*

Then I will come to your aid.

Ravi stirred on the floor. His beard, always so perfectly coiffed, looked matted and flattened against the floor while he groped for his sword. His fingers found the blade and then walked down until he could grip it. He rose to his knees slowly, wearily. A shell of the unstoppable force that Keel had seen so many times before.

You have a plan, Ravi communicated.

Just get me a shot at his heart. I'll take it from there.

As the Golden King turned to see how his prey was faring, Ravi leapt at him, sword flashing as it caught the glow of the vault's lights. He sought to drive the blade downward across the armored chest, slicing it away to reveal the Savage beneath.

The Golden King simply turned once more, denying Ravi the target.

But for only a moment. Summoning all of his will, Ravi twisted his body in mid-jump so that he landed face-to-face with the Golden King. He brought his sword down in that same moment, slicing at the only opening he had and cutting the stump of the severed arm off at the shoulder. The Ancient then fell away, his strength, and perhaps his life, exhausted entirely following the blow. He lay on his back, galaxies upon galaxies swirling in his eyes.

Keel summoned the last of his strength as well. He leapt onto the Golden King's back, suffering an awkward blow as the enraged Savage attempted to throw him off. He shoved his blaster into the wound opening and aimed it downward, firing six scoring bolts that depleted the pack, all the while riding the bellowing Golden King down to the floor as the Savage's heart liquified under the blast.

The smuggler rolled off the dead body and crashed onto his back. His hand and blaster were covered in the peculiar blood. "Sket," he mumbled, exhaustion and pain threatening to overtake him completely.

The curse was for what he had to do next. He wanted nothing more than to sleep. Even to die so long as it meant stillness and an end to the pain and fatigue.

He activated screaming abdominal muscles and forced himself to sit up. Then, after rolling over onto his hands and knees, he rose, unsteadily, to his feet. Keel staggered toward Kel Turner, and wasn't surprised when he found a thermobaric grenade and remote detonator clipped to Turner's kit. That operator was the most prepared that Dark Ops had probably ever produced.

Turner moaned as Keel removed the grenade. "Gonna borrow this," Keel said. "I'll be back."

Keel limped back to the body of the Golden King, vowing not to see the resurrection trick twice in one lifetime. Taking no chances, he set a fifteen-minute timer in the device while also slaving it to the remote detonator. Whether by a countdown or because Keel pressed the boom button, the thing would go off.

Now to bury it deep enough that the Savage couldn't free himself of it.

The blaster bolts had burned a path through the Golden King's chest that Keel followed as he shoved his arm inside the corpse all the way up to his throbbing shoulder. Jagged and broken ribs popped and snapped as Keel pushed his way in. They lacerated his arm as he pulled it free, but the primed weapon was ready. It would suck out all the oxygen in the room as it super-heated its epicenter, turning most of it to slag and leaving the Golden King as little more than ash and atoms. Let him try and resurrect from that.

Keel needed only to get clear.

Bloody, battered, bruised, and beyond all the limits that Legion selection had told him he had, he went to Ravi. Keel bent over at the waist, fearing that if he dropped to a knee again he might not be able to get back up.

"Tell me you can hear me," he said. "Because if I close my eyes and try to communicate that way, I'm not gonna be able to open 'em back up."

Only Ravi's mouth moved. "I can hear you."

"Good. Now tell me you can walk out of here. Or hell, jump your way back to the *Six*."

"Myself, yes," Ravi confirmed, moving his head and neck now as well. "But I lack the strength to take—"

"Go," Keel commanded.

Ravi gave a nod and disappeared. Not quickly like all the times before. It was more like he faded from reality.

Keel then turned and began his zombie-like shuffle to Kel Turner. He wondered if he'd set enough time on the thermobaric grenade.

"Can you walk?" he asked Turner. When the man couldn't even muster a grunt, Keel groaned. Somehow he managed to stoop and hoist the old legionnaire into a fireman's carry, though he nearly toppled over as he stood back up.

The shuffle to the vault's front door was riddled with pain. Keel's feet and ankles ached with every step. Every part of his body hurt when he thought of it. And he was sure fifteen minutes had passed if a second had gone by, but the fragger hadn't exploded, so that couldn't be true.

When he reached the vault door, he found that it was locked. "Oh, come on."

A clumsy, punching inspection showed that it had been hard-locked from the outside, the external controls destroyed, preventing anyone from entering, but he could still operate it from within. He opened the door and staggered out, Kel Turner on his shoulders, and was greeted by the sounds and smells of a fading battle.

The doors closed behind him just as the grenade ignited into a firestorm that reduced the Savage king into a pile of ash and broken dreams.

Keel found himself in the some kind of cave. Forward, just outside the mouth of the cave, was a burly operator with sunglasses, a dark beard, and curly dark hair. Several Gomarii prisoners were uncomfortably bound in ener-chains and gagged behind him, so the operator out there was probably on the same team as Keel. At this point, it didn't matter.

Keel stumbled up behind the man, who turned.

"Holy karking sket," Carter said, his eyes wide in surprise. "Captain Fast?"

Keel handed Turner off to the man. "Guess so."

43

It was when Fish was blown apart on Ankalor by a suicidal zhee, right in front of him, that Chhun first started to wrestle with the dark feeling that his life meant a curse for the leejes with him. He knew that wasn't how the galaxy worked, but sometimes it felt that way. He'd even talked it over with Sergeant Major MakRaven.

"All I can say is use it," MakRaven had said. "I ain't no priest of Oba and I can't absolve you of none of them feelin's, but I met more than a couple leejes who felt like they were livin' on time borrowed from their dead brothers. Drove at least one good man from the Legion altogether. 'Nother one couldn't stop riskin' his neck—that was Hannibul, and he paid the price. Best ones did their jobs with a sense that they ain't dead because they ain't done. 'S how I see it. How you need to see it, too, General."

Which was what Chhun had been doing anyway. From the raid to free Dark Ops prisoners only to see them—but not him—cut down by the Cybar, to all of Article Nineteen and every conflict since.

But now, as he stood alone in a corridor aboard the Savage hulk, surrounded by the dead, he didn't know what to think.

It had come as a storm. A tangible one. He could *see* the wind. He'd even fancied ghoulish, demonic faces in it. Like in the old family spooky stories that had followed his clan's migration to Teema. That wind had passed over him, around him. But not so the others with him.

On his left lay his N-4. Andien Broxin lay dead on his right. Every legionnaire that followed, every hullbuster he could see behind him, likewise had been killed. The HUD in his Legion bucket told him that every corridor in the ship was the same. No leej with a life sign. Victory Company lost. A second time. The ship was quiet now. A tomb.

And him still standing.

Aboard the *Centurion*, they knew something was wrong; he was being pinged incessantly. Chhun didn't answer. He could think of nothing to say. Could comprehend no report to give. Years of training to give the Legion ACE reports were simply shrugged off.

He killed his comm. It didn't matter.

Why had he survived this?

When the wind came and blew around him and took the souls of all who were with him in an instant, he had turned to watch it ravage its way down the corridor. He had seen the men behind him halt their running and fall like puppets with their strings cut. Then he watched the wind turn and rush back the way it came, and he thought...

This time... this is it.

But the demonic faces in the wind passed over him again. He turned and watched them go.

Again, Chhun had survived when so many others had died.

Why?

The voice of MakRaven, another good man that Chhun had outlived, came to him with an answer. *You ain't dead because your job ain't done, Leej.*

Chhun lifted his rifle and resumed his run, churning toward the throne room. Unsure of what he'd find, but thinking:

This'll be it. It has to be.

The throne room swirled with the malignant wind, which rose to the cavernous ceiling like smoke looking to escape its confines. Below was carnage. Several Savage marines lay dead. Blood was everywhere. A headless woman in a beautiful white dress, stained red, lay cold on the floor. And a girl lay sprawled out in a puddle of her own blood. A girl with raven-dark hair. She held something in her hand that seemed to be cast in a permanent shadow that defied the light in the room.

Chhun removed his helmet to be sure his eyes weren't playing tricks on him. The supernatural shadow remained, and seemed to pulsate now.

Wasn't this the girl? The one who had been with Ford's crew? Prisma.

Chhun walked purposefully toward her, rifle still up and ready for any Savages in the room who might not be dead. But they all were. The Dark Ones had torn away the life of everyone here, everyone save Prisma.

And him.

He knelt at her side and felt for a pulse. This seemed to stir the girl to life. She moaned, rolled over in his arms, and slowly opened her eyes.

"Help," she said, weakly, fearfully.

Chhun wondered if this was why he'd lived. If this was what MakRaven's idea of living long enough to complete that unbriefed mission was leading him toward. Overhead, the dark wind continued to swirl.

"I'm here," he said, and checked the girl over. Her wounds were... substantial. Anyone could see that just from the blood. Her skin was pale and cold and her teeth were coated in red. And yet Chhun could find no wounds on her body. It was as if the blood was effusing out of her body, directly through her skin.

"Help," she whimpered again.

There were still ships waiting in the docking bay. Chhun cradled Prisma in his arms. "I'm gonna get you out of here."

His eyes went up to the visible wind overhead. Prisma's did the same. She groaned.

Chhun rose to his feet. "It's okay. You'll be okay."

He carried her, his armor washed in her blood. It dripped down his front and soaked his gloves.

"You'll be okay. It's okay."

He took more steps. She whimpered as one jolted her with pain. Her arm fell limp, but her hand gripped something tightly. An amulet, maybe.

"Help..."

"I'm helping you," Chhun said. "You'll be all right. It's okay."

They passed the trigger-nuke, though Chhun didn't recognize what it was as he moved around it.

"N-no," Prisma moaned.

"It's okay."

"No..." The girl lifted her arm and tried to point toward the trigger-nuke. The gesture was weak, but Chhun turned and looked.

Now he recognized the weapon for what it was.

"Blow the ship," he said.

She nodded, her eyes fluttering.

"No, it's okay. The crew is dead. I need to get you out of here."

Prisma gurgled. More blood washed out of her mouth and over her chin. She pointed to the swirling mass above them. Chhun looked up.

"Help," she said. "You... see? Help."

Chhun watched the demonic faces snarl and swirl, held seemingly at bay overhead. "I see them. You can kill them? Stop them?"

"Help." Prisma gestured to the trigger-nuke. "Must... stop... them. Have to."

Chhun stood there for a moment, looking down at the girl, painful memories resurfacing as he held her in his arms. Then he gazed up at the darkness. The demons. Those old stories coming back.

The legionnaire turned and carried Prisma to the device. "I'll have to put you down."

"Down," the girl repeated, her voice a ragged whisper.

As gently as he could, Chhun set Prisma down. He didn't lie to her. Didn't tell her it was okay. He activated the control panel. Unsure if he'd even be able to give the proper command to get the thing to blow. To his surprise, the device was full and free. Whoever had put this most illegal piece of munitions here had set it up to blow easily. Irresponsibly so. He worked his way through the simple control screen, smearing it with blood with each press of his finger. The screen beeped, and the trigger-nuke began to hum.

A sinking feeling formed in the pit of Chhun's stomach. Sitting next to a trigger-nuke when it detonated was not on his list of possible ways to die, but as he slid down the device to sit beside Prisma, he realized that was exactly how it would end.

"Okay," he said. "That's that."

"How... long?" Prisma asked, lying on her side, still gripping the amulet tightly. Chhun was amazed at how much more blood had pooled beneath her already.

She should be dead, he thought.

He smiled down at the girl, hoping it would cheer her. There hadn't been any sense in a long countdown. "Thirty seconds."

She nodded once, then struggled to lift her head. "Thank... you."

And then Chhun was no longer aboard the Savage hulk. He was sent through the folds of reality, through the Quantum. His eyes were open to what passed before them. He viewed the other side. And he saw the men whose missions in life had ended. Nobly. With purpose.

Exo and Major Owens. Fish. Twenties. Pike. Others. More.

They were waiting. Somewhere. A good place.

Chhun saw the passage in a way that Keel had not. He became aware of the bright light of Kima. Aware that he was lying at the edge of a swamp on the edge of a dying battlefield. Instinctively he looked up to the sky, unsure why he did so.

He saw the tremendous flash as the Savage hulk exploded.

EPILOGUE

The man once known as Wraith kept the strength of his youth much longer than most men. But even he was not immune to the demands of age, and in time his strength faded, formerly tireless muscles slowly replaced with the dull aches and lingering pains that were the toll for wisdom. Aeson Ford was still handsome, though. His beard was silver and clipped close to his face except for around the chin, where the hairs clung stubbornly to their color. He let those grow longer as a reward for their loyalty. A healthy hairline and a thick head of gray hair took off some of the years that his beard added. His body was trim, and though less imposing than it once was, it maintained an aura of danger. Behind his bright eyes was still something of the Wraith that communicated a caution for those who took him to be an old man. But stronger was the gleam of Keel, whose mischief both delighted and frustrated his family.

They were all here now, which was rare. Everyone was busy, both with professional duties on Enduran and with the daily duties of having your own family and living your own life. Still, today called for everyone to be together. Some official visits could pass without notice, but not this one.

Ford had woken up alive with excited memories of bygone years. He'd had trouble falling asleep, a thing that usually gave him no trouble at all. All the night before, he'd lain listening to Leenah's quiet breaths in bed next to him while he remembered faces and names and the feelings associated. But despite the remembered sorrows and pains, chief among that parade of emotions was an eagerness he hadn't felt in a long time.

When he woke up the next morning, he remembered he was old. A lingering pain in the Achilles of his left foot was reminding him of that again. It grew tender any time the tendon was given enough time to tighten up. Most mornings started with a limp that disappeared once he moved around the palace that he called a home long enough for everything to "get lubricated," as he described it.

Now it was evening, with the sun stretching its light across the distant mountaintops, giving a sparkling blaze to their white snow peaks. Keel had been waiting all day, as patiently as he could, for the time when they would take the speedlift up to the receiving pad. They were finally here, but he had sat too long, and now the tendon was tight again. He stretched his foot back and forth and must have appeared nervous because of it.

"You're fidgeting," Leenah told him. She was as beautiful as ever. Her skin was unlined, though some of its brilliant pink color had faded, which was common to Endurians. "Are you really that nervous?"

"Just my foot," Ford quickly explained. "But... it has been a while."

He hadn't realized that he was nervous until Leenah suggested it. And "a while" was understating things. Ford hadn't seen Cohen since it all ended and the galaxy was finally free to travel whatever path lay before it. They had stood against the Dark Ones where the Ancients had fled, and now this galaxy was theirs because of it.

A strong hand gripped Ford's shoulder. His son pointed to the horizon. "Looks like you don't have to wait much longer, Dad."

Keel shot his son a look. "I'm not blind yet."

A small atmospheric transport sled hummed on a steady course for the restricted landing zone. It was entirely at the mercy of a tractor system that guided the custom vehicle in—a security precaution. The palace defense systems needed only to turn off the tractor beam and the ship would drop helplessly, and any ship that attempted to fly into the palace airspace under its own power would have been shot down several kilometers out.

The Endurians were serious about protecting their leaders.

As soon as the sled appeared, a spark of excitement grew uncontrollably in the toddling grandchildren who had been pressed into waiting for this most important of visitors and who had been just as fidgety as their grandfather. Now they danced back and forth in anticipation, turning little heads in search of confirmation from their parents that yes, now was the time.

The grandchildren were beautiful. The mix of human and Endurian tended to result in exotic and beautiful combinations. Skin color seemed to be largely determined by the human parent's eye color, which introduced new shades of green, blue, brown, and hazel not common to the species. In most cases tendrils remained instead of hair, but sometimes the children kept the hair, and in those cases their skin color would match the human parent's—although sometimes tinted slightly by the shade of the Endurian parent. There were long-studied scientific and biological reasons for all of these things—which Ford had never bothered to study. All he knew was that his grandchildren were cuter than even his children had been, and he smiled as they whispered excitedly with broken, half-formed words.

Leenah grabbed Ford's hand and squeezed. His son stood on his opposite side, and his daughter was next to Leenah. Those two had both already married and started families of their own, which was a mystery to Ford because time was not meant to pass so quickly as it had. Their spouses stood together, a few paces off to one side and caring for the youngest children, though they hadn't been asked to separate themselves.

The ship landed in front of them, accompanied by a gust of salt wind that blew in from the ocean to the west. The breeze chased the creases from Ford's trousers and sent his cape flapping behind him. Leenah's dress twirled and whipped at her ankles. The gust died down as the sled door opened.

The man who stepped out was too old to be Cohen Chhun. His hair and beard were both gray and long, though not unkempt. Ford smiled inwardly; he'd never seen the legionnaire ever let a single follicle of hair on his body grow more than a quarter inch. He kept looking, expecting to see another passenger emerge from the other side.

"Ravi," Chhun said, "sends his apologies."

Years of leadership prevented Ford's shoulders from slumping the way he wanted them to. "Oh."

"Well," said Leenah, springing into action. "That doesn't make it any less wonderful to see you, Cohen."

Ford recovered. "Good to see you, pal." Expecting a handshake, he was instead pulled into an embrace. Chhun had kept some of his strength, too, and he still wore armor beneath the simple gray robes worn by all those seeking peace in the sanctuary of En Shakar.

"You too, Wraith." Chhun hugged Leenah next. "And you, Leenah."

"Who's Wraith?" asked one of the grandchildren.

"Forget you heard that," Keel mumbled. He reached for his son. "Here. This is my oldest. Ellek."

Chhun smiled and shook the man's hand. "That's a good name."

"Yes, sir," Ellek Ford said. "I've tried to live up to it."

Ford looked lovingly at his son. "You've succeeded."

Leenah pushed herself into the men, wrapping her arms around Ford's midsection. "Aeson wanted at least seven boys, and he had a legionnaire lined up to name each of them after. But we only had one more after Ellek." She smiled and pulled her daughter, twice as beautiful as she was, in close. "Prisma."

"Of course," Chhun said, a brief sheen coming across his eyes as he stared at the woman. "That's a good name, too. Very good."

Leenah introduced the in-laws and grandchildren, and then suggested that the family head back down the speedlift so the little ones could get out of their official clothes and be free again. "The royal uniforms aren't tailored for comfort," she explained.

She stepped away to see her children off, promising to rejoin the men in just a moment.

Chhun took the opportunity to wipe away a tear before it could form. "Sorry. Don't know why that got to me."

"Yeah you do," Ford said.

"Yeah."

Changing the subject, Ford brought a mischievous smile to his face. They seemed to come easier at his age than they had when he'd been gallivanting around as Captain Keel. "You know, I never thought I'd see the day when a switched-on legionnaire like Cohen Chhun would go up and hug a Mid-Core Rebel like my wife."

"Well, I'm not a legionnaire any longer."

"Uh-huh. I myself decided to stop being human."

Leenah swatted Ford's arm as she returned to his side. "You really are going to hold those six months over my head for the rest of my life, aren't you?"

Ford gave a half smile. "Or the rest of mine."

"If we're talking about surprises," Chhun said, "seeing you here, like this, is about as surprising a turn of events as I can think of... Your Majesty."

Keel laughed long and warmly. "I knew rescuing a princess would be a good move in the long run. No matter what Ravi said at the time."

Leenah rolled her eyes.

Ford continued. "There's a saying on Enduran. Marrying a princess won't necessarily get you elected king, but it's a good start."

Leenah looked at her husband with admiration. "*All* Endurians are princes or princesses by birth. To become a king, especially a non-Endurian king, takes more than connections."

"You still have to be married to an actual Endurian," Keel insisted.

"Endurian citizen. And those aren't automatically the same thing anymore like it used to be. That's a good thing." She held her head high and explained to Chhun, "The last king who wasn't a full-blooded Endurian was half human, and that was nearly eight hundred years ago. But with everything Aeson did for my planet and people... there was no one else they would have even considered once the old regent died and the time came. I don't know if you heard about the Scale Conflict or not; it happened after you left."

Chhun shook his head. "Not much news reaches En Shakar, but that's sort of the point."

"I wasn't trying to get involved," Ford said. "Just another of those things that sort of happened and I got swept up in it is all. So now we've both made general, which is something when you consider where we started."

"I guess they'll let anyone in," Chhun said, and then laughed and took a quick step back when Ford raised his fist. "Honestly, Ford, I'm not surprised at all. You can't help but go running into trouble."

Keel shrugged. "There's been a lot of it, even with the Savages gone. And look who's talking."

The conversation began to fade, but the silence wasn't awkward. Chhun folded his arms, a warm smile resting on his face.

Ford was used to seeing the former Legion commander as sober, serious, and driven. When he'd been an NCO in the 131st, he'd been angry and sarcastic as well. But never... content. Never at peace. Seeing him that way now was a relief to Ford. Chhun had crested a wave of death from Kublar to Earth and seemed to have finally found a cove of rest. A sanctuary.

"It's a nice evening," Leenah said, pulling a sheer shawl over her shoulders against another ocean breeze. "Why don't you two enjoy it together for a while? The sunsets on Enduran are more magnificent than on any other planet in the galaxy."

Ford took his wife's hint and motioned for Chhun to come around the transport sled to see the view at the edge of the covered landing pad. A great, carved stone rail circled the round pad. It sat waist-high, with pillars shooting up four meters to hold up a golden, conical roof. Despite sitting in the sun, the blue stone was cool to the touch, and its carvings looked as though they had been lifted from deep inside one of Enduran's lofty mountains, a gift from the mythical dwarven people once imagined to live at the root of the planet.

When Leenah reached the speedlift down to the palace, she paused. "You'll be joining us for dinner I hope, Cohen?"

The contented look fell from the legionnaire's face. "I'm sorry, no."

Surprise and puzzlement flashed on Leenah's face, but she quickly recovered her composure. "Another time then. Our table is always open to you. Goodbye, Cohen."

"Goodbye, Leenah."

When she had gone, Ford set his elbows on the stone rail and stared out at the snow-capped peaks of the Plynth Mountains. "You know, Endurian food is actually pretty good. Or are you afraid of eating Leenah's cooking? Because we have a bot who does most of that..."

Chhun laughed. "No. Nothing like that. I'm sorry I can't stay. I'd meant, for a long time, to come sooner and spend more time with you. Now... I can't."

"So why didn't you before?"

Chhun shook his head. "I don't know. I used to dream about everyone getting back together, just to talk about the old times. I wanted to remember it with the people who knew what it was like. Who knew what happened."

Keel nodded. He knew that feeling. In fact, it was part of what had gotten him so excited about Chhun's unexpected message that he was coming.

"And then... I started to realize that I didn't need that. Not that it wasn't important. It was all important. I'm not sorry for any of it. But I just... I don't know. The past... I don't need the past in order to do good in the future. Is that... am I wrong?"

"I don't think so," Ford said after a time. "But if you are, I'm wrong with you. I still don't know all the ins and outs of whatever it was I doing. And now, I've spent more time in *this* life with Leenah and the kids than those years before. I don't think our lives boil down to a stretch of a few years, no matter how important they were."

A silence followed.

"I was hoping Ravi would be with you," Ford said at last. "How is he?"

"Ravi is Ravi. He wanted to come. Said it had been a long time."

"Prisma was just a baby."

Chhun nodded. "Right. He said to tell you that it wouldn't be fair. To you."

Ford raised an eyebrow. "He's not *that* annoying."

Chhun laughed softly, because there was nothing else in that moment to do. He grew serious again. "He felt as though he'd put your life through the repulsor wash enough times already and has it in his mind that if he came again and went through his pitch, you'd feel like you needed to leave everything you have."

"Leave for what?"

"It's why I can't stay. Why I'm out of time for those reunions. I'm searching, Ford. And I'm close. Ravi is leading me."

"Searching for what?" Ford was beginning to feel uncomfortable. The last thing he wanted to hear about was another lost tribe of Savages or some other extra-dimensional nihilistic force threatening the galaxy. At this point he was just about ready to stand aside if that was the case.

But Chhun's answer put those fears to an immediate rest. "For peace."

Keel closed his eyes and didn't open them for a long time. When he did, he said, "I have that. Now. With Leenah and the children. Tell Ravi not to worry. I'm sure he'll spout off some odds and explain why he's worried for me anyway, but you can tell him."

"Peace and... understanding," Chhun said. "About why we're here. What we're supposed to do."

"Oh. Yeah, I got all that figured out, too."

Chhun laughed and changed the subject. "Your son Ellek certainly grew into his namesake. Not quite as tall as Major Owens, but he does have a presence to him. Needs to grow a beard."

"He can't. Endurian genes. But otherwise, yeah. He's a major in the planetary defense forces. Should get his first bird before the year is over. That's how they do it on Enduran. More birds, fewer leaves. Also, for the record, he's an inch taller than the major was."

Chhun shook his head and smiled. "Heh. I suppose certain people grow larger in your memories as time goes on." He gripped the edge of the cool blue stone and then looked west toward the ocean, where large flying creatures glided atop the air currents coming in from the breakers. Licking his lips, he thought he could taste the slightest spray of salt from the air.

"They always do," said Ford. He could sense that Chhun still had something he needed to say. Perhaps just to say goodbye for good, but maybe something more. He let the silence settle in, ushering with it a faint crash of waves.

"It took me a decade to find even the slightest peace," Chhun said at last. "I think that's why Ravi had me stay at En Shakar for so long. I needed to heal. Mother Ree, she passed a few years back, but she was good at that. Healing. Helping others."

Keel nodded. He thought of that planet and of the little girl they'd tried to help by placing her under the same Mother Ree. Had it helped? Or had that choice been what ultimately brought about Prisma's demise?

The question sometimes kept Keel up at night.

"I got to this point where I was sure that my number was up and I was next in line to get dusted. This was back when I was still leading KTV. Every op and mission, I had this feeling like I wouldn't survive. I'd remember Kags and Twenties laid out on that shuttle and think: *That's gonna be me.* Only it wasn't. Someone else would buy it. Just feet away. Someone else and not me."

"Well, you and Masters," Keel added, regretting at once his tendency to be the contrarian.

Chhun laughed. "Yeah. I think he was right all along: too beautiful to die."

Both men laughed, and Keel relaxed despite what he still felt was a mistake. "We're all old now, so I'm not sure how much longer that's gonna hold. He's probably had to change his strategy and focus on the more *mature* attractive women of the galaxy. Or the dumb ones."

"He actually came to En Shakar a while back. Still there."

Ford's jaw dropped. "You're kidding."

"Actually, he was the one I most expected to see there. I was surprised it took as long as it did."

Keel shrugged.

Chhun regained his focus and picked up his story as if the interlude hadn't occurred. "I think I'm getting dusted, but instead the other guys do. Every time. I can't help but notice. At first it feels like the breaks, but on Herbeer when Pike went, I remember feeling off about it. Then on Ankalor, I see Fish get blown up right in front of me. That donk was gunning to blow me up, Aeson. And then... boom. He's gone and Fish is gone and I'm still alive. It all stuck in my head and I saw it happen again and again. Exo, MakRaven... hell, even young leejes I barely knew who dropped dead in my proximity. You know what happened to Broxin. I was inches from her, Aeson."

Keel nodded. "Yeah."

"My mind kept saying that even though I was the one who'd outlived the odds, they were the ones paying the price."

Both men stared straight ahead at the mountains, snowy heads before snowy peaks.

Chhun pulled his fingers through the long shocks of his hair. He turned and looked at Ford. "Do you know that feeling? Like people are dying *for* you? Like the galaxy is sacrificing them so you can keep living?"

"Just one," Ford said. "Prisma. She drove me nuts. But I wanted to help her. I wanted to save her. So did Leenah. Even more than me. You believe in destiny?"

Chhun looked down the dizzying distance on the other side of the stone banister. He couldn't see the palace from this vantage point, only the mountain it was set upon. "I'm not sure."

"Neither am I. But I think for Prisma, at least, it was real. I couldn't save her and neither could you... because she needed to save all of us."

Chhun didn't respond to that. Instead he turned away from the vista, as if closing that chapter. "Ravi says you should come with us," he said. "And Leenah. We're all going. We need to find out. Bombassa, too. There are others. Ravi wants you to come but he doesn't want to force you. He sent me to ask."

Ford straightened up and walked Chhun back to his sled. "Tell Ravi that I can't come along. Tell him that my daughter is living the life we wanted for Prisma. I'm still saving her, Cohen. I have to see it through. Tell him that. He'll understand."

Chhun stood at the vehicle's door for a moment, and then nodded. "The galaxy is changing, Wraith. Not for the better. Article Nineteen won't do it next time."

Ford smiled. "Don't I know it."

"No matter what happens, there'll always be a Legion. Remember that. Don't let it be forgotten."

Ford put a hand on his friend's armored shoulder. "I won't."

ABOUT THE MAKERS

Jason Anspach is the co-creator of Galaxy's Edge. He lives in the Pacific Northwest.

Nick Cole is the other co-creator of Galaxy's Edge. He lives in southern California with his wife, Nicole.

HONOR ROLL

Jason and Nick would like to thank those who whose Galaxy's Edge Insider Subscriptions saw the conclusion of Galaxy's Edge, Season Two.

Cody Aalberg
Sam Abraham
Guido Abreu
Alex Acree
Chancellor Adams
Myron Adams
Chris Adkins
Garion Adkins
Ryan Adwers
Kyle Aguiar
Elias Aguilar
Morgan Albert
Neal Albritton
Aleksey Aleshintsev
Willis Alfonso
Jonathan Allain
Bill Allen
Byron Allen
Justin Allred
Paul Almond
Larry Alotta
Tony Alvarez
Christian Amburgey

Joachim Andersen
Galen Anderson
Jarad Anderson
Levi Anderson
Taylor Anderson
Pat Andrews
Robert Anspach
Melanie Apollo
Benjamin Arguello
Thomas Armona
Daniel Armour
Omar Arroyo
Linda Artman
Nicholas Ashley
Jonathan Auerbach
Sean Averill
Nicholas Avila
Albert Avilla
Tisianna Azbill
Benjamin Backus
Matthew Bagwell
Christian Bailey
Marvin Bailey

Daniel Baker
Sallie Baliunas
Nathan Ball
Kevin Bangert
Christopher Barbagallo
John Barber
Brian Bardwell
Logan Barker
John Barley
Brian Barrows-Striker
Richard Bartle
Austin Bartlett
Robert Battles
Eric Batzdorfer
John Baudoin
Adam Bear
Nahum Beard
Michelle Beaver
Mike Beeker
Randall Beem
Matt Beers
John Bell
Daniel Bendele
Royce Benford
Mark Bennett
Ryan Bennett
Edward Benson
Hjalmar Berggren
Matthew Bergklint
Carl Berglund
Brian Berkley
Corey Berman
David Bernatski
Gardner Berry
Tim Berube
Michael Betz

Kevin Biasci
Shannon Biggs
Gregory Bingham
Brien Birge
Nathan Birt
Francisco Blankemeyer
Trevor Blasius
David Blount
Liz Bogard
James Bohling
Evan Boldt
Rodney Bonner
Rodney Bonner
Thomas Seth Bouchard
William Boucher
Aaron Bowen
Brandon Bowles
Alex Bowling
Keiger Bowman
Michael Boyle
Clifton Bradley
Chester Brads
Scott Brady
Richard Brake
Ryan Bramblett
Logan Brandon
Evan Brandt
Ernest Brant
Daniel Bratton
Chet Braud
Dennis Bray
Robert Bredin
Christopher Brewster
Jacob Brinkman
Geoff Brisco
Wayne Brite

Joysell Brito
Spencer Bromley
Paul Brookins
Raymond Brooks
Zack Brown
RFC Brumley
Jeff Brussee
Benjamin Bryan
Marion Buehring
Wendy Bugos
Johncarlo Buitrago
Nicholas Burck
John Burleigh
Tyler Burnworth
Donald Butler
Noel Caddell
Daniel Cadwell
Brian Callahan
Joseph Calvey
Decker Cammack
Van Cammack
Chris Campbell
Mark Campbell
Danny Cannon
Zachary Cantwell
John Cappleman
Spencer Card
Brett Carden
Brett Carden
Daniel Carpenter
Rafael Carrol
Brad Carter
Robert Cathey
Brian Cave
Brian Cheney
Brad Chenoweth

Caleb Cheshire
David Chor
James Christensen
Robyn Cimino-Hurt
Cooper Clark
Kelly Clark
Rebecca Clark
Rebecca Clark
Casey Clarkson
Ethan Clayton
Jonathan Clews
Beau Clifton
Sean Clifton
Morgan Cobb
William Coble
Robert Collins Sr.
Alex Collins-Gauweiler
Jerry Conard
Robert Conaway
Gayler Conlin
Michael Conn
James Connolly
Ryan Connolly
James Conyers
Brian Cook
Devyn Cook
Dustin Coons
Terry Cooper
Jacob Coppess
Michael Corbin
Alex Corcoran
Robert Cosler
Anthony Cotillo
Ryan Coulston
Seth Coussens
Adam Craig

Andrew Craig
Zachary Craig
Adam Crocker
Ben Crose
Justin Crowdy
Christopher Crowley
Jack Culbertson
Phil Culpepper
Scott Cummins
Ben Curcio
Thomas Cutler
Tommy Cutler
Christopher Da Pra
John Dames
David Danz
Matthew Dare
Hayden Darr
Chad David
Alister Davidson
Peter Davies
Walter Davila
Ashton Davis
Ben Davis
Ben Davis
Brian Davis
Ivy Davis
Nathan Davis
LeRoy Davis
Joseph Dawson
Andrew Day
Ron Deage
Nathan Deal
Jason Del Ponte
Anthony Del Villar
Tod Delaricheliere
Wayne Dennis

Anerio (Wyatt)
Deorma (Dent)
Aaron Dewitt
Isaac Diamond
Alexander Dickson
Nicholas Dieter
Christopher DiNote
Matthew Dippel
Gregory Divis
Brian Dobson
Samuel Dodes
Graham Doering
Gerald Donovan
Ward Dorrity
Dustyn Down
Noah Doyle
Michael Drescher
Adam Drucker
John Dryden
Garrett Dubois
Josh DuBois
Ray Duck
Marc-André Dufor
Cory Dufour
Thomas DuLaney II
Brendan Dullaghan
Trent Duncan
Christopher Durrant
Evan Durrant
Chris Dwyer
Virgil Dwyer
Brian Dyck
Brian Dye
Nick Edwards
Travis Edwards
Justin Eilenberger

Brian Eisel
Jonathan R. Ellis
William Ely
Michael Emes
Paul Eng
Brian England
Andrew English
Dakota Erisman
Stephane Escrig
Ethan Estep
Dakota Estepp
Benjamin Eugster
Richard Everett
Jaeger Falco
Nicholas Fasanella
Christian Faulds
Steven Feily
Julie Fenimore
Meagan Ference
Brad Ferguson
Hunter Ferguson
Adolfo Fernandez
Rich Ferrante
Austin Findley
Ashley Finnigan
Rhys Fitzpatrick
Matthew Fiveson
Daniel Flanders
Waren Fleming
Kath Flohrs
Daniel Flores
Geoffrey Flowers
William Foley
Charles Ford
Steve Forrester
Skyla Forster

Joshua Foster
Kenneth Foster
Jacob Fowler
Bryant Fox
Chad Fox
Doug Foxford
Martin Foxley
Mark Franceschini
Dennis Frank
Greg Franz
Kris Franzen
Luke Frazer
Evan Freel
Erik Freeman
Kyle Freitus
Griffin Frendsdorff
Josh Frenzen
Bob Fulsang
Elizabeth Gafford
David Gaither
Seth Galarneau
Matthew Gale
Zachary Galicki
Christopher Gallo
Richard Gallo
Robert Garcia
Joshua Gardner
Michael Gardner
Alphonso Garner
Mackenzey Garrison
Cordell Gary
Nathan Garza
Marina Gaston
Robert Gates
Brad Gatter
Tyler Gault

Angelo Gentile
Cody George
Stephen George
Nick Gerlach
Eli Geroux
Christopher Gesell
Joshua Gibson
Kevin Gilchrist
Dylan Giles
Joe Gillis
Oscar Gillott-Cain
Jason Ginzkey
John Giorgis
Jodey Glaser
Johnny Glazebrooks
Bob Gleason
Martin Gleaton
James Glendenning
William Frank Godbold IV
Justin Godfrey
John Gooch
Tyler Goodman
Zack Gotsch
Justin Gottwaltz
George Gowland
Mitch Greathouse
Gordon Green
James Green
Matt Green
Shawn Greene
Stephen Greene
John Greenfield Jr.
Dan Griffin
Eric Griffin
Eric Griffin
Ronald Grisham

Paul Griz
Preston Groogan
Auguste Gumbs
Jeff Haagensen
Levi Haas
Joshua Haataja
Owen Haataja
Michael Hagen
Tyler Hagood
Kelton Hague
Levi Haines
Michael Hale
Andrea Hamrick
Brandon Handy
Erik Hansen
Greg Hanson
Jeffrey Hardy
Ian Harper
Jordan Harris
Revan Harris
Akoni Harris
Shane Harris
Brett Harrison
Brandon Hart
Matthew Hartmann
Adam Hartswick
Reese Harvey
Mohamed Hashem
Matthew Hathorn
Ronald Haulman
Joshua Hayes
Ryan Hays
Adam Hazen
Richard Heard
Colin Heavens
Jon Hedrick

Jesse Heidenreich
Brenton Held
Kyler Helker
Jason Henderson
Jason Henderson
Anders Hendrickson
Fynn Hendrikse
John Henkel
Daniel Heron
Bradley Herren
Felipe Herrera
Paul Herron
Sven Hestrand
Kyle Hetzer
Korrey Heyder
Matthew Hicks
Anthony Higel
Dustin Hill
Samuel Hillman
Craig Hiltbrunner
Lance Hirayama
Ty Hodges
Jonathan Hoehn
David Hoeppner
Aaron Holden
Brad Hollingsworth
Joe Holman
William Holman
Clint Holmes
Jason Honeyfield
Charles Hood
David Hoover
Garrett Hopkins
Tyson Hopkins
William Hopsicker
Jefferson Hotchkiss

Aaron Hough-Barnes
Caleb House
Ian House
Jack House
Ken Houseal
Nathan Housley
Jeff Howard
Nicholas Howser
Mark Hoy
Kirstie Hudson
James Huff
Dante Hulin
Aaron Huling
Mike Hull
Donald Humpal
Daunte Hunter
Bradley Huntoon
Bobby Hurn
James Hurtado
Wayne Hutton
Gaetano Inglima
Antonio Iozzo
Randy Islas Jr.
Wendy Jacobson
Paul Jarman
Bobby Jeffers
James Jeffers
Michael Jenkins
Jacob Jensen
Robert Jensen
Tedman Jess
Eric Jett
Anthony Johnson
Cobra Johnson
Eric Johnson
Gary Johnson

James Johnson	Robert Knox
Josh Johnson	Eric Koeppel
Nick Johnson	Andreas Kolb
Nick Johnson	Steven Konecni
Randolph Johnson	Christian Koonce
Timothy Johnson	Ethan Koska
Bryan Jones	Evan Kowalski
Jason Jones	Byl Kravetz
Jason Jones	Bodhi Kruft
Micah Jones	Mitchell Kusterer
Paul Jones	Nathan Laidlwe
Tyler Jones	Clay Lambert
Tyler Jones	Jeremy Lambert
David Jorgenson	Mark Landez
Ryan Kalle	Andrew Langler
Chris Karabats	Travis Larsen
Ron Karroll	Dave Lawrence
Timothy Keane	Alexander Le
Cody Keaton	Jacob Leake
Tyler Keaton-El	David Leal
Brian Keeter	Andy Ledford
George Kelly	Nicholas Lee
Jacob Kelly	Joseph Legacy
Noah Kelly	David Levin
Caleb Kenner	Luke Lindsay
Zack Kenny	Ruel Lindsay
Darin Keuter	Eric Lindsey
Daniel Kimm	Eron Lindsey
Kennith King	Paul Lizer
Zachary Kinsman	John Lloyd
Jesse Klein	Andre Locker
Kyle Klincko	Dominick Loele
Brendan Klingner	Michael Lofland
Albert Klukowski	Maxwell Lombardi
Marc Knapp	Richard Long
William Knapp	Oliver Longchamps

Litani Looby	Joseph Markey
David Lopez	Cory Marko
Joseph Lopez	Alexande Martin
Matthew Lopez	Bertram Martin
Kyle Lorenzi	Bill Martin
David Losey	Christopher P. Martin
Doug Lower	Edward Martin
Steven Ludtke	Jason Martin
Johan Lundberg	Logan Martin
Caleb Lunsford	Lucas Martin
Andrew Luong	Pawel Martin
Jesse Lyon	Trevor Martin
Brooke Lyons	Christopher Martin
Taylo Lywood	Tim Martindale
David MacAlpine	Joseph Martinez
John Machasek	Michael Martinez
Brian Machimbira	Phillip Martinez
Sawyer Mack	Cory Masierowski
Patrick Maclary	Michael Mason
Daniel Magano	Nicholas Mason
William Mahoney	Tao Mason
Richard Maier	Wills Masterson
Ryan Mallet	Mark Mathewman
Chris Malone	Michael Matsko
Jake Malone	Justin Matsuoko
Adam Manlove	James Matthews
Andrew Mann	Ezekiel Matze
Scott Mann	Mark Maurice
Aaron Manning	Simon Mayeski
John Mannion	Joseph Mazzara
Brian Mansur	Timothy McAleese
Brent Manzel	Sean McCafferty
Robert Marchi	Logan McCallister
Jacob Margheim	Kyle McCarley
Deven Marincovich	Mac McCleary
John Marinos	Timothy McCoy

Quinn McCusker
Matthew McDaniel
Shane McDevitt
Alan McDonald
Caleb McDonald
Connor McDonald
Jeremy McElroy
Dennis McGriff
James McGuire
Hans McIlveen
Rachel McIntosh
Ryan McIntosh
Richard McKercher
Ryan McKracken
Jacob Mclemore
Jason McMarrow
Wayne McMurtrie
Colin McPherson
Daniel Mears
Christopher Menkhaus
Jim Mern
Dylon Merrell
Robert Mertz
Jacob Meushaw
Brady Meyer
Pete Micale
Christopher Miel
Mike Mieszcak
Ted Milker
Corrigan Miller
Daniel Miller
Patrick Millon
Reimar Moeller
Ryan Mongeau
Jacob Montagne
Ramon Montijo

Dale Moody
Mitchell Moore
Sherry Moore
Josue Rios Morales
Nicholas Moran
Matteo Morelli
Joe Morgan
Todd Moriarty
Matthew Morley
Autumn Morris
Daniel Morris
William Morris
Christian Morrison
Alex Morstadt
Nicholas Mukanos
Bob Murray
David Murray
Jeff Murri
Joseph Nahas
Vinesh Narayan
Colby Neal
James Needham
Ray Neel
Merle Neer
Kristian Neidhardt
Adam Nelson
Timothy Nevin
Ethan Nichols
Travis Nichols
Bennett Nickels
Trevor Nielsen
Andrew Niesent
Timothy Nixon
Sean Noble
Otto (Mario) Noda
Brett Noll-Emmick

Michael Norris
Ryley Nortrup
Greg Nugent
Christina Nymeyer
Brian O'Connor
Matthew O'Connor
Sean O'Hara
Patrick O'Leary
Colin O'neill
Ryan O'neill
Patrick O'Rourke
Colin O'Rourke
Jacob Odell
Grant Odom
Conor Oehler
Quinn Oehler
Kevin Oess
Nolan Oglesby
Gary Oneida
Max Oosten
Anthony Ornellas
Gareth Ortiz-Timpson
Christian Owens
James Owens
James Owens
Will Page
John Park
David Parker
Matthew Parker
Shawn Parrish
William Parry
Eric Pastorek
Anthony Patsch
Andrew Patterson
David Patzer
Yahya Payton

Thomas Pennington
Aaran Pereira
Hector Perez
Daniel Perkins
Kevin Perkins
Toby Permezel
Chase Barret Perryman
Trevor Petersen
Zac Petersen
Marcus Peterson
Nicholas Peterson
Chad Peyton
Corey Pfleiger
Peter Pham
David Phillips
Jon Phillips
Sam Phinney
Tim Pickett
Dupres Pina
Michael Pister
Jared Plathe
Pete Plum
Luke Plummer
Matthew Pommerening
Stephen Pompeo
Jason Pond
Nathan Poplawski
Michael Portanger
Chancey Porter
Rodney Posey
Brian Potts
Jonathaon Poulter
Daniel Powderly
Matt Prescott
Thomas Preston
Matthew Print

Aleksander Purcell	Thomas Rogneby
Joshua Purvis	Thomas Roman
Max Quezada	Aaron G Rood
Adam Quinn	Elias Rostad
Scott Raff	Rob Rudkin
Shahik Rakib	Arthur Ruiz
Joe Ralston	Jim Rumford
Frederick Ramlow	John Runyan
Jason Randolph	Nick Rusch
Aindriu Ratliff	Chad Rushing
Beverly Raymond	Sterling Rutherford
T.J. Recio	RW
Ron Redden, Sr.	Justin Ryan
Blake Rehrer	Mark Ryan
Ryan Reis	Matthew Ryan
Cannon Renfro	Greg S
John Resch	Zachary Sadenwasser
Nathaniel Reyes	Connor Samuelson
Paul Richard	Lawrence Sanchez
Cody Richards	Dustin Sanders
Augustus Richardson	David Sanford
Eric Ritenour	Joshua Sayles
Paul Rivas	Jaysn Schaener
Tina Rivers	Shayne Schettler
Michael Roach	Jason Schilling
David Roark	Daniel Schmagel
Grant Roark	Andrew Schmidt
John Robertson	Ray Schmidt
Walt Robillard	Thomas Schmidt
Edward Robinson	Kurt Schneider
Joshua Robinson	Peter Scholtes
Daniel Robitaille	Theodore Schott
Christopher Roby	Kevin Schroeder
John Roche	Michael Schroeder
Paul Roder	Alex Schwarz
Zack Roeleveld	William Schweisthal

Anthony Scimeca
Cullen Scism
Connor Scott
Ethan Scott
Preston Scott
Andrew Scroggins
Robert Sealey
Aaron Seaman
Dan Searle
Phillip Seek
James Segars
Kevin Serpa
Dylan Sexton
Austin Shafer
Mitch Shami
Timothy Sharkey
Curtis Sharp
Kevin Sharp
Christopher Shaw
Charles Sheehan
Wendell Shelton
Lawrence Shewark
Logan Shiley
Ian Short
Glenn Shotton
Emaleigh Shriver
Dave Simmons
Dave Simmons
Joshua Sipin
Chris Sizelove
Andrew Skaines
Chris Slater
Scott Sloan
Steven Smead
Jesse Smider
Anthony Smith

Daniel Smith
Ian Smith
Lawrence Smith
Michael Smith
Michael Smith
Neal Smith
Sharroll Smith
Timothy Smith
Tyler Smith
Cory Smith
Caleb Smith
David Smyth
Tom Snapp
David Snowden
Alexander Snyder
Alain Southikhoun
Briana Sparh
Robert Speanburgh
John Spears
Anthony Spencer
Thomas Spencer
Troy Spencer
Jeremy Spires
Peter Spitzer
Dustin Sprick
Super Squirrel
George Srutkowski
Cooper Stafford
Travis Stair
Graham Stanton
Paul Starck
Jolene Starr
John Stephenson
Thomas Stewardson
Tanner Stewart
Maggie Stewart-Grant

Edmond Stone	David P. Thomas
Fredy Stout	Marc Thomas
Rob Strachan	Vernetta Thomas
James Street	Jacob Thomas
Joshua Strickland	Chris Thompson
William Strickler	Jonathan Thompson
Shayla Striffler	Steven Thompson
John Stuhl	William Joseph Thorpe
Brad Stumpp	Beverly Tierney
Louis Styer	Yvonne Timm
Ned Sullivan	Michael Tindal
Kevin Summers	Russ Tinnell
Joe Summerville	Daniel Torres
Ernest Sumner	Justin Townsend
Randall Surles	Matthew Townsend
Michael Swartwout	Jameson Trauger
Aaron Sweeney	Dimitrios Tsaousis
Bryan Swezey	Scott Tucker
Tiffany Swindle	Oliver Tunnicliffe
Lloyd Swistara	Eric Turnbull
George Switzer	Ryan Turner
Carol Szpara	Brandon Turton
Travis TadeWaldt	John Tuttle
Allison Tallon	Dylan Tuxhorn
Daniel Tanner	Nicholas Twidwell
Blake Tate	Joshua Twist
Joshua Tate	O'brien Tyler
Lawrence Tate	Nerissa Umanzor
Kyler Tatsch	Jalen Underwood
Dave Tavener	Barrett Utz
Justin Taylor	Paul Van Dop
Robert Taylor	David Van Dusen
Tim Taylor	Erik Van Otten
Jonathan Terry	Andrew Van Winkle
Anthony Tessendorf	Patrick Van Winkle
Stavros Theohary	Paden VanBuskirk

Patrick Varrassi
Daniel Vatamaniuck
Jason Vaughn
Jose Vazquez
Brian Veit
Daniel Venema
Marshall Verkler
Abel Villesca
Cole Vineyard
Ralph Vloemans
Jeff Wadsworth
Anthony Wagnon
Wes "Gingy" Wahl
Christopher Walker
David Wall
Joshua Wallace
Justin Wang
Andrew Ward
Wedge Warford
David Warren
Scot Washam
Tyler Washburn
Christopher Waters
Zachary Waters
John Watson
Bill Webb
William Webb
Ben Wedow
Garry Welding
Hiram Wells
Jack Weston
William Westphal
Ben Wheeler
Paul White
Paul Wierzchowski

Grant Wiggins
Christopher Williams
Jack Williams
Taylor Williams
Justin Wilson
Dominic Winter
Scott Winters
Evan Wisniewski
Nicholas Withrow
Matthew Wittmann
Reese Wood
Ryan Wood
Tripp Wood
Robert Woodward
Sean Woodworth
Robin Woolen
Michael Woolwine
John Wooten
John Work
Bonnie Wright
Jason Wright
Anthony Wulfkuhle
Elaine Yamon
Ethan Yerigan
Matthew Young
Phillip Zaragoza
Brandt Zeeh
Kevin Zhang
Pamela Ziemeck
Attila Zimler
David Zimmerman
Jordan Ziroli
Nathan Zoss

HISTORY OF THE GALAXY

Explore over 30+ Galaxy's Edge books and counting from the minds of Jason Anspach, Nick Cole, Doc Spears, Jonathan Yanez, Karen Traviss, and more.

LAST BATTLE OF THE REPUBLIC

REBIRTH OF THE LEGION

JOIN THE LEGION

FOR UPDATES ABOUT NEW RELEASES, EXCLUSIVE PROMOTIONS, AND SALES, VISIT INTHELEGION.COM AND SIGN UP FOR OUR VIP MAILING LIST. GRAB A SPOT IN THE NEAREST COMBAT SLED AND GET OVER THERE TO RECEIVE YOUR FREE COPY OF "TIN MAN", A GALAXY'S EDGE SHORT STORY AVAILABLE ONLY TO MAILNG LIST SUBSCRIBERS.

INTHELEGION.COM

EPITAPH

After letting the Kublarens off his ship to join the battle surrounding the vault on Kima, Skrizz flew a long, looping pattern away from the fight. War was an odd thing. As crazy, deadly, and chaotic as an entire planet embroiled in war might be, there were still areas of peace. There was too much surface.

War is a thing near.

That was another wobanki proverb, meant to remind young cubs that violent destruction could only harm those in its direct path. The moktaar might slaughter a mother and her cubs, kill the warriors, butcher all and consume raw. But only they—the dead—knew the war.

Skrizz had been taught to be ready for war. With tooth and claw. At all times. Because war is a thing... near.

The wobanki had always believed that. The truth was inalienable. It had proved itself repeatedly, regardless of circumstances. The debt to Hogus paid when the nearness of war bored a hole through the fat captain's chest. Tyrus Rechs had found out as well.

And then things changed with a simple touch. A radiating sense of otherworldly comfort that came from Prisma. One that somehow swept away the nearness of war, the violence of survival, and offered... something.

Skrizz could not explain what it was. Only that it was true.

He thought, for a while, that if he could rid himself of Prisma, it would all fade away. Those very un-wobanki feelings.

They did not.

He thought, for a while, that if he could find Prisma, he might somehow understand the depth of those feelings. Through understanding, perhaps he could *then* walk away. Or maybe he would stay and dedicate himself to the mystery.

Mystery. That was how Skrizz saw what had happened. It was a thing beyond Prisma and beyond himself.

But it was true. And it was... good.

Prisma was going to die. Skrizz knew it. The girl knew it as well. She had to die. Skrizz knew that, too. He would not argue the point. She *did* have to die. To live would be to become the lowest of all living. Morally destitute and hopelessly selfish. Beneath even the moktaar.

She had to die.

But...

She didn't have to die alone.

The naval battle was almost over when Skrizz sensed that the time had come for him to leave his lazy holding patterns above a vast and deep blue ocean once called the Pacific. Back when those names meant something, and the people of Kima understood the meanings. Back before everything that had ever made sense ceased to. Before the madness had gripped and the end came quickly.

The *Obsidian Crow* glided out of orbit, its bulk handling the departure from atmosphere with ease. Skrizz had always liked flying this ship.

The Savage hulk's hangar was lifeless. Not empty, but lifeless. It was littered with dead.

Skrizz picked his way past the bodies. He moved silently, his whiskers back against his face, his ears up and straining to hear some evidence that he wasn't alone, the last of the living on a floating graveyard.

He passed more bodies in the corridor. Some he recognized. Andien Broxin lay there.

Then, the throne room. He saw neither Captain Keel nor Ravi, and gave no time to consider whether that was a good or ill omen. It didn't matter. For there, next to the grave monolith that was a trigger-nuke, sat Prisma, barely able to remain upright. Blood pooling beneath her small legs. Blood dripping from her chin and soaking her clothes, arms, hands.

Skrizz didn't speak. He padded in and sat next to her, seeing that his time left to live could be measured in a few scant seconds. He held up her drooping face and licked her forehead. She looked at him, and her dull eyes brightened with recognition.

With a trembling hand, she reached up and petted him, smearing her blood on his luscious fur.

Their worlds... ended.

Made in the USA
Las Vegas, NV
21 December 2022

63772775R10256